THE CHILD UPSTAIRS

PROLOGUE

ANGEL

Yorkshire, Age 13

Daddy always came back, didn't he? That was the main thing.

Angel was supposed to be calculating the area of a hexagon. But instead, she was lying curled up in bed with the duvet pulled up to her chin, eyes fixed on the alarm clock on her bedside table. Waiting for Mickey Mouse's white-gloved hand to inch up towards the hour. It was almost ten o'clock. Which meant Daddy had been gone for three full days.

Mum had said earlier not to worry. She'd enfolded Angel in a big, soft hug and said that Daddy just needed to have his 'wild days', his bit of freedom, like all men did. He'd be back before they knew it.

The *Dallas* theme tune drifted up from downstairs. Angel heard the hesitant thuds of Mum's rubber-tipped walking sticks on the kitchen lino, the gush of water into the kettle. She sat up against her pillows and twisted her necklace – a gold-plated pendant in the shape of an 'A', threaded onto a fine chain. Proper grown-up jewellery, Daddy had said when he'd presented it to her on Christmas Day.

She opened her bedside drawer and took out the small photograph she'd found in the pocket of Daddy's leather jacket last night. The girl who gazed out from the glossy paper looked like a pretty, perfect princess. She sat with her chin tilted up, as if her posh school tie was tied too tightly around her neck. Her hair, the colour of tarnished gold, had been brushed into a ponytail, a few curls escaping at the sides.

Angel's stomach twisted. Perhaps her worst fear, the one she'd held inside for as long as she could remember, was finally coming true. Maybe Daddy had gone off to live with *the others*. His other girls. She could hardly bear to think of it.

She examined the photo again. This was clearly the younger of the two, the pretty one, the 'bobby dazzler'. The smug cow. The smug... *bitch*! Mum had told her off for saying that word, but it gave her a fizz of satisfaction even to think it. She flipped the photo over to read the pencil writing on the back. It said 'Steffi Woodgrove', underlined twice. And the name of a school – St Otterley's.

Mickey Mouse's hands were now pointing to six minutes past ten. She knew she was too old for a clock like that. She'd had it since she was eight, and it would have to go in the cupboard if anyone from school came round. But sometimes she wished she could go back. That she could take some Alice in Wonderland potion and get smaller again, rather than bigger.

Angel could hear Mum calling. She probably wanted

Angel to carry her mug of tea through to the living room. She couldn't do that herself any more, not on a two-stick day like today. Her rheumatics were definitely getting worse. Daddy had promised to arrange an appointment with a top specialist, who would finally give her the right medication. Then her aching joints would ease, and all that weight would just melt off. The sticks wouldn't even be needed. But he'd promised that months ago and it hadn't happened yet.

'Coming!' Angel tried to summon up the energy to move. She'd travelled to St Otterley's today, while she was meant to be at school herself. It had taken three buses and a forty-minute walk to get there, including ten minutes just to walk up the long, tree-lined drive. It had been easy enough to hide behind a wall and watch the comings and goings from the main entrance. She'd heard the noise of instruments – trombones or something – floating out from a row of arched windows. She'd watched three boys in burgundy uniforms hurrying across the courtyard with cello cases. Another had followed behind, trundling something along that looked like a harp. All boys, though. No sign of *her*. The stuck-up bitch.

She'd go back tomorrow. She'd go back every day if she needed to.

She picked up her maths set and took out the compass, twisting it out of the plastic moulding that lined the tin. She had a sudden urge to score the sharp point across the face of the perfect princess. To erase her, to go back to a time before *the others* existed, even though that was further back than she could remember. But she knew she had to put the photo back in Daddy's jacket. He'd want it when he got home.

Headlights swept the bedroom wall – a wash of bright light across the peeling pink wallpaper. She heard car doors clunking shut – one, two. She knelt up on her bed to look out of the window, her homework jotter sliding onto the floor, the maths set tin rattling down after it.

It was the police. She could see two hats, with black and white checks, bobbing along above the garden hedge. Her first thought was that it was something to do with Barry, her big brother. Perhaps he'd been stealing cars again. But no, that was impossible. He'd been in a young offenders' institution since the summer. Mum still cried about it, most days.

Maybe there'd just been another burglary in the area, and the police were going round warning everyone. She lifted the 'A' of her necklace and held it to her lips, offering up a silent prayer.

Then came the shrill burst of the doorbell. The clack of Mum's sticks, the hall floorboards creaking. Angel crept out of her bedroom to listen, crouching behind the banister at the top of the stairs. She didn't want the police to see her in her old, faded but beloved Snoopy nightshirt.

'Keith's not here,' she heard Mum saying.

But the police officers asked to come in anyway. They went into the living room, walking slowly to match Mum's wobbling pace. Angel sat down on the top step of the stairs, trying to listen.

Did this have something to do with *the others*? She realised the photograph of the pretty, perfect princess was still in her hand and she was crushing it. She pressed it against her thigh, just below the hem of her nightshirt, trying to smooth it out. It felt tacky against her hot skin.

She heard the word 'accident'. Something about a motorway bridge.

Then came a horrific shriek. It whooshed and distorted in her ears, like the feedback from the mics when a band played down at Daddy's club. She wished, for a moment, that she

THE CHILD UPSTAIRS

LUCY LAWRIE

For Jane and Lesley, my partners in crime.

could just run out of the house and not come back. Not hear whatever was coming next. `

If *the others* had done something to Daddy, she'd find them and she'd... she'd *kill* them. No matter how long it took, or how well they hid.

Something pinged. She looked down and saw that she'd torn off her necklace – her fist was wrapped tightly around the pendant, the flimsy chain swinging below. With the sharp apex of the 'A', she scored a line across the face in the photograph. The paper creased but didn't tear. So she scored harder, until the metal pierced both paper and skin, and a bead of blood sprang up on her thigh. And then harder, still harder, until the pain began to dull the sound of the screams from the living room.

PART I

1

STEFFI

Edinburgh, Present Day

I t made no sense that I didn't want to go home, that my stomach was crawling as I pushed the pram past the café, the two artisan bakeries and the entrance to the park.

Edie and I had been booted out of the 'Mummy and Me' class again.

'Don't you like yoga?' I reached down to stroke a lock of hair away from her flushed, contorted face. 'That's the second week in a row, my love.'

Most days, the crying started at teatime and went on until midnight. Today, it had begun mid-morning, just as I was 'flowing forward' from a downward dog position, trying to aim a kiss at my baby's forehead, something the other class participants seemed to manage with ease. Edie, lying spread-eagled on the yoga mat, had screamed in terror at my rapidly advancing face, and that had been that. Game over. After fifteen minutes of shushing, jiggling and pacing, the teacher had gently suggested that we try again next week.

We turned onto our street, a wide, tree-lined avenue with views of the Royal Botanic Gardens and the Edinburgh skyline beyond. I was lucky to live here, I knew that. It made no sense that Tom's house – *our* house – our beautiful, tastefully decorated Victorian villa, made me think of a grey stone mausoleum. Or that some voice inside me was urging me to run. To just turn around and run.

Sleep deprivation, I told myself. The postpartum brain could play tricks on you.

Stooping to unfasten Edie's straps, I saw that she'd fallen asleep. I manoeuvred the pram carefully up the steps to the front door and wheeled it inside, trying not to think of Tom's reaction the last time I'd left it in the hallway, leaving muddy marks on the antique floor tiles.

I longed to simply collapse on the sofa, pull a blanket around me, and close my eyes while Edie finished her nap. But when I'd signed up for the 'Mummy and Me' yoga classes, I'd made a vow to myself. A promise to try and find the old Steffi again. I had to believe she was still there inside me, somewhere. Underneath the extra pounds and the skin that had gone grey from exhaustion. I picked up the TV remote and searched for a workout video on YouTube.

I took off my hoodie, the hairs on my arms lifting in the chill of the high-ceilinged room. Feeling ridiculous at first, I punched the air in time to *Take On Me* by A-ha. But as the chorus came in, something inside me kicked into gear. Before I knew it, I was whirling around the living room, wiggling my hips, accenting my hands like a dancer.

A wail came from the hallway. Edie had woken up. Still dancing, I scooped her up and sashayed back into the living room. She looked startled for a moment and then she giggled. A full-throated baby chuckle.

My heart soared. What miracle was this?

It was a bubble of pure joy, an Instagrammable moment. Marie Godfrey-Carruthers, from the yoga class, was always posting ominous updates about how motherhood would be over in a flash, and we should cherish every moment of this short, sweet season while we still had the chance.

Holding Edie firmly around the waist, I dropped into a squat and then pushed upright again. She squealed and kicked her chubby legs.

Knee lifts next. 'Go Edie! We're smashing this! Yes! We! Are!'

A noise came from behind me – the nasal explosion of a laugh that had been held in too long. I spun around, clutching Edie to my chest.

It was Tom. He was bent over at the waist, gasping with laughter, his forehead creased in disbelief.

I reached for the remote and silenced the TV. Edie writhed against me and began to fuss again.

'So *this* is what you two get up to all day?'

I tried to catch my breath. 'Edie got us booted out of baby yoga again.'

'Goodness me!' He tutted at his daughter. 'A mini delinquent.'

'What are you doing home?'

'I forgot my other laptop. I need it for my presentation this evening. You are remembering I'll be home late again?' He paused. 'I'll just phone the zoo quickly, before I go.'

'What?' I wiped the sweat off my brow with the back of my hand.

'I think a mother and baby hippo may have escaped.' He

jammed his lips together, as if trying to suppress another wave of mirth.

'Very funny,' I muttered.

He turned into the hall and began to walk up the stairs, still shaking with laughter.

'Want to try again?' I asked Edie. Maybe we could recapture the moment. But she wailed in frustration, stretching her arms out towards Tom.

When he reappeared in the living room doorway, he was holding his laptop bag in one hand and a bottle of disinfectant floor spray in the other. He tossed the bottle into the room, rolling it along the carpet towards me.

'What have I told you about bringing the pram into the house?'

I shivered suddenly, the sweat cooling on my skin. 'I... Edie was...'

'It stays in the garage. Which part of that do you not understand?' A moment later, the front door banged.

AT FIVE O'CLOCK, during a brief pause in the crying, I phoned the health visitor.

'She wakes up every forty-five minutes during the night.' I paced up and down the room, jiggling Edie, the tendons in my knees aching. 'And she's been screaming all day. I've given her extra feeds. I've tried dancing with her. I've massaged her tummy and given her colic drops and gripe water. I've played baby chill-out music. I've tried baby yoga...'

As if triggered by the mention of baby yoga, Edie started up again.

Wah... wah... waaaaahhhh!

The health visitor's voice was weary. 'As I said last time, don't worry. This is completely normal.'

Wahhhh!

'What was that, sorry?'

'It's NORMAL.'

'But what should I do? I've got a step-daughter to look after, too.' Poor Tilly had gone up to her room to escape the noise as soon she'd arrived home from school.

'Have you tried leaving Edie to settle herself?'

'Yes,' I snapped, untruthfully.

'Well, all I can say, really, is to hang on in there. It's ages and stages, that's all.' Her voice was brisk now, and she ended the call without her usual assurances that she was always at the end of the phone.

Perhaps ear plugs would block out the screams a little bit. Or even better – Tom had some expensive noise-cancelling earbuds that his mother had given him when Edie was born. My heart sank, though, as I realised they'd be in his study. Upstairs.

First, I strapped Edie into a sling on my chest. Then, humming *Dancing Queen*, I clasped the banister with both hands and went up slowly, bringing my feet together, side by side on each step, trying to ignore the sickening sensation in my stomach. I found the earbuds in his desk drawer and I wiggled them in, as deep as they would go, before embarking on the descent back down to the kitchen. Still, the screams vibrated through me, rattling my skull.

Stop, baby. Please, please stop.

I thought about texting my sister. Sarah must know about this stuff, with two children of her own. But I'd have to word the message carefully to make sure Sarah didn't actually come over, like that time she'd bought round that white noise machine during dinner. Tom hadn't spoken to me for two days.

At six o'clock, Tilly and I ate a lasagne ready meal for dinner while Edie continued to wail. While we were clearing the table, Edie flung her head back so that her skull knocked hard against my upper lip. Pain bloomed through my face and the taste of blood filled my mouth. I ran my tongue over my front teeth to check if they were intact.

It popped into my head – just out of nowhere – that maybe my sister could adopt Edie. I would still be able to see her. I wouldn't be giving her up completely. Sarah would be better at this than me.

Consumed by shame, I buried my face into Edie's neck, breathing in the scent of baby skin and the soured milk that collected in the folds of her neck when she dribbled. 'I'm sorry. I didn't mean it. I love you.'

'Didn't mean what?' Tilly's voice was anxious.

'Come on,' I said. 'Let's get out of the house for a bit. We can go for a drive. You can bring your iPad.'

After five minutes of driving, Edie fell asleep and I pulled up in the car park of a retail estate. I turned to Tilly, who was bundled up in her anorak in the back seat, her legs looking cold in her school skirt and ankle socks. I felt a pang of guilt – she should be settled in her cosy PJs at home.

'Okay?'

Tilly nodded, glancing nervously out of the car window. A group of lads in hoodies were kicking an empty can about near the recycling bins.

'They'll go away in a minute.' I pressed the button to engage the central locking and set an alarm on my phone for thirty minutes. Any longer in the car seat and I'd be seriously risking Edie's health. That's what the health visitor had said, when I'd once told her, with a rueful laugh, about driving around to try and get Edie to go to sleep. I laid my head against the cool glass of the window.

When the alarm woke me, I was even more tired than I'd been before. Groggy and with a splitting head, I started to drive home. Tilly had fallen asleep too, so she probably wouldn't settle tonight, either. She would drift around the house after bedtime, appearing in doorways, worrying about monsters or looking for water.

How did other women do this?

At the junction with Ferry Road, the world seemed to slip and slide for a moment. A bus glided towards us, its windows all lit up. I thought of the Harry Potter night bus. I thought...

'BRAKE!!' screamed a voice.

Adrenaline fired through me. I slammed on the brakes. The bus kept moving towards us, its headlights blinding, in a split second that seemed to last forever. There was a hideous metallic squeal as it swerved and came to a stop, mere centimetres from my car.

The lights were red. They had been red. I had driven through them.

My heart thumped against my ribs. I tried to suck in a breath. Another. My chest was too tight to take in the air.

The bus moved. The lights were green now. A horn blared behind us.

The lights were green but I couldn't move. My legs were jelly.

Move. I had to move the car out of the junction. My foot was shaking so much that I could barely press down on the accelerator. But I managed to manoeuvre the car to the kerb just past the traffic lights.

I twisted around to check the girls were okay in the back seat. Tilly was rubbing her eyes in confusion.

'What happened?' she asked sleepily.

It didn't make sense. If Tilly had still been asleep, who had shouted 'BRAKE!!'?

'Are you okay, Tilly? Is Edie okay?'

As if in response, Edie's pudgy hand unfurled like a little starfish, and then tightened again.

'She's fine,' said Tilly, leaning over to check. 'But her straps aren't fastened.'

I must have undone them in the retail estate so that I could unzip her coat. If the bus had crashed into us, she would have been tossed out of her seat. And Tilly's sleeping head had been resting on the car window – the side of the car where the bus would have hit.

Images flashed into my mind. Broken necks. Shattered skulls. Gruesome facial injuries.

'There,' said Tilly, fastening the harness and pulling the shoulder straps snug around Edie. 'I've done her up now.'

I drove back to the house and pulled up in our driveway, still shaking, my hands stiff from gripping the steering wheel.

Tilly piped up from the back seat: 'Who was that lady?'

'What do you mean?'

'That lady in the car park when you were asleep.'

I'd been dead to the world for those thirty minutes. I had no idea what she was talking about. 'A lady? What lady? What did she do?'

Tilly shrugged. 'She just peered through the car window to look at you.'

A cold tingle crept down my spine.

It must have been some concerned passer-by, walking back to her car with her shopping – the supermarket at the far end of the retail estate had still been open. She'd have seen what a bad mother I was, risking my baby's life by leaving her to sleep in the car seat. I imagined someone who looked just like our health visitor, shaking her head and tutting.

'What did she look like, Tilly?'

'She was wearing a sort of hoodie.'

'Maybe it was one of the boys who was kicking cans around when we arrived?'

Tilly shook her head, adamant. 'No. It was a lady.'

'Did she look into the back of the car? Did she see you and Edie?'

'I'm not sure,' said Tilly. 'I was pretending to be asleep, too. Then she wrote something on the car and went away.'

'She *wrote something* on the *car*?'

Tilly nodded, frowning.

Heart hammering, I got out of the car to look. There, on the side of the driver's door, carved into the red paintwork with a sharp point, was a single word.

BITCH

2

STEFFI

Edinburgh, Present Day

Tom appeared in the kitchen at just after seven the next morning, shaved and suited, already radiating boardroom energy.

'How's my little princess?' He kissed Edie, who was hoisted up on my hip. 'And my big princess?' He planted moist lips on my forehead too.

'Good,' I lied. In my fleecy pyjamas and with puffy, bedhead hair, I felt like a bloated ugly sister, not a princess. And I was feeling slightly sick at the thought of having to tell him about the damage to my car door. One-handed, I filled the kettle and put one of his herbal tea bags into a mug.

'Did we keep you awake? I've been up and down all night with her.' Every time I'd got back into bed, Tom had sighed and tossed around under the covers. 'She's –'

He held up a hand, cutting me off. 'Not a problem.'

'Have you got a lot of meetings today?'

'Yep.' He puffed out a breath of air. 'Three this morning, and then a meeting over lunch. I've got a presentation to the Board this afternoon as well. We need their buy-in for the next round of M&A targets.'

I shuddered, thinking of all the ways that Tom was protecting me from the real world outside this expensive house.

'Edie and I could move into the guest room for a while. Then we won't wake you in the night.' I'd made the suggestion several times over the last few months. I loved the idea of having Edie's cot right next to the bed. And maybe even pulling her in beside me, if she was restless. The warmth of skin against skin, helping us both to settle. And it was safer, down on the ground floor. Away from the stairs.

I pulled Edie closer and held my cool cheek against her rosy warm one. She felt like velvet, this little miracle creature. How on earth had I made her? How was my body capable of such a thing?

'No, I draw the line at that, Steffi.' He rubbed his hand over his newly shaven jaw. 'We're not going to be one of those couples who sleep in separate rooms.'

'She was crying *all day* yesterday. Literally. You have no idea.'

'Hmm,' he said distractedly.

'Actually, there's something I need to... run past you. About my car.'

'Have you seen my earbuds? I was trying to find them last night.'

I felt hollow, suddenly. I'd taken them, of course, but where had I put them?

'I borrowed them.'

His frown deepened.

'I could still hear Edie, don't worry. She was perfectly safe.'

'Where are they, honey?'

Honey sounded all wrong in his posh, boarding school accent.

'I just need to look for them. I'll do it after I've changed Edie.'

'Can we go to school now?' Tilly had appeared in the doorway. 'I don't want to be late for breakfast club. It's pancakes today.'

Tom shot me a dirty look, as if it were my fault they were serving pancakes and not the kind of carb-free, sugar-free breakfast he would have favoured for her.

'Two minutes, darling.' He downed the rest of his herbal tea. I envied him the luxury of his anti-caffeine stance.

'Good morning, Tilly,' I said, patting her shoulder awkwardly. She was still funny about hugs. 'Thank you for getting ready all by yourself.'

She shrugged. She did it without prompting every morning, trained, no doubt, by the nannies who had cared for her before I'd moved in. As she picked up her schoolbag, I noticed her blouse was gaping a little bit around the buttons. I'd need to order some in the next size up. But she noticed me looking and frowned, pulling her blazer tight in front of her chest.

I turned to Tom. I wanted to get this over before he left. 'My car got scratched. When we were in a car park.' Would he march me out to the driveway to show him, like the time I'd kerbed one of my alloys? Would I have to tell him about 'the lady', the mysterious late-night shopper who'd felt compelled to tell me I was a bitch?

But Tom's body sagged in his chair. 'Do I have to deal with *every little thing* that goes wrong in this house?'

'Is it okay to get it fixed? Is it okay to put it on the credit card?' I felt like a child, asking for extra pocket money.

'Fine,' he said, throwing up his hands. 'Good idea. You can actually do something for once. I've got to get to work.'

LATER THAT MORNING, Edie had some time in her jungle gym, kicking at the soft monkeys, snakes and parrots that dangled from its green foam arches.

She seemed happier than yesterday – thank goodness. She'd had a morning nap after Tom had left for work, taking Tilly with him to drop her at school on the way. This had given me time to look for the earbuds, rifling through drawers and cupboards, stripping all the covers off the bed and emptying the laundry basket onto the floor.

The house looked as if it had been turned over by burglars. I'd have to look again later, if and when Edie had a nap, and then tidy everything up again. And I'd have to phone the garage about getting my car fixed, too.

I still didn't understand why anyone would have vandalised my car in that way. But I'd come to the conclusion that Tilly must have been mistaken about the 'lady'. It must have been one of the lads who'd been mucking around near the recycling bins. Trying to replay events, I wondered if I'd shot them a disapproving look as I'd driven past, and this was some form of retaliation.

I could feel my eyelids closing. 'Hey look, it's a cheeky monkey.' I gave the monkey a half-hearted squeeze and it squeaked mournfully. Edie blinked and kicked a chubby leg.

I bent over to kiss her, inhaling her milky, powdery smell. She gave a little gurgle, her dark blue eyes earnest, as if she was trying to tell me something important.

'Oh God, I love you. I just love you so much.' I kissed her nose again and then laid my head down on the play mat beside her. I closed my eyes, just for a second.

When I woke, I had the strangest feeling that someone had poked me on the shoulder. The room had gone quiet, and the gurgles and shuffling noises had stopped.

I sprang up onto my knees. Edie's eyes were bulging, her face turning red.

Jesus Christ – she was choking.

No. No no no no no...

I'd watched some videos online about baby first aid. Was I meant to turn Edie upside down and shake her to dislodge the object? Or do some sort of Heimlich manoeuvre? Or should I call an ambulance?

I lifted Edie and struck her between the shoulder-blades. Nothing happened.

'Help!' I croaked, uselessly. There was nobody else in the house.

Pick her up and lay her on your thigh, face down, so her head's lower than her bum.

It was as if someone was beside me, talking to me. The voice was in my head but not in my head. I sat down on the edge of the sofa and turned Edie over.

That's it. Head lower than her bum. Now hit her between the shoulder blades.

I just did as I was told.

Harder. A good old whack.

My hands were shaking. 'I can't... I can't.'

Come on, now – one, two... and whack.

'It's not WORKING!' Edie was turning blue around the mouth.

One more time. Come on.

There was a small coughing sound, and then a loud, furious cry.

I snatched her up, watched her draw in a deep breath and let it out again in a cry. The skin around her mouth began to return to its normal colour.

'Oh my little love.'

A thought materialised. What would it have been like – telephoning Tom at work to tell him Edie had died? I could almost hear the impatient, clipped sound of his voice when he answered, followed by... what? What would his voice sound like when I told him? Then I fast-forwarded to another scene – Tom and I sitting on low chairs in a funeral director's office, looking through a brochure of children's coffins.

I clutched Edie to my chest and wept. I wept for everything I'd gone through in the last few months, the loneliness of it all. I wept at the thought of what had almost happened... at the thought of mortuaries, and how cold Edie would have been in one of those steel drawers. I thought of choosing hymns, and a reading. And I wept at the thought of my own reprieve, and because somewhere out there, there were mothers who hadn't been so lucky. How could they go on?

How could anyone, when something like this could happen at any moment?

You're exhausted.

Releasing Edie and wiping my face on my sleeve, I noticed an earbud on the carpet by my feet. No... surely not?

I picked it up. It was damp with saliva. Edie must have seen it, picked it up, and put it in her mouth. I hadn't even noticed.

My first thought was that Tom would be furious if he found out. I went to the kitchen and took a long swig from my bottle of multi-vitamin tonic for new mothers. And then I swallowed six caffeine tablets.

∼

LATER, sitting in the rocking chair while I gave Edie her bottle, I collected my thoughts.

The voice I'd heard – twice now – was probably just a reaction to stress. A biological thing, an evolutionary throwback. My own motherly instincts, made audible.

Edie stared up at me trustingly, her mouth sucking and releasing the plastic teat.

I thought back to the few days after Edie had been born. I'd just come home from the hospital and was having a rest in bed, with Edie asleep in her little Moses basket beside me. I'd asked Tom why there was another baby crying somewhere in the house – was there a television on somewhere, or the radio?

Tom said it was probably a hangover from the hospital. There'd been babies crying all day and night long in the ward.

It had gone on for a week or so – I would rush to the nursery, convinced Edie was crying, only to find her fast asleep. Once, disorientated after waking from a nap, I'd searched the whole house from top to bottom, trying to find the crying baby, when in fact Tom had taken Edie out for a walk in her pram. He'd returned to find me curled in a ball at the top of the stairs, my hands over my ears.

And then I'd read an article saying this was something that often happened with new mums. It was because they were programmed to be super-sensitive to their babies' needs. It was something to do with hormones. There was even a name for it – 'phantom crying'.

This would be something like that... phantom voices.

I drew my phone out of my pocket and searched for 'hearing voices new mum'. It would probably turn out to be a well-documented thing, too. There'd be hundreds of search results that would show how normal all this was.

The results that appeared on my phone screen – things about postpartum psychosis and schizophrenia – well, they didn't apply to me. I scanned through an article about a mother who'd nearly drowned her own baby and ended up on a psych ward for six months, and closed the page down quickly. I added the words 'NHS' to my search – surely they would be less sensationalist. But the page I found failed to provide any reassurance, going on grimly about 'auditory hallucinations' and the various causes for these, none of them good.

I wondered, briefly, about searching for whether it was normal for new mothers to be frightened of the stairs in their own home. To worry that they might suddenly feel an over-whelming urge to throw themselves – or their fragile-skulled little babies – down them.

Probably best not. I'd conquered my strange childhood fear of the stairs before, and I could do so again. It was only natural that, caught up in the sleep deprivation and upside-down craziness of this postpartum world, it had come back. It was a susceptibility, that was all. Like how I'd been prone to eczema as a child, and it sometimes came back if I was run down, erupting in painful patches on my wrists and elbows.

Self-care, that was what was needed. That was what Marie Godfrey-Carruthers, from the baby yoga class, would say. A bubble bath or two would see me right. And maybe I could install stair gates, just for additional peace of mind. I could justify it to Tom on the basis that Edie might be crawling soon. My sister, Sarah, had crawled at six months minus eight days, as my mother had liked to inform people at any opportunity – it had been the first sign that she was going to be an exceptional child.

I, on the other hand, had started to crawl at some vague, unspecified age: 'At about the usual age, I think, Steffi. Please stop pestering.'

And then I seemed to hear the voice again, as clear as if someone was sitting beside me.

It's only me. Don't you remember me?

3

STEFFI

Yorkshire, Age 8

Steffi's first Appalling Fuss came out of nowhere, one rainy Saturday afternoon.

There was no rhyme nor reason for it, as Daddy said afterwards. Steffi had been absolutely fine before the guests arrived. Just singing and playing with her Lego in a corner of the dining room.

'The cream of the cream,' she sang as she fixed a red tile to the roof of the house she was building. 'The cream of the *cream!*'

In the living room across the hall, Sarah's Brahms *Intermezzo* came to a sudden stop. 'Mu-um! Make Steffi be quiet!'

'Pipe down, Steffi!' Mum called from the kitchen.

Steffi drew her tartan blanket around her shoulders, tying the corners under her chin to make it into a cloak. Her sister was playing the piano in a big concert at Central Hall tonight, even though she was only thirteen years old. The leaflet said the concert was a showcase for the cream of the cream – the best young musicians from all the schools in Yorkshire and Humberside. Steffi had carefully propped the leaflet against her bedroom window, unfolded and facing outwards, held in place by two piggy banks, to catch the attention of passers by on the street. She'd thought Sarah would be pleased, but she'd just given her a withering look.

Anyway, Mum was making just as much noise as Steffi, with the Kenwood Chef going, mixing up the horrible mixture for the mushroom vol-au-vents.

When Steffi heard the doorbell ring and then voices in the hall, she ignored them. She was busy scrabbling in the Lego box for the oven, with its tiny hinged door.

'Should it go here?' she muttered, hovering the oven over a space in the kitchen.

No, replied Dodo inside Steffi's head. *It goes here by the back door.*

Steffi nodded and pressed the piece into place. She'd been trying to get this house right for weeks.

Dodo, invisible, flung out her arms dramatically: *Cream of the cream of the CREAM!*

Steffi flung out her arms too and gave a single piercing shriek.

Sarah put her head around the door. 'Steffi! Come on! We've got to say hello to The Relations. And no, you can't bring Dodo. Nobody's impressed by your silly imaginary friend. It's not cute and it's not funny.'

The queasy smell of the vol-au-vents was stronger in the living room.

'Hello, everyone,' said Sarah.

'Hello, everyone,' echoed Steffi in a tiny voice, hovering behind her in the doorway.

'You remember Uncle Geoffrey?' said Granny, pointing to a big, balding man whose face was the grey-pink colour of old ham. He was sitting on the sofa next to Aunt Veronica. She'd been going out with him for a few months now and she had been *transformed*. Steffi had heard Mum saying so on the phone: '*She even got her colours done at Debenhams. I know – can you believe it?*'

'Geoffrey, you remember the girls – Sarah and Steffi?'

Uncle Geoffrey leaned forward. 'Ah! Splendid.'

'That's the musical one,' said Granny in a loud whisper, pointing at Sarah. Then she looked at Steffi, working her mouth so that the loose skin under her jaw wobbled. 'And that's... the other one.'

Daddy appeared at Uncle Geoffrey's side, gangling over him with a bottle of sherry. 'Just a spot,' said Uncle Geoffrey. 'Just a spot.' But he held out his glass for a long time until it was up to the top.

Aunt Veronica turned to Mum. 'Oh, Jill, I meant to say. Did you hear that Marjorie Dennis has had another turn?'

'Oh *no*,' said Mum. 'Is she back in hospital?'

'Well...' Aunt Veronica went over and sat next to Mum, leaning in. Steffi heard her say something about tests. Steffi thought of Marjorie Dennis, lying bandaged in a hospital bed, being grilled on times tables or Viking longboats.

'So what do *you* like doing, then?' said Uncle Geoffrey to Steffi.

Her tummy felt wobbly. She wondered if she could say she needed the toilet. But Mum had said she needed to try and be more pleasant with The Relations. More smiley. Less shy.

'I like Lego,' she managed.

'Oh, do you indeed? What are you making?'

Astonished that somebody was actually interested, Steffi darted into the dining room and carefully dragged through her Lego house, arranging it at Uncle Geoffrey's feet. It took three goes, as it was on three different bases.

The conversation about tests was still going on, Mum and Aunt Veronica talking in quick whispers, heads bent together like they were making a spell.

'I'll go and see to the food then, shall I?' said Granny to nobody in particular, making a big deal about having to step around the Lego. Steffi held her breath as the legs came past, dark veins bulging through milky-tea tights.

'My word!' said Uncle Geoffrey, peering down at the Lego house.

'It's got an oven.'

'Now, I think I have some toffees somewhere...' He started rooting around in his pockets, pulling out a crumpled tissue, a paperclip and a pound note. 'Why don't you come here and tell me all about school.' He patted his knee.

Did he mean that she should go and sit on his lap? Steffi's body stiffened with uncertainty. He handed her a toffee, warm and slightly soft from being in his pocket. She placed it carefully it on the arm of the sofa. Uncle Geoffrey laughed, and she caught a whiff of his eggy breath. 'Come here. I don't bite.' He snaked an arm around Steffi and pulled her onto his knee.

'Don't touch, please,' she said, squirming off.

Granny, who was just coming back into the room with bowls of crisps and nuts, gasped. 'Steffi! Manners!'

Mum laughed, her voice high and strangled. 'Talk nicely to Uncle Geoffrey, please, Steffi.'

Steffi sat back down on the sofa, leaving a space between herself and Uncle Geoffrey – Dodo could sit there. She took a gulp of air and re-tied her tartan blanket under her chin, smoothing its ribbony edge between her fingers. Nobody spoke. The big clock on the mantelpiece ticked on.

Suddenly, Sarah was at the piano, playing something loud and fast, elbows flapping, plaits swinging.

'Ahhh!' Daddy smiled in relief. It was a wide, delighted smile showing both rows of teeth, crowded and sharp like a T-Rex's. Steffi felt protective of him, wanted to run over to him and hide him.

'*Con brio!*' he cried in an Italian accent, jerking his hands in time to Sarah's playing. 'That's it! With vigour. Haha.'

'Ah, splendid,' said Uncle Geoffrey. 'Rum-pa, rum-pa...' He reached over and patted Steffi's knee in time to the music. 'Rum-pa-PA!'

Steffi jumped up, quick as a jack-in-a-box. 'Fook off!'

What had she said?! She felt her face turn red, and then crumple. Pulling her blanket over her head, she ran upstairs to her bedroom, collapsing onto her bed just as her legs turned to jelly.

It was Daddy who came up first, his forehead creased and his legs too long as he perched on the edge of her bed. He put a cool hand on her cheek. 'I think she's got a temperature, Jill,' he called out. 'Steffi, poppet? Shall I get you a nice glass of water?'

Mum came in. Steffi held her arms out, longing to be enveloped in her softness and her Fairy soap smell. 'Not until she explains herself. What a performance!'

Steffi turned over, away from Daddy's hand and the look on Mum's face. 'Dodo made me say it.'

Her mother took a sharp breath in. 'I told you before. That's a silly game and we won't tolerate it in this house. Come on, Rob, you can help me dish up. Steffi, you can jolly well stay here and stew until you've found your manners.'

So she would miss the vol-au-vents at least.

But Steffi knew she'd still have to go to Sarah's concert. Nothing would get her out of that. Even if she was in prison, they'd come and fetch her and make her go. Steffi imagined herself, chained to a prison officer, sitting in the back row of Central Hall. The clanking noise as she clapped dutifully for the Brahms *Intermezzo*.

It was beginning to get dark outside when she heard her name being shouted. She came out from her bedroom. Mum was standing at the top of the stairs, her hand on the banister. The stairs were shadowy behind her. 'Are you not *ready*? Put on your shoes. We're leaving now.'

'Come on, folks,' boomed Daddy from the hallway below. 'Wagons roll!'

But the banister didn't look right. It was twisting – slowly, slowly. Steffi thought of snakes. Snakes waking up.

'Mummy –' She rubbed her eyes.

'*Well*?'

The stairway seemed to stretch, opening up like a great gaping mouth.

She dropped onto all fours, digging her fingernails into the carpet.

Her head was spinning. Like the metal spinning top in her toy box. The one with the faded circus pictures that turned into a rainbow blur when you pumped the handle.

She pushed her face into the carpet, breathing in the

tickly smell of dust, her hands making a cage for her head. She could hear a sort of high wailing that might be coming from her.

It's okay, said Dodo's voice, close and warm. *I've got you.*

And an outside voice – her mother's – followed: 'For heaven's sake, what's the matter? What an appalling fuss!'

4

STEFFI

Edinburgh, Present Day

I'd been wondering if Tom would remember that it was the second anniversary of our first date. But he came home with a present – a box wrapped in gold paper with a red bow.

'Aw! Thank you!' I gave him a kiss on the cheek. It was nice to know I was appreciated. It had been yet another bad day with Edie – there'd been six wake-ups last night, and an explosive diarrhoea incident in Sainsbury's that afternoon. It had taken a whole package of baby wipes to sort out, and a staff member with a mop.

'You open yours first,' I said.

My present to Tom was a framed sketch of him, asleep on the sofa with Edie curled on his chest. I'd drawn it from a photograph using watercolour pencils. I thought Tom looked adorable, his face relaxed in sleep, his glasses squint from the way he was resting his head on the cushion. Edie had been just a few weeks old, her whorls of hair duckling-soft.

His face spasmed briefly in a micro-expression that I couldn't fully read. It looked like amused revulsion, or embarrassment, as if I'd presented him with something deeply inappropriate – a naked photograph or something. He quickly corrected his face. 'It's lovely, honey,' he said, putting it face down on the bed. 'You open yours.'

It felt like a physical blow. It had taken me weeks to finish the sketch, in snatched moments during Edie's naps. I'd sung along happily to the radio as I'd worked on it, enjoying the thought of Tom's delighted reaction. I wasn't the world's greatest artist, by any means, but I felt I had captured something in the picture. A moment of peaceful contentment between father and daughter. A moment to cherish.

#Blessed, as Marie Godfrey-Carruthers, from the baby yoga class, would have said.

But maybe he was distracted, anticipating my reaction to the gift he'd got for me. I told myself I should give him the benefit of the doubt.

Inside the wrapped box I found a framed photograph of myself, taken a good few years ago, before I even met Tom. I was stretched out on a sun-lounger in Cyprus, holding a Margarita with sugar crystals around the rim of the glass, the last of the sun's rays kissing my lightly tanned legs.

'I had it framed,' he said, his eyes boyish and excited.

'That's... really nice. Thank you.'

'You said that was your favourite photo of yourself.'

I nodded. That's because I'd been two dress sizes thinner back then, with no saggy bits. And that golden, cocktail-hour light had caught me just right, somehow making me look better than I did in real life. With my sun-flushed cheeks and that surprised half-smile, I looked, well, lovely.

Tom meant well, that was the main thing. He'd been paying attention to the things I said. He was trying. When had he even had time to go through all the old photos I'd uploaded onto the computer?

Then I noticed there was a gold envelope tucked behind the photograph.

'Oh.' A piece of paper fluttered out onto my lap.

It was a voucher for Bootcamp Betty, a women's personal trainer. I'd seen her advertised on Facebook – *Blast that baby bod!*

'It's for ten sessions, but I'm happy to pay for more, if...' He trailed off delicately.

If what? If I lost weight? If I blasted my bod to oblivion? I sat stock still, feeling a hint of a wobble in my chin.

'Deborah said this Bootcamp Betty is the best. No messing around. She forces you to be accountable.'

Of course, *Deborah*. His bloody PA.

'Well? Do you like it?'

I bit my lip, hard. Harder, till the skin felt as if it might burst like a grape. Didn't they say you couldn't feel two kinds of pain at once?

'You said you've been wanting to get back into shape.' Tom's tone wasn't quite defensive, not yet. He was just reminding me of the facts. Explaining why I should like the present.

I'd said that after polishing off two slices of chocolate cake on Tilly's birthday. Wasn't that what everybody said? I'd been fishing for reassurance, if anything, hoping he would say I was perfect, just as I was.

'She offers sessions from six am,' he said. 'And she comes to the house if you like. So I was thinking, you could get up and do that for an hour before I've left for work, and I'll look after Edie.'

How could I say it, without sounding ungrateful? The best present he could possibly give me was to look after Edie for an hour before work so I could *sleep*.

'You always said you were too busy to look after her in the mornings,' I whispered.

He smiled, seeming to think I was whispering because I was overcome by his generosity. 'I'd do anything for my princess. I know you've had your mind set on getting fit again.'

How could he have got this so wrong? How could he have got *me* so wrong?

A tear shot down my cheek. I nudged it away with my shoulder.

'What's wrong?' His voice was clipped and quiet now.

I didn't trust myself to speak. I bit my lip again, tasting the iron tang of blood. I was being stupid. Over-sensitive. 'Nothing.'

I looked up at him and saw that his face had changed.

'Oh for God's sake, Steffi. I thought you wanted this? You said...'

'I was going to wait until she's sleeping a bit better before trying to get fit again. I'm just so exhausted.' My voice came out high and reedy.

'What about that vitamin prep I got you? Have you been taking that?'

Another of Deborah's recommendations – her sister had taken it after having her twins. Sixty pounds a bottle and worth every penny, apparently.

'I don't think vitamins are going to fix this,' I said. 'Or bootcamps.'

'Fine.' He whipped the voucher out of my hands. 'Give it here. I'll cancel it and get a refund. If I can.'

I thought of the articles I'd read online about how to improve your relationship. Communication was key. I should try and explain my feelings. But what were the words you were supposed to avoid? 'Should' was one, wasn't it? Or starting sentences with 'you always...' or 'you never...' And I should focus on explaining how I felt, rather than criticising what he had done.

'Getting the voucher made me feel like... maybe you preferred me how I was, before Edie. I'm worried that I'm not *enough* any more.'

'Don't be so ridiculously sensitive, Steffi. I was trying to do something nice.' The final word emerged as a hiss through gritted teeth.

I chose my words carefully. 'I know. I just feel like... What about tennis membership? That's something we could do together. It would be fun as well as exercise. I think there's even a creche at that club down the road. And Tilly could join in too.'

Surely he'd go for that – he was always saying how she needed to get more exercise. I had once tried to explain that it was normal for young girls to grow outwards a bit before they grew upwards, but he'd ruffled my hair and said I was 'spouting old wives' nonsense'.

Now he looked at me as if I'd gone mad. 'What, leave Edie with strangers? And do you have any idea what tennis membership would cost? In fact, do you have any idea how hard I have to work, to keep you in the lifestyle to which you've become accustomed? Try walking in my shoes for a day, Steffi. Try living in the real world. Just for once.'

Prick, muttered a voice, right behind me.

I spun round. Nobody there.

I turned back to Tom. It was important to keep calm. 'I'm just trying to –'

'You know what? I give up.' He held his hands up on either side of his head, boxing himself in. 'I can't do anything right.'

I heard him go into his study, slamming the door with a force that seemed to shake the whole house. Moments later, noises of shooting and frenzied shouting echoed through the hallway. He was playing one of his video games – probably that horrible violent one about the Korean war. He needed it to unwind, apparently.

Tilly appeared in the bedroom doorway, making me jump. 'Could you please ask Daddy to turn the volume down? I'm trying to do my homework.' She spoke in a flat, resigned voice, almost as if she knew there was no point in asking.

'Oh, darling... Shall we give him a minute? He'll probably realise and turn it down.' What a failure I was. Scared to ask my own fiancé to stop doing something that was upsetting his daughter. Our daughter. My step-daughter, if we ever ended up actually marrying.

A particularly loud burst of gunfire sounded through the study door. From the nursery, Edie began to wail.

Tilly's face remained blank, her eyes as dead as a doll's. Anything could be going on inside that head. A shiver moved over my skin.

'Are you okay, Tilly?'

Then corners of her mouth turned up into a slight smile.

'Yes. Never mind. Do you want me to walk around with her for a bit?'

I pictured Tilly walking around with Edie on the upstairs landing, close to the vertiginous drop of the stairs. I shivered. 'Don't worry. I'll get her. Thank you, though.'

5

JOANNE

Yorkshire, Present Day

Nobody would call Joanne a people person. No, she wasn't fussed about people at all and she had her reasons. But showing members of the public around the rescue centre was a crucial part of her job, so she had to stick a pleasant expression on her face and get on with it.

Her badge said 'Animal Care Worker', but privately, she considered herself an *advocate*. Somebody had to make a case for the cats that nobody wanted, the ones people would just walk past without noticing. She couldn't entrust that delicate work to the spotty, mumbling teenagers doing their Duke of Edinburgh volunteering, more was the pity.

Blackie chirped and trotted over as soon as Joanne opened up the door of the enclosure. He wound himself around her legs with such enthusiasm that she had to pick him up to let the visiting couple come in.

'Blackie's one of my favourites,' she explained. 'He's very gentle. Very sweet. Aren't you, boy?'

Blackie's purr grew stronger and louder, a little engine under her hand. The hopeful look in his eyes tore at Joanne's heart, even though she knew he was probably just hoping he might get a handful of treats, and would have no thoughts of finding his forever home. He'd been here so long he'd probably forgotten there was even a world outside Willoughby Bridge Cat Rescue.

'Oh,' said the woman – a thin creature with big, bug-like eyes, who wore yoga leggings and a long cardigan. 'He's... lovely.'

Joanne smiled sourly. People never went for black cats. And poor Blackie had a bit of a dandruff problem, God love him.

'He's six years old,' she persisted. 'Owner died. Nice old lady by all accounts. A university lecturer in Old English literature, I think they said.' Joanne had no idea whether this was true. The lady could have been a foul-mouthed sewage plant operative for all she knew.

But the woman brightened a little. She stuck out a tentative hand towards Blackie, although she curled her pretty little fingers in again before she actually touched him.

This was a Cushion Couple – that much was clear. Joanne had categories for would-be adopters, based on long years of experience. Once, soon after she'd started here, a couple had come in every Saturday for a month, until she showed them a silver tabby kitten who'd just been brought in.

'Look, Marcus!' the woman had said, turning to her husband. 'She's perfect!' and she had actually pulled out a photograph of a sofa with soft grey velvet cushions.

'He's a *he*, actually,' Joanne had said, clanging the door

shut. 'And he won't be ready for a while. Bad case of worms. Resistant to treatment.'

That cat had gone later the same day – to a nice Polish couple with a pair of shy little girls. The kittens always got snapped up, especially the ones that looked nice.

Although the silver kitten must have died by now, from old age if nothing else. And those shy little girls would have grown up and flown the nest to goodness knew where. Joanne pulled her purple fleece closer around her body.

'The thing is,' said the bug-eyed woman now, with an apologetic wince. 'We were really looking for something younger.'

Some*thing*?

Joanne reached for Blackie and rubbed the soft fur behind his ears, giving him a little massage by way of apology. His purring became ecstatic, and he pushed his head hard against the bobbled sleeve of her fleece.

'The website said you had some kittens?' Mr Cushion was clearly used to getting whatever he wanted in life.

Joanne pondered. There was that pair of feral kittens a council worker had brought in that morning. She led the couple through to the next hut. 'This area's just been sprayed for fleas,' she said, as the couple began to cough and cover their faces. 'They'll be a handful, mind.'

The creatures hissed and arched their backs. Painfully thin, with oversized leathery ears, they had an alien look about them.

'Can we go in and see them?'

'No,' said Joanne. '*Sorry.* Trained staff only.'

The woman didn't bother to say they were lovely. Poor little mites. They'd been found living behind some over-flowing bins at a motorway service station.

'Is that all you've got?' said the man, frowning.

'We've got a waiting list for kittens,' said Joanne, feeling a sensation of satisfaction build under her ribs.

Mrs Cushion filled in a form at reception, covering the page in her neat, looped handwriting. Joanne told them she'd be in touch as soon as any suitable animals were found.

'Thank you so much,' said the woman, flashing a bleached smile.

Joanne ran her tongue around her own mouth, feeling the crumbled molar at the back, which she was putting off seeing the dentist about. Her heart sank at the thought of it.

As she watched the car pull out of the car park, the silver rings of its Audi logo flashing in the sunlight, she lifted the form, crumpled it in one hand and tossed it in the bin.

6

STEFFI

Edinburgh, Present Day

'I've invited Sarah and the boys over this afternoon,' said Tom, looking at me coyly.

'Really?' I understood that this was his way of saying sorry. Neither of us had mentioned the argument since it had happened, but he had been more attentive than usual, throwing his arms around me periodically, saying he loved me. He was packing a small suitcase for a trip to London – he was on the red-eye flight the next morning.

He nodded. 'I thought it would be nice for you. And you could ask her about the sleeping thing. Just make sure you keep them in the kitchen, yeah?'

Tom liked to refer to Ben, Sarah's seven-year-old son, as his 'nemesis'. Last time he'd been here, the child had emptied a carton of Ribena onto the living room carpet. He'd simply upended it and watched as the purple liquid pooled onto the pale oatmeal twist. Tilly's mouth had fallen into an 'O', and she'd flown into the kitchen for paper towels.

'Come here.' Tom pulled me round so I was facing him, and then rubbed his thumb back and forth over one of my eyebrows and then the other. I gritted my teeth, suppressing a surge of irritation as I heard the scritch of the hairs being pulled the wrong way, felt the stretching of the skin. 'That's better. You suit the natural look. I keep telling you.'

I did my eyebrows every morning, meticulously adding in fine, natural-looking strokes with a sharpened eyebrow pencil. I'd done it every day of my life since a girl at school told me that my face looked like a boiled egg, with my high forehead and pale skin. But I knew from experience that it would be easier to submit to Tom's thumb-rubbing routine, and re-apply the eyebrows later, than to endure the sulk that would ensue if I pushed him away.

'I was thinking we could go out for a walk?' I suggested, as soon as Sarah and the boys stepped over the threshold. 'It's a lovely day.'

I noticed my hands were making tight little circling movements. I was desperate for them to leave and they'd only just arrived.

'Oh. Yes... okay,' said Sarah, leaving a little pause, a micro-expression of annoyance. 'Is it okay if I just get Ben a glass of water?'

I realised my mistake – if they were heading out again straight away, Sarah wouldn't feel the need to take off her shoes.

'I'll get it,' I said, flying to the kitchen.

When I came back with the water, Sarah reached into her bag for a bottle of yellow gloop and a dosing syringe. 'Thanks. He's got to take his antibiotics.'

My heart sank. Antibiotics for what? Something infectious?

'Oh dear. Is he okay?'

'And I need the loo, Mummy,' said Adam, Sarah's four-year-old, folding over and clutching his middle. In one hand, he held half a tuna sandwich – he called them 'Tudor sandwiches', and they were the only thing he would eat.

I caught Tom's eye as Sarah hustled the boys into the bathroom. He did a comedy grimace and held his outstretched hands in a hovering motion as if to say, 'Breathe...'

As if we were in this together, facing this horrifying invasion. I relaxed, just a little.

On cue, Edie began to scream, and threw up half-digested milk down my top. It was the fourth top that day. I'd have to go upstairs to get another. And then I'd have to put this one in the overflowing laundry basket (first putting it in one of the plastic 'wet bags' that Tom insisted upon) and then load the washing machine later while Edie napped, or grizzled in her bouncy chair. And while I was there in the utility room, I'd end up folding the clean clothes from the tumble dryer and I'd take them upstairs to put them away – Edie's baby-grows, vests and dresses in her wardrobe, Tilly's things in her room, Tom's pants and socks in one drawer, mine in another. His shirts in the ironing pile. Which reminded me – there was that button on the collar of his pink striped shirt that was loose and needed sewing back on. And the whole house needed a good clean too. This morning I'd found a message, written with a finger in the dust on the bathroom mirror: *I love you.*

'Steffi, are you okay?' asked Sarah, emerging from the bathroom. Ben ran ahead of her down the hall making aeroplane noises, holding aloft the yellow-stained medicine syringe.

It was another thirteen minutes until we left. Finally, Sarah got her two out the door and began to shepherd them down the driveway, hauling a buggy out of her car boot for Adam.

I wheeled Edie's pram round from the garage and crouched down to strap her in.

Tom came up close behind me and lifted the hood of my jacket, pulling it back with a tug, so that I had to grab the frame of the pram to keep my balance. 'I hope Sarah knows that you have to keep dogs on the lead in the park.'

I frowned, and opened my mouth to ask what he meant.

But another voice sounded in my head: *Fuck you, asshole.*

'Love you. Bye.' Tom ruffled my hair, like you might ruffle the ears of a spaniel, before he turned and went indoors.

THE BOTANIC GARDENS WERE BUSY, families drawn out by the September sun.

Sarah walked hunched forward, pushing the buggy, her face set with grim determination. Adam was way too heavy for his buggy now, but he hated walks, so had to be pushed at least some of the way. Ben circled around them, still holding the gloopy syringe, making siren noises. Tilly walked at my side, a little shadow. Edie was quiet for once, asleep and missing the company and the beautiful day. I glanced around, counting the children, making sure we hadn't left anyone behind.

I noticed Sarah's frown line had deepened into a perma-nent groove, and her eyebrows were reverting to their natural, untamed state, with some stubbly hairs in the middle that hinted at a monobrow. I felt a protective twinge. Was she struggling? Surely not – she had a lovely German girl who collected the children from school and nursery, and got the tea ready. And a cleaner three times a week. The family's life ran like clockwork, even while Sarah held down a high-powered job as an actuary in one of the big firms.

'So how are things?' I ventured, when we reached the top of the hill, near the café. Our shadows moved in front of us on the path, black as burnt matchsticks. I glanced behind us again, surveying the path that wound up the hill, the sunlit expanse of lawn. The high whispering trees and the shrubbery beds with their neat labels. The yew hedge with its dark spaces where I had once lost Tilly, one dreadful afternoon. Why did it feel like there was someone missing?

'Oh, you know,' said Sarah. Then she swung round. 'Ben! Put that down! We don't eat things off the ground! Wait for your lunchbox!'

Once we'd queued up in the café and sat down with our trays, Sarah pulled out her phone. 'Did I send you those pictures from Adam's birthday? There's a lovely one of you and Edie.'

She turned the screen around to show me. I stared. That couldn't be me.

My face was a starburst of lines where I'd forced a smile. My jawline – well, I didn't have one from this angle, my face merged into a Weeble-style double chin. And my hair... I'd noticed it had been thinning a little, since Edie's birth, my scalp more visible beneath the hair at my parting. I'd been hoping it wasn't obvious to anyone else, but there it was in the picture for all to see.

It was no wonder Tom wasn't bothered about our sex life any more. Who could blame him?

I tried to pull myself together. The photo was nice – it was *nice*, for God's sake. I'd barely bothered to look at Edie, as cute as a button in her little stripy dress. Or at Tom, standing to the side with his proud smile and smooth jaw, like a man from a Gillette shaving advert. It was one of those family moments you were supposed to cherish.

Just this morning, Marie Godfrey-Carruthers had posted a link to a piece saying how you shouldn't waste time folding the laundry, or doing the washing up, because your babies would be grown up and gone in the blink of an eye. It showed a photo of a beautiful young woman in a lacy vest top, her upper body curled around a sleeping baby, glossy chestnut curls tumbling everywhere.

I wondered what Tom would say if I left the house to descend into a chaos of unwashed dishes and dirty laundry so I could spend my time cherishing moments. I pictured his nostrils flaring, the muttered swear words as he swept errant pants and socks into the washing machine. The emphatic slam of the dishwasher door.

I exhaled, making a conscious effort to relax. Edie was sleeping and Tilly had taken Adam over to the play kitchen in the corner. Ben was running in circles with the aeroplane-syringe, drawing disapproving looks from a group of elderly ladies at the next table. I was about to drink a coffee while it was still hot, for once. This was *good* – as good as it got.

Sarah was fussing around with the things on the trays. 'Why did you get so many glasses? We've got one too many. And an extra box of raisins.'

'Edie doesn't sleep,' I blurted out. 'She wakes up every forty-five minutes. I don't know what to do. Sometimes it feels like she's doing it on purpose, testing me.' I felt my hands circling again. Heard my voice rising.

Sarah frowned and glanced at Edie, as if the fact she was asleep disproved everything I'd just said. I had always been the dramatic one. The annoying one. I had a sudden image of the four of us sitting round the dinner table – me and Sarah, our parents – as I related some injustice from the school playground.

I could almost hear my father's voice, the words deepening, the tone becoming authoritative: 'Come on now, Steffi, I think that's a bit of an exaggeration.'

'Please, Big Sarah,' I said, softly. I hadn't called her that for years. 'I need help.'

She picked up her phone again. 'I saw something on Facebook the other day, on that Edinburgh group. It was somebody recommending a baby sleep coach. People were raving about her.'

I imagined the raving mothers, senseless with sleep deprivation, arms waving like zombies.

'Damn, I can't find it. You could always put up a post yourself, looking for recommendations?'

'You're right,' I said, picking up my phone.

'Help needed!' I typed, then paused, thinking of Tom's horrified reaction if he ever saw this. The Buchanan-Smiths never had to ask anyone for help. 'I can't think what to say. I'll do it later.' I slid the phone back into my pocket.

'Here, let me do it.' Sarah reached for my phone, waggling her fingers.

'Sarah...? Do you remember Dodo?' My mouth felt dry. I ran my tongue over my lips to moisten them.

'Oh God,' said Sarah, keying in my passcode. 'How could I forget Dodo? I had to sit next to her every day at dinner.'

'What?'

She laughed. 'Don't you remember? You went through a phase when you insisted on setting an extra place at the table for Dodo.'

'*Did* I?'

'It used to drive Mum mad. You always wanted Dodo to get a portion of pudding so that you could eat it when nobody was looking. Mum always said no, and that she wouldn't "pander to your ways".'

'A very Mum thing to say.'

'But you'd get your way sometimes with Dad. He would say you were only little.'

A memory bobbed up in my mind. The family sitting around the table, the eager clatter of spoons scraping yoghurt pots. And Sarah's voice, dripping with teenage scorn: 'It's interesting how Dodo's never bothered about having a portion of lamb stew, or broccoli...'

And me, throwing a napkin ring at her, the clunk as it ricocheted off her eyebrow and hit the fireplace surround.

Screams. Tears. Me being sent to my room. (What an Appalling Fuss!) Whispering to Dodo under the covers that they could all die for all I cared, because they'd never loved me anyway. And then crying with shame, hating myself for thinking such terrible thoughts.

And now they *had* died, Mum and Dad. Sarah was all I had left.

'Sarah?' My heart pounded in my chest. 'I think Dodo has come back.'

'I've drafted up a post for you,' she said, handing my phone back. 'Have a read of that and see what you think.' Her head whipped to the side. 'No, Ben! No! Put that down! We don't throw cups!'

7

STEFFI

Edinburgh, Present Day

'How was it, then?' asked Tom. 'Are the glass houses still standing? Did he lay waste to the herbaceous borders?'

'Who?'

'My nemesis. Young Ben.' He put on a low, dramatic voice: 'The agent of my downfall.'

'Ha! He wasn't too bad today. The café was in pretty bad shape by the time we left, though.'

'You'll be barred from that place, you lot,' Tom said fondly. He placed his knife and fork neatly together by the side of his half-eaten shepherd's pie. He'd left the topping – the 'stodge', as he called it – even though I'd made it with sweet potato and cauliflower, rushing to put it together while Edie napped.

I could hear the sound of faint singing from the hall. Tilly, who'd finished her dinner already, including the stodge, was walking Edie around. The colic hadn't started in earnest yet – she was just grumbling a little.

'Yes. We were having an interesting discussion, actually. About baby sleep coaches.'

There had been one particularly promising response to my Facebook post – a woman had recommended somebody called the 'Sleep Fairy', and the fairy herself had joined the thread, with gracious thanks and a link to her website.

'Loads of people are saying they've used sleep coaches, and that it was, well… a game changer.' One of the articles I'd read about improving relationships had suggested mirroring the kind of language your partner would use.

But he just sighed. 'So this is what you've been cooking up. I thought you were up to something.'

'Sarah suggested it when we were on our walk.'

I realised I sounded like a child… *Sarah made me do it.*

'I'll have a look later.'

'Mmm…' I didn't want to show him the actual post on Facebook. Although the comments had started well, with the Sleep Fairy posting her link, another group member had posted a damning review of another sleep guru, whom somebody else happened to know, and the comments had got a little fractious. An admin had needed to step in.

'Most of them are booked up for weeks. But this Sleep Fairy one, she says she has a slot coming up on Thursday – a cancellation.'

'I'll have a look later,' he repeated. 'What do you actually know about this woman?'

'People have recommended her.'

'What *people*?'

'People on Facebook.'

He closed his eyes and pinched the top of his nose. 'I'll ask Deborah. She'll know someone. This isn't something to just launch into with abandon, Steffi.'

Deborah. His PA, again. I dug my nails into my palms.

'You see, I wondered if... you know the, er, the vouchers you gave me? Well, if you were okay with it, I could use the money for this instead?'

'How much will it *be*?' He let his mouth fall open.

'Two hundred pounds for the initial consultation,' I said quietly.

'Sweet Jesus.'

'I can't go on like this, Tom.'

'And *I* wish you'd stop making such a drama out of things. I said I'd look into it. I don't appreciate being ambushed.'

I picked up our empty plates and carried them over to the sink. 'But this Sleep Fairy person, she's got a slot this week. If we wait until Deborah has looked into it, the slot might be gone.'

'You can't just invite somebody off Facebook into our *house*, to look after our *child*.' He rose suddenly, scraping his chair back, whisking his plate away to put it in the dishwasher. Over the clatter of crockery, I heard him mutter: 'I mean, surely that would be obvious to anyone with half a brain.'

I had a sudden image of myself with my face shot off. Skull shattered, half my brain missing. Like in one of those awful video games Tom liked to play.

I wondered if I could just go ahead anyway, cover the cost myself. The problem was I didn't have any money of my own. My redundancy money had run out soon after Edie was born, and Tom had been covering all our joint expenses for a while now – mortgage, bills, food. He'd given me a credit card for anything I needed myself and he paid it off each month. But it was already close to its credit limit this month, since I'd had to pay the garage four hundred pounds to remove the word 'Bitch' from my car door, and two hundred to get the new stair gates fitted.

From somewhere overhead, floorboards creaked. Had Tilly gone upstairs with Edie? I tried to track her footsteps... she seemed to be walking towards the back of the house. Maybe she was taking Edie to look out of the big window at the back, the one with the stained glass panels at the top. No – she was heading the other way now, walking along the galleried landing. Had she closed the stair gate behind her? I pictured her struggling with the mechanism, Edie balanced over one shoulder.

'Now it all becomes clear.' Tom grabbed my plate and glass off the table.

'What does?' I felt an unpleasant flutter in my chest – my heart skipping out of rhythm.

'Why you sneaked off with Sarah this afternoon instead of having coffee here like you said you were going to.'

'I thought you would prefer it if we went out, so we wouldn't make a mess. I mean, you wanted us to stay in the kitchen and not go into the living room.'

'Oh, Steffi. That was a JOKE. I'm not going to stop you going into the living room with your own sister. For *FUCK's* sake.' He shoved the plate and glass into the dishwasher with such force that all the dishes inside it rattled.

Then he turned – slowly, wearily – and faced me. 'Am I such a monster?' he said softly.

Yes, said a voice.

'Of course not.'

Get away from him. Get out of his space.

'Come here.' He stretched out his arms and wiggled his fingers. I stood up and went to him, stiffly giving myself up to be held.

'There we go,' he said, pulling on my arms and tucking them around his waist. 'That's it, my love. There we go. I'm sorry I'm grumpy. It's just work stuff. You mean the world to me. You and Edie and Tilly. My beautiful princesses.'

It was okay, I told myself as I made my way carefully up the stairs to find Tilly and Edie, my hands leaving sweaty prints on the polished wood banister.

It was okay, I told myself when I found them cuddled up together on Tilly's bed. Tilly was reading *That's Not My Bear*, while Edie waved her little legs in their stripy woollen tights.

This was my family now. And Tom loved me. He loved me so much. He had a strong personality, that was all. He was an alpha male. Which had its pros and its cons – two sides of the same coin.

I would remind myself, in moments like these, how he had literally picked me up and put me back on my feet, after Mum died. I'd been 'made redundant' from Slater & Beeny, the property company I worked for, six weeks after her funeral. A woman from HR had called me in to her office to give me the news. They insisted it had nothing to do with the important client presentation during which my mind had blanked, or the times I'd had to go home early because I couldn't stop crying.

On my way out, my legs folded under me and I sank to the marble floor of the entrance lobby. I'd never had a panic attack before and I didn't understand what was happening. The security guard came over and tried to escort me from the building, but my legs were shaking too much to stand up, and I had no air in my lungs to explain. He muttered something into his headset, and a few minutes later the woman from HR appeared, dithering, keeping a safe two metres away. A cleaner materialised with a mop and bucket, her eyes grim and expectant over the top of her face-mask, as if waiting for me to expel some bodily fluids.

And then a man strode over. He was tall and broad, with a rugby player's build, wearing a dark suit and a pink shirt with a faint stripe, unbuttoned at the collar. Even in my panicky state, I recognised him as Tom Buchanan-Smith, someone high up in Breitling-Brown Investments, the company that was in the process of buying out Slater & Beeny.

Without a thought for his bespoke Prada suit (as he liked to point out in subsequent retellings of the story), he knelt down beside me on the floor. He shooed the other onlookers away. He told me to breathe with him, counting to four on the in-breath and six on the out-breath. As my breath returned, I found I wanted to lay my head on his chest. To feel those arms close around me, to feel the warmth of his skin through the pink cotton.

Once my legs were working again, he helped me to my feet and I stood there like a wobbly lamb, a newborn thing. He ordered a taxi home for me on his own account. As it pulled away into the traffic, I looked back at him through the window. He was standing there in the middle of the pavement, watching me, his feet planted firmly, hip width apart. He raised his hand in a confident wave and held it there, while passers-by weaved around him, until the taxi turned a corner and he was out of sight.

Presence. That's what he had. He wasn't afraid to take up the space around him.

Later that day, a box of delicious frozen meals from an

organic farm shop arrived, and a package containing cashmere bed socks, hand cream and soothing herbal tea.

And a note: 'Please allow me to take you for dinner when you're feeling better.'

Within weeks, he'd arranged the early termination of my lease on a horrible, expensive little flat in Canonmills, and hired a van to move all my stuff over to his house in Inverleith. He'd said he was honoured to be my 'port in a storm', and that I could stay as long as I liked. Or forever. He liked to relate this story often, as if he was telling an old and beloved fairy tale.

And our love story had to go on. Tilly was a part of it now, and Edie.

I watched as Tilly faltered over the last few words of *That's Not My Bear*, and Edie reached up to grab a fistful of her hair.

An unhappy ending simply wasn't an option.

8

JOANNE

Yorkshire, Present Day

Cushion Couple returned the next week, like the smell from a semi-blocked drain.

Joanne did the tour herself, even though it was her lunch hour and she'd been about to nip over to the Greggs on the market square to get a cheese and onion pastie. It was important to give the two new kittens in the back shed a wide berth. She'd privately earmarked those for a single mum of twin girls who'd phoned up that morning.

'You saw Blackie the last time,' said Joanne, ushering the visitors briskly through the first hut. 'And Twinkletoes.' It was an unfortunate name for the poor eight-year-old female, a tortoiseshell with a comfort-eating problem. Join the sodding club.

'No kittens have come in?' The woman actually pushed her bottom lip out.

'Nothing suitable,' said Joanne, shaking her head slowly, pretending to think.

The man went over to a cage near the back where a pair of skinny tearaways were tumbling around each other, making a right racket.

'What about one of these?'

'They're littermates. We're rehoming them as a pair.'

'They're adorable,' said the woman. 'What kind are they?'

'They're known as tuxedo cats,' said Joanne. 'They're not any particular breed, though. That's just the name for those black and white markings. See, they look like they're wearing white shirts and dinner jackets?' She felt herself softening a little when she saw the woman smile.

'They're seven months old, these two. Brothers. They came from –' She stopped, letting the story come to life in her head. 'A lovely chap who had to move to LA. He was in the film industry, I think.'

The couple exchanged a smile.

'It's up to you, babe,' said the man indulgently.

'We'll take this one!' The woman pointed at Felix, the one on the left.

Joanne froze. This couldn't be happening. Not again.

'They're to be rehomed as a pair.'

'We don't have room for two,' said the man. 'We've only got a small flat.'

Fiddlesticks. With that top-of-the-range Audi out front?

'Felix and Gus come as a pair,' she repeated. 'They've got an unusually strong bond. They're always playing together, grooming one another and everything.'

When they'd come into the shelter, they'd huddled together, shaking, at the back of the cage, and she'd found them asleep later, Felix's head resting on Gus's flank. They hadn't come in from some fancy film producer, they'd been found in a soaking cardboard box outside Pets at Home. If the couple had been Softies, or Saviours, she'd have told them that and laid it on thick. But Cushions never went for damaged goods.

It was just her luck that Mei-Ling chose that moment to come into the hut to refill the food bowls.

'We do prefer to rehome littermates together,' she said. But Joanne didn't miss the warning look she shot her.

'Oh,' frowned Cushion Woman.

'We can only take one,' insisted the man.

Mei-Ling looked at Joanne. 'I'll deal with this, please.'

Joanne turned and walked away slowly, her fists clenched in her pockets.

She just couldn't fathom it. How could people be so heartless? And bloody Mei-Ling was... what was the phrase again? Enabling them. Enabling them to be selfish pricks.

An hour later, Joanne watched from the staff room window as the couple left the shelter, the man gripping a cat carrier. Poor Felix cried loudly, his paws skittering on the newspaper as the carrier tilted. They hadn't even bothered to line it with a blanket.

Joanne wondered if he'd cry that night, or if he'd settle.

She felt two little pats on her arm.

'You know the score,' said Mei-Ling. 'It's management policy. We're bursting at the seams.'

Joanne nodded curtly. She knew it wasn't Mei-Ling's fault, not really. Underneath the woman's brisk exterior, she was a decent human being. She'd even asked Joanne over to her house for tea once. But Joanne had made some lame excuse. It was better to keep work and personal life separate. Even if her personal life consisted of a poky cottage in the lane behind the Co-op and two little cats.

And the mere idea of friendship felt dangerous to her – creaky and uncertain, like rotten floorboards in an abandoned house. Nobody would want to be friends with Joanne if they knew what she'd done.

She winced as the man slammed the boot shut. Poor Felix would be jumping out of his skin. The couple got in the car, so pleased with themselves that they hadn't noticed the long scratch along the side of the Audi's paintwork.

Joanne waited for the leap of satisfaction in her chest – for any kind of feeling at all other than this crushing weight – but it didn't come.

'That Facebook thingie we talked about,' she said, finally. 'Will you help me?'

'Yes.' Mei-Ling gave a deep nod, as if she'd been waiting for this moment for a long time. 'Although I'm not sure why you need me. You do an amazing job with the kitties' profiles.'

Joanne flapped away the compliment. She'd taken over the task of keeping the rescue centre's website updated, and had spent her recent annual leave redoing the profile pages for all of the cats they looked after, starting with the residents who'd been with them the longest. She'd taken three hours over the profile of an unfortunate soul called Bruiser. He'd been a hard sell, what with his missing eye and the chunk torn out of his ear. Joanne had renamed him Rocky, and had photographed him having his tummy rubbed, his head stretched back and his front paws flexed in delight. He'd been adopted within the week. Mei-Ling had declared Joanne 'the IT-savvy one' and sent her on a training course about social media for charities.

'We'll need a decent photo of you,' added Mei-Ling, with a warning look.

Doubtfully, Joanne looked down the length of her body, at the jeans with dirty patches on the knees, and the bulky purple 'Willoughby Bridge Cat Rescue' fleece.

'Smile!' Mei-Ling was already holding up her phone.

Joanne tried to think of something funny. Something happy. But all she could think of was Felix. How long before he forgot about Gus? A day? A week? Or would he always think of him when he curled up at night, aware of the empty, brother-shaped space beside him?

9

STEFFI

Edinburgh, Present Day

E die's cry burst through the darkness.

Groggily, I checked the clock. It was just after two o'clock, only forty minutes since I'd last got her back to sleep. I laid my head back on the pillow. Pain coursed through my body, zipping down every nerve. It felt like a physical assault, to be woken again so soon.

I lay and observed the baby monitor with one eye open, watching the green lights at the side going up and down with her whimpers.

Was that... whispering?

Had Tilly gone through to Edie's room to comfort her? Or was I just hearing things in the staticky background noise of the monitor?

Hush...

Hush...

Edie fussed again, her cry tailing off into a thin wail.

I'm here.

Jesus, that was definitely a voice. I hurried through to the nursery. But all was peaceful in there. Edie must have been dreaming. She was asleep on her back, chubby hands resting at the sides of her face. She was fastened into a quilted white baby sleeping bag which poppered over her shoulders and formed a triangular shape around her body and legs, like a child's drawing of an angel.

My heart settled and filled with love. And then guilt – how sad that it was easier to love Edie when she was asleep.

Just think how much I'd love her if she died.

The thought came into my head before I could stop it.

I laid my hand, very gently, on her chest, wanting to feel the rise and fall of her breathing, to let it settle me.

MY EYES SHOT OPEN.

Why was I standing in the dark at the top of the stairs? And holding Edie, still in her baby sleeping bag? Tilly was behind me, one hand on my arm, the other grasping the waistband of my pyjama bottoms.

'W-what happened?'

'I woke up to go to the loo,' squeaked Tilly. 'You were just standing here with Edie. Just staring down the stairs. I asked what you were doing but you didn't answer.'

I looked down. Below my feet, the stairs seemed to disappear into blackness, into the the unlit space of the downstairs hall. For a moment I had the dizzying impression that the dimensions of the house had changed while I'd slept, that the hall had shrunk into a narrower space, held tight between high walls.

And that there might be a figure down there in the dark, standing at the bottom of the stairs, staring back. Was that the glint of their eyes, reflecting the half light from the cupola above? I blinked and looked again.

As my eyes adjusted, I found I could make out the hallway – the open doorways into the dining room and the living room, the glass panels of the door into the vestibule, the Victorian patterned tiles. The shape of the coat stand with its curved hooks. My head seemed to swoop. I took a step back from the edge.

'Steffi?'

'Sorry,' I murmured. 'I must have been sleepwalking or something. Let's get Edie settled down again. Perhaps you could watch her for a minute while I get her a bottle.'

Tilly followed me into the nursery. Edie fussed a bit as I placed her in the cot, sensing the open space around her, the cool air where there had been warm arms. I curved my hand over her rounded head, the fragile bones of her skull, not yet fused into place. I thought of the sound of it, cracking off the tiles in the hallway below. Of what those eyes might look like with all the light gone out of them.

'Oh God...' A shudder moved through my body.

I felt Tilly's hand, tentative on my back. 'It's okay, Steffi.'

Edie's sleeping bag bunched as she drew her knees up to her chest. Her face crumpled.

'I'll get her a bottle,' I said. 'She won't go down without one.'

But Tilly placed her hand – fingers splayed into a star shape – onto her sister's chest and held it there for a few moments. Edie's eyes closed.

What? That never happened. *Never.*

We stood for a few moments watching the front of the quilted sleeping bag move up and down beneath Tilly's palm, the movement almost imperceptible.

'You wouldn't have fallen,' said Tilly. 'You wouldn't have... dropped her. You were quite far from the edge, really.'

I took Tilly back to her bed. 'Thank you,' I said, as I leaned in to hug her.

'Thank you,' she parroted back, stiffening under my touch like a little wooden doll.

'It must have been scary waking up in the night and finding... well, me. Like that. At the top of the stairs. I'm sorry if I frightened you.'

'It's okay. You didn't,' she replied flatly.

I wanted to say so much more.

Sorry for coming into your life and turning everything upside-down.

Sorry for not loving you the way I love Edie.

'You seem unhappy,' I ventured.

She looked away from me and down at her chest, making a pudgy little double chin. Then she pulled her covers up to her neck.

'No, I'm fine. Goodnight.' She rolled away from me and closed her eyes.

I retrieved my phone from the bedside table, taking care not to wake Tom, and went to the bathroom.

Sitting on the toilet, I opened up Facebook, only to find that my post about sleep coaches had been deleted. But there was a message in my inbox, which had been sent three days ago.

I think your thread may have been deleted!
But see below the link to my website again. I
do have a free slot next Thursday morning so
please let me know if I can help. Either way,
wishing you and your little one all the best.

Somebody was finally going to help. Tears blurring my eyes, I messaged her back.

10

STEFFI

Yorkshire, Age 8

It was going to be a good day. Sarah's usual Saturday piano lesson wasn't on, so she'd invited her best friend over, and Steffi would be going swimming with them.

Mum had bought a whole pineapple from the greengrocers, because Georgina was staying to tea.

'It's a bit of an extravagance, I know,' she said, unpacking the shopping.

Steffi pictured her father, standing over the table, smiling his kindly dinosaur smile and carving the pineapple proudly like it was a Sunday roast. She felt her insides squirm, just a little. Maybe she could suggest to Mum that he could cut it up in advance.

Still, today was a good day.

Mum crouched down to put the cold things away in the

fridge. Steffi noticed the way her dark hair curled against the collar of her blouse, how pretty it was.

'Will you plait my hair later?' asked Steffi. 'After swimming?' Her mother put complicated French pleats into Sarah's hair every day before school.

'Hmm, well, let's see.' She swivelled round to look at Steffi, a pot of yoghurt still in her hand. 'Yes, I suppose so. Your hair looks long enough now.'

'I love you!' It just burst out of Steffi's mouth. Then she hesitated a moment. Would she do it? Yes. She threw her arms around her mother's neck, trying to plant a kiss on her face.

Mum stood up, squirming out of Steffi's grip, trying to save the yoghurt. 'Steady on! You'll pull me over! Now off you go and get your swimming things ready.'

Steffi still had a funny feeling about the stairs, since the day of Sarah's concert when the banisters had twisted around like snakes and she'd dropped to the floor in an Appalling Fuss. But she'd discovered that she could go up them safely, as long as she sang *The Lord of the Dance* while doing so. She knew all the words because she had to sing it in assembly every week – Mrs Mountbatten, the tone-deaf headmistress, liked it best of all the hymns in the book.

Daddy had made a pitying face when she'd told him. Not about the stairs, but about Mrs Mountbatten. At St Otterley's, the boys' school where he was Head of Music, they sang choir music every morning in assembly, and a tone-deaf headteacher would never have been given the job.

Steffi made her way up the stairs, carefully placing her feet in time to the words. Up in her room, she found her swimming costume, towel and goggles and shoved them in an old Woolworths bag. She couldn't wait to get to the swimming pool, to go into one of the little changing cubicles that lined the poolside. Then she'd swim into the part of the pool where the sun streamed in through the glass of the Victorian roof, making ripples of light that shimmered under the surface.

They would play games, maybe timing each other to race across the pool, watching the Speedo clock that hung over the deep end. Once, they'd played synchronised swimming and Sarah and Georgina had clapped and cheered when Steffi had managed to float on her back with one leg stuck in the air, before sinking down under the water in a semi-controlled fashion.

And this trip would be even more exciting than usual. The three of them were going to get the bus to the swimming pool by themselves, because Mum and Daddy were going to be busy painting the spare bedroom, ready for Aunt Veronica and Uncle Geoffrey visiting next weekend. Last night she'd overheard a whispered debate between Mum and Daddy about whether Uncle Geoffrey should be allowed to share a room with Aunt Veronica, since they were not married. Daddy – who'd said yes, of course, they were grown adults – had won.

Steffi knocked on Sarah's bedroom door. 'Are you nearly ready?'

'No.'

Steffi opened the door, even though she knew that would make Sarah cross.

'I'm a monster! *Roar!*' she cried in an endearing voice aimed at Georgina. She ran in and launched herself at her sister's friend.

'Hi, pest.'

'You've got new braces!' said Steffi. And more spots than before, she thought, but didn't say. She loved Georgina.

'I'm a monster!' she repeated.

'You're pathetic,' said Sarah, wearily. 'Go away. We're getting ready.'

'Can I get ready with you, too?' She made her voice high and soft. 'Please, Big Sarah!'

'Go away.'

Steffi tried again after five minutes. She banged on the door with both fists. '*Ro-oarrrr!*'

'Go AWAY!'

Steffi swung open the door and leaned in. 'DANCE, then, whoever you may be!'

Last time Georgina had come over, she and Sarah had taken turns to sing *The Lord of the Dance*, seeing who could best imitate the high, wavering tones of Mrs Mountbatten. They'd fallen about in helpless giggles, setting each other off again and again.

'That's not even the right words,' said Sarah, in withering tones. 'I can't find my goggles. Can you find them, please? I'll give you five pence.'

'Where did you last see them?'

Sarah looked thoughtful. 'In the shed.'

With a loud sigh, Steffi went downstairs and pulled on her trainers. The shed was horrible – it smelled funny, and there was a spider's web in one corner of the roof, with fuzzy lumps that Steffi thought were probably baby spiders ready to hatch. What would Sarah's goggles be doing in here?

Steffi rummaged through a box of old flower pots and pushed aside a bag of compost with her foot. A bit of old trellis fell down on her, scraping her leg.

She ran back into the house. 'They're not there!' she
shouted up the stairs.

But Sarah's bedroom was empty, sunlight falling in pale
columns across the beige carpet. Steffi flew into the spare
room to find her mother and father, clad in old shirts, paint-
brushes in their hands. The bedroom was empty of furniture
apart from the bed, with its old-fashioned headboard and
ruffles around the sides. For a moment she imagined Uncle
Geoffrey sitting up in the bed, dressed in a frilly granny's
nightcap like the wolf in Little Red Riding Hood. And Aunt
Veronica beside him, in the flower-sprigged BHS nightie
Mum had bought her for Christmas, with its terrifying 'Keep
away from fire' label.

'They've gone!' Steffi cried. 'Sarah and Georgina have
gone without me!'

Bitches.

That was Dodo, muttering inside her head. Steffi closed
her mouth into a thin line so that word wouldn't come out.

Daddy looked up, wiping a smear of paint off his face
with the back of his hand. 'Oh, Steffipops. Let the girls have
some time to themselves. You know how busy Sarah is. She
hardly ever gets time with her friends.'

She stamped her foot hard on the floor. 'But you *said*!'

'Steffi!' snapped her mother. 'You're going to have to stop
these outbursts.'

Steffi ran to her bedroom, diving under the duvet and
pressing her face against the soft fabric of her tartan blanket.
No swimming pool. No sunlit water. No synchronised
swimming.

Sarah and Georgina didn't think she was cute. They just
wanted her to disappear. She cringed at the thought of her

monster impression and pulled at her hair until strands of it came away in her hands.

How could she make Big Sarah care about her?

She wept until she was exhausted and her eyes felt puffy and swollen. The sky grew darker and rain began to fall – hard, sideways rain, spattering itself against the window. She thought of Sarah and Georgina getting soaked as they waited for the bus, and felt calmer. She wrapped her tartan blanket around her shoulders and wrote in her notebook for a while – she was writing a story about some children who lived in a house near a railway line, a house you could see from the train. Their father had gone away, a bit like *The Railway Children* but different. But today it seemed like a stupid story.

Pointless and stupid. She heard Sarah and Georgina come in, the front door slamming behind them, and she pulled the duvet over her head again. She wasn't a cute monster. She was like Gollum, in the *Lord of the Rings* picture book that Sarah had on her bookshelf. A pale, ugly, creeping thing that lived in dark places.

But eventually her mother rescued her. She came in to ask if Steffi would like to help cut up the pineapple. Steffi rose from her bed, weak with relief. She wrapped her arms around her mother's waist, pressing her face against her stale, floury apron.

Her mother reached for the doorframe to steady herself. 'Ouff! Steffi, don't *attack* me!'

Steffi followed her out of the room, waving a quick apology to Dodo. Who was still angry and sad and invisible, sitting on the floor by her bed.

11

STEFFI

Edinburgh, Present Day

The moment I saw the woman standing on the doorstep, I had the overwhelming sense that everything was going to be fine. Apple-cheeked and smiling, she was wrapped in a long grey coat, buttons securely fastened against the September wind.

She radiated quiet confidence. Capability. All I had to do was hang on. Just hang on for a few more nights, and things would get better.

'Joy?'

'Indeed I am,' she said. 'And this must be Edie?'

Perched high on my hip, Edie glowered at the lady who'd come to sort her out.

I ushered Joy into the hall and took her coat, hooking it onto the antique coat stand with my spare hand. Then I stood jiggling Edie, hovering in anxious indecision. Tom insisted that everybody take their shoes off in the house, even the people who came to read the meter, and the plumber who came to fix the shower last week.

As if she'd read my mind, she leaned over to unlace her sensible shoes. Then she stood up, patted down her silvery-blonde helmet of hair, and plucked a piece of fluff off her cardigan, which was navy wool with a repeating pattern of cherries. 'Right, then. Shall we get started?'

I led her through the hallway to the cavernous kitchen at the back of the house, where sunlight from the tall windows fell across the polished oak flooring. I ran water into the kettle and put mugs out on the worktop to make tea.

'We've only got an hour or so, I'm afraid. I need to collect Tilly from school at three.'

'That's plenty of time for the first session,' said Joy. Then: 'What a remarkably beautiful house.'

'Thanks.' I gave an awkward laugh. 'It's...' I always had to stop myself explaining to everybody that this was Tom's house, not mine. As if I were the nanny or something.

We sat down with cups of tea. I positioned mine a good eighteen inches away, out of grabbing reach. I'd have to let it go lukewarm before I could risk drinking it.

'So how can I help?' asked Joy.

I didn't think I could say it with Edie sitting right there on my knee. Or maybe I couldn't say it at all. Joy would be shocked. Her soft, lined eyes would widen in surprise.

I'm at the end of my tether.

Sometimes I wish I could hand her back.

I would kill for a few hours of uninterrupted sleep.

I rested my gaze above Joy's head, where shadows danced on the pale grey wall, a delicate tracery of branches. Tom wanted to cut down the old magnolia tree that stood at the edge of the terrace because he was worried its roots would be encroaching into the foundations of the house. I'd persuaded him to give it a stay of execution.

What could I say?

I'm going crazy.

There's an invisible person living in my house.

Edie's outstretched hand swiped my face, the edge of a fingernail catching my lower eyelid.

I gasped, my hand flying up to my eye. Edie arched back dangerously on my knee, and I grabbed her round the middle.

A tear shot down my cheek and I smudged it away with my shoulder.

'Has it been a hard old few months?' said Joy.

'It's – it's just my eye. She caught my eye.'

'Ouch.' Joy winced and unclipped her handbag – it was one of those granny-ish ones with stiff leather and gold clasps. She handed me a clean, folded tissue.

'She won't sleep,' I managed. 'I've tried everything. It's all getting too much.'

'Too much in what way?'

I opened my mouth to tell her about my auditory hallucinations, the sleepwalking incident, my dependence on caffeine tablets to get through each miserable day, but I couldn't find the words. Instead, I pushed some sheets of paper across the table to Joy.

'I've been keeping a sleep log. This part shows the times of all her feeds, how many mils she drank, whether she was sick, what times she slept and woke up, and what I did to try and get her back to sleep. This column shows what activities we did during the day... a walk, or baby yoga or whatever. I've been trying to find a pattern, to work out what helps her to sleep or not.'

Joy frowned down at the sheets of paper. Each day, the writing started off neat, and then descended into barely legible scribbles, with words snaking into the margins. One of the sheets had a brown stain in the corner. Another was wrinkled with spilt milk.

Joy flicked through the last couple of sheets, nodded, and pushed them back across the table.

'I can help,' she said simply.

I looked away, fixing my eyes on Edie's hair, on a perfect little curl behind her ear that caught the light like spun gold. I could feel another tear wobbling, about to fall.

'And we won't need any of that,' went on Joy. 'No more lists or logs. Once she's sleeping better, everything will be easier, I promise.'

I gave a small nod.

'I trained as a nursery nurse when I left school,' said Joy. 'It was all I'd ever wanted to do. And then in my mid-twenties I went to work in a unit for mums who had postnatal depression. I helped the mums learn how to play with their babies, and manage day-to-day routines. Then I took the plunge and trained as a therapist, specialising in family dynamics.'

'Oh goodness,' I said.

She nodded, a little shyly. 'So I'm coming at this from two angles. I know babies, the monkeys. I know their ways.' She shot me a conspiratorial look. 'I can give you all the practical advice there is about babies and sleeping and routines. But my training means we can do deeper work together, too. I set up my little Sleep Fairy business because I've seen what a difference it can make, using this combined approach.'

I nodded. 'That makes sense.'

'What is it you would really like to get out of this?' she asked. 'How would you like to *feel*?'

I thought of Marie Godfrey-Carruthers and her Facebook posts. 'I want to cherish every moment. I know she won't be a baby for long. But I just spend all day longing for her to go to sleep.'

Joy spoke softly. 'How can you possibly cherish each moment when you're in such distress?'

I shook my head. If I said anything, my voice would go. This woman saw me. She'd seen, in a few minutes, what Tom hadn't seen in five months.

But what was that sound? A key in the front door? Was Tom home early? I lurched out of my chair, clutching Edie against my chest, and grabbed the charts off the table with one hand. But then came the sound of something shuffling and then dropping onto the doormat. It was just a delivery.

'Silly delivery people gave Mummy a fright!' I kissed the top of Edie's head. Placed the trembling sheaf of papers on the table again.

'Oh yes,' said Joy. 'It can sound like somebody's in the house. I nearly got the fright of my life last week when my Veet strips arrived from Amazon.' She pointed to her upper lip and widened her eyes.

I smiled. 'Oh.'

'You mentioned... Tilly? Was she a good sleeper, as a baby?'

'Tilly is Tom's daughter. I'm just her stepmother. Except I'm not officially that, because Tom and I aren't married. Yet. We're engaged.' I was gabbling.

'So you weren't around when Tilly was a baby?'

'No. Not till the last couple of years.'

'And is Tilly's mum... is she...' Joy left a delicate pause, lifting her tea cup to pursed lips. 'Is she still with us?'

'She lives in a special community down south. A sort of community for, well, for...' I tried to find the right words. I could hardly say it was for loonies, like Tom had said. 'It's for artists. It's a safe place where everybody supports each other.'

I was embarrassed at how little I knew about Adeline, except that Tom couldn't divorce her – even after several years of separation – because it would 'push her over the edge'.

He didn't like to talk about her, but phrases had stuck in my head from the bits and pieces of almost-conversation we'd had about it.

Resistant to treatment...

Relapsing episodes...

Postnatal psychosis...

Tom had said that she was happier living in the community place – they were like a family to her. She'd never been able to cope in the real world. She was one of those fragile artist types, only interested in 'flinging paint around'. She certainly hadn't taken to motherhood. She'd acted more like a disinterested, much older sister to Tilly, rather than her mother.

'So she's not around,' I explained to Joy. 'But she does keep in touch.' The community was 'off-grid', Tom had explained, so communication options were limited. But Adeline wrote twice a year, at Christmas and on Tilly's birthday. Sometimes she sent paintings she'd done. Last birthday she'd sent a painting of a screaming face, which Tom had picked up by its corner between finger and thumb, and dropped into the wheelie bin. Tilly had gone quietly off to her room. 'It just upsets her,' Tom had said, shaking his head.

'And Tom,' said Joy. 'Does he help out with the baby at night?'

'He's very busy at work. He really can't function without proper sleep.'

Joy's face contorted into a pitying expression. 'Dear oh dear. Men are so helpless, aren't they?'

I nearly laughed. In my relationship with Tom, I was the helpless one. Right from the day when he'd picked me up off the floor, the day I'd been made redundant from Slater & Beeny.

And now look what I was doing – going behind his back, hiring the Sleep Fairy when he had expressly forbidden it. I had withdrawn cash on the credit card and told Tom I'd needed it to pay for some dental treatment – the surgery's card machine had broken. I'd held my hand up to my cheek as a sort of corroboration. He'd frowned but hadn't pursued it.

I pushed my guilt away. Tom would support me, if he knew how much I needed this. And anyway – what was it he'd said when I'd talked about getting my car paintwork repaired? That I should 'actually do something for once'?

'So... how do we do this?' I asked Joy. 'How can we get her to sleep through?'

'Why does Edie cry in the night, do you think? Why does she bother?'

'Because –' Suddenly I thought of those silent Romanian orphanages where none of the babies ever cried, because nobody ever came.

I thought of a cot painted with faded yellow giraffes. Of looking through the bars towards a dark hallway. The image flickered in my mind and was gone.

'Because she *trusts* you, Steffi,' said Joy. 'Crying is her language, and she is asking you to help.'

'Help her with what? She can't really be hungry. I feed her before I go to bed. And the doctor has said there's nothing physically wrong with her.'

Joy inclined her head towards Edie. 'Ask her.'

I sat Edie upright on my knee. 'What do you need, my love?' Suddenly, as I looked deep into her dark blue eyes, I had a rush of understanding. 'You're tired too, aren't you? Is that it? You just want to sleep. Just like me.'

I glanced at Joy, who was grinning broadly.

'So here's my idea,' I said to Edie, suddenly feeling that she and I were in this together. 'If you cry at night, I'll come and stroke your back, and sit with you. But you need stay in your cot. Because we stay in bed if we want to go to sleep, don't we?'

'Look at you! You're doing my job for me! So when do you want to start? I usually come round for a few hours on the first night when you're starting the new routine. Just to give you some moral support and get you started.'

I thought quickly. Tom was going to be visiting his mother in Pitlochry on Friday night, and was taking Tilly with him.

'Friday night? Could you do Friday night?'

Joy smiled. 'Yes I can.'

'The only thing is... payment. I've got a limited budget. I've got two hundred in cash here for the initial consultation, but...'

'We'll sort all that out later,' she said, waving me away. 'We'll work something out. I'm not in this for the money.'

12

JOANNE

Yorkshire, Present Day

J oanne held her fingers crossed behind her back. This was the first person in weeks to show any real interest in Blackie.

The woman in the cream silk blouse and suit trousers – Cheryl, she'd said her name was – had got right down onto the floor of the enclosure to pet him. Joanne crouched down too, even though she knew her knees would crack something terrible when she stood up again.

'Oh, you adorable thing!' Cheryl squeezed her eyes shut and leant forward to kiss the top of Blackie's head. Her hair – faded red Bonnie Langford-style curls – tumbled around him. Joanne caught sight of the cat's eyes, his pupils huge, peering through the ringlets.

Joanne curled her fingers around his tail and stroked it to

the tip. 'I'd take him home myself if I could. But it wouldn't be fair on my other two.'

'Have you got cats yourself?' The woman's voice was high in pitch, rather timid.

Suddenly, Joanne realised where she'd seen the woman before. She'd been in front of her in the queue at the bakery a couple of weeks ago. She'd been kind to the young girl behind the counter, a nervous new hire who'd given her a steak bake instead of a cheese and onion pastie, and then dropped her change on the floor. Cheryl, gracious and unhurried, had stooped to retrieve the coins and then put them into the tip box on the counter.

Joanne didn't normally give out details about her own cats – her family, as she thought of them – to any old stranger, but Cheryl seemed decent enough.

'Mitski's five. She's a right madam, a Bengal-tabby mix. Gorgeous – and she knows it! And Albie's ten, bless him. Just a gentle soul. Took him ages to adjust when Mitski came in. It wouldn't be fair to add another one to the mix. And before that, I had Whisky and Sherry. Littermates. They lived till fourteen and then went within a week of each other.'

Cheryl's face creased. 'Oh, good Lord.'

Joanne had thought she'd never recover. She'd brought Albie home from the shelter a month later. He'd been living in a one-bed flat with a pair of drug addicts and he'd pulled half his fur out. She'd cried like a baby that evening, when he'd come to lie quietly on her lap during *Coronation Street*, and she'd realised that she could let herself love another cat.

'Blackie's ever so sweet,' she said, running a hand along his back and up the length of his tail. 'He's got a touch of dandruff and unfortunately I think that's put off some of our would-be

adopters. The less experienced ones, you know.' Joanne
sensed that Cheryl was the sort who'd go for an undercat. She
categorised her as a Saviour type, under her meek exterior.

'I used fish oil supplements for my last cat,' said Cheryl, a
note of determination entering her voice. 'So I could try that.
And lots of grooming and brushing. That'll sort you out,
won't it, Blackie? Hm?'

Blackie pushed his nose into the lady's cupped hand,
marking her with his scent. He pushed so hard that Joanne
could see his legs quiver with the effort.

Please, she thought.

'Come on then, you,' said Cheryl, bending again to kiss
the top of his head. 'Let's get you home.'

JOANNE WENT over the forms with Cheryl in the office. She
learned that she had just recently moved to a bungalow in a
quiet cul-de-sac, with a large garden that backed onto woods.
Blackie would be the only animal in the household.

'We normally do a home visit,' said Joanne, 'before
releasing an animal for adoption. But I'm happy to arrange
that over the next few weeks if you'd like to take him away
today.'

'Oh, of course! Pop over any time. We've still got one or
two packing boxes about the place, but we'll be shipshape in
no time. We only moved in a few weeks ago.'

Joanne's pen hovered. 'Have you got a partner? Children?'

'No,' said Cheryl. 'Just me and my dad. He was desperate
to come along today, but it's hard for him to get out.'

Joanne nodded happily. A housebound oldie was good.

Plenty of company for Blackie and the house would be kept warm all day.

'And your occupation?'

'I'm a private investigator.'

Joanne's eyebrows shot up before she could help it. She'd always imagined private investigators as hard-nosed types with nicotine-stained fingers, their cars littered with take-away food wrappers. Not like this gentle, hesitant woman in front of her now. Her cream silk blouse had a ruffled bow at the collar. It made Joanne think of the tired department stores of her childhood, of smooth, faceless shop mannequins.

'Really? What sort of private investigating do you do?'

'A fair bit of marital. Some court work. We find lost people, sometimes.'

'Lost people?'

'Yes. Missing persons. AWOL fathers. Long-lost family type stuff. Not as exciting as it sounds, I'm afraid. It's mostly online these days – desk work.'

Joanne thought of her new Facebook profile, and the post that Mei-Ling had helped to create. It had been shared just five times, and had generated no leads. And what a time of it they'd had, trying to take a profile photo that satisfied Mei-Ling. 'Too grumpy!' she had scolded, repeatedly.

The picture they'd finally settled on had been the best of a bad bunch. Mei-Ling had pulled Joanne's greying brown hair out of the harsh ponytail she always wore for work and fluffed it around her shoulders, but it had done nothing to soften the frown lines, the thick set of her features, the jowly chin. Christ, she was only forty-nine and she looked sixty. And nothing to show for it except two cats in a cottage that smelled of damp, and a job that paid less than McDonalds. How had that happened?

'Will my driving license do for my ID?' asked Cheryl, waving it in front of Joanne.

'Sorry, I was miles away.' Joanne took the little card and placed it under the lid of the photocopier. Something was building inside her – an urge that was hard to ignore.

'How much do you charge?' she asked, trying to sound casual. 'For your investigating?'

'It depends.' Cheryl eyed her with curiosity. 'But we offer a free initial consultation. We ask for all the information you've got and give an honest view on whether we think we can help.'

How would a 'people person' react, Joanne wondered. She could feel the stirrings of a liking for this woman who'd been kind to Blackie. And she wanted her to like Joanne back. So she stuck a smile on her face, and made her voice soft and cooing. 'I'd love to book an initial consultation. If that would be okay.'

13

STEFFI

Edinburgh, Present Day

I woke suddenly to a stinging pain in the centre of my scalp.

'Ow!!' My hand flew to my head, eyes watering.

Tom was propped up on one elbow, grinning, holding a couple of strands of my hair between his fingers.

'You had a grey,' he said.

'What?'

'I got it, don't worry,' he added with a satisfied nod.

As if he'd captured a head louse or a flea.

I closed my eyes and took a deep breath. Tom didn't know I was paranoid about the thin hair at my parting. He probably hadn't noticed the specialist shampoo, lined up with the other bottles in the shower. He wasn't doing it to annoy me.

What would the relationship articles say?

'I'd quite like to keep *all* of my hairs, thank you,' I said, forcing a light, playful tone.

'Not the grey ones,' he said, still grinning like a loon. 'You don't want to be a grey old granny, do you?' He un-pinched his fingers to drop the hairs. They drifted down onto my chest.

'I don't have any grey hairs yet, as far as I know.' Which was a miracle, given the last few months.

'Ooh, a wee bit sensitive, are we?' He leaned over to peer into my hair again and started raking through it with his fingers. 'Let's see.'

'Actually, Tom. Just leave my hair, please.'

He sighed. 'Okay, okay. How about I bring you tea in bed? And one of those yoghurts you like.'

He meant the fat-free, sugar-free yoghurts he had added to the supermarket order.

But I smiled. 'That would be nice. Thank you.'

'Look at you, eh? A lie-in and breakfast in bed.'

I glanced at the clock. It was just before seven. I'd been up between ten past three and four with Edie, and again between about five and six. I actually wanted to cry. If Tom hadn't woken me, I might have managed another precious half hour of sleep.

He leaned forward to kiss me. 'Do you love me?'

'Yes,' I mumbled.

'No, say it properly.'

'I love you.'

He winced and turned his face away with a little cough. 'Ugh. Can I suggest you either brush your teeth or close your mouth.'

When he'd left the room I lifted the hairs from my chest

where he'd dropped them. I held them up to the light to check. They weren't grey.

I heard him going into the bathroom and getting into the shower, turning on the water. Breakfast in bed obviously wasn't happening after all. I decided to go downstairs and make myself a cup of tea, hoping I might be able to drink it in peace before Edie woke. I took the stairs slowly, humming *Dancing Queen* and holding onto the banister, bringing my feet together carefully on each of the steps.

Tilly was down in the kitchen, already fully dressed in her uniform. But one of the buttons had come off her shirt. She was definitely developing in the chest area, the poor soul. The other nine-year-olds in her class at school were as flat as washboards.

'Oh darling,' I said gently. 'One of your buttons has popped off. Can you go upstairs and put on another shirt? I'll sew it back on later for you.' An unexpected, warm feeling went through me as I thought about getting out my mother's button box and searching through it to find one that matched.

Tilly nodded. I watched her as she left the kitchen and stood in the hallway just outside. She took a deep breath and ran. I followed her into the hall, watching her run to the foot of the staircase and all the way up, a dark blur on the other side of the banister. I heard her releasing her breath in a big puff as she reached the top.

A wave of dizziness passed through me. What if she tripped and fell? I thought of her, a little heap in her school uniform at the bottom of the stairs.

When she reappeared in the kitchen in a new shirt, I spoke to her gently. 'Please be careful on the stairs, Tilly. You don't want to trip.'

'Why are you scared of the stairs?' she asked, curious.

I opened my mouth to say I wasn't scared of them. But then I stopped. I thought of my first Appalling Fuss, at the top of the stairs in my childhood home. My mother's face contorting as she tried to get me off the floor to go to Sarah's piano concert.

'I've never liked stairs. I don't really know why.' I gave a little laugh, trying to make light of it. 'If you think about it, stairs are weird, aren't they? A bit like having a huge cliff in the middle of your house.'

Tilly's eyes widened.

'You just need to be careful, that's all,' I said. 'And you don't need to hold your breath when you go up. You might make yourself dizzy.'

'Okay, Steffi,' she said, her voice wooden. Suddenly, I wanted to sweep her up into a hug.

'By the way,' I said. 'I saw those amazing drawings in your room. The ones of the cats and kittens? You really like cats, don't you?'

She nodded, looking up at me warily. 'Dad says we can't get a cat. I've already asked him. Because of the hairs and the smell and everything.'

Arsehole, said a voice in my ear.

'Did he? Oh dear. But you're so good at drawing. You've got a real eye. And actually, I've been thinking and I've got an idea for something we could do together. A little project.'

Her face lit up.

THERE WAS a new mum at the school gates that afternoon, deep in conversation with one of the other mums, Cassie. She was gesticulating wildly, and I caught the words 'homework' and 'impeenge on family time', spoken in an Australian accent.

Cassie introduced me: 'Steffi, this is Zara. Her little girl, Aurelia, has just started at the school.'

Zara stepped towards me and held out a confident hand, the movement causing her mass of dark curls to tumble forward over the shoulder of her smart navy blazer jacket. 'Hi! You're Tilly's stepmother, aren't you?'

'That's right.' I didn't go through the whole loop of explaining that Tom and I weren't married yet, so I wasn't anybody's step-anything. 'Hello! And this is Edie.'

Zara glanced briefly into the buggy. 'Oh, lovely. The next generation of sprogs coming up, eh?' She touched my arm lightly. 'I'm soooo glad that Tilly's doing so *well* these days.'

I smiled vaguely, wondering if I was missing something. Was there a suggestion that Tilly *hadn't* been doing well before?

'I knew Adeline,' she said, with a little sympathetic crinkle of her nose. 'We used to go to the same baby massage class.'

Adeline. She put the stress on the final syllable instead of the first and it took me a moment to realise that she meant Tilly's mother. This was interesting. I'd never met someone who knew Adeline. Other than Tom, of course. And Tilly, although she couldn't remember anything much about her.

'So terrible, what happened.' Zara peered in at me, fixing me with gooseberry green eyes. Perhaps she was trying to gauge how much I knew.

I could either nod knowingly, or I could use the opportunity to... well, gather information. I left a pause, just long enough for it to feel awkward.

'We don't talk about it very much,' I said finally. 'I know that she went away to live in some kind of artists' community when Tilly was younger. I know she'd had some... *episode* of some sort. Tom doesn't like to talk about it. It still upsets him.' I had a sudden image of Tom as some kind of present day Mr Rochester, brooding and mercurial, with a mad wife or two tucked away somewhere in our vast Inverleith pile.

Zara nodded and wrinkled her nose again.

'In fact, you may well know more about it than me.' I tilted my head and gave her a sad, sweet smile.

She seemed to swell with self-importance. 'She had a rip-roaring case of postpartum psychosis. Didn't you *know*?'

A tingle moved down my spine. 'I wondered if it was something like that. Poor Adeline.'

'She thought it might have been linked to her difficult childhood – growing up in care, and everything,' Zara added, observing me closely for a reaction.

'Oh dear,' I said.

'Yeah. It was so difficult for Tom,' Zara went on.

It had been difficult for *Tom*? A dart of annoyance went through me. 'Was it?' I said lightly.

'She was an inpatient for a few months in a special unit. He had to cope all on his own with Tilly, taking her in to see Adeline most days. Not at the start, of course, because she wouldn't see him. When she was first admitted, she believed that Tom was a secret government scientist and that he had filled the house with poisonous gases as an experiment. Apparently, she'd been online trying to order gas masks from Amazon.'

I thought of Tilly as a baby, a gas mask strapped over her little white face. I had a sudden urge to pull her close. I scanned the playground, looking for her.

'When Adeline came out, her hair had gone completely white!' Zara stepped back on one of her high-heeled boots and folded her arms. 'An extreme stress response. I barely recognised her. She seemed to have aged terribly, the poor thing. Some of us from the baby massage class went to visit her a few times. But we could see something still wasn't right. The maternal bond, it never recovered. Or it was never properly there in the first place. There were... question marks.' She looked at me knowingly.

'What do you mean, question marks?'

'About how well she was coping with Tilly.'

'Oh?' Join the club, I thought.

Zara nodded. 'Once she left Tilly alone in the house and went out. Although it turned out she was in her car, parked at the end of the driveway. A neighbour saw her there, fast asleep. Adeline had taken sleeping tablets, seemingly, and dihydrocodeine. She was rambling, telling the police she would die if she didn't get a few hours uninterrupted sleep.'

Poor, poor Adeline.

'And it was dangerous to take all those tablets, with her heart condition. Really reckless. They kept it all very hush hush. I only know all this because the neighbour's sister used to go to our tennis club.'

'Heart condition?'

'Yes. She had to be rushed to hospital. When she got back, there was talk of Children's Services getting involved. But then she went off to that community place. I think, at the end of the day, she accepted that she wasn't cut out for motherhood.' Zara pulled her face into a sad yet smug expression.

'Poor Tilly.' I felt a strange, hollow ache in my chest.

'You're doing a fantastic job,' said Zara, putting a hand on my arm. I wasn't sure how she would know this, having only met me five minutes ago. 'Blended families aren't easy,' she continued. 'My sister remarried three years ago. Her step-daughter cried through the entire wedding. And she still asks every day when she's leaving. Every. Single. Day.'

A shudder went down my back.

'How did Tilly take it when you guys got married?'

'Oh, we're still planning our wedding, actually.'

Which was a lie. But Tom had promised it would be soon. He'd just have to pick the right time to raise the divorce issue with Adeline. His lawyer had advised him to tread carefully because of the possibility that Adeline might 'make things difficult', or even go for custody of Tilly. Whenever I probed further, he'd shake his head and say I didn't understand what I was dealing with. The woman was 'like an unexploded bomb,' he'd said.

The school doors were flung open and small children spilled out into the playground, running up to their parents for hugs, or thrusting school bags and gym kits into their arms before running off to play again. Tilly appeared quietly beside me.

'Hello!' I smiled and gave Tilly's shoulder a little squeeze.

'Ah, lovely.' Zara shot me a syrupy, meaningful look over the top of Tilly's head, as if to congratulate me on the 'fantastic job' I was doing. 'Hey, how about getting Aurelia and Tilly together for a play date? Do you guys still live in the same house – the one down near the Botanics?'

I put on a well-practised smile. 'That would be so lovely! Let me check the calendar and I'll get back to you.'

I'd just have to hope she didn't bring it up again.

'It's my *space*,' Tom had whined, the last time I'd raised the subject of playdates. 'I just don't want it overrun with kids. Or *mums*, spilling coffee and crumbs everywhere. Does that make me such a monster?'

'But it means Tilly doesn't get invited to playdates at other children's houses,' I'd explained. 'Even the birthday party invitations have dried up, now that they're getting older and people aren't inviting the whole class. If we want her to make friends then we have to let her have people over. And I have to make friends with the mums, too.'

'Don't make a drama out of it, Steffi, please. We've got the Botanics right on the doorstep,' he'd said, sweeping an arm in the direction of the bay window, where rain was running in rivulets down the panes. 'Take them there.'

'Tuesdays are good for us,' said Zara now, her face expectant.

'Perfect,' I said, using my smile again. 'We have one or two things pencilled in over the next couple of weeks, but maybe towards half term?'

Tilly tugged on my sleeve. She was looking up at me, her face alight. I resolved to speak to Tom again about playdates.

14

STEFFI

Edinburgh, Present Day

My nerves were shredded. It was half past midnight and Edie had just gone to sleep for the third time that night after an hour and a half of screaming.

Joy and I were sitting on the floor in the hall outside the nursery, talking in low voices.

'Maybe she's unsettled by that wind.' Joy looked up at the cupola, where rain rattled against the glass. 'It's blowing a hoolie out there.'

'Maybe.' If only Edie's sleep patterns could be explained by something as simple as the weather.

'So where's Tom tonight? Is he away on business?'

'He's taken Tilly to visit his mother.' I pictured the dreaded 'Granny Vivienne', festooned in Van Cleef & Arpels, leaving vapour trails of Dior *Poison* in her wake.

She nodded emphatically. 'Oh, quite right, quite right. It's always easiest to do these things when they're away. Doing their golf or whatnot. They'll just get in the way otherwise. Or think they're helping.' She waved a dismissive hand. 'You know what men are.'

I changed the subject quickly. 'I'm not keen on the controlled crying thing, just leaving them to cry it out on their own. I'm glad you're not suggesting that.'

'Ach, these things go in and out of fashion. My mother used to leave me in my pram at the bottom of the garden for most of the day while she got on with the chores. That's just what they all did in those days. They believed babies needed fresh air – that it would help them to sleep, and give them healthy lungs.'

I thought about Edie, lying in the dappled shade of the magnolia tree, blue eyes gazing up into the canopy.

Joy left a pause, and then said softly, 'Did your own mother ever talk about her experience of motherhood? About how you were as a baby? Sometimes we can pick up messages about parenting from our own parents, without even realising it.'

'I can't really remember. Mum sometimes talked about my sister, Sarah, having asthma and how scary that was when she was a baby. Hospital trips in the middle of the night and so on.'

'And what about her experience with you?'

Had I been a difficult baby? An easy one? I realised I had no idea.

'I don't think I had any particular problems.'

'So you had a normal, happy childhood?'

'I guess?' I shrugged.

Joy kept her gaze fixed on me, eyebrows raised slightly, as

if waiting for me to say more. I remembered that she'd trained as a family therapist. Perhaps she wasn't going to be satisfied until I'd dished up some childhood trauma that would explain my ineptitude with Edie.

'I suppose Sarah was always the favourite. She knew all her numbers by the age of two and a half, and could sight-read music by the time she went to school. She's an actuary now. I think she got all the mathematical genes.' I gave a rueful little laugh. 'I'm more... artistic, I guess. Or I was, as a child, anyway. I used to like drawing. I was always writing stories and doing pictures to go with them. I used to staple them together into little books.'

Joy looked confused for a moment. Perhaps I had strayed off topic.

'Where do you get that from, then?' she asked. 'Was someone in your family artistic?'

I tried to think. 'My Aunt Veronica did a pottery class once.' I laughed, suddenly remembering how her gentleman friend, Uncle Geoffrey, had arranged it for her birthday. He'd put the course leaflet inside her birthday card, with a note inviting her to 'unleash' her artistic side. Aunt Veronica had blushed deeply. Granny had looked aghast, as if he'd organised a pole-dancing class or something.

'I like to take a holistic view,' said Joy eventually. 'Sometimes sleep problems in babies are all bound up with deeper rooted psychological issues. Chatting to family members can be useful – to help us reflect on different parenting styles, and our own experience of being parented.'

'My parents passed away some time ago. I guess I could ask Sarah, my sister.'

'You could look through some family photos. That's how I got to talking about all this with my own mother. She had a photo of me in my pram, looking grumpy and all trussed up in a woollen bonnet.' Joy gave a tinkling laugh. 'Have you got any old photos?'

'I've got a few in the bureau downstairs. But they're school photos, mainly.'

In fact, I'd had them out to show to Tilly just the other day, because she'd been asking what people used to wear for school uniform 'in the olden days'.

And Tom had come in. 'What are those photos?' he'd demanded. 'Where did you get them?' He'd calmed down once I'd shown them to him, and said he'd leave his 'princesses' to it. I wondered, afterwards, if he thought we'd found some photographs of Adeline.

'Sarah's got most of the family photos in her attic. But there aren't many. My parents didn't have a camera until I was about three.'

'Oh?' said Joy.

'Yes. Cameras were expensive. Getting the films developed and everything, too.'

Even as they came out of my mouth, the words sounded odd. They had an automatic quality about them, as if I was repeating something I'd been told as a child. Something I'd never questioned.

An image popped into my head – Sarah's face, gaping and furious, looming over me.

You've ruined it. You've ruined it.

And I suddenly remembered a rainy day stuck in the house, having to listen to Sarah plonking away on the piano for hours. I'd explored Sarah's room and found a photo album at the bottom of her wardrobe, and a black magic marker in the pot of pens on her desk…

I remembered looking down in horror at what I'd done –

it had been like waking from a dream, seeing the black figure I'd drawn onto every one of the photos, the telltale black smudges on my fingers. Feeling sick and shaky about the row I'd get from Mum.

But when Sarah had called Mum up, and shown her what I'd done, Mum had barely reacted. She'd simply prised the marker pen out of my fingers, her lips pressed into a thin, pinched line.

'She'll have to get them reprinted,' Sarah had hissed, as we'd watched Mum retreat down the stairs with the photo album tucked under her arm. 'So *expensive*.'

'I'm sorry, Steffi,' said Joy, breaking into my thoughts. 'I didn't mean to be nosy, honestly. It's just that this is a special area of interest for me. I think I mentioned that I'm doing a diploma in perinatal mental health?'

I nodded vaguely.

'As part of that, I need to complete a little research project of my own. I'm doing mine on how child-rearing beliefs are passed down from mother to daughter, and how that impacts on mental health.'

'Interesting.'

'In fact...' she looked a little sheepish now. 'I was wondering if you would agree to be one of my case studies. As a thank you, I'd be happy to enrol you in my Platinum Package, free of charge.'

'Platinum Package?'

She nodded earnestly. 'That's ongoing support with sleep training, weaning, tantrums and other toddler issues... basically, support in person or at the end of a phone, any time you need it, until Little Miss reaches age four. We'd start with a session every two weeks, at least until she's in a really good routine.'

'For no charge? It would be free?' I wouldn't need to invent any more dental treatment. And having Joy at the end of a phone... it would be almost like having a mother. I swallowed hard.

Joy nodded. 'Indeed it would. Including this session, too. And you'd be doing me a favour. I'm a wee bit behind, you see. I should have started all my case studies by now.'

'Would it be... anonymous?'

'Of course. Completely confidential.'

'The only problem is... Oh God, I'm sorry. This is ridiculous. But Tom doesn't know about our sessions. He's not...'

Joy nodded, her double chin bulging, her eyes conspiratorial. 'He's not on board yet? No need to explain.'

'But if you were able to come round when he's at work...?'

Edie's cries started up again from behind the wall.

Joy patted my shoulder. 'Come on, you go in and settle her. I'll make us both a cup of tea.'

15

STEFFI

Edinburgh, Present Day

'Wake up, sleepyhead!' Joy was smiling down at me, holding out a cup of tea and a cashmere throw that she must have picked up from the sofa downstairs. I'd nodded off on the floor outside Edie's room.

'Here, wrap this round you. Keep warm. I'd say she might just settle for the night now. She's been quiet for about ten minutes now, the monkey.'

I took the mug from Joy and sighed a grateful thank you. I caught her glancing at her shadowy reflection in the ornamental mirror that hung on the wall opposite. In a fussy little movement, she patted her hair down, smoothing it into place around her ears.

'Yes, let's hope so.' I put the mug of tea down and closed my eyes. I just wanted to curl up on the carpet and go back to sleep. Had Joy really needed to wake me?

A noise came from the hall downstairs – the inner front door rattling in its frame.

I pitched forward onto my hands and knees and scrambled to my feet. 'Shit! He's back. Oh shit, shit...' My mind was racing – how would I explain Joy's presence? Maybe she could pretend to be a friend who'd come round to visit me. Maybe she could pretend to be the GP or the health visitor. I could say I'd been worried about Edie...

Joy was up on her knees, listening hard, her head straight up like a meerkat. 'No. It's just the wind, dear. It's shaking the house, that's all.'

Of course it was. Why would Tom be coming back home in the middle of the night? I sat back down, the adrenaline subsiding.

A wash of light moved over the wall above the stairway. This time it was Joy who reacted, drawing in a quick breath. Her face was a frozen mask in the half dark.

'It's just a car,' I said. 'Their headlights catch the wall sometimes if they do a three-point turn at the end of the road. It looks like someone's waving a torch around, but they're not.' I laughed uneasily. 'It can get a bit spooky in this big old house at night.'

As if in answer, the wind howled in the chimneys. I sat back against the wall again and pulled the blanket over my hunched knees. From the corner of my eye, I could see the dark drop of the stairs. Joy hadn't fastened the stair gate when she'd come up.

The woman appeared to be thinking hard. She frowned and pressed her forehead with both hands. 'If you don't mind me saying,' she said eventually, 'you appear to have two problems here. The fact Edie doesn't sleep, which we can sort.

And the fact that Tom doesn't seem to be supporting you. When's the last time he took a night shift with Edie?'

I shook my head. 'He's got a very demanding job. He needs his sleep, in order to function.'

Joy sighed. 'Men are such hopeless creatures, I find.'

'He's a good man, honestly. A decent, hardworking man.'

He's an arrogant pig, said a voice in my ear.

'Be quiet,' I muttered.

Joy sat back and crossed her arms, observing.

'I'm sorry,' I muttered. 'I didn't mean you.'

'What's going on?' she asked, her eyes narrowing in concentration.

I thought of mental hospitals with locked corridors and doors that buzzed when people were let in and out. Social workers with heavy brown files.

But the words spilled out anyway. 'I think I'm going mad. I hear voices. I can hear someone speaking.'

'What someone?' Her voice was sharp, suddenly.

'It's Dodo.' The words came out automatically.

Joy's frown deepened. She gave two tight little coughs, as though her throat had gone dry. 'Dodo?'

'Yes. She was... she was an imaginary friend, when I was little. But she's come back.'

I heard Joy's mouth unsticking as she prepared to speak. 'What kind of things does Dodo say?'

'She comforts me when I'm upset. She warns me sometimes, if there's danger. She helped me once when Edie nearly choked.'

There was a long silence. When Joy spoke there was a slight tremble in her voice: 'I've come across this before.'

'You have?'

'Have you heard of Third Man Syndrome?'

'No.'

'You know of Ernest Shackleton, the explorer? Well, when he went on his expedition to the Antarctic, he and his team had to survive dreadful, appalling conditions. They were at the edge of human endurance. Freezing temperatures. Facing death from exposure and exhaustion and starvation. They just had to keep walking and walking, day and night.' She cycled her hands round like she wanted to fast-forward over all that and get to the good part. 'Later, when they got home, they reported a... an unexplained presence. They said that there was another person with them. They all said that there was *one more person with them than they could count.*'

She leaned forward in her chair, eyes fixed on me.

I thought of the walk in the Botanics with Sarah, and my feeling that another person was with us, just outside of my field of vision. The way I'd counted the black shadows that fell on the path ahead of us.

'And now it's a recognised phenomenon,' Joy went on. 'There are similar reports from all through history. In all cultures and religions. You see it in the accounts of soldiers and explorers, and the people who survived 9/11... even in the Bible. When people are at the limits of their endurance, they report the same thing. The human mind creates a sort of psychological guardian angel. Someone to get you through.'

The limits of endurance. That's where I'd been, for the last five months. Pushing through the wilderness of motherhood alone. Days and nights cycling in an endless blur.

'So you don't think I'm mad?'

'Bouf!' She batted my question away. 'Not a bit of it. You've been doing exactly what you need to do in order to cope. Just like Shackleton, or those people who escaped the Twin Towers. You're a survivor, Steffi. A survivor.'

The doorbell shrilled, making us both jump.

'What the hell...' I glanced at the clock. It was half past three in the morning.

Had there been an accident, or something? I lurched up, my legs weak with panic. I descended the stairs, holding the banister with both hands. Joy walked behind me, her hand on my shoulder. 'Take it easy now, dear.'

There were two police officers at the door. A man and a woman.

Edie...

Tilly...

'What's happened?' I demanded.

'Sorry to disturb you at this hour," said the male officer. 'We've had a couple of calls from concerned members of the public.'

'*What?*'

'One caller reported incessant crying.' He glanced down at his notebook. 'As if a baby or young child was in unusual distress. Or had been left unattended.' He glanced behind me into the hallway.

Joy began to speak. 'Now let –'

The policeman held up a hand. 'I've got two little ones myself. I know what it's like. But the other call was rather more concerning. The caller reported seeing a figure. A woman, they thought it was, standing up on the roof.'

'On the roof of this house?' I said, incredulous.

He nodded.

'What, like someone trying to break in?'

The officer shrugged slowly and shifted from one foot to the other. 'It wasn't clear to the caller what the person was doing up there.'

I thought of the noises of the wind and rain, shaking the house. Could there have been someone up there?

'There's no way up to the roof from outside,' I said, trying to think clearly. 'There is a flat area up there, a bit you can stand on, but you can only get to it through a hatch in the upstairs hall ceiling. It's got a ladder that pulls down. It takes you up into the attic space and then you go out of a little door onto the roof itself.'

Specialist workmen had been up there in spring to clean the cupola. It had cost more than I used to earn in a month at Slater & Beeny.

'And nobody's been up there,' I said. 'They couldn't have been. We've been here in the house the whole time.'

I thought, suddenly, of Tilly's hooded 'lady' from the retail estate. The one who'd carved the word 'bitch' onto my car. Had that been something personal, after all, rather than a random act of vandalism? Was it possible? Had that person waited until Tom had gone away for the night and then tried to break in?

The female officer was staring at me, waiting for me to elaborate.

Then I realised. The caller must have thought it had been *me*. Teetering up there on the roof. Trying to block out the sounds of my baby's screams. Deciding whether to step off into thin air.

She spoke gently. 'We're just following up. Checking if any assistance is required.'

'Assistance is *not* required.' Joy stepped forward, her nostrils flaring. 'I've been here with Steffi the whole time. Every single minute of the last several hours. And I can assure you there's nothing untoward going on. Nothing whatsoever. I'm an accredited sleep expert and I'm helping with the baby's routine.'

The male officer nodded, seeming to visibly relax.

Joy wrapped an arm tightly around my shoulders and gave me a reassuring little jiggle. 'Now, officers, you're welcome to come in and see if we're harbouring any poor distressed souls or abandoned babies. But all you'll find is a Little Miss who's rather put out with her new routine.'

The woman officer's mouth twisted, as if she was trying to hide her amusement. 'Sleep training, eh? Right you are. Well, we'll take a quick look around the back just to make sure there's nothing amiss.'

When they'd gone, Joy tutted. 'What nonsense. Your neighbours must have way too much time on their hands.'

Which of the neighbours had it been, I wondered? There was a High Court judge and his wife on one side, and a famous but reclusive writer on the other. I'd never spoken to them at all. I'd planned to drop Christmas cards round once, but Tom had told me to respect their privacy.

'Now, how about some fresh tea?'

I smiled and let her fuss around me. But Joy hadn't been quite straight with the police, had she? She hadn't been with me every single minute. Not when I'd fallen asleep. And I did have form with sleepwalking, didn't I?

I tried to dismiss the possibility. Joy would have heard me clattering around with the ladder, wouldn't she? But still, I glanced uneasily up the stairs to the hall above, at the ominous square of the hatch in the ceiling.

16

JOANNE

Yorkshire, Present Day

Joanne had made tea for Cheryl and shown her into the living room, acting as if she had visitors all the time, as if she hadn't just spent the last two hours making the place look vaguely presentable.

She'd scooted a sulky Mitski off the sofa to make a bit of space and she'd even forced out some small talk, as best she could manage. She'd asked about Blackie and how he was settling in... whether he was on wet food or dry, whether he liked going outside, whether he'd brought anything in. He wouldn't be much of a hunter, she was willing to bet. Too soft, just like her Albie. Cheryl smiled and nodded without carrying the conversation on. Joanne opened her mouth to ask what brand of worming treatment Cheryl was planning on using, then closed it again.

And so now here they were. Joanne knew she'd have to go through it all quickly. To skate over it like thin ice.

Cheryl drew a notebook and pen out of her bag. 'I'm just going to make one or two little notes, if that's okay?'

Joanne nodded, and folded her hands to keep them still. 'Our mum tried her best.'

The story contained certain elements that had to be true, that held it up like load-bearing walls. 'She tried her best, but she had problems, and she didn't get the help she needed. Sadly, she died.' Her voice sounded wooden, as if she was reading from a script.

'I was eleven and my sister was just coming up for three. It happened suddenly and the social workers had to find emergency foster care because we had no family we could go to.'

Cheryl closed her eyes briefly and nodded, as if it was a story she'd heard too many times before. She'd pinned her curls up today, into an opal-effect hair clasp, but they looked tired and faded. Joanne could see pale bits of scalp under the teeth of the clasp. She wore similar tailored trousers to those she'd worn at the rescue centre and a powder-blue silky blouse.

'And that night, the night it... happened, they couldn't find an emergency foster family that would take the two of us together. They were all full up. So I went to a family on Dalby Crescent, who had four already, and she went to a family who lived on the other side of town. The social worker kept saying I'd be able to see her soon, but there were procedures that would have to be followed, first. Forms to be filled.'

Joanne took a sip of her tea, noticing white flecks floating on the surface, wondering how long the milk had been open, wondering if she could really do this.

Cheryl shook her head in sympathy as she wrote something in her notebook. 'Did you see her again?'

'I saw her all the time,' Joanne said with a dry little laugh. 'But it was never really her.'

She remembered a rainy afternoon she'd spent on the peeling bedroom windowsill at Dalby Crescent, squashed between the glass and the net curtain, trying to give her hard-faced foster sisters a wide berth.

She'd peered through the window, wishing she was out there instead of in here. Down the street, towards the main road, she could see a woman at the pelican crossing, the one with the entrance to the park on the other side. With her was a little girl who was wearing an ugly pink raincoat with brown flowers on it. Her arm was stuck up at an awkward angle, holding the woman's hand. Her legs looked thin in dark tights, her shoes clumpy.

The little girl's hood slipped down for a moment and Joanne glimpsed her face.

In an instant, she launched herself off the windowsill. She ran down the stairs and flew out of the front door, not even pausing to put on her shoes.

She ran to the crossing, socked feet slapping on the wet pavement. Her head swung wildly from left to right, checking up and down the street – no sign of them.

She ran on to the park entrance and across the soggy grass, calling her name again and again, even though the park was all but empty. Just an old man walking his dog, and two boys kicking a football around. The play park area was empty, rainwater pooling at the end of the slide and in the seats of the swings.

Where had they gone?

But her legs wouldn't work any more. She folded onto the

grass, her hands clasped over her head. She wanted to pull her sister into her arms, to hold her so hard that the little arms and legs would squirm beneath the ugly raincoat. To see trusting brown eyes lifted to hers.

'I've got you,' she'd say. 'I've got you.'

And it would all be okay. She'd never let them take her away again. She'd never believe their lies about paperwork, and procedures, and getting to see her soon.

But the woman and child had gone. Had they used the other exit, out onto Malton Street? Or maybe they'd gone down the steps into the lane behind the shopping centre. She wished she could split herself into a dozen different parts, so she could run down every street, bang on every door, until she found her.

'Are you okay?' asked Cheryl now, reaching a soft white hand across the coffee table towards Joanne.

'Yes,' said Joanne. 'Anyway, after about a year the social worker told me that she'd been adopted by another family. It was a closed adoption, which meant that I wasn't allowed any contact with her. They said they always tried to place siblings together but it wasn't always possible.' Joanne's voice sounded rigid, robotic, just like the social worker's when she'd told her the news. 'I got a photo, a while later. And then that was it. Nothing.'

'Did you ever try going through a specialist intermediary who could access the adoption records?'

'I did look into that once. But the circumstances that led to her being taken into care were... difficult. Very difficult. I think it's unlikely that her adoptive parents would have made her aware. So I felt it would be unfair to open it all up. To land all that on her. I realised that I owed it to her to... well, to leave her be.'

Cheryl's brow crinkled. 'So why now?'

'What I really want...' Joanne swallowed. 'Is to know that she's okay. If I knew she was safe, and happy, and grew up in a nice family, then I think I could leave it at that.'

'Are you saying you want me to find her, but without her knowing?'

'Exactly.'

Cheryl simply nodded, and made a note in the notebook. Joanne's heart soared. She remembered the collapsing face of the adoption support specialist when she'd asked if such a thing would be possible.

'Without her consent? *Absolutely* not. Not under any circumstances,' the woman had said. She'd spoken so forcefully that a fleck of spittle had landed on the lapel of Joanne's jacket.

'Can you do that?' Joanne asked.

'I can certainly try,' Cheryl said, still writing. Joanne noticed she had an opal ring that matched the hair clasp.

Maybe the woman's meekness, and the invisibility afforded to her, as a late middle-aged woman, gave her an edge as a private investigator. Nobody would give her a second thought.

'Sometimes people can be found through social media,' said Cheryl. 'I assume you've exhausted those avenues, though?'

'I don't have enough to go on,' said Joanne. 'I don't even know what surname they gave her.'

'Okay. I'd like to take down all the details you have,' said Cheryl. 'Names and last known addresses, dates of birth, birth parents' details... everything you know.'

Joanne told her everything she could remember, which wasn't much.

'And how do you spell her first name?'

'S-T-E-F-A-N- I-E.'

'Stefanie? That's useful – an unusual spelling. And how old was she when she got taken into care?'

'She was just about to turn... three.' Her voice thinned on the final word.

Joanne remembered Steffi's third birthday quite clearly. She'd wanted to buy her a present, ready for the next time she saw her. But she hadn't had any money, not even enough for one of the tired-looking teddy bears in the window of the local Oxfam shop. Instead, she'd mended Steffi's blankie – a square of soft tartan material that she'd taken everywhere with her, before... well. She'd borrowed a needle and a reel of red cotton from the art room at school, and spent two evenings working on it, trying not to think about how Steffi would be managing without it. Trying not to think about the dull, horse-faced social worker who'd packed it in the wrong sodding case while Joanne had been on her knees on the pavement, trying to comfort her sister. *Inconsolable*... it was a word she had never truly understood until that evening.

Anyway, she'd mended the tear with the neatest little stitches she could manage, sponged off the sticky marks with a soapy flannel, and ironed it on the lowest heat setting. She had even wrapped it up, ready to hand over. She still had it now, in a box on top of the wardrobe.

'You mentioned a photograph,' said Cheryl. 'Would you mind showing that to me?'

Joanne went and fetched it from a little box on the mantlepiece, and handed it to Cheryl. It showed Steffi beaming, showing both rows of her little white milk teeth, peeping out from behind a tall ice cream sundae.

'She's in a café of some sort, I think.'

Cheryl looked closely at the photo. 'See the window? There's a reflection there, right in the corner. I think it's a reflection of a sign behind the counter.' Joanne could hear a note of determination enter her voice, reminding her of the moment the woman had decided to adopt Blackie.

'I know,' said Joanne, peering at the photo upside-down. She could see the dark, rain-streaked window, a smudge of headlights on the street outside. The blurred, curly lettering of a pink neon sign reflected in the glass. 'I've tried to read what it says. Marinello's, or Maricello's. Or Marinella's, maybe. I looked it up online and couldn't find anything.'

'It looks like Mannello's to me,' said Cheryl, squinting. 'Do you mind if I take this away with me? I can try and get it sharpened up. If we could narrow down her whereabouts to a city, or a town, that would make all the difference.'

'Please take care of it. I've only got the one copy.'

Cheryl got out her phone and carefully photographed the snapshot. 'I'll message this to you. So you've got something, at least, until I can give you the original back.'

'Thank you.' Joanne had already photographed it several times, saving the images in various folders and drop boxes, but she didn't say anything. Albie twined around her legs and she lifted his sleek, elastic body onto her lap. He'd be looking for treats.

'And I know this might be very hard, but what can you tell me about the circumstances that led to the adoption?'

Joanne concentrated on stroking Albie. From the top of his head, down his back, along the length of his tail.

Top of his head, down his back, along his tail.

Top of his head...

'Anything that you can tell me would help,' coaxed Cheryl.

Joanne swallowed. 'Our mother died suddenly. In an incident at home. Keith was charged and found guilty.'

'Keith being...?'

'Our mother's boyfriend. Steffi's father. My biological father, technically, too, as I understand it.' She shuddered. 'He used to come over and stay, once or twice a week. He'd bring drink with him and they'd have a bit of a session, usually. But he had another family. A wife and children, I believe. He wasn't a pleasant character.'

Cheryl left a pause. Albie yawned widely, squeezing his eyes shut and revealing four sharp canines and rows of jagged molars. A tiny squeaking noise emerged before he closed his jaws again.

'I... I had to testify against him, when he was on trial for killing my mother.'

That was why she'd had to leave the foster family on Dalby Crescent. A brown envelope had arrived through the letterbox, with Joanne's name on the front. And inside, a long, muscular, obscene-looking length of meat, crawling with maggots. The police had confirmed later that it was a cow's tongue.

Joanne had told the police about Keith's teenage thug of a son, Barry, who'd once had a Saturday job at the butcher's. She'd heard Keith boasting about it to her mother, saying the lad could get his hands on cheap meat – meat that was just starting to turn but would be fine once cooked. The police had said, very carefully, that nobody could prove the cow's tongue was connected to Keith, but all the same, it was a stunt that bore all the hallmarks of witness intimidation. The implications of a chopped-off tongue were perfectly clear. So she'd been moved to an emergency foster family, further away.

'Keith went to prison,' went on Joanne. 'One of mum's cousins took me in eventually, after the trial was over. But Steffi's adoption had been finalised by then.'

'And is your father, Keith, still alive?' Cheryl's pen was poised, ready to write down the details.

Joanne cleared her throat. 'Would you mind... *not* referring to him as my father? I never thought of him in that way. And certainly not after what happened.'

For a moment Joanne wondered if she'd offended Cheryl. But then the woman nodded vigorously, curls bouncing. 'Of course, of course. I'm sorry.'

'I did some searching a while back. Ancestry sites and whatnot. It seems he died in 1991, just a few years after it happened.'

'And Keith's other family? You said he had children?'

'He had a wife, who was disabled, I believe. And Barry, the son I mentioned. And a younger daughter – Angel, I think her name was. I don't think that's going to help you find Steffi, though. The whole point of her adoption was to get her as far away from that rotten lot as possible.'

'Okay. We'll move on for now,' said Cheryl in a whispery voice. 'But this makes me wonder – have you thought about adding your details to the adoption contact register?'

'I've told you,' said Joanne. 'I don't want to dump all of this on her. It's not fair.'

'I understand,' Cheryl assured her. 'But remember, with the adoption contact register, you'd have control. The adoption records wouldn't necessarily be opened up. You could decide exactly how much to tell Steffi about what happened. You could even say that you don't want to meet, or have ongoing contact, but you just wanted to know that she was well.'

Having found Steffi, could she just let her go again? 'I'm not sure,' she said.

'But think about it, Joanne. If Steffi *has* put her details on the adoption contact register, it means she is *already looking*. She wants to know about her birth family and is taking steps to find out the truth. Wouldn't it be better if she found you first? Then you could control the narrative, couldn't you? If she draws a blank with the adoption contact register, she might well try and access her files. If she hasn't already.'

Joanne imagined Steffi in some soulless room at the council offices, someone setting her social work file on the table in front of her. The look on her face when she realised what had happened. And nobody there to explain. To tell her that, no matter what had happened, she had been loved in that first life of hers. Adored.

Joanne felt her heart speed up. Her guts churned, suddenly, with the urgency of it. 'Okay then. I get it. Let's put my details on the adoption contact register.'

'Right. I've got the forms here. I'll need some ID from you as well before we do this.' She paused, reached out the white hand again. 'Are you okay to continue, Joanne?'

She'd bloody well have to be, wouldn't she? She pulled Albie closer onto her lap and nodded.

17

STEFFI

Edinburgh, Present Day

Sarah, Ash and the kids lived in a neat white bungalow in Blackhall, perched on a windy corner plot at the top of a hill, with high hedges to shield it from the road. The dining room looked out onto a shadowy wedge of garden with a weeping willow and a gnarled Victoria plum tree.

Sunday lunch had started at eleven o'clock. Nobody really had the appetite for roast chicken at that time, let alone crumble and custard, but Ben had football practice at two, and Sarah would have to drive him there.

Sarah always hosted a traditional Sunday lunch on the third Sunday of September, because of Mum and Dad. It was a tricky time of year. Dad had died on the eighteenth of the month. A lorry had ploughed through a red light into his car, while he'd been driving home from a school choir rehearsal. I could never think of it without remembering the phone call, the harsh ringing disturbing the quiet of a Sunday afternoon.

And Mum's fixed face, brittle as porcelain, during the six days it had taken for him to die in hospital.

She'd waited another ten years to go – ten years and two days. It was as if she'd set herself a target and grimly hung on. Getting up every morning, going to sleep every night, disturbing only one side of the double bed with its stiff floral bedspread. Preparing modest meals and a succession of hot drinks – two cups of tea in the morning, three to stretch through the afternoon and an Ovaltine at night.

In the end, she'd been whisked off neatly by an aortic aneurysm. No fuss. When Sarah and I went through her house, she'd already packed most of her belongings into boxes labelled for different charity shops.

And now it was just us. There was no generation ahead of us, to show the way or to make it easier. The four of us – me and Tom, Sarah and Ash – we were the grown-ups now.

I looked at Tom, who was sitting beside me at the table, and felt a sudden tenderness towards him. Although he was perfectly groomed as always, he had purple shadows under his eyes from yet another week of working ridiculous hours. He held a forkful of potato halfway to his mouth, nodding as he listened to Ash going on about an intellectual property conference he'd attended recently.

Adam, swinging his legs under the table, munched on a pungent 'Tudor sandwich' – he didn't like chicken. Ben, thinking he was unobserved, flicked a stray pea at his brother.

Tom turned to me, one eyebrow raised slightly. When no-one else was watching, he crossed his two forefingers together and raised them up towards Ben, as if warding off evil.

'*Nemesis*,' I whispered. But he'd already looked away.

Tilly, dutifully sawing through a dry piece of breast meat, looked up in curiosity. 'What's "nemesis"?'

'Oh, nothing, darling,' I said.

'Yeah, what's "nemesis"?' demanded Ben, pouting.

Tom shot me a withering side-eye. In a mere second, his mood had curdled.

By my feet, Edie made a little sucking sound. We'd decided to put her in her car seat for a bit so we could both eat at the same time, and she'd fallen asleep there – *guilt, guilt*.

I wondered about lifting her out and settling her warm, dense little body against my shoulder. There was a small chance that she'd finish off her nap. If not, she'd probably fall asleep in the car on the way home and that would be her new sleep schedule knocked off for the next twenty-four hours.

'Tell them about our book,' I said to Tilly, when we'd moved on to pudding and there was a lull in the business chat.

She looked away shyly.

'Shall I, then?'

Tilly lifted a shoulder in a tiny shrug.

'Well!' I looked around the table. 'Tilly and I are writing a book! Our plan is to get some copies printed, and sell them at the school fair, with the profits going to charity. We could sell it on Amazon too, and maybe at the local bookshop – you know, the one that Suzy's mum runs – they might take a few copies.'

'Oh!' said Sarah, raising an impressed eyebrow at Tilly. 'What's it about?'

'Cats,' whispered Tilly. She reached for the custard jug and poured another helping onto her crumble. Tom looked at her pointedly and shot me a frown.

'So you know that book you gave Tilly for her birthday – the one about how to draw cats? Well, she's amazing at it. Absolutely amazing. She's been practising and practising. So I'm going to write the story and she's going to do the illustrations. It's about a girl who is a normal schoolgirl by day, but at night she changes into a witch's cat!'

I looked at Tilly for encouragement but she was concentrating on her crumble.

'We might even do a series,' I added. 'Tilly's got two notebooks full of drawings already.'

Sarah and Ash nodded politely. At my side, I could sense Tom seething. I didn't understand why. What had I done wrong this time?

'And the witch's cat, Gobbolina, has all sorts of adventures with a witch called Gertrude, and the other witches' cats in the coven!'

'That's brave subject matter,' said Tom.

'What do you mean?'

'Do you know that in seventeenth century Europe, over fifty thousand women were tortured and executed as witches? Fifty thousand.' He winced, and paused to let it sink in. 'It was an obscene sort of collective psychosis.'

My insides shrank a little. Oh God, was he right? Was it in poor taste to write a story about a witch's cat? But what about *Harry Potter*? What about *The Worst Witch*?

'Little girls have always liked stories about witches, though,' I said. 'And black cats and spells and cauldrons, and all that stuff.'

'You used to dress up as a witch all the time,' said Sarah, frowning slightly, as if she was worried I might be implicated in the 'collective psychosis'. 'Mum cut up one of her old jumpers to make it into a raggedy witch's outfit and you had a big tantrum one day because she wouldn't let you wear it to school.'

'Exactly. The magic powers are... a sort of metaphor for empowerment.' I felt my cheeks redden. 'For using your innate abilities to overcome things that are bigger than you. And finding your own personal magic that is unique to you. Even if other people don't like it.'

Tom kept talking as if he hadn't heard me. 'Many of the women who were tortured and killed had mental or physical disabilities.'

'Not *that* kind of witch, though.' My voice sounded high and childish. 'The witches in our book are more about...' My mind went blank. 'Yes, empowerment.'

'*Empowerment* comes from putting in the work,' said Tom, with a dry little bark of a laugh. 'Sixteen-hour days and working weekends.' He nodded across the table to Sarah and Ash, as if they, as fellow professionals, would agree.

'Well, the concept is still quite fluid at the moment,' I said. 'The main thing is to showcase Tilly's drawings. Have you seen them?' I directed this to Sarah and Ash. 'They're amazing. Here, I've got some photos of them on my phone.'

But Tilly had gone bright red, staring down at her empty bowl.

'Yes, we'll have to have a proper look at those in a bit.' Sarah stood up, gathering up a pile of bowls. Ash fled too, grabbing the crumble dish and the custard jug. Ben and Adam remained at the table, fixated on their tablets.

Tom leaned over to me, so close that I could smell the chicken fat on his breath. 'If you want to pursue some kind of vanity publishing project, then that's up to you. But my daughter's name is not getting dragged into it.'

'Okay... but –'

I wanted to tell him all the reasons why I wanted to do the book. Because Tilly drew so well for her age – like I had, once. I wanted to nurture her talent, to make a quiet little girl feel *seen*. And most of all, this would be something she and I could do together, to strengthen our fragile bond.

'Sorry. I should have spoken to you first.'

Tom sighed in exasperation, and patted my hand. 'What are we going to do with you, eh? We'll say no more about it.'

He peered at me intently, as if noticing something amiss on my face. Then he touched his finger to the tip of his tongue to moisten it, and rubbed it back and forth over one of my eyebrows and then the other. 'That's better.'

My skin prickled. I needed to get away from him. I turned to Tilly. 'Hey, Tils. Do you want to help me with something?'

She nodded, and I took her through to the kitchen to find my sister. 'Sarah? I was wondering – have you still got the family photos here?'

She sighed gently and scraped peas and gravy from a plate into the bin. 'They're in the attic. Why?'

I'd planned my answer. 'I'm making a baby book for Edie. It's got a little family tree page and you can stick in photos, so I was looking for some nice ones of Mum and Dad.'

It was partly true, because I was planning to get on with the baby book – I really was. I'd started it after Edie was born, and had written in a short, sweet account of the birth, with all the horrific bits edited out. I'd even tucked Edie's hospital bracelet, and a feathery wisp of her baby hair, into the little transparent pockets on the first page. But the rest of the pages were blank. I hadn't recorded the day when Edie had first held her head up, or the day she'd first smiled, or the day she'd moved into her own bedroom. I hadn't written down the names of all Edie's 'friends' in the 'Mummy and Me' baby yoga group. I should be cherishing all these moments and pinning them down into the book. I would need some memories to look back on if Edie...

If she died.

'Are you okay?' Sarah put down the plate and reached out to touch my shoulder. 'You look awful.'

'I'd get copies of the photos. I wouldn't cut them up or... or damage them or –'

'Ash!' called Sarah.

He popped his head into the kitchen.

'Can you go up into the attic and bring down the box of photo albums? It's on the left by all your old hi-fi stuff.' She rolled her eyes and muttered to me: 'Never throws anything away.'

Tilly and I followed Ash through to the hall, where he pulled down the folding ladder to the attic.

'Shall we just come up?' I called. 'Save you lugging it down here? And we haven't seen your attic since you had it all floored.' There had been weeks of mournful tales about builders and mess.

Tilly nodded excitedly and climbed up the ladder, me following close behind.

'Right,' I said to Tilly. opening one of the albums and turning the pages till I found what I was looking for. 'That's my mother and father. I want to find the very nicest photos of them. About this big, for Edie's baby book.' I held up my thumb and finger to show the size.

'Okay,' said Tilly. And after a minute of flicking through the pages: 'Who's that?'

'That's Auntie Sarah when she was a baby!' I said. 'Look at all that dark hair she's got!'

'She looks like Adam,' said Tilly. 'Are there any of you when you were a baby?'

I felt a little rush of warmth that Tilly was interested – it wasn't as if she would bear a resemblance to anyone in the photos.

'I'm not sure. I don't think Mum and Dad had a camera back then. Cameras were expensive. You keep looking, though, and see if you can find any.'

'Did you have spiky black hair too?'

A strange, blank feeling came over me. An emptiness, where there should be... *something*.

'Do you know, Tilly, I'm not sure! Maybe we should ask Sarah.'

A few minutes later, Sarah's head popped up through the hatch. 'Getting on okay?'

'Why are there photos of you when you were a baby, but none of Steffi?' asked Tilly with a frown. She had a very pronounced sense of fairness.

'Our parents didn't have a camera when Steffi was a baby.'

'But there are baby photos of *you*. And you're *older*, so they must have had a camera.'

'Maybe our granny and grandpa took them,' said Sarah smoothly. 'Mum and Dad didn't have much money in those days. Cameras were expensive. Getting the films developed and everything, too. And I think some of the albums got lost. When we moved up from Yorkshire.'

'But –' began Tilly.

'Anyway, I've got to head out now to drop Ben at football. I won't be too long.'

'Is Edie okay?' I asked.

'She's still asleep. Tom's with her.'

I felt a prickle of anxiety. What if Edie had slept *too* long?

She usually only had an hour or so at this time. But I had to finish going through the photos.

Ash came up in a while to offer us a cup of tea.

'Is this definitely the only box of photos?' I asked. 'I think there must be some missing.'

He screwed up his face in the effort of trying to remember. 'I think I might have seen another album at the top of our wardrobe,' he said. 'I'll go check.'

A few minutes later, I heard the creak of the ladder, saw his balding head emerging through the hatch. 'I was right,' he said, looking pleased with himself. 'There's this one.'

Tilly reached over, took it from him, and opened it at the first page.

This was the one I'd remembered when I'd been talking to Joy – the one where I'd drawn on all the photos with marker pen. Sarah had kept it.

In one of the photos on the first page, she was blowing out a cake with seven candles, with Mum, Dad, and a black scribbly figure seated at the far side of the kitchen table, looking on.

If Sarah was turning seven, then I would have been two. So where was I?

There was Sarah on the back of a donkey on a sandy beach somewhere, with Mum and Dad carefully walking alongside. And a black shape wedged in behind Sarah, arms and legs spiking in all directions.

And then there were Christmas photos. Sarah in front of the Christmas tree, showing off some new white skating boots she'd been given. And a stick figure beside her, holding a massive box with wobbly criss-crossed lines and a bow on the top.

I flipped over the page to see Dad, asleep on the sofa with

a paper hat on, his mouth open, his gangly legs stretched out in front of him, crossed at the ankles. Sarah snuggled in at his side, her thumb in her mouth.

A smudged inky figure loomed behind them with a manic smile.

With a thud of certainty, I understood that the black figures were me. I'd drawn myself into all these scenes.

So where had I been? Had my family been doing all these things without me? Celebrating birthdays and Christmas and summer holidays? I had a sudden childish horror that I'd been shut up in a dark, empty place, miles and miles away from home. That I'd been shouting and shouting but nobody could hear.

From downstairs, I heard a jagged little cry. Edie had woken up.

'Why don't you go and find Daddy,' I said to Tilly. 'He might need help with Edie.'

18

STEFFI

Edinburgh, Present Day

I heard the slam of a car door, the noise of feet on gravel, and the kitchen door closing. Then the murmur of voices, and Sarah shouting: 'You did WHAT? Bloody hell, Ash!'

Moments later, Sarah appeared at the top of the ladder, her face slightly flushed.

'You okay up here?'

'What's the story with this photo album?' I waved it weakly in front of me. 'I mean... why am I not in the photos?' I felt a churning low in my stomach, sweat prickling on my back. Perhaps I was going to be sick. How long would it take to get down the ladder and into the bathroom?

Sarah gave an exasperated sigh. 'I don't know, Steffi. It was a long time ago. I can't even remember those photos being taken.'

So I was the annoying little sister again. The one who always made a fuss over the slightest thing. Who didn't know when to let things go.

And Sarah was the one who was always dismissing me. Who would never give a straight answer to a straight question. I had a sudden image of her as a child – lifting her chin and turning her head away, plaits swinging.

'Sarah. No – look at me! There is something YOU ARE NOT TELLING ME!'

She swayed backwards a little, rings clinking as she grabbed the rail of the ladder with both hands. 'There's no need to *shout*.'

'Come up,' I demanded.

She came and sat beside me, eyes cast down to the floor.

'Please, Sarah.'

She sighed again. 'You weren't in those photos because you didn't live with us until you were three.'

It was very quiet in the attic. Sarah pivoted her foot from side to side, rubbing away the dust from a small semicircle of floor. My own feet, in patterned Nordic socks, seemed like heavy blocks, strangely disconnected from me. I wiggled my toes. The patterned toes moved. I swallowed hard.

'Adopted?' It sounded fanciful. Overdramatic. Like a word from a children's story.

She nodded.

My first thought was that I wanted Mum. I wanted to find her and bring her back, so she could tell Sarah to stop this nonsense. She would have a sensible explanation for the photos, for all of it. I tried to picture her – holding me, comforting me, tutting at Sarah.

But suddenly all my thoughts of Mum seemed to shrink to one single, sharp memory – of getting off the coach after a long, hot week away at summer camp. Cool air hitting my face as the doors hissed open, late afternoon shadows stretching across the crumbling tarmac of the church carpark. Sarah dropping her rucksack, running into Mum's arms. Mum squeezed her eyes shut and hugged her so tightly that her muddy white trainers lifted off the ground. I stayed back at first, and then copied Sarah, launching myself at Mum, only to feel the pressure of her hands on my arms as she gently disentangled herself. 'Right, then. Let's get home, shall we? It's getting late!'

'Steffi?' Sarah put her hand on my arm, bringing me back. 'Are you okay?'

I shook my head. 'That can't be right. I just can't believe it.' But I did believe it. Some part of me, layered deep down, beyond the reach of memory, recognised the shape of this. Knew it to be true.

'But it doesn't make any sense. I mean, Mum and Dad had you, right? Why did they need to adopt?'

'Mum couldn't have any more children after me.'

'How do you know that?'

'She told me she'd had "a baby that didn't work out", and that she'd had to have her "insides sorted" afterwards.'

That rang a distant bell. She'd once said something similar to me, when one of my friend's mums got pregnant and I'd asked, excitedly, if we would ever have another baby in our family. She'd said it in a tone of voice that closed down all further discussion on the subject.

'But wouldn't I remember, if I was three?'

She shrugged. 'I don't know. I don't think I can remember much, if anything, from when I was that age. The memories I do have, well, they're just memories of memories. Family stories. Things that we've talked about again and again until they're sort of... fossilised. You know what I mean?'

Sarah looked a bit red in the face. She didn't normally talk in this way.

'I mean, even I can't remember much about when you first came to live with us.' She shot a sideways look at me. 'All I remember is that Mum and Dad bought a doll for me to give to you when you arrived, but you just dropped it on the floor by the door. And you had a suitcase of clothes that smelt funny, and Mum bundled them all into the wash. They didn't smell *bad*,' she added quickly. 'They just... they smelt of another house.'

I closed my eyes and willed myself to remember something – anything – about that other house. That other life.

But all I could think about, again, was Mum. And one time when I'd lifted my face to hers to give her an 'eskimo kiss', after seeing it on *Blue Peter*. 'Do you know how many different types of bacteria can be found in the human nose?' she'd said, shrinking away and tipping me off her lap.

It was just one of the odd little things that I'd filed away under the heading of 'Mum's squeamishness'. Like the way she always summoned Dad to clean me up, if I'd been sick. He would flap around, asking what cloth and bucket to use, rummaging in the airing cupboard for clean bedding, while she just stood there, with her cardigan held over her face.

Or the way my toothbrush was kept in a separate tooth mug on the bathroom shelf while Mum's, Dad's and Sarah's were all thrown in together. Sarah had told me that it was because I had a 'different blood type,' so the toothbrushes couldn't mix.

A dull pain began to spread behind my ribs.

'It's okay, Steffi.' I felt Sarah's hand on my shoulder, tentative and awkward. 'Try and stay calm.'

'But why didn't they *tell* me?' My voice trailed off into a high, thin wail.

Sarah shushed me, rubbing my back in long strokes, asking if I needed a glass of water, or a cup of tea.

The rungs of the ladder rattled and Tom's head appeared through the hatch. 'I'm taking Tilly home.' His voice was quiet and clipped. 'She has homework to do. I can see you're otherwise engaged.'

'Yes, she is,' returned Sarah. 'I'll drive her home in a bit.'

Normally I would have gone after him, trying to please and pacify him, saying of course we would go now, and goodness me, was that the time? But this time I just watched him leave.

Sarah turned to me again. 'I think they were just trying to protect you.'

'From what?'

Sarah shrugged. 'From... from upset?'

Upset. It had been one of my mother's favourite words. She'd used it as a noun, a word to cover a multitude of sins. Like the neighbour's daughter's teenage pregnancy. Or the sudden dismissal of two teachers at our school after the police were seen going into the head's office one lunchtime.

'And what about *you*? You could have told me.'

She shifted uncomfortably. 'I've thought about it. Quite a bit, since Mum died. But I guess I was trying to honour what she would have wanted. She went to some lengths to make sure that you wouldn't find out.'

'What *lengths*?'

'She got a fake birth certificate from somewhere. To replace your adoption certificate.'

'She did *what*?' My mother, who was the treasurer for the local Brownies, and headed up the PTA for six years in a row?

'Once I asked her where she'd got it and she went all white and furious-faced, you know?'

I did know.

'She said something about getting it from the lawyers. And then she sent me up to my room for the rest of the day.' She gave a rueful laugh. 'I didn't ask her again.'

'Do you know anything about my family? My...'

Birth family? Was that what I should call them? Again, it sounded like something from a television programme, or an article from a woman's magazine.

Sarah shook her head. 'I don't.'

'What about Mum and Dad? Did they know anything about them?'

'I'm not sure. They never really talked about it. I think that... well, I got the impression that perhaps your birth mother had... died.'

The pain in my ribs spread wider. Emptiness, cracking me open.

'I'll get you that cup of tea,' said Sarah, with two firm pats on my shoulder.

When she'd disappeared off down the ladder, I folded myself over, pushing my chest against my knees, rocking.

Alone in that attic, it made no sense that I could feel warm breath against my hair. And a whispered *Hush... hush...* that rose and fell in time to my own breathing.

19

STEFFI

Yorkshire, Age 8

Steffi was drawing the house again, the same one she'd been trying to make out of Lego, but hadn't been able to make quite right. It was going to be the front cover for her book. She'd decided to draw it from the back, as if she was standing on the edge of the railway cutting that you could see from the bedroom window. There wasn't much she could do to cheer up the dreary grey walls with their black drainpipes, or the dark grey roof, but she drew in the purple and yellow pansies in the strip of soil under the kitchen window. Humming softly, she added a rectangle of grass, a tree, and a washing line with a small tartan blanket hanging up to dry.

'When can we go back to this house?' she asked her mother, who was sitting at the kitchen table beside her, running a pair of home-made curtains through her sewing machine. Mum was really good at sewing. It was she who'd made Steffi's blankie for her, after Steffi had spotted a big roll of the soft tartan material, reduced to clear in the haberdashery shop. Mum had bought a piece and sewed on a ribbony edge so it didn't fray. That had been a few years ago now, and the fabric was starting to wear a little thin in places.

Her mother didn't reply to the question. There was a purring, rattling noise as the sewing machine ate up more of the curtain.

'Where is this house?' insisted Steffi. 'The one near a railway line. I'm writing a story about it.'

'Oh... I think that's Auntie Anne's house. Her old house, before she moved. We used to visit sometimes when you were younger.'

'Auntie Anne?' Steffi closed her eyes and tried to cast her mind back. She remembered the rattle of trains at night, their lights glowing like eyes in the dark. She thought she remembered a swing with a scrubby bit underneath where the grass had worn away. And dry summer pavements with weeds growing between the cracks, and the hot metal smell that happened after thunderstorms.

'Where's the house?'

'Oh, down beyond Doncaster.'

'Can we go there?'

'Auntie Anne died, darling.'

Steffi put on her best sad face and left a polite pause. 'We could still go there, just to see.'

'Daddy and I were thinking we might go to the Lake District next summer. I think you can go to Beatrix Potter's house and see where she made the Peter Rabbit books. And you can go and see Esthwaite Water, where Jeremy Fisher lived.'

'The Lake District – really? Oh Mamma, I'd love that!'

Mum looked up from the sewing and smiled.

Steffi's heart was full to bursting at the thought of going to Beatrix Potter's house. She thought of going round with her mother, of buying a fluffy Peter Rabbit in the gift shop, if it wasn't too expensive, and bringing it home.

'Can we go to that house in the Christmas holidays, then? Before we go back to school?'

'No, darling. We're busy then, remember? Daddy and I are going to a wedding near Oxford. Aunt Veronica and Uncle Geoffrey are coming to stay and they're looking after you while we're away. Veronica said she was thinking of taking you on an outing to the Jorvik Viking Centre.'

'Oh but *Mum*! They're so boring.' The last time they'd come, Uncle Geoffrey had talked for nearly two hours about the fundraiser for the church roof. Daddy had actually fallen asleep, his head jerking up again when someone asked if he wanted another cup of tea.

'Don't be so rude, Steffi.'

Steffi kept on drawing. But a feeling had crept into her chest, like cold fog.

Something was going to go wrong. She wasn't sure what it was yet. It was something to do with Mum. A bad thing.

What was the worst thing that could happen?

Well, Mum could die.

'Can you go and get some more pins from the other sewing basket, Steffi? It's in the cupboard in the hall upstairs.'

Steffi made her way up carefully, singing in her head.

Dance, then, whoever you may be...

She lifted out a cushioned tray of cotton reels and a spool of scarlet embroidery thread. A pair of sharp scissors with black handles.

Careful, whispered Dodo in her ear.

'There are NO PINS!' Steffi bellowed.

She heard Mum sighing and coming up the stairs, her shoes shuffling on the stairs. Granny always said she didn't pick up her feet properly.

'Out the way,' she sighed. Steffi stepped back, holding the scissors open with their terrible steel jaws. A cold feeling moved through her body and she thought she might need the toilet.

She was standing just a few steps away from the top of the stairs. She pictured herself pointing the scissors at Mum, making her step backwards. Making her fall down the stairs. Her neck would crack and snap.

She tried to remember the words to *The Lord of the Dance*, but they'd gone. Disappeared from her head. Steffi closed both hands around the scissors and placed them – slowly, slowly – on the shelf. She turned round and went into her bedroom. She shut the door.

There would only be one thing worse than Mum dying.

That worse thing would be Steffi killing her.

Maybe she was going to do it. Maybe she wouldn't be able to stop herself. She thought of how much she'd had to concentrate, to put the scissors back on the shelf and walk away. But she couldn't put the stairs away. They would be there, waiting, every hour of every day until the Bad Thing happened.

THAT EVENING, lying in bed with her tartan blanket pulled right up under her chin, she made a bargain with the Bad Thing. She would only go out of her room to go to school, to have meals or go to the bathroom. She would go down the stairs three at a time, so her feet had to touch them as little as possible. She would not touch any scissors or knives. It wouldn't be easy. Eating a pork chop with only her fork at dinner had been a challenge and Daddy had done his disappointed face.

A story kept going through her head. It was a story in which she stabbed Mum and pushed her down the stairs. She had to go to court for a trial, and when the judge found her guilty of murder she was led to a prison van with bars on the window. Daddy and Sarah had to go home alone, to the cold empty house without Mum, and without Steffi. She thought of them sweeping away all the Lego because nobody would be playing with it any more, and she wouldn't be allowed it in prison. She thought of Daddy reading the instructions on a tin of tomato soup and then breaking down in tears while Sarah comforted him, her hair wild and unplaited. This tragic image set her own tears flowing, for the third time that day. They trickled into her ear and made it tickle.

Mum came in and asked if she would like to help make apple crumble. Maybe just this once... If she stayed three feet away from any knives or scissors, maybe that would be okay. Or four feet? How long was a foot anyway?

'No thanks,' she mumbled, turning on her side to face the wall. There was no point making bargains with the Bad Thing. Not when the Bad Thing was her.

She closed her eyes and sang *The Lord of the Dance* in her head until the words began to drift and separate. She thought she felt the mattress springs shift as Dodo curled in behind her, the damp warmth of her breath against her hair.

20

STEFFI

Edinburgh, Present Day

Tom was lying on the sofa in the living room when I got home, pinned under Edie, who was sleeping on his shoulder.

Even in my turmoil, I felt a flash of irritation. It was too late in the day for her to be sleeping now.

'Can you help Tilly with her homework?' he said in an urgent whisper. As if all other tasks were impossible, all duties suspended, while he was in charge of the baby. Edie was moulded onto the contours of his body like she was part of him, breathing noisily into the hollow made by his collarbone. Father and daughter. She bore a definite resemblance to him, something to do with the shape of her forehead, the determined set of her mouth. Although she was all me around the eyes.

I sat down on the sofa beside him. 'I'm sorry about earlier. Sarah had some news for me. I've had a bit of a shock.'

Tom's face creased with concern. 'What is it, honey? Look, you're trembling. What's wrong?'

I exhaled loudly. 'So... I'm just getting my head around this, but it seems that Mum and Dad weren't my biological parents. I was adopted.'

It still sounded stupid. I half expected him to roll his eyes.

But his mouth fell open. 'Oh my *God*! Steffi!'

'I know.'

'How did you find out? And why has this come up *now*?'

I told him about Tilly and me looking through the photos in the attic. And how I'd pushed poor Sarah to tell me the truth.

He seemed to be thinking hard. His eyes flicked from side to side, from me to the fireplace to the window. Back again.

'Do you know anything about your parents? Do you remember them, if you were three?'

I shook my head. 'I think my biological mother died.'

He looked down at Edie, and back at me again. 'I mean... do you know their medical history and so on?'

'No. But there are ways I can try and track down biological relatives. Apparently you can request a copy of your original birth certificate. Or there's an adoption contact register you can sign up for.'

'So... you're not related to Sarah at all?'

That ache again, behind my ribs. 'No.'

He frowned heavily, as if my genetic link to Sarah – the sensible, professional actuary – had been part of the deal. Like he'd bought a dog and found out its pedigree was fake.

Then his face softened. 'My poor, poor Steffi. Come here.'

He reached out his spare arm and gathered me against his chest, dropping kisses onto the top of my head.

'I just can't believe it.'

'We'll sort it out,' he said. 'You don't need to worry. We're your family now. Me and Tilly and Edie.'

I pressed my face against his shirt, breathing in the familiar scent of his skin beneath the cotton.

'I'm thinking of doing the adoption contact register thing, as a first step.'

'Hmm...' he said doubtfully, his words vibrating against my cheek. 'Just don't expect too much, my princess.'

'I might be able to find them. My birth relatives. Maybe they've been looking for me all this time. Waiting for me to put myself on the register.'

'Oh Steffi. That's a tiny bit naïve, isn't it?'

'Why?' I said sharply, jerking back to look at him. 'Why is it naïve?'

'You're exhausted,' he went on. 'I'll look after Edie tonight. You need a proper night's sleep.'

'But your meetings tomorrow...'

'I've got a report to write anyway,' he said. 'Edie will keep me company. I'll set up her bouncy chair in my study.'

I opened my mouth to tell him that Edie wasn't supposed to stay in her bouncy chair for more than half an hour at a time. But then, from the hallway outside the living room, we heard a loud gasp.

Tom turned his head. 'Is that you, Tilly?'

'Oh,' I said. 'Yes. She's started holding her breath when she runs upstairs.' As soon as the words were out of my mouth, I wished I could take them back.

'Tilly!' he called, his voice ominous.

She appeared in the doorway and blew out the air from her puffed cheeks. 'Yes?'

'What's this I'm hearing about you holding your breath?'

'Oh...' She held onto the door frame with one hand and swung on her heel. 'Nothing. It's just a game.'

'You know you shouldn't run up the stairs?'

She looked uncertain for a moment. Then she gave a high, slightly strangled little laugh. 'I know. Steffi said stairs are scary. Like having a big cliff in the middle of your house that you could fall down at any minute.'

Tom took a deep breath and let it out slowly. When he spoke his voice was low: 'Just walk, please, Tilly.'

When she'd gone, he turned to me, his eyes dark and narrow. 'That?' He waved his hand in the direction of the hall, the stairs. 'That needs to stop. I'm not having you pass your neuroses, or whatever they are, on to my daughter. Whatever it is you've said to the child, unsay it.'

'I didn't mean –'

He held up his hand. 'Just sort it.'

I had a sudden urge to snatch Edie out of his arms. To take her, and Tilly, and go far, far away.

Run, said the voice in my head.

Run as fast as you can.

21

JOANNE

Yorkshire, Present Day

Joanne had her Friday night microwave curry on the sofa, vaguely watching the comings and goings on *Eastenders* before remembering she had an important task to do.

A couple had returned a cat to the rescue centre that day – a shy, seven-year-old tabby called Lady. It had taken Joanne ages to bring her out of her shell when she'd first arrived at Willoughby Bridge a few weeks ago – her devoted ninety-year-old owner had been taken into a care home – but, as she'd told the couple, Lady had a sweet temperament and made delightful chirping noises when she received attention. The couple had taken her home, only to bring her back within a week. A friend-of-a-friend's cat had given birth to kittens and they'd decided to 'upgrade' (unbelievably, the man had actually uttered that word).

Joanne had processed the paperwork, making a note of their details on a piece of paper which she took home. Now, one by one, she brought up the websites for twenty charities, inputting the couple's names, phone numbers, email addresses and home address, sending enquiry forms and ticking boxes to confirm they were happy to be contacted to discuss how they could support the charities. That would keep them busy for the next few weeks.

She also wrote an email to Lady's former owner at her care home, explaining that the adoption had fallen through, but that she was safe and well at Willoughby Bridge until they found a new home. And they would – Joanne would see to it personally. She attached a photo she'd taken of Lady that afternoon, curled up on a blanket. Joanne hoped she looked contented, rather than exhausted and bewildered.

She yawned and sighed. She was starting to get a crick in her neck, since Mitski had been draped around her like a scarf for about an hour now. Her front paws, with their delicate striped markings, rested on Joanne's right collarbone, kneading her lightly now and again. Joanne reached up to pat each paw in turn.

Mitski was such a needy little soul. She'd been taken away from her mother too soon. She'd been found, soaking wet, in a sack by the side of a canal with her two dead sisters. Joanne had worn her in a baby sling for the first few weeks, feeding her with a miniature bottle.

It had reminded Joanne of when Steffi's fourth birthday had come round, and she'd gone to WH Smith's and bought a Tiny Tears doll which came with a bottle which looked just like that. It had white filmy liquid inside the plastic that seemed to disappear if you held the bottle upside down. She wrapped it up in shiny striped paper, ready for when she saw

Steffi again. At that point, she still believed that the social worker was 'working very hard' to try and arrange contact.

Mum's cousin, Sharron, had taken Joanne in by then. Keith's trial was over and done with, and the social worker had said the change of scene – Sharron lived miles away, in Sheffield – would do her the world of good. At first, it had been a relief. Joanne could stop listening for the rattle of the letterbox, the unwelcome surprises. And nobody shouted foul names at her from across the street.

Sharron was an Avon lady with a thick layer of beige foundation and a stiff brown bob that made her look like a mushroom. Uncle Pete was a lorry driver who worked away a lot. They lived in a pebble-dashed semi with a scrubby garden, old bikes and scooters left to rust amongst the weeds. Joanne would have liked to play with them but wasn't allowed to because Tansy – Sharron and Pete's real daughter – would collapse to the ground and cry.

It was a long time before she made any friends at school – not till she was studying for her exams and the maths teacher put her next to a new girl called Nancy, who had big brown eyes, and a permanently worried expression. She smelt, just a little, and the other girls at school avoided her. Joanne started a rumour that there'd been a fire at Nancy's house, and the family couldn't get the smell out of their clothes. She could almost picture the tragic scene – the burnt-out washing machine, the soot hanging in the air, and only one school blouse left un-scorched.

One Friday, when Tansy was away staying with her nan, Nancy was allowed to stay the night. She came home from school with Joanne, carrying an Adidas holdall with a torn strap that smelled of football boots when she opened it. But just before bed, she started crying, said she couldn't stay.

'Why not?' Joanne had asked, desperately.

She couldn't get it out of her. Nancy shook her head, over and over, until she whispered: 'I've started my... my *time of the month*. It hurts. It's the first time.' She clutched her stomach.

Joanne ran her a bath, found her clean underwear to borrow and some pads. Nearly bursting with the satisfaction of being able to help, she gave Nancy a fresh bar of Johnson's baby soap, still in its waxy paper, and a peach-coloured bath towel.

Afterwards, Joanne helped Nancy to dry off her hair with a hand towel – a matching peach one – and she tugged her own brush through Nancy's hair, tutting gently at the most stubborn tangles. When she was finished she knelt by the bed and rubbed Vaseline Intensive Care into Nancy's hands, which had red ragged skin around the fingernails.

'There we go,' she said, screwing the top back on the tube. 'How are you feeling now?'

Nancy leaned over suddenly and threw her arms around her, wet hair falling around Joanne's face and neck, heat and soapy scent enveloping her. That was when Sharron opened the door. Nancy gasped and scrabbled to pull the towel tighter around her chest. Sharron's face changed colour beneath its thick layer of foundation.

Ten minutes later, Nancy was out the door with her Adidas holdall, and Sharron was standing in the door of Joanne's room again.

'You're unnatural, that's what you are.'

'I was just helping her dry off. She was upset.'

'Dry off, my arse,' said Sharron. Joanne had to stop herself making a smart comment.

'Don't think you'll ever be having a *friend* round here again,' said Sharron. 'I've got my Tansy to think about.'

'Fine,' mumbled Joanne, as Sharron flounced away.

But a moment later, Sharron stuck her mushroom-shaped head round the door again. 'You know that's why they separated you from your sister, don't you? Because you're not normal. And they knew she'd have a better chance of growing up normal without you.'

'No,' said Joanne.

'Yeah,' said Sharron. 'You might as well know. The social work report said you weren't right in the head. Said you'd corrupt her, or disrupt her or something. Bad patterns, that kind of thing. You'd stop her having right relationships with other carers.'

'Bad patterns?' Joanne thought of sewing, and wanted to laugh. 'Piss off.'

Sharron stepped forward so she was just inside Joanne's room. 'You know what I think?' Her voice was quieter now, sly. 'Keith's family were on to something, weren't they? You killed her, didn't you? You killed your own mother and blamed your father.'

Joanne took a step towards the door.

'Keith was found guilty.' She would never call him her father. Never.

'You wanted rid of them both, didn't you? And you wanted your sister all to yourself. Thought you could do a better job?' Sharron shook her head in disgust. Her hair, sprayed into submission with Elnett (extra firm hold), remained rigid. 'But the social workers, they saw through you, didn't they? Even if the jury didn't. That's why they made sure you'd never see Steffi again.'

Joanne began to shake. She wouldn't cry in front of Sharron. She would not.

'Just tell me,' whispered Sharron. 'You did it, didn't you?'

Rage boiled up inside her. 'So what if I did? Why do *you* care?'

Sharron's coral-lipsticked mouth curled up at one corner. She looked plain cruel now. Even uglier than usual. She nodded, as if she'd made a decision, and turned and left the room.

JOANNE TURNED sixteen the following week. She'd known it wouldn't be much of a birthday, and she had to work a shift after school. She'd got herself a kitchen job at one of the B&Bs on the road into town. She did four weekday evenings and the Saturday and Sunday breakfast shifts.

Walking home in the dark, she hoped that Sharron had kept some dinner for her. She wasn't a great cook but Joanne had overheard her saying something to Tansy about cottage pie.

When she got back to the house, she rang the doorbell – Sharron had never given her a key to the house – but there was no answer. She tried it again – three more times, until she saw in the half darkness that the letterbox had been taped over.

And there was a sign in the narrow pane of glass that ran the length of the door. 'No mail – gone away.'

Gone away?

They'd... moved?

While she'd been out, they'd *moved*?

Her legs trembly all of a sudden, she went to the neighbour's house and rang the bell. Mrs Biggs just shrugged. 'There was vans here earlier. Men in and out. It's nowt to do wi' me.'

'Where have they gone?' pleaded Joanne. If nothing else, she needed her stuff. Her clothes, her school books. She had a maths assignment due in tomorrow.

'If you see that Sharron, tell her I want my plunger back.' She gave a dignified sniff, and closed the front door.

Joanne went round the side of the house. Perhaps she could break in. Perhaps she could live there for a while until someone made her leave. She found two black rubbish bags by the bins. Her clothes were in one, together with a pair of trainers and a single flip-flop. The wrapped parcels from the top of Joanne's wardrobe, containing the Tiny Tears doll and the presents Joanne had bought for Steffi's other birthdays, weren't there. Sharron must have kept those for Tansy. She continued to scrabble around, her heart leaping when she finally found it – the carefully mended tartan blanket.

She'd been too proud to tell anybody what had happened – the teachers at school, or even Nancy. And that useless lot at the social work department washed their hands of you once you were sixteen.

It was Mr Singh from the B&B who'd given her a lifeline. He'd let her stay in a little room off the kitchen in exchange for doing a bunch of daytime shifts, which had been fine as she'd been thinking about ditching school anyway. It had been a store room, really, with white tiled walls and a scratched lino floor, and a shelving unit with industrial-sized tins of tomatoes and baked beans. Mr Singh had provided a camp bed and a duvet and pillow from the linen store. His wife had even brought down an electric fan heater when there was a cold snap in December.

She remembered icy mornings trying to wash her hair in the tiny sink in the staff toilet; the sprinkle of lukewarm water produced by the little plastic water-heating unit above the sink. She'd just shorn her hair off in the end because it was easier. Her colleagues in the kitchen had cheerfully referred to her as a dyke after that. Only when Mr Singh wasn't in earshot, though. He'd been decent to her, and his wife had volunteered at the cat shelter, which was how she'd got into all that. Which showed that there was a reason for everything.

Almost everything.

Mitski made a chirping noise – an outraged little protest – and sank her claws into Joanne's jumper.

Joanne thought of her bed, which she hadn't made that morning. The sheets she hadn't washed in a while. And the dreams she'd had last night, the feeling of dread every time she woke in the dark, soaked in cold sweat.

She opened up her laptop again, and reached up for Mitski's paw, pressing the toe beans one by one so that her claws poked out. The cat's purr deepened into an ecstatic rumble. 'Let's see if we can jazz up Lady's profile, eh? And maybe Tigger's and Marmalade's? I haven't looked at them for a few weeks.'

22

STEFFI

Edinburgh, Present Day

'So I've got some news,' I told Joy when she came round the following Thursday, and I'd plied her with tea and Viennese Fingers. Tom had deleted them from our Sainsbury's order but I'd bought a pack at the corner shop with some loose change I'd found in my pocket.

'After our discussion last time, I went to my sister's house to look through our family photos. And it turns out... I'm adopted.' I gave a short, hollow laugh.

Edie, curled asleep against my chest, made a snuffling noise. It was strange to think she carried the mystery of my birth family inside her too, in every cell, their DNA laced into hers.

Joy's eyes widened. 'Good Lordy.'

'Yes. A bit of a surprise.'

'I can imagine. My goodness. How did you find out?'

I told her about the Sunday afternoon in the attic with the photograph albums, the information I'd learned from Sarah.

'Do you know anything about your birth family? About the circumstances?'

I shook my head. 'Sarah didn't know much, except that I was three when I came to live with them. *Three*. And yet I remember nothing.'

'How odd that they never told you. I know that used to happen, in the old days. Adoption was all hush-hush. Shameful, even. But if you were three years old? It seems like... like you had a right to know.' She shook her head and brushed a crumb off her jumper. Today she was wearing one with geometric squirrel-like shapes knitted into the pattern. 'I mean, what about your birth certificate? Don't adopted children have something else... an adoption certificate?' She screwed up her face, unsure.

'Apparently – I can hardly believe this – Mum arranged to get a fake birth certificate. From some dodgy lawyer or something.' Suddenly, I had to stifle a giggle. It sounded so ridiculous.

But Joy clearly wasn't seeing the funny side. She gasped, held a hand over her mouth. 'Wicked,' she whispered. 'How *wicked*.'

'I don't think it was wicked, exactly. She was just trying to protect me.'

Joy closed her eyes and shook her head.

'Apparently, I can request my original birth certificate. I can ask to see my adoption file, if I can find out which agency or social work department handled the case. Or I can sign up to the adoption contact register. If any of my birth relatives have also signed up, then I'll get contacted to say there's a match. Their details get passed on to me and I can decide if I want to make contact. But I've got a bit of a mental block about doing it.'

'Well, let's see – what are the pros and cons?'

'The cons are... well, I might find out something upsetting.'

She nodded. 'That's certainly possible. Nobody wants to give up their child, after all. There's probably a sorry tale behind that.'

'The pros are... I just want to know.'

'I think you should ask yourself the deathbed question,' said Joy. 'That is to say, which would you most regret, if you were looking back at your life? Would you regret finding out the truth about your birth family, even if it was difficult? Or would you regret it more if you died having never found out? If you'd given up the chance – however small – of having some sort of relationship with your birth relatives?'

'I do want to do it,' I said quietly. 'I want to know. I've spent all of my life so far *not knowing*.'

'And it's no wonder you're having trouble settling into motherhood, if you were separated from your own mother.' She made a little clucking noise and shook her head. 'It may be bringing up all sorts of unconscious feelings. Feelings about separation and abandonment.'

'I guess.' I tried to stifle a yawn. For a moment I wished she would just go away so I could try and get Edie down for a nap, and curl up beside her myself.

Her eyes widened. 'For example, it makes perfect sense that you can't stand to leave Edie to cry. Not even for a second.'

I felt a prickle of annoyance. I wasn't *that* bad, with Edie. I'd been following all of Joy's instructions about not picking her up at night, not that it was making much difference. I released a long sigh. 'I should speak to Tom about it first, though. Check he's happy for me to go ahead. I guess, in a way, they're his family too.'

Joy gave a quick, dismissive shake of her head. 'This adoption contact register,' she said. 'Is that the starting point? The easiest way?'

'I think so.' I yawned again.

'What are you waiting for, then? Let me take Little Miss. I'll walk her around while you get started.'

'I might do it later today.' I went over to the fridge and took out my vitamin tonic.

'What's that you've got there?'

'Oh, it's for new mothers. A vitamin tonic. It's got iron and ginseng and whatnot. It costs about sixty quid a bottle, apparently. But it comes highly recommended.'

I imagined the bottle rebranded with Victorian-style lettering like Edie's gripe water: 'Bloody Deborah's Vitamin Tonic'.

Joy gasped. '*Sixty pounds*? What a racket. A scam, if you ask me. All a new mum needs is a good steak dinner once a week. That'll see you right.'

'Well, it's that, or the caffeine tablets,' I said ruefully. But then, when she wasn't looking, I rattled out four caffeine tablets and swallowed those too.

SARAH and I took the little ones to Inverleith Park the next day, finding a nice spot on the hill overlooking the pond, the grass dappled in the autumn sun. Tilly sat on a picnic blanket eating a lemon muffin, with Edie propped up between her legs. The boys, fuelled by oversized chocolate cookies, played some noisy game where they pretended to be fighter planes, which mainly involved kicking up a lot of leaves. Sarah and I supervised from a park bench, takeaway coffees in hand.

'We don't have long, I'm afraid,' said Sarah, looking at her watch. 'Ben's got his piano lesson at four and we've got to get across to East Calder.'

That would take at least an hour in Friday afternoon traffic. They'd have to leave in about fifteen minutes. I felt a dart of annoyance. 'Why don't *you* just teach him?'

She snorted. 'His mother teaching him? It would put him off for life.'

'Do you ever play yourself, these days?'

She shook her head and laughed, as if I'd said something ridiculous. 'No. No time, I guess. I've forgotten it all anyway.'

'But you were so good.'

She shook her head. 'I was above average for a schoolgirl my age. Nothing special.'

What had it all been for, I wondered? The hours of practising. The evenings and weekends my parents had driven her around the country. She used to vomit, sometimes, before competitions. She'd made me promise, with dagger eyes, not to tell Mum.

'I used to like it when you played.' It was sort of true. I hadn't particularly liked it at the time, but I liked the memory of it. Playing with my Lego on the floor while she practised.

'Thank you.' She smiled shyly and I saw that she was still there, squashed underneath the successful actuary, the busy mum of boys – Big Sarah, who'd loved her piano so much.

My Big Sarah.

Suddenly, it made sense why I'd always called her that. Because I'd known perfectly well, back when I was first adopted, aged three, that Sarah wasn't my big sister. But I was supposed to act as if she was. So I'd used my own variation on the words: 'my Big Sarah.'

On impulse, I leaned over and kissed her on the cheek.

She jumped in surprise, and laughed nervously. 'What was that for?'

'I've made a decision. I'm going to put my details on the adoption contact register.'

'Okay.' The groove between her eyebrows deepened. 'Oh, Steffi. Are you sure that's a good idea?'

'I've got to know where I came from. Or at least try to find out. Otherwise I'll always wonder.'

'But there will be a *reason* you were given up for adoption. It will probably be sad and depressing and awful. Nobody wants to give their child up.'

'Hmm. I know.'

'What does Tom say about it all?'

'Nothing much.' He'd barely looked up from his phone when I'd mentioned it to him. He'd just said, 'You know I'm behind you, whatever you decide.'

On the blanket, Edie whimpered and reached for Tilly's muffin. Tilly put it back in the paper bag and held on to Edie's chubby wrists, moving her arms around in time to the *Five Little Ducks* song. Edie gave a delighted shriek and propelled herself back and forth. She was getting so big – nearly sitting up by herself now.

'Can you remember anything else?' I pressed Sarah. 'About when I arrived? I mean, didn't I say anything? About my other family?'

'You didn't talk all that much, and when you did it was quite difficult to understand. I remember Dad telling me that your language was a little bit delayed for your age.'

I thought of Romanian orphans again. Mute in their cots, staring at the walls.

'What, because I hadn't been... talked to enough?'

'I don't know. "Chaotic" was the word Mum and Dad used. You'd come from a "chaotic" family set-up.'

'What was I like, though? Did I like dressing up? Ice cream? Cuddly toys?'

'You seemed to like ducks,' said Sarah, still frowning. 'You used to say "Fee kisses de duck".'

Those words – they were familiar, somehow. I smiled, and relaxed back on the bench.

'We thought you were saying "Steffi kisses the duck." Aunt Veronica got you a toy duck for Christmas but you didn't like it. You screamed and threw it at the wall.'

'Oh dear.'

I thought of Sarah and Ash with their kids. The 'do you remember...' conversations they always had.

'Do you remember when Adam threw his Tudor sandwich out the car window and the police pulled us over?'

'Do you remember when Ben put his pants on his head after swimming and Mummy didn't notice until we got home?'

'We'd been told Ben was a girl! He had to wear pink baby grows for the first week.'

And they would laugh at the absurdity of it, no matter how many times the story had been told. Ben would oblige everyone with a horrified expression.

We'd never had those conversations in our family.

I realised then that we didn't have them in my new family, either – Tom and Tilly never reminisced. Tom probably didn't want to raise the subject of Adeline. I resolved to try and find out more about Tilly's early childhood, to find some safe areas of discussion. Maybe I could ask him to dig out some photographs, and use them as a starting point. Surely he must have kept some photos of Adeline, for Tilly's sake if nothing else.

'What else do you remember?' I felt like a child again, pestering my sister.

'We took you to the park once, not long after you came to live with us. We went down to the duckpond with some stale slices of bread in a red and yellow Sunblest bag. You got excited when we saw the ducks and you tried to take your shoes off – you hated shoes and you would have gone everywhere barefoot if you could. Mum told you to stop – I think she thought you were about to get into the pond! So I pointed at the ducks and said "Fee kisses de duck?", but you had an almighty tantrum.'

'Mum would have loved that.'

Sarah laughed weakly. 'Yes. People were looking. So Dad had to pick you up and carry you all the way home, tucked under his arm. You pulled one of your shoes off and threw it across the road. I picked it up for you.'

Sadness throbbed in my chest. I looked out over Inverleith Pond, letting my gaze drift up over the Edinburgh skyline.

'It must have been so difficult for you,' I said. 'Keeping quiet.'

Sarah frowned. 'The problem was, it was difficult for me to be your sister, in the normal sense. Because I was always on the parent side of the equation. You on one side. Mum and Dad and me on the other. With the adoption – the big secret – in the middle.'

Typical of Sarah to try and understand our family in terms of a mathematical problem. A problem that couldn't be solved. A family that had never quite worked.

'Thank you,' I said suddenly, the words catching in my throat. Over the Pentland Hills, far in the distance, grey clouds were gathering. Rain would fall tonight.

'We did our best.' She looked sad for a moment. Terribly, desperately sad. As if our family was over, now the truth was out. As if she was saying goodbye.

I shivered and pulled my coat around me. 'Come on. You'd better get going or Ben will be late for his lesson.' I glanced at my watch. '*Really* late. The traffic will be crazy.'

She turned to me, her face suddenly determined. 'Let's go back to yours. I'll help you with this adoption contact register thingy.'

I did a mental calculation. Tom wouldn't be home until at least six. Sarah and the boys would probably be gone by then, with enough time for me to tidy up. 'But what about Ben's piano lesson?'

'You're right, we'll never get to East Calder in time now. He can miss it just this once.' She gave a high-pitched, slightly crazed giggle. 'He hates it anyway. He'd much rather play with Tilly.'

SARAH and the boys had just left when the notification came through. I had Edie in a sling on my chest, and was pushing the vacuum cleaner around the living room. Tilly was collecting the cups and plates we'd used and was carrying them, one at a time, into the kitchen to put into the dish-washer. I heard a ping on my phone and I pulled it out of my pocket. It was an email from the adoption contact register. There'd been a match.

My legs almost folded under me. I let go of the vacuum

cleaner and stepped backwards, dropping down onto the sofa.

It seemed that my birth sister, Joanne, had also placed her details on the register. The email included her contact details and explained that the ball was now in my court – I could decide to make contact if I wished. It was suggested that I might benefit from counselling to support me through the process.

Joanne. She lived somewhere in Yorkshire – Willoughby Bridge. I closed my eyes and tried to picture her. Was her hair the same colour as mine? Did she have my blue eyes? And Willoughby Bridge – was that near my first home? I tried to picture a house, a garden, a family. Nothing came.

Tilly came back into the room. She looked at the vacuum cleaner, abandoned on the floor but still running, and then she looked at me, her eyes full of fear. 'Steffi? What is it? What's wrong?'

'I'm fine, darling. I just need a minute.'

'Would you like me to look after Edie?' She switched off the vacuum cleaner and pulled the bouncy chair out of the cupboard. I released Edie from the sling and handed her over to her sister. Tilly took her carefully and strapped her in. Kissed her once on the forehead.

A single word bobbed to the surface of my memory.

Jo-Jo.

Then it came to me. Not as a shock or surprise, but rather as a clearing away of noise. Dodo hadn't been an imaginary friend. She'd been Jo-Jo. My sister. My lost sister, who I'd carried with me always, on the edges of my memory.

23

JOANNE

Yorkshire, Present Day

Joanne lay back on her pillows, damp and sweaty. Her stomach was churning so badly, her heart racing so fast, that she couldn't sit up. Far less get up and get showered and dressed. Cheryl would just have to take her as she found her.

Her mind ran over what had just happened, and whether it was possible that she might still be dreaming. Saturday lie-ins were usually her favourite part of the week, but the phone had woken her just before nine.

'Joanne? It's Cheryl.' And she'd known, right there and then, from her voice, the way its pitch dropped on the last word.

'I've got some news.' Cheryl left a long pause. 'I wondered if I could pop round later and have a chat?'

Remembering it now, a soft moaning noise escaped her.

Albie, curled on the end of the bed, twitched an ear in her direction and then turned to face her. Slowly, he made his way over the duvet – over the useless lumps of her feet, her legs – and came to settle on her chest. He stretched out one of his front paws, flexed his claws, and rested it on one side of her neck.

'Albie. Lovely boy. Lovely, lovely boy.'

He stretched out his other paw, grazing her cheek with his claws as he brought it down to rest on the other side of her neck. His rumbling purr vibrated through her chest. The sick feeling subsided, just a little. She laid one hand on his back, feeling the nubs of his spine beneath the soft fur, and stroked his silky head with the other.

'How will I cope, Albie? How will I stand it?'

Albie held her gaze, then closed his eyes slowly and re-opened them.

It took an hour to work herself up to it, but finally she tipped Albie off her chest and heaved herself out of bed. She picked up some trackie bottoms and a fleece from the floor, where she'd dropped them last night, and she sniffed them before pulling them on. She brushed her teeth with just water, as she'd forgotten to buy new toothpaste. Again. What a disaster she was. She swallowed down some painkillers from the back of the medicine cabinet, to help the ache that had been building behind her ribs since Cheryl's call. And she was in the process of tugging a brush through her hair, cursing its greasy roots and frizzy ends, when the doorbell went.

'Hi Joanne. How are you doing?' Cheryl's voice was soft and sympathetic, like it had been on the phone. Uninvited, she took off her pastel pink coat and matching scarf, and shook out her droopy auburn curls.

'I'll make some tea.' Joanne turned away from Cheryl and made her way down the hall, suddenly not wanting to hear the news after all. What you didn't know couldn't hurt you, right?

But Cheryl followed her into the kitchenette, hovering in the doorway. Joanne felt trapped. She thought of the feral cats that were sometimes brought into the shelter, how they would hiss and spit from the back of the enclosure. Or try to bolt past you if given half the chance.

'What is it, then?' she snapped.

Cheryl swallowed and then continued, in a high, flutey voice. 'So I managed to trace a member of Steffi's adoptive family. Her adoptive sister, Sarah. She's written a letter for you. I'm afraid it's not good news, about Steffi.'

Joanne's legs felt weak, as she shoved two teabags into mugs, nearly knocking one off the counter with her shaking hands. Bloody Cheryl. Weren't you supposed to get people to sit down before you told them bad news?

'Let's see it, then?' She supposed she should be making an effort to sound polite, given that Cheryl had come over at the weekend to deliver the news. Why couldn't she have waited till Monday?

Cheryl handed her an envelope. She removed the letter – barely aware of something fluttering down to the floor as she opened it – and spread it out on the worktop.

Dear Joanne,

I understand that you are looking for information about your half sister, Steffi, who was adopted into my family

*shortly after her third birthday. I became Steffi's adoptive
sister at that time (I was aged eight).*

*Sadly the adoption was not a great success. Steffi never
warmed up to us and she was detached and distant – except
when her anger issues got the better of her. Once she pushed
me down the stairs and I broke my leg, which needed pinned in
two places. Social workers and psychologists put all this down
to the trauma of separation from both of her birth parents at a
crucial time in her development. One said she had developed a
personality disorder which I have to say I agree with.*

*My parents tried their best but Steffi never bonded with
them in the way they had hoped. My mother used to say
she was 'blank behind the eyes'. Sometimes I wonder if I
could have done anything to change that – played with her
more or something.*

*I am sorry to have to tell you that Steffi took her own life
when she was fifteen years old. My mother came into the
hall and found her hanging from the banister. She'd used
her dressing gown cord.*

*We never knew why she did it. We wondered if she had
been bullied at school or something like that but the school
just said she always kept herself to herself.*

*I realise this will not be the news you have hoped for and I
am sorry. But there is not much more I can tell you. My
parents have both passed away now. They never really got
over the guilt, or the sense that they had failed her. It*

wasn't their fault, though. They had no idea what they were taking on at the time.

This was a painful and difficult time in my own life too and it has put me in a dark place even thinking of this again. I must protect my own mental health and so I would ask you to respect my wishes NOT to be contacted again.

I haven't hung onto much from those days, but I am enclosing a school photograph of Steffi when she was about five or six in case you want to keep this.

Yours sincerely
Sarah Livingstone

THAT WAS THAT, then.

Stupid.

There must have been a splodge of butter or something on the worktop because a greasy mark had come through on the paper, smudging the 'S' on Sarah. Not that it mattered. It wasn't a letter that would bear reading more than once. It could go in the bin.

You see – *this*. This was the reason she should never have started looking in the first place. She felt irritated with herself. Angry.

Bloody stupid, Joanne.

Cheryl's hand on her arm stung like an electric shock. 'Here's a photograph. It fell out as you were opening the letter.'

For an instant, Joanne felt a flare of hope. That it wouldn't be her. That this was all a mistake.

But there she was. That was her. Her stiff, pinched little face. Anxious eyes staring straight into the camera, her lip tethered between her teeth. Hands squeezed together in her lap.

This was *her*.

This was her last – her very last – glimpse of her sister.

It was like looking back through time. Back through all those murky years of not knowing. Nobody had told her it would get harder, and not easier. For each year, as Steffi's birthday had come and gone, Joanne's grief had compounded, like the interest on a bad debt. She would never know Steffi aged four. She would never know her aged five. Christmases, Easters, school terms, summer holidays, all went past in a blur. Stretch upon stretch of wasted time, wasted life, her loss like an impossibly high wall that she could never hope to get over. And yet here she was, her Steffi. Here she had been, on the other side, if she could only have reached her.

She stared into the picture, imagined reaching out and sweeping that severely cut fringe away from Steffi's eyes. She imagined the warm little cheek bobbing against her own, as she carried her up the stairs to bed. The lips whispering breathy toddler secrets. The soft fingers holding out small treasures. A pure white feather found on the carpet. A velvet pansy petal carried in from the garden, sheltered in cupped hands. A marble retrieved from the back of the airing cupboard, which glowed sapphire-blue in the sunlight, a colour to match her eyes.

Something surged in her chest. Leaning forward, she gripped the worktop.

'Are you okay, Joanne?'

She nodded curtly. 'So that's it, then.'

'Yes.'

'How did you find her? This... *Sarah*?'

'The café in the picture you gave me – Marinello's. It's in Harrogate. That narrowed the search.' She sounded almost apologetic.

Joanne nodded again.

When Cheryl had gone, she swallowed another couple of painkillers and filled a coffee mug with brandy, spilling some of it on the worktop as she tried to pour it out with shaking hands. She went and sat down on the sofa, where Albie was lying curled up in a thin sliver of sunlight that filtered through the grubby net curtains.

She leaned over and pressed her face into his flank, breathing in the warm hay scent of his fur. Then she turned her head to the side so that she could hear his heartbeat and the sound of his breath in and out.

It made sense to her now, why she'd never really tried as hard as she could to find Steffi. Why she'd resisted, when Mei-Ling kept coaxing her to do it. Why she'd slammed shut her old laptop again and again, while trawling through Facebook looking for Stefanies who might be about the right age. Because somewhere deep down, she'd known that she wouldn't be able to bear it, if her hope was taken away.

The big question of Joanne's life had finally been answered. It had been the wrong call. Her decision to get Steffi away from her father, whatever the cost, had been a mistake. Those words in the letter... 'the trauma of separation from both her birth parents'. *Both*. That's what had caused her personality disorder or whatever it was. That's what had destroyed her. And that had been down to Joanne. If she hadn't lied about what happened that night, Keith wouldn't have gone to prison. Steffi would've still had a family, such as it was.

What must it have been like for Steffi? To decide she didn't want to go on. To tie her dressing gown cord around the banister and climb over the side...

Her chest hurt. It throbbed with a sadness so heavy, so absolute, that she could hardly breathe. It's happening now, she thought. Her heart was finally breaking after all these years.

She took another gulp of brandy. Albie turned his head to lick the place where her tears had soaked into his fur, and she closed her eyes and concentrated on the warm rise and fall of his flank, the rasping sound of his tongue. His little cat heart beating in the safe dark space beneath his ribs.

24

STEFFI

Yorkshire, Age 8

Over the long summer holiday, Steffi did tennis camp – Improvers Level. Mum had seen it advertised in the local paper and had decided it would keep Steffi busy while Sarah worked towards her Grade Eight piano.

The tennis club became Steffi's new favourite place. The background noise gave her a nice, comforting feeling – the gentle pock of balls against rackets, the polite voices calling out 'Deuce!' or 'Nice shot!' or 'Sorry!' when a ball bounced into somebody else's court. She loved the way the shadows lengthened on the faded red asphalt as summer afternoons edged into evening.

Although she'd been shy at first, she'd found it was nice to make new friends, who didn't know she was the younger sister of a piano star. And she'd discovered that tennis gave her a warm glow in her arms and legs, and a cosy sort of heaviness at night. She wasn't thinking about the Bad Thing so much. One morning, she was able to sit in the kitchen and eat breakfast in the chair nearest to the knife block, and not think anything of it. And before they left the house to get in the car, she ran up the stairs to get her sunglasses, and ran down again, without even remembering to sing *The Lord of the Dance.*

When she got home that day, Steffi decided she would do something she'd been meaning to do for a while – write her own advert for the local newspaper. People did that all the time. Bikes for sale. Dead people announced. Lonely hearts. Aunt Veronica had even tried that once, before she'd met Uncle Geoffrey at the church and been *transformed*. She'd heard Mum telling Granny about it on the phone, one night when she was supposed to be asleep.

She hurried up to her bedroom, carrying a slice of buttered malt loaf on a plate. Kneeling forward on her bedroom floor, bottom in the air, she filled in the form. She'd cut it out from the back of the paper a couple of weeks ago.

The pen – she'd only been able to find one black biro in the house – had nearly run out, and it threatened to poke through the paper at one point so she fetched The Illustrated Children's Bible to lean on. Carefully, she inserted block capitals into the row of small boxes:

'TO ANYONE WHO KNOWS ME, PLEASE REPLY.'

She added her name and address underneath, going over and over the letters to make them clearer.

Stuffing the rest of the malt loaf into her mouth, she pulled two crumpled five pound notes and four fifty-pence pieces out of her piggy bank and ran downstairs to the kitchen, where Mum was opening a tin of corned beef, turning the little key.

'Mum, could I have a cheque please? If I give you this money? A cheque for twelve pounds?'

'Is it for tennis club?' Mum asked.

'Yes.' Steffi thought quickly. 'We're having a trip. A picnic at the beach. They need money for the food. And the coach.' Her insides fizzed a little at the lie. 'I can fill the cheque in, if you want. To save time.'

Mum turned around, wiping her hands on her apron. 'Let me see the letter about the picnic. Twelve pounds seems like an awful lot.'

'Oh... it's upstairs.' As soon as she said it, she realised her mistake. 'Actually, I might have left it at the club. I'll get it tomorrow.'

Steffi followed her mother – three careful steps behind – as she climbed up the stairs to Steffi's bedroom and started shuffling around in her rucksack. 'Are you sure there's a trip? It's the first I've heard of it.'

She turned to Steffi and her eye caught the Illustrated Children's Bible, and the completed form. She snatched it up.

Her face went white and then blotchy-red. 'The local newspaper! An advert? Such a STUPID thing to do! *Anyone* could have replied.'

'It *isn't* stupid!' Steffi returned in a high, piping voice.

Daddy came into the room. 'What on earth is going on?'

'This child,' said Mum, 'has been trying to put an advertisement in the local paper. "To anyone who knows me, please reply."' The paper made a snapping sound as she thrust it towards Daddy.

He shook his head sadly. 'Oh dear, Steffipops. That was

silly. We don't do that kind of thing, do we? It can lead to trouble.'

'Why did you do this?' demanded Mum.

'I was just *interested*. Laura from tennis club found out she had a cousin she'd never met – a tennis star who almost got into Wimbledon once. We might have someone like that.'

'Did somebody put you up to this?' Mum's voice was thin, shaking.

'Yes. Dodo.' She didn't even know why she said it, except that Dodo had always been happy to take the blame for everything.

It was a terrible, sad feeling, watching Mum tearing up the form. It was like at Easter when she'd opened up a beautiful, foil-wrapped chocolate Easter Bunny, nearly as tall as a long ruler. It had made a hollow sound when she'd tapped it, so she'd snapped off its head eagerly. But there'd been nothing inside it – no mini-eggs, no coins, no sweets, nothing. Just an empty chocolate shell, where there should have been something. And a snapped-off head and ears that couldn't be put back on.

Mum huffed off downstairs and Daddy sat down on the edge of her bed. It was too low for him and his knees and elbows stuck out at sharp angles, like a daddy-long-legs.

'I'm going to ask you a special favour, Steffi,' he said quietly. 'This business about Dodo, blaming things on Dodo. It has to stop. You're far too old for it now, and it really upsets Mum.'

'Sorry.'

'And you don't want to hurt your mother, do you?'

Steffi thought of Mum, with her neck at a funny angle, at the bottom of the stairs.

'No,' she whispered. How did Daddy know about the Bad Thing? She hadn't told a soul apart from Dodo.

'Well, then,' said Daddy. 'Dodo has to go.'

After he'd gone, she retrieved her tartan blankie from where it was balled up under her duvet. She held it to her face for a moment. Was Daddy right? Would the Bad Thing stop, if Dodo went?

Nameless feelings rushed through her, making her eyes smart and her chest feel tight. But she gathered her resolve – she wasn't a baby any longer, who needed blankets. Look at how her tennis was improving. Maybe one day she would be as good at tennis as Sarah was at piano. She pushed herself up off the bed.

Then she walked down the stairs, and out the kitchen door to the black bin. She thrust the tartan cloak deep into the rubbish, into eggshells and teabags and last night's lamb stew. Then she walked back upstairs, as hollow and useless as the Easter bunny with no head.

25

STEFFI

Edinburgh, Present Day

The email arrived while I was standing waiting for Tilly at the school gates, with Edie strapped into a baby sling against my chest. I'd been refreshing my phone every few minutes for most of the week, ever since I'd sent my own initial message to Joanne to establish contact.

I did a double take at first. The subject line of the email said 'Joanne Graham', but the message was from somebody called Cheryl Black. My hands shook as I clicked on the message, and then opened an attachment.

Dear Steffi,

I know you'll be expecting to hear from your birth sister, Joanne Graham. By way of introduction, I'm a private investigator based in North Yorkshire. Joanne engaged me recently as an intermediary when she decided to embark on a search for her birth sister. I understand that is you.

Joanne's decision to search for you was not an easy one. The circumstances leading to your adoption were difficult. But Joanne knew that you might go looking for your birth family one day, and she wanted you to hear the truth from her. Not from social work files or court reports or the newspaper reports from the time.

When we started the search, Joanne prepared a letter for you, in the event that we should find you. I think it's best that I let her tell you what happened in her words:

"Our mother's death was a tragic accident. It happened one evening when you were acting up and our mother was in a deeply intoxicated state which, sadly, was not unusual.

I was trying to put you to bed but you were shouting for 'Mama'. You picked up the kitchen scissors and you were running around with them, still naked and wet from the bath. I told you to stop, but you ran away from me and out onto the landing.

Our mother was standing at the top of the stairs. She'd come up to see what all the noise was. And you flew at her, holding the scissors. She stepped back and fell down the stairs. She landed badly and the impact broke her neck.

I still don't know why I lied. It is something that tortures

me every day. Partly it was to protect myself. I was supposed to be looking after you, so I wanted to deflect the blame. And I suppose I was trying to protect you too. So I rearranged the story. It was a simple swap – our father at the top of the stairs and not you.

I told everyone – the police, the social workers, the court – that he had pushed her. The jury believed my account. They were only too willing to swallow the hook that he was a violent abuser. They didn't want to believe that a little child could have caused a woman's death.

You were placed with a family for a closed adoption, and I disappeared into the care system.

Our father went to prison. He never managed to clear his name and that destroyed him. I can never put it right, what I did to him. The shadow of it follows me everywhere."

The letter was never finished. Joanne told me she didn't think it was possible to have any sort of future relationship with you, but she was unsure how to phrase this so as not to hurt your feelings.

Very sadly, Joanne died just over a week ago. She was found in her flat. She'd consumed alcohol with strong opiate painkillers. The police say it is unclear whether she intended to cause her death, or if she died by misadventure.

It may be that hearing from you, and reflecting on those difficult times, caused her to spiral. Or maybe she decided

*she could finally let go, once she'd received the confirmation
she'd been seeking – that you were safe and well. Unfortunately, she hadn't been a happy lady in recent years.*

*I'm very sorry to be writing to you with such difficult
news. I wish you all the best for the future.*

*Your sincerely,
Cheryl Black
Private Investigator*

~

I READ the email twice and then closed it down.

Joanne – *Dodo* – was dead.

I'd found her, only to lose her again.

No, it was worse than that. I'd pushed her over the edge.
Just like I'd pushed my mother.

My fear of the stairs... it all made sense now.

Children began swarming out of the school gates. Tilly
would be one of the last to come out since she was cloakroom
monitor this week. I pulled Edie's body closer against mine.

My cheeks flooded with heat. Shame.

I'd imagined myself as a victim of tragic circumstances,
torn from my mother's arms like in some heart-wrenching
episode of *Long Lost Family*. But her death had been a conse-
quence of my own actions. My own *personality,* even. I'd been
acting up. Making a fuss. Seeking attention.

Sarah had been right. It would have been better if I had
never found out. It would have been better if those photograph albums had stayed neatly stacked in their boxes in her
attic, covered in a benign layer of dust.

Don't cry. I've got you.

I pushed the voice away. I'd been enchanted, a few days ago, by the idea that Dodo might have been an echo of my sister. Love, internalised.

But she'd been a tortured, fragile soul, and now I'd killed her.

I felt a shrinking, a hollowness in my chest. A shutting down.

Tilly appeared by my side, shyly waving a handful of drawings.

'Let's go, then.' I couldn't muster my usual enthusiastic smile. I couldn't even be bothered to ask what the drawings were.

Tilly's face fell. We headed for home.

PART II

26

ANGEL

Yorkshire, Present Day

Sometimes she wished Daddy would just stop talking altogether. She imagined draping a blanket right over his high-backed armchair, like you might with a canary that sang too much. Or a foul-mouthed parrot.

He'd followed her into the garden that day, which was unusual. He seemed to be getting stronger with age, in some strange reversal of how it was meant to be. And he'd certainly got louder, more insistent, since Mum had died. It was as if he was drawing energy from somewhere. Sapping the thin warmth out of the October day, leaving the air cold and bitter.

Now, just as she was sitting down after clearing away the dinner things, he started up again.

'It's just you and me now,' he said. 'Me and my Angel.'

'I know.' She kept her eyes down, staring at the patches where the tweed had worn thin on the arms of his chair.

'You know what I'm going to say,' he coaxed.

Oh yes. Oh yes, she did.

'We're running out of time. How can you stand to see her, going around like a princess? Completely oblivious? Like butter wouldn't melt?'

'I know, Daddy,' she whispered.

'Come on, pet. I'm counting on you. It's not much to ask, is it? After everything? Why can't you just do it?'

Angel tried to think back to her old psychotherapy sessions. She tried to conjure that peaceful room with the box of tissues on the table. And the therapist, with her daft cardigan with the cherries on it, sitting there with her hands folded in her lap, her eyes kind.

'Try and become aware of your body,' she would have said, in her gentle voice. 'Place your feet more firmly on the ground. *Feel* the breath going into your lungs. Listen to the sounds going on around you.'

But all she could hear was Daddy's words, in the blood that rushed through the soft inside parts of her ears.

Do it. Do it. Do it.

She put her hands over her ears, trying to shut him out.

'We can do it together, can't we?' he said. 'Set things straight? Get this family back on track?'

What family, though? Barry had another ten years left to serve on his sentence. And poor Mum was never coming back, was she? Angel thought of her – her big, soft, cuddly mum. She wondered what she'd look like now, after two months rotting in her oversized coffin.

As for perfect princess Steffi, and that hard-faced bitch, Joanne – they would *never* be family, in anything other than a biological sense. And biology – the genes, the fiddly, twisting DNA in their cells – would be obliterated once they were ashes too. That horrible link would be severed forever.

It would be like going back to the time before any of it had happened.

That's what Daddy said, anyway. Although, in truth, she couldn't remember a time when they hadn't been around. *The others.* A blot on the edges of the family, impossible to get off, like the black mould marks around her bedroom window.

She remembered Mum trying to comfort her when Daddy went round to their house, to his other family.

'He'll be back,' she'd always reassured Angel. 'That's the main thing.'

Angel had understood, even as a small child, that her mother had reached an uneasy acceptance of the situation. She'd heard her on the phone, telling some friend that she just couldn't give Keith everything a man needed. Not any more, not with her crippling rheumatics, and the size she'd reached. And she'd decided it was better to share him than lose him altogether. Angel had hung onto the hope that things would be different once the new treatment was available. Mum would wear pretty summer dresses, like she used to, and Daddy would dance around the living room with her again.

And then she'd thought it would stop after the other woman died – the 'drink-addled floozy'. Mum had promised that Daddy would settle down after all that business, after his stretch in prison. He'd be happy to stop at home. Angel had counted down the days until his release, crossing them off her Disney Princess wall calendar. But almost as soon as he'd got back, he'd started disappearing again.

'Just get on with it,' said Daddy now from his chair.

His words were like a parasitic worm, burrowing through her brain. Hungry, so hungry, never satisfied. Eating it from the inside, leaving great gaping spaces where Angel had once been.

27

STEFFI

Edinburgh, Present Day

Tom had placed a black rectangular box on my pillow, tied with a glossy red ribbon. I lifted the lid to reveal a basque laid between sheets of tissue paper – a concoction of black lace with panels of scarlet silk. And a pack of whisper-thin black stockings and a suspender belt with tassels.

Tassels.

The silk slid through my fingers, arterial red.

What was he playing at? He hadn't touched me in months. Was this him trying to resuscitate our sex life? I cleared my throat, imagining what I was going to say to him.

'It's so lovely, but –'

'Gosh! This is amazing. I'm totally blown away. The only thing is –'

I jumped when I saw his shape in the doorway.

'Do you like it?' He stepped into the room with a bashful smile.

'It's lovely,' I said. 'It's just... well, it's too small, I'm afraid.' A full two sizes too small.

Tom waved an impatient hand. 'Oh, come on, Steffi. You're not going to be that size forever.'

I stood there, unsure. 'Well, I just thought...'

He sighed, his shoulders deflating.

'What?'

He muttered the words so quietly that I could barely hear them: 'Here we go again.'

I thought of the self-help articles, of how I could use positive language.

'I would love to have something that I could wear *now*. Perhaps I could keep this and also order a bigger size?'

'You could at least try it on.' He'd reverted to his charming, bashful schoolboy voice again.

I imagined myself squeezing into it. How the seams would dig into my flesh like the string around a raw gammon joint. The tassels swinging as I manoeuvred onto the bed to take my position.

I shook my head dumbly.

He let out a long, slow puff of breath through pursed lips, his face pained like a woman in the throes of labour. Then he turned and left.

HE'D GONE UP onto the roof. That was where he went to smoke the odd cigarette every now and again – his guilty pleasure.

He sat there now with his head resting back against the

chimney stack, eyes on the sky, feet planted in front of him, a cigarette balanced between two fingers of his right hand.

'Carefffful,' he said, breathing out a puff of smoke with the word. 'Watch your step.'

He reached down and moved the bottle of beer that stood near his feet.

I held the baby monitor to my ear to check it was working, and pressed the button that showed you the battery level. A row of reassuring green lights appeared – it was nearly fully charged.

The Edinburgh skyline stretched before us, windows and street lights glinting in the dark. A couple of feet to my left, a sheer black drop to the garden patio.

I shuddered silently. I hadn't told Tom about the visit from the police when Joy had been here. The neighbour's report of a madwoman teetering on the roof.

I sat down carefully. 'Like I was saying, it would be nice to have something I could wear now.' I touched his leg softly. 'I miss you,' I whispered. 'I miss... *connecting*.'

Was it true?

I knew, somewhere deep down, that it wasn't. I knew it in my muscles, the way they tightened even when I willed them to relax. I knew it in my skin, in the way it shrank from his fingers. But I missed the *idea* of connecting. The trying. The optimism of it.

No marriage was perfect, right? You had to work at it.

'I want you to know,' he said, 'that it doesn't change how I feel about you. This adoption business, I mean.'

I was confused. Why *should* it change anything, as far as he was concerned? I hadn't even told him about the letter I'd had from the private investigator. I hadn't told him that I'd caused my birth mother's death, with one of my tantrums. I hadn't told him that my birth sister had died in misery, just a few weeks ago, in large part due to me. What was the point?

'It's not as if you kept it from me,' he said. 'It's not as if you knew.'

'I didn't know I was adopted. I had no idea.'

'I don't know why people can't just be straight with each other,' said Tom. 'That's what bothers me. Your parents knew, all this time. Your sister knew.'

'They were trying to protect me, I expect.'

'Adeline was never straight with me.' He said it almost flippantly, with a half shrug. My ears pricked up. He barely ever mentioned Adeline. We normally had to skate around her like a big black hole that might swallow our family up.

'Oh?' I said.

'She saw people.'

Saw people? I thought of Dodo. 'Really? What kind of people?'

'Other men. I know of at least one. There were probably more.'

'Oh.' I racked my brain for something to say. That she wasn't in her right mind? Did that make it better or worse?

'She'd grown up in care,' he said. 'In and out of foster homes and care homes. I think lying had been a way of surviving, for her. And it had become part of her character. You should have seen her. She would lie, perfectly straight-faced, whenever it would get her out of trouble.'

What kind of trouble, I wondered. 'That's so awful. Poor Adeline.'

'I knew *you* were different,' he said. 'I could see that right from the start.'

'Really?' I snuggled against the side of his arm, pushing my face against his sleeve like a cat.

'God, yes. I never believed what people said about you.'

'What?' I raised my head. 'What did people say about me?'

He was silent for a few moments. 'I didn't mean to say that.'

'No, what do you mean?'

He shrugged. 'Nothing, really. One or two people said they didn't understand why we were together.'

'Meaning?'

'They thought you might have had... an agenda, I guess.'

'What agenda?'

'Well, you gave up work almost straight away, didn't you?'

'What, they thought I was with you because I wanted some life of luxury?'

'Just forget I said anything. Please. I don't want to cause a...' He winced and wiggled the fingers of his non-cigarette hand. 'A *thing*.'

An upset. An outburst.

'You encouraged me to leave, Tom,' I said quietly. Reasonably. 'You said that if I took too much time off sick it would go on my record and it would go against me if I was looking for a job in the future. You said it would be better if I took some time out completely to recover.'

He raised an eyebrow. 'And you don't think that's a luxury? To be able to do that?'

I thought of how I'd been after Mum died. The days when I couldn't bring myself to get out of bed. I drew in a slow breath and widened my eyes, trying to let the tears evaporate into the night air.

'You're misunderstanding me, Steffi. I'm saying there's nothing wrong with it. You wanted to be looked after. I was happy to give that to you. I wanted us to be a proper family unit.'

'I was thinking that I might look into going back to work when Edie's a bit older. I thought I might get in touch with Sandra.'

Sandra, my old boss at Slater & Beeny, with a face that looked like an enraged horse. A long nose with flaring nostrils.

He made a face, pausing to blow out smoke. 'Honey. This might be hard to believe but I think they'll be managing just fine without you... and your hour-and-a-half-long lunch breaks.' He ruffled my hair affectionately.

'I never had...' And then I stopped. There was no point.

'I mean, let's face it. It was hardly like you were going to set the world of property on fire.'

It was true that I'd hated Slater & Beeny. I had never seen my future there. That must be what he meant. I had to give him the benefit of the doubt.

'There's no shame in it. Some people are just not made for the cut and thrust of life. Business and high-powered careers and whatnot. It's really tough out there. You'd be going back in there at entry level, competing against kids straight out of university.'

I imagined myself getting dressed up for a job interview, having to ask Tom for money so I could go and buy a suit that was two sizes bigger than I'd been when I was last in work. I imagined myself being asked some question about the property market and my brain just freezing. The pitying looks of the interviewers. Then my mind jumped ahead and I saw myself broke and homeless. Cold and hungry. All the things I'd be without Tom.

'I could do something else. Like work in a nursery or something.'

'Hmm,' he said doubtfully. 'Maybe you could help Sarah out? Isn't her German girl going back to Germany soon? You could collect the boys from school for her. That way you wouldn't have to leave Edie.'

I sighed. 'But I could hardly take money from Sarah for that sort of thing.'

'Remember when you looked after the boys when their nursery had to close because of the norovirus outbreak? She gave you a very generous spa voucher, as I seem to recall.'

Another image flashed into my head. Of me trying to pay down the first month's deposit on a flat with an envelope stuffed with spa vouchers. Or trying to pay for a week's groceries. The vouchers slithering onto the checkout with their gold-foiled lettering.

Where did that come from?

I seemed to hear my mother's voice: *Good Lord, Steffi. No marriage is perfect.*

'Maybe I could do some training. An Open University course or something. From home. While Edie's asleep.'

Tom snickered softly, and drained the last few drops of beer from the bottle. 'I thought Edie never gave you a moment's peace? Is that not right? You've made very sure that I know how difficult your life is, haven't you?' He ruffled my hair again. 'You poor thing, eh? You need to get your story straight.'

I jerked my head away. 'Tom –'

'Relax! I'm only joking.' He gave a warning huff of a sigh, and then began again, his voice softer. 'What I'm *saying* is... I know it's hard. But you're good at it. You're a natural, and you don't even realise it. Your mothering instincts kicked in straight away.'

I thought, inexplicably, of dogs.

'Not every woman's do. Adeline's certainly didn't.'

I remembered that Zara woman at the school gate. 'Did Adeline have mental health issues? Postnatal depression?'

He shrugged. 'Who knows. According to her, she had everything under the sun.'

'So how did she end up going to the artists' community?'

'One afternoon I got a call from the nursery to say that Tilly hadn't been collected. I had to leave work to go and get her – a merger was going through and it was a bastard to get away. I had the police out looking for Adeline for three days before she deigned to get in contact.'

'What did she say?'

'Nothing. She got the leader of the community to phone me. Some moon-worshipping nutter, but smarmy with it. Said his name was "Wolf". He said Adeline had "exercised her sovereign right" to find her own path in life. Some shit like that. I asked to speak to Adeline and this... *Wolf*... said the residents didn't have access to phones.'

He looked down at his hands. For a moment I wondered if he was about to well up.

'Was it some kind of cult?'

'I spoke to the police again. They said that due to further information received, Adeline's disappearance was no longer considered to be a police matter.'

'It must have been torture for you.'

'She wrote a letter, some weeks later. She said she regretted having to leave Tilly, but she knew it was the right decision. She felt "held" by the community, in a way she never had before. Her creativity had simply "erupted".' He rolled his eyes. 'Drugs, most probably.'

In a flash of understanding, I thought I knew what Adeline had meant. She'd found her tribe. A place where she was accepted. Where she was enough.

But to leave Tilly...

'Did you try and find out about it? About the community, I mean?' I ran my tongue over my lips – my mouth had gone dry suddenly. 'What was it called?'

'Something to do with Selene, it was called. The Selene Community... No – The Circle of Selene, I think.'

I placed a gentle hand on Tom's back. 'It sounds like she was unwell.'

He shrugged. 'I think I told myself that, to excuse the worst of her behaviour. Now I wonder if she was just spoilt. She had no grit. Wasn't cut out for motherhood and couldn't hack it.' He turned to me with a lopsided smile. 'Not like you.'

I thought of the time Edie had choked on Tom's noise-cancelling earbud. The times I'd been terrified I might hurl her warm, dense little body down the stairs.

'I just can't understand why she would just... *abandon* Tilly.'

Tom shrugged sadly. 'She knew I would look after her. That I would do the right thing. She took me for a mug, in that respect. But to be honest? She just didn't seem to love her, the way a mother should. Tilly seemed to irritate her.'

'No! Surely –'

That's when I heard a sound. Saw a shape silhouetted in the attic door.

'Daddy? Steffi?'

Oh sweet Jesus, she'd heard.

'What's up, Tilly?'

She paused for a moment. 'Edie's been crying.'

I looked at the monitor – it was dead. I held it to my ear, and then pressed the battery check button. No green lights appeared. How the hell had that happened?

I scrambled over to the attic door, nearly tripping over my feet. 'Did you climb up that ladder yourself, Tilly?'

She nodded. 'But I didn't try and carry Edie.'

'Is Edie in her cot?'

'Down there,' said Tilly, inclining her head.

I peered down through the hatch. Edie was lying on the carpet, wrapped loosely in her cot blanket, less than two feet from the top of the stairs. And the stair gate was undone, the gate suspended over thin air. Panic surged through my body.

'Fucking hell!'

Tilly flinched.

'Did you undo the stair gate, Tilly?'

Her chin dipped, the bottom lip sliding out.

'Tilly?'

'I was looking for you,' she whispered.

'Edie can roll over now! She could have rolled down the stairs! Jesus Christ, Tilly!'

I climbed down the ladder and snatched Edie up to my thudding chest. A sick, rushing sensation went through me, like going too fast over a bump in the road or missing a step. Somewhere, in some shadowy other world, some parallel version of reality, I jerked my arms forward and threw my baby down, down into the dark.

28

STEFFI

Edinburgh, Present Day

'Oh. Hi, Joy.' I'd actually forgotten she was coming today. 'Come on in.' I turned and hobbled towards the kitchen, leading the way. Edie's cheek, flushed and hot from teething, bobbed against my shoulder. Having clung to me all morning, she'd finally fallen asleep. But she wasn't fully relaxed, even now – whenever I moved, her little hands clenched, fingers digging into the fabric of my fleece.

Joy's voice rang out behind me. 'Good Lord! What have you done to yourself?'

My thoughts flashed back to the day before. Edie had been asleep, flat on her back on her play mat, with an hour to go before we had to pick up Tilly. I'd stretched out on the sofa and tried to fall asleep myself. But I just lay there fidgeting, counting the repeating shapes in the cornicing.

Finally I went through to the kitchen and took the marble rolling pin – a present from Granny Vivienne for my last birthday – out of the drawer. I hated it, the stupid thing. I whacked it against my ankle. Once, twice, three times.

I needed bruises. My ankle had to be black and blue. The pain was exhilarating at first. It felt real. Powerful. When I couldn't force myself to continue, I squeezed my ankle instead. Squeezed it with both hands as if I was strangling the life out of it. Strangling left bruises, didn't it?

'I sprained my ankle,' I told Joy now, wondering how long it would be before she'd go away. I waved away her concerned noises, her questions about how I'd done it. 'It's nothing, really. I've been having trouble with vertigo – you know, head spinning, that sort of thing? I tripped on the stairs. Can I get you some tea?'

'Lovely, thank you.' Joy settled her ample behind onto one of the kitchen chairs. 'Shall I take Little Miss?'

'She's a bit drooly, I'm afraid.' Edie woke briefly as I transferred her, her arms jerking out in a startle reflex. 'I think she's teething.'

'Did you try cooling a facecloth in the freezer, like I suggested?'

'Oh... no, actually. I'll try that. Lemon and ginger tea?'

'Perfect. And how have things been going?'

'A bit better, actually,' I lied. I busied myself with the cups and teabags, avoiding Joy's eye. 'Edie and I have moved into the guest bedroom downstairs.'

'Oh?' I could hear the concern in her voice.

'I can't manage the stairs in the night,' I explained. 'What with my ankle and everything. She's in her travel cot, next to the bed.'

I wasn't going to tell Joy that I'd pulled Edie in beside me last night for a sleepy cuddle. I'd been astonished to wake at seven, after three hours of undisturbed sleep.

Joy wouldn't approve, I knew that. Bringing Edie into bed, or even sleeping in the same room, would only sabotage the sleep training we had been doing. The whole point of that was to teach her that she could sleep without me. But what about *me*, I'd been wondering recently. What if I couldn't sleep without *her*?

I took Edie back so that Joy could drink her tea. She took out a folder with her notes in it and laid it on the table.

'Now, where were we last time?'

I wondered how she'd react if I told her about the stairs. About my urge to stand at the top and feel those waves of dizziness, the spinning sensation, to watch the banisters writhing like snakes. To see if I could remember ending my mother's life.

To see if I might throw myself down after her, and be done with it.

It wouldn't leave me alone, that urge. It pulsed through me in miserable waves while I was trying to get to sleep. It prickled my legs and the soles of my feet so they wouldn't stay still. The only way I could settle was to wrap Edie in my arms and slow my breathing to match hers.

Edie woke with a gurgle and placed one soft, exploratory hand on my cheek.

'Hello, my darling.' I reached for my cup of tea, to move it further away, and knocked it over. Steaming liquid flooded over the table towards Joy.

'Christ!' I jumped up.

She moved her chair back but the tea had already spilled over the table edge onto her skirt.

'Are you okay? I'm sorry. You're soaked.'

I went over to the counter to grab the roll of kitchen towel but there were only a couple of sheets left. 'Oh no... I'll go and get some more.'

She motioned me to sit down. 'I'll get this, dear. You just sit there and make sure Edie's okay. Don't worry. I'm *absolutely* fine.' She began mopping up the tea. A little gold cross-and-chain necklace swung forward from her throat.

'There's more kitchen roll in the cupboard under the stairs. I'll just get some.' I had to remember to hobble, as I made my way out of the room. 'Don't tell,' I whispered into Edie's little pink ear. But the kitchen roll wasn't in the cupboard. Tom must have moved it.

That was right – I vaguely remembered him saying it shouldn't be kept in that cupboard because it was a fire risk, with the fuse board being in there. I hobbled into the garage and found it in there, in a pack of twelve, wrapped in plastic. I had to tear the plastic apart with my teeth and, with one hand, pull out one of the rolls through the hole I'd made.

When we got back to the kitchen, Joy was making fresh tea. 'Are you alright now, dear?'

'Yes. I'm sorry about spilling the tea. I'm feeling a bit shaky.'

'You do look a bit peaky. Have you eaten anything today?'

I shook my head miserably.

She tutted. 'Have you got a wee biscuit or something, somewhere?'

'I think there's some in that cupboard by the dishwasher.' I'd put them at the very back, hidden behind the sugar-free rice cakes that Tom insisted on ordering for Tilly.

While Joy was on her knees, rummaging in the cupboard, I half-heartedly mopped up the tea on the table. I moved her folder to the side, and a few of the pages cascaded out.

I reached over to move them, and Edie's name caught my eye. Craning my head round, I managed to read the first few lines on the top page.

Thursday 11th. Seemed very distracted. Didn't remember my suggestion last week of getting cream for the spot of eczema on Edie's arm but became agitated when talking about Edie's sleep chart. Seems to swing between 'zoned out' state and heightened anxiety.

Thursday 18th. Constantly checking stair gates. OCD?

Thursday 25th. Low mood. Had not tried frozen facecloth for teething. Ankle???

I pushed the papers back into the folder, my face burning. Eczema? Edie didn't have eczema. Or had I forgotten that too? I checked both her arms. The skin was smooth and healthy, although there was a slightly dry spot on the back of one elbow. I kissed it and she gave me a solemn look.

Had Joy mentioned buying cream? I honestly couldn't remember. And OCD? She had told me she was making notes for her dissertation, but this? This just seemed to document what a useless mother I was. Or even worse, that I'd somehow lost the plot. And I hadn't even told her about the stairs. Or how I'd shouted at poor Tilly, seconds after she'd overheard Tom saying that her own mother had found her irritating.

Joy pivoted round, holding the biscuits aloft. 'Bingo!'

She looked so warm, so friendly. It just didn't make sense.

'Do you think I'm a bad mother?' I managed.

'What?' She looked genuinely shocked. 'No! Of course not!' She came over and folded me and Edie into a hug. I let myself be held, my cheek pressed against the shoulder of her jumper. She smelled of something familiar – Yardley soap, maybe. Or talcum powder. I closed my eyes briefly.

'Parenting is tough,' she said. 'You'll get through this, I promise. And I'm here to help.' She stepped back and looked me in the eye, appraisingly. 'It's been such a tough time for you, finding out about your adoption. You must be at sixes and sevens. Have you heard anything further?'

'No,' I lied. I wasn't having her make more notes about my precarious mental state. I just wanted her to leave.

She nodded slowly. 'Is today just one of those days? Would you like me to come back another time?'

'Would that be okay? I think I might take her out for a walk. Get a bit of fresh air and exercise.'

But as soon as she'd left, I went back into the kitchen and ate four of the biscuits. Maybe the sugar would help me to stay awake. Imagining Tom's disapproving face, I also swallowed a swig of Bloody Deborah's Vitamin Tonic.

'See, Edie?' I said. 'We've got this, haven't we? Now, how about watching a nice episode of *In The Night Garden*?'

29

STEFFI

Edinburgh, Present Day

I woke with a rush of panic, disorientated.

Why was I lying on the floor in the living room? Where was Edie? And Tilly? What time was it? I wiped a string of saliva from my chin and checked my phone – it was four thirty.

I must have fallen asleep. But the time leading up to that – the whole day – was a blank. I tried to piece it together, my brain struggling to hold the thoughts in my head.

Edie had been teething. And it was Thursday, because Joy had visited – that had been today, hadn't it? Yes. And then I'd got rid of Joy, and Edie and I had watched some television before going to collect Tilly. When we'd arrived home I'd made Tilly a bowl of strawberries and apple slices and started her on her homework. And then I'd put Edie down on her play mat. And then I must have closed my eyes for a second...

'Tilly?' I pulled myself up off the floor. The house was quiet. Too quiet.

They weren't in the kitchen. Or the downstairs bathroom or the guest room. The stair gates were both undone. Clinging to the banister with both hands, I forced myself to go upstairs.

'Tilly? Edie?' My head swam. 'Come out now, please!'

A minute later, I was on the phone to Tom. 'They've gone!' I managed to croak, even though no air was reaching my lungs.

'What are you talking about?'

'They've gone. They're not – in the house. They're not. Here.'

'Haven't you been watching them?'

'I fell asleep.'

A barely audible mutter came down the line: '*Fucking useless.*'

'I –'

'Call 999. I'm leaving now.'

'I'll go out and look –'

'Stay where you are,' he barked, hanging up.

This couldn't be happening. It must be some kind of nightmare. I had the sensation that I was watching myself, hovering somewhere overhead, as I dialled 999 and managed to explain that the girls were missing. They said someone would be with me in a few minutes.

I sat on the bottom step of the stairs, eyes on the front door, fighting waves of nausea. The clock in the hall ticked round. One minute past five. Two minutes past. I could hear the traffic from the main road. Rush hour. Maybe the police couldn't get through. Would they put their blue lights on or was this not urgent enough? Two little girls, missing.

I tried to focus on getting breath into my body. Beyond that, I knew I was absolutely helpless. Like a patient, opened up for surgery, my chest cracked open wide. A great gaping hole where Edie should be.

And Tilly was out there somewhere, too. Poor little motherless Tilly.

Always second on my mind.

I heard my own voice – a thin wailing – echo around the empty hallway.

What an Appalling Fuss.

The minute hand crept to twenty past... twenty-five past. Where were the police? Where was Tom?

I had a sudden thought – perhaps they'd all conspired to leave me here alone. I'd be here forever at the bottom of the stairs with the clock ticking past. With nobody to look after me. I held my head in my hands, fingers clutching at my scalp as if I could tear off this face, this mask. As if I could go back. Back to that other time. That other house. As if I could undo it all and start again.

The doorbell rang and I flew to open it.

And there they were. Edie in her pram, and Tilly, face streaked with tears, holding the hand of one of the two police officers.

'Thank God. Thank God. Thank God.' I caught Tilly up into a hug. She was limp as a rag doll in my arms. I lifted Edie out of the pram and held her, burying my face in her neck. She grabbed a fistful of my hair.

Tom's car turned into the drive, his tyres sending up a spray of gravel. He ran up the steps. 'Here you are,' he said. 'Here you all are.'

The female police officer explained, over a cup of sugary tea, that they'd had a call from the staff at Costa. Tilly had gone in there, pushing Edie in her pram. She'd been told off in the queue by an old man who she'd bumped with the pram, and had been close to tears as she'd tried to buy a double shot latte and a lemon muffin. Then she hadn't had enough money to pay for it. The girl behind the counter had noticed that she seemed very young to be out by herself, in charge of a baby. She had settled her in at a table near the counter, with a drink of juice and a biscuit, and had made a call to the police.

Tilly had told the police that her stepmother was asleep and needed a coffee to wake her up. She'd explained that Edie had been crying so she'd brought her along in the pram, hoping she might fall asleep.

'You always say she needs to be down for her nap by four thirty or she won't sleep at night,' said Tilly now, looking at me anxiously. 'Any later and it's a full-on disaster scenario,' she added, echoing my own words back to me.

Poor Tilly. Struggling with the pram. Not having enough money to pay. Trying to be a mother herself. Suddenly my heart broke for her, this solemn, private little girl who I'd never really learned how to love. Hot tears flooded down my cheeks. I put my face in my hands, my body shuddering.

'Steffi,' hissed Tom.

'You're alright,' said the police officer. 'It's just the relief, eh?'

'I'm so sorry. I must have dozed off this afternoon. Edie hasn't been sleeping too well. I'm a bit sleep deprived.'

'No harm done,' said the police officer, standing up. 'Looks like you could do with a decent night's sleep. Maybe hubby can take the night shift tonight?' She gave me a conspiratorial wink.

Tom stood up and arranged his face into a smile. He held an arm out towards the door. 'All's well that ends well, eh?' he said. 'We'll let you get on.'

On the way out, the police officer turned and spoke to me. 'Just to make you aware, we will need to make a report to Children's Services. It's standard practice when a child has been reported missing. It's possible they may want to have a wee chat.'

I nodded, but I felt sick. Maybe they'd also tell Children's Services about the other police visit a few weeks ago. The visit concerning reports of a child in distress and a crazy woman on the roof. The visit that Tom knew nothing about.

Once the front door was closed, Tom turned to me. 'What the hell, Steffi?'

'I'm so sorry. I was just so tired.'

'What's got into you? Sleeping on the job? Are you depressed or something?' He hissed the word, keeping his voice low so that Tilly wouldn't hear.

But she emerged from the living room. 'Are you cross with me?'

'You shouldn't have left the house,' said Tom. 'And you shouldn't have taken Edie. It was dangerous.'

'I didn't answer the door,' she said.

He rounded on her. 'What part of "You shouldn't have left the house" do you not understand?'

Tilly's lip started to wobble again. She turned to me. 'But the lady said.'

A wave of tingles moved down my spine. I crouched down in front of Tilly. 'Hang on – what lady?'

'The lady who came to the door. She said that I should go and get you a coffee to wake you up.'

'WHAT lady?' repeated Tom.

Tilly shrugged. 'I don't know.'

'What did she look like?' I persisted.

'I don't know. I only spoke to her through the letterbox. I didn't answer the door because you said I should never answer the door to strangers.'

'So you spoke to a lady through the letterbox and she told you to go out and buy a coffee for me?'

'I don't know. I think so. She said she knew you. But I still didn't let her in. That was right, wasn't it?' She looked up at me with worried eyes.

Someone who knew me? Could it have been one of the mums from baby yoga?

'It wasn't Auntie Sarah? Or one of your friends' mums? That woman... what's-her-name... Zara?'

Tilly shook her head. 'Don't think so.'

I thought of the hooded 'lady' in the car park. The woman on the roof... Although there hadn't been a woman on the roof, had there? Because that would have been impossible. It was all too much to make sense of.

The front door slammed behind us, shaking the stained glass panels. Looking through the hall window, I saw Tom get into his car and drive away. Where the hell was he going? Leaving us in the house with this 'lady' at large?

I moistened my lips. 'Tilly? It wasn't... the same lady who was in the car park that time? The one who wrote the thing on my car?'

'I didn't *see* this lady today,' she answered with a frown. 'She was on the other side of the door, remember?'

'Come along,' I said. 'You can help me make up Edie's bottle and then we'll do dinner.'

She sniffed and wiped her nose with the back of her hand. I wanted to give her a cuddle, to make it all okay again. But I couldn't face the thought of her shrinking away, stiffening again. So I just patted her shoulder. 'I'm so glad you're back.'

Half an hour later Tom was back, standing on the front door step surrounded in plastic packaging and tools he'd brought in from the garage.

'Where have you been?'

'Argos,' he said. 'I've been meaning to get one of these for a while. A doorbell camera. We'll be able to see if this "lady" comes back,' he added grimly. 'I'll get a phone notification whenever someone comes to the door.'

I pulled my cardigan around me. 'Who do you think she was?'

'I don't fucking know. She could have been *anyone*.'

TO ANYONE WHO KNOWS ME, PLEASE REPLY.

I shivered. 'Well, I suppose a doorbell camera's a good idea. Do you want a cup of tea?'

'No, I'm about to go and pack.'

'*What?*'

'I'm taking the girls to my mother's for the weekend. Give you time to sort yourself out. You can sleep for forty-eight hours straight if you want to.'

'Tilly's got school tomorrow. And you've got work.'

'We'll take a long weekend. I'll let the school know.'

'But what about Edie?' She'd never been away from me before.

'Yup. She's coming too. My mother will be only too happy to look after her.'

'But I don't want –'

'Give me STRENGTH!' he burst out. He stretched out his hands and looked up, as if seeking divine intervention. 'You whinge on about sleep. I'm *giving* you sleep, by taking the girls away. Discussion over.'

30

STEFFI

Edinburgh, Present Day

I didn't like the feeling in the house that night.

The house never usually felt quiet, even when Edie and Tilly were tucked up and asleep. It always hummed with their presence. The imperceptible sounds of the breath moving in and out of their bodies as their chests rose and fell. Limbs wriggling under the covers as they dreamed.

Tom hadn't even let me pack for Edie. He'd gone round the house throwing things into bags. I'd felt as if I'd been dropped into some sort of parallel universe. One where I was watching him leave me.

'*Please*,' I'd kept saying, following him around each room, close to tears. I'd thrust a bundle of things at him in the hall – Edie's bunny blanket, her bath sponge. Tilly's colouring pencils.

'Sorry,' Tilly had mouthed, silently, as she'd been corralled out the door.

Knowing I should try and catch up on some sleep, I lay in bed watching a Scandi noir drama on my tablet, with my headphones on and Edie's second favourite blanket draped over my chest.

I turned my head suddenly, thinking I'd seen a movement from the corner of the room, by the chair where a bunch of clothes had been dumped – a mixture of Edie's things and some hoodies and leggings I hadn't bothered to stick in the washing basket. But there was nothing moving. It was just my eyes playing tricks on me.

What if the clothes were to lift themselves off the chair to form the shape of a figure? I imagined it hovering there as I kept my eyes on the programme, too scared to turn my head and look at it full on.

I thought of Dodo, that sweet, shadowy version of my birth sister. As a child, I used to think I could see her sometimes – shapes flashing across my peripheral vision. It wasn't so much of a leap to go from hearing voices to seeing things.

My mother had often commented, with a frown, about my tendency to be 'fanciful' – an affliction that had never affected her, Dad or the ever-sensible Sarah. Maybe it was something I'd inherited from my other family.

Hallucinations. Psychosis. Plain old madness.

I closed my eyes and turned away from the chair, lying on my side. Uneasiness crept through my body in unpleasant tingles. With a sinking heart, I thought of the stairs. Maybe I should stand at the top and test myself again, now that the children were out of the house.

Then I thought of them returning on Sunday night.

Finding me crumpled and blackening at the bottom of the stairs.

It seemed possible that I wasn't entirely well. I couldn't blame Tom for taking the children away. I tried counting my breaths on my fingers.

One, two, three. One, two, three.

Had Adeline felt this way? Had she been terrified of losing her grip on reality? I tried to imagine a scenario where I would voluntarily leave my child, go and live somewhere else, and couldn't. What kind of mental torment had she suffered, to get her to that place? I thought of the picture of the screaming face that Tom had dropped in the bin, on Tilly's last birthday. I remembered Zara's story about Adeline and the gas masks. Her admission to a mental unit.

Had it all started like this for her?

It's possible they may want to have a wee chat.

At half past three in the morning, I gave up on the struggle to fall asleep. I picked up my phone and did a search:

How to pick a filing cabinet lock.

The hardest part about it was getting up the stairs. Once in Tom's study, I found a paperclip and bent it into the shape suggested by the website. Wiggled it around until something clicked and the top drawer slid open a crack. I imagined Tom's face, if he could see me now, and pushed the thought away.

I was looking for anything about Adeline. Medical records, financial stuff. I strongly suspected that Tom had destroyed any photographs of her, but I'd look for those too. I didn't even know what she looked like, my ghostly predecessor.

Or maybe there'd be legal correspondence about the

divorce Tom had promised he'd get, and why it all had to be handled so carefully.

The invoices were in the third drawer down, filed neatly in a plastic wallet. They were from Selene House, somewhere down south. Not 'Circle of Selene', as Tom had said. The basic fee was £6,000 per month. 'Extras' were also listed:

- Hairdresser: £60
- Farm shop delivery (2x raspberry jam, teacakes, 2x Dundee Cake, butter with sea salt flakes): £24.55
- Oil colours: (Burnt Umber 200ml, Van Dyke Brown 200ml, Rose Madder Genuine 200ml): £36

The way Tom had talked about it – an 'off-grid' artists' community – it had sounded almost like a strange cult. But what kind of cult had visiting hairdressers and farm shop deliveries?

There were monthly invoices covering a period of three or four years, all labelled 'paid' in Tom's small, square handwriting.

I wondered if he was still paying for all this, even now. Maybe they'd moved over to email invoices, or some online system. If not, who *was* paying? Other family members, perhaps? Although Zara had said she'd grown up in care. Without Tom, she had no-one.

Back in bed, I couldn't find anything on the internet about Selene House, or 'Circle of Selene'. But a place called 'Chesters' came up in the second page of search results. Was it linked, somehow? I clicked onto a landing page showing a carousel of photos – an English manor house with glowing windows and red ivy climbing the walls, a view of sunlit lawns and a rose garden. A painter's easel in a room full of morning light, and a tea tray by a crackling log fire. But it required you to log in to access the rest of the site.

I googled the address that had been printed at the top of the invoice: 'The Old Coddenham Road', and scoured the satellite map view. It looked like a rural road that ran for two or three miles, with a few properties situated along it. There were a couple of farms, by the look of it, and a sort of manor house with outbuildings.

Zooming out on the map, I saw that this Old Coddenham Road wasn't far from Doncaster.

My heart leapt in my chest. I was completely free all weekend. I could get the train to Doncaster, jump in a taxi at the station and ask them to take me to The Old Coddenham Road. I could try and solve the mystery of what had become of Selene House. Maybe I could even find Adeline. She might still be there, busy and happy in her painting overalls. She could reassure me that Tom wasn't a monster, that it just hadn't worked out between them. I could tell her about Tilly and how fast she was growing up.

Tom couldn't know, of course. I'd have to pretend I was at home, if he called. Or say I'd been sleeping, if I couldn't answer. And I'd have to leave the house by the back door so he couldn't see me on the doorbell camera. But it was *possible*.

Before I'd even made a conscious decision, my fingers moved on the keyboard, searching for train times. There was a train at seven in the morning. I could just about get there and back in a day. I still had the money I'd been going to use to pay Joy for the initial session, before she'd offered it free of charge. I could use that for my ticket. But I'd have to leave in just over an hour.

A shadow seemed to move again, in the corner by the chair with the clothes piled on it. I rubbed my eyes. Anything would be better than staying here on my own.

31

ANGEL

Yorkshire, Present Day

'She's like a princess, that one. A right bobby dazzler. You should see her face. Like peaches and cream.' Daddy gave a wistful sigh followed by a little chuckle. He was starting up again, just when she thought he'd settled down for the night.

Angel wasn't going to listen to this. She turned up the television, an old episode of *Songs of Praise* she'd found on the BBC iPlayer. She could feel him standing behind her. She knew he was pointing over to the kitchen cupboard where the drain cleaner was kept. The extra strong bottle with all the warnings, the one he'd made her order online, standing over her until she did it.

'And that's okay with you, is it?' he said in a croaky whisper. 'The fact she's still swanning around?'

'I did what you asked, Daddy.' Her voice was patient, coaxing. 'You – *we* wanted to set the record straight. That's what we've done.'

'Why can't you do anything properly? It's always got to be half-arsed with you, hasn't it? *Useless bitch*,' he added, under his breath.

'Why don't you go and sit down,' she suggested. 'We can watch this for a bit and then I'll put on the football.'

'You need to get off your backside and make it *happen*.'

Get off her backside? What did he think she'd been doing, all these weeks?

She began to sing along to the hymn, following the words that were shown on the screen, drowning him out. She wasn't religious, exactly, but she found hymns comforting, especially Christmas ones. She enjoyed noticing the many references to her own name. Once she'd learned *O Little Town of Bethlehem* on the keyboard in the school music room, and had been allowed to play it at a Christmas assembly. She'd begged her parents for piano lessons for weeks afterwards. Mum had said maybe – once she'd got her medicine sorted, and could go back to her job at Tesco. But it had never happened.

One day, not long after that terrible day when the police had come to the door, Angel had stayed behind after her Religious Studies lesson to ask the teacher whether hell really existed. Mr Munro had leaned back in his chair, linking his fingers and resting them on his round belly. He'd stared at the ceiling for a moment and Angel could see up his nose, where a pale blob of something hung suspended in the hairs.

'Christians would say that God doesn't want anybody to go to hell. He longs to welcome us into His light, even the most base, wretched sinners.'

'What, so you're saying the people choose to go to hell?'

The teacher's eyes were sad. 'The Christian view is that God gave us the gift of free will. The most precious, and the most dreadful, of gifts. He won't force us to accept His light.'

'So what happens to those people?'

'CS Lewis wrote something on this point, as I recall. About hell as separation – separation from God. From our fellow humans. From love, if you will.' He rose from his chair and approached the bookcase in the corner. 'Let me see if I can find the passage I'm thinking of.'

Angel thought that didn't sound so scary. Not like a lake of burning fire or devils tossing you about with pitchforks or something. She'd already been separated from everyone who mattered.

Mr Munro crouched down to peer at the titles on the bottom shelf. 'And, if I remember it rightly, his idea was that those poor souls would simply become more and more self-absorbed. They would become smaller and smaller. Until they were not really souls at all, any more. And maybe God, in his infinite mercy, might allows them eventually to just... disappear.' He turned to her, holding his hands out in a wide shrug.

Angel thought, rather oddly, of crisp packets – how they crumpled if you threw them into a fire. The sudden shrinking and twisting. The distortion and blackening. Someone had told her that people's faces went black after they died.

Without a second of warning, her senses were filled with it again. Ambushed. Taken over. It was as if she was back there and it was all happening again – the sweep of car headlights on the wall of her bedroom. Her maths homework slithering off her bed onto the floor as she kneeled up to look out of the window. The two police hats, their black and white blocky patterns bobbing along, just visible over the top of the garden hedge. The sharp burst of the doorbell. And then Mum screaming, the sound distorting into a tinnitus screech.

'Bother. I can't seem to find it.' Mr Munro had risen to a standing position, his face reddened from the exertion. 'But you get the gist.'

'Okay. Thanks.'

'What about you?' the teacher had asked, suddenly curious. 'What would hell mean to you? What would *heaven* mean?'

She'd thought of dirty water spiralling down a plughole. A cleansing. A washing away.

A head empty of thoughts.

'Dunno,' she'd said. 'Lakes and pitchforks and angels and that, I suppose. I've got to go now.' She'd hauled her schoolbag onto her shoulder and left.

Angel hadn't envisaged, back then, that Daddy would come to live with her again. That she'd be bringing him newspapers and buying his favourite sweets. Making sure his slippers were by the chair in case he needed them.

Work – that was the answer. She turned down *Songs of Praise* and brought up the details of her latest case on her laptop. It concerned a bin man, *a waste management and disposal technician*, who'd been signed off work for the last eight months with a bad back. But he'd promised – on Facebook, the stupid clown! – to help his brother move flat tomorrow, and he'd even hired a white van.

She looked up the address on the map, and went into street view mode. These cheaters, these liars, she'd pick them out one by one.

'Gotcha,' she whispered, identifying a parking spot that

would give a perfect view of the door to the brother's flat – not too near and not too far.

From his chair, Daddy nodded in approval. 'Good girl.' His voice was full of warmth now, to the point where she wondered if she'd imagined his unpleasant mutterings a few moments ago. 'You go get 'em, girl.'

32

STEFFI

On a Train, Present Day

The taxi came early, when I was not long out of the shower. I had to drag a brush through my hair, pile a few things into a bag, and rush out of the house, leaving clothes on the floor and a smear of toothpaste on the bathroom sink. I tried to suppress the thought of Tom's face, should he come back early, for some reason, and find all that mess.

I found a window seat on the train, one with a table. I settled in there, watching people milling about on the platform. Huddled down in my coat, I felt an uneasy thrill, like a child running away from home.

My parents, Sarah and I had always gone to stay with my grandparents in the countryside near Doncaster every Christmas. After we'd moved from Yorkshire up to Edinburgh, when I'd been about eight, that had meant going by train. A black taxi would materialise, rumbling on the street outside our house, headlights slicing through the early morning dark. We'd climb in with our suitcases and Sarah and I would take the backward-facing seats that folded down. We'd catch the eight o'clock train from Edinburgh Waverley.

Now, as the train began to move, I took out my phone and searched the web again for references to Selene House, and Chesters. I googled Adeline's name. I searched for her on Facebook and Twitter and LinkedIn. I found nothing. It was as if she had never existed.

An elderly lady got on at Berwick-upon-Tweed and sat opposite me. She ordered a tea and a KitKat from the refreshments trolley, and opened her newspaper to the crossword page.

My mother had always packed bits and pieces to amuse me on the long train journey south – Connect Four and colouring books. Word searches and playing cards. Dog-eared *Famous Five* books that I'd read a dozen times. But I remembered sitting with my face pressed to the window, looking into the lighted windows of houses that we passed. Watching the dark fading into the grey of dawn. There were long stretches of countryside, winter trees edging silvered fields. And dreary outskirts of towns, where crowded red-brick terraces backed onto the tracks. We stopped at stations, where announcements came over the loudspeakers. 'The train arriving at Platform 2 is the ten forty-two to London King's Cross, calling at Darlington, York, Doncaster, Peterborough...'

I knew what I'd been looking for, on those old childhood journeys. I'd been looking for the white house in my drawings, the one that backed onto the railway line. The one I put in all my stories, with a red-tiled roof and a washing line and pansies growing in a strip by the back door. The one I'd tried to build out of Lego, again and again. The one that my mother had told me was Auntie Anne's old house.

'Help me look, Mamma,' I'd say.

'Our house wasn't anywhere near a railway line,' she'd frown, trying to foist more games and books onto me.

'Not that house. Not our Yorkshire house. The *other* house.'

I realised now that I'd been searching for the house I'd lived in before my adoption. I knew it with absolute certainty, like a jigsaw piece flipping into place, or the clunk of a Rubik's cube.

I had a sudden, sharp longing for my mother, who'd loved me and lied to me. She'd been trying to protect me, trying to write over my memory of the white house and its shadowy occupants. I wished I could ask her about it.

There was nobody alive now who could tell me where I'd come from. Not now that my birth sister had died.

Joanne.

Jo-Jo.

Dodo.

'Are you all right, dear?' The elderly lady slid a liver-spotted hand across the table.

I looked up, and realised my face was wet with tears.

THE TAXI DRIVER blew air through his teeth when I mentioned The Old Coddingham Road, and that I'd like him to wait for me and bring me back to the station. Then he shrugged and put the taxi into gear. 'It's your money.'

'Do you know Selene House?'

He frowned. 'You'll be looking for Chesters. That place changed hands years ago.'

It took half an hour to get there, inching through the traffic in town before the road opened out into the countryside, a landscape of pale stubbly fields and belts of woodland, dotted with old, red-bricked houses.

Chesters, when it came into view, looked like a country hotel, with extensive grounds contained within a high stone wall. Ornate wrought iron gates opened to allow the taxi through.

We approached the house along a winding driveway, bordered by mature trees. Wide lawns stretched on either side and I noticed a man in a blue sweatshirt and jeans, raking leaves. To the side of the house, a gravelled path led towards a row of outbuildings that looked like workshops.

Assuring the taxi driver I would be back, I climbed up the steps to the front entrance.

I was buzzed into an entrance hall with wood-panelled walls and a stained-glass window at the turn of the wide staircase. Behind a large mahogany desk, a receptionist was talking on the telephone in hushed tones. I surveyed a rack of leaflets about wellness activities and a multicoloured timetable which had been fixed onto an A-frame display board. Today there would be yoga classes, nutrition workshops and meditation sessions. At three o'clock there would be a visit from 'Buddy and Jess' – who appeared from the photo to be a golden retriever and a brown-spotted spaniel. At the top of the timetable there was a note of the psychiatrist on duty for that day.

I realised with a little jolt that this was some form of mental health facility. A very upmarket one.

'Hello?' The receptionist was an owl-faced woman, peering at me over the top of her glasses, eyebrows raised.

'Hello. I wonder if you can help. I'd like to visit Adeline Buchanan-Smith.'

The receptionist continued to stare at me, her face expectant.

'I think she stays here? Or... she might once have stayed here?'

'I'm sorry.' She offered a fixed smile. 'We don't give out patient details.'

'But can you just tell me if she's here? I've travelled all the way down from Edinburgh.'

'*Absolutely* not.'

'Okay.' I tried a different tack. 'If there *is* an Adeline Buchanan-Smith here, could you please inform her that I'm here to see her?'

The receptionist shook her head. 'Visits are strictly by patient request only.'

I felt a childish rage welling up inside. Then hopeless exhaustion.

'Please. I've travelled all day to get here.'

A figure emerged from a wood-panelled door behind the reception desk. I looked up to see a forty-something woman wearing jeans and a silk floral blouse.

'Please,' I said. 'I need to see Adeline Buchanan-Smith. It's urgent.' The energy seemed to drain out of my legs. I gripped onto the reception desk.

The woman in the flowery blouse stepped closer and placed a hand on my arm. I saw she had a name badge which simply said 'Bea'.

'You seem upset. Why don't you take a few moments in our garden? I'll show you the way.'

Bea led the way back down the stone steps and behind the main house to a rose garden surrounded by a box hedge. The rose beds formed four quarters of a circle with grass pathways between. In the centre of the circle stood a wooden pergola. Most of the roses were finished, but there was a pink climbing rose still in bloom, clinging onto the silvered wood.

She motioned me to sit down beside her on a wrought-iron bench. It shifted slightly as we sat down, its feet not quite even on the grass.

'Ah, there's Muriel.'

She nodded towards an elderly lady in overalls who was kneeling on a gardening mat, weeding the rose bed and humming.

'Is this a mental health facility?' I asked.

'A therapeutic community,' she corrected. 'Rebuilding lives is a slow process. A mountain climb, not a sprint. We like to think of this as a home from home. A *human* place. Because in the end, it's our humanity that heals us, isn't it? Our capacity for connection with other humans.'

'Mmm. If you can afford the fees, I guess.'

She closed her eyes and nodded. 'I hate that it's out of reach for most people. We have one or two funded places. Not enough, of course.'

A robin landed on the arm of the bench, stayed for a few seconds and then flew off again.

'It's so peaceful here.' I thought of Tom, sending Adeline to this kind place, and the fortune that it must have cost him over the years. He was a good, caring man. Why was it that I kept thinking such awful thoughts about him?

'Modern life can be an assault on the senses,' went on

Bea. 'It can feel like being attacked from every angle. Our soft, human souls just weren't built for it.'

Maybe that's what Tom had meant when he'd said that about my job. About how I was too fragile for the real world.

'I couldn't cope with my job.' I could feel the shame rising in my cheeks. 'And then I couldn't cope with having a new baby.'

'Our hearts still beat to a much older rhythm.' She tipped her head back and looked at the sky. 'The healing of the slow, dark winter months. Unfurling into life again in the spring.' Her voice was soft and monotone. 'Imagine a life with no clocks, waking with the sunrise and going to sleep when it gets dark? A life that is simple – just eating, sleeping, growing. Old and young, weak and strong, living side by side.'

Then she turned and looked me straight in the eye. 'You have a deep, ancestral memory. And it knows you should have your women-folk around you in the months after giving birth. Mothers, aunts. Grannies. Sisters.'

A blackbird began to sing from the top of the pergola, its song spilling into the air.

I suddenly remembered a little bird that I'd been given as a child, a hollow thing made of green transparent plastic, the colour of a lime-flavoured boiled sweet. You filled it with water and then blew into it like a whistle to make a low, warbling sound.

And I remembered green shadows lengthening across a lawn. Bare feet on cool evening grass. A summer dress with heart-shaped buttons.

Had that been in my old life, my lost life? Or my later one, with my parents and Sarah?

'I was hearing voices.' I felt a quick, slippery relief in saying the words, in getting them out of me. 'In my head. After I had my baby. I thought there was something wrong with me. I've wondered if it might be... well, postnatal... a postnatal...thing.'

Postnatal psychosis.

The words hung in the air, unsaid. A breeze moved through the garden and, somewhere far off, a wind chime made a soft tinkling noise.

'What makes you think it's wrong to hear voices?' Bea's voice held no judgement – it was simply full of curiosity.

'Well, it's not exactly normal, is it?'

'In some cultures, voice hearing is viewed quite differently. It's considered an ordinary part of life. Sometimes it's even revered or celebrated.' She leaned back against the bench again and stretched out her legs, easing off one of her sandals so that the top of her foot was exposed to the weak sun. 'In fact, I read a paper recently suggesting there might be a genetic element to voice hearing or experiencing visions. That particular combination of genes may have given our ancestors an evolutionary advantage, hence being passed down.'

'It was almost like having an imaginary friend.' I didn't know how to put it into words – that Dodo had been an echo of someone I'd lost.

Bea nodded enthusiastically. 'Children have it right, don't they? They're less rigid than we are, in the way they interpret reality.'

'I think I was lonely.'

She simply nodded. A long silence fell between us. Just the wind stirring the leaves in the treetops.

'I want to find Adeline because she was my fiancé's first wife. My step-daughter's mother. I thought that he... that he...' I paused, and then blurted it out: 'Sometimes he scares me.'

'Does he?' Bea's voice was soft, relaxed.

'And sometimes I scare myself.'

She shifted beside me, transferring her weight from one hip to the other. Surely now she would recommend that I speak to my GP, or phone some helpline.

'Our ancestors would have been scared of lions or wolves. But we are scared of what we see in the mirror.'

'Maybe.' I thought of my thinning hair, my baby weight.

She put her hand on my arm again. 'I'm heading over to the workshops now. Art therapy class.'

'I need to get back to my taxi.' I thought of the long journey back to Edinburgh. The train windows turning black as we sped further north into the evening.

Bea called across to the lady weeding the flower bed. 'Muriel, could you show this lady back to reception?'

'I hope that you find Adeline,' said Bea, turning back to me. 'And I wish you all the very best.'

'You're looking for Adeline?' said the old lady as we walked back around the side of the house. 'If you see her, will you tell her I was asking after her?'

I stopped and spun towards her. 'Adeline Buchanan-Smith? You know her?'

She nodded. 'Of course. She was here a few years ago. She stayed for quite a while. But then she left.'

'Was she... better?'

'Oh yes. She was ready. She'd been ready for a while. We all wished her well, we wished her all the luck in the world.'

'Did this place used to be a sort of artists' community?'

Muriel shrugged. 'You could think of it in that way. The workshops are a big thing here. Some people do upholstery or pottery, or make furniture. Others paint or sculpt. Others help with the gardens, like me. There's a market garden here where we grow a lot of our own produce. And we keep chickens and ducks, and collect the eggs for the kitchens. The idea is that the work helps us to get better.'

Maybe it had been easier for Tom to tell Tilly – or tell the world – that Adeline was in an artists' community, rather than a mental health facility. I could sort of understand that. But why hadn't he mentioned she'd left?

'Was there someone here called Wolf, a while back?'

Muriel's face split into a wrinkly smile. 'Dr Wolfe? He was one of the psychiatrists here. Lovely, lovely man. He's retired now. But he comes to our Christmas fair every year.'

'I see.' My head throbbed, trying to understand all this. Hadn't Wolf been some strange, moon-worshipping type, almost like a cult leader? Had Tom's version of things been deliberately twisted, or had I just misunderstood him? 'Do you know where Adeline went? Or why she left at that particular time?'

She smiled again. 'She was leaving for love. That's what she said, anyway. I think she had met someone, because she had a baby after she left. She sent photos a while back.'

A baby? Did Tilly have a new brother or sister out there somewhere? Maybe that's why Tom hadn't been forthcoming with the truth. He was trying to protect Tilly from knowing her mother had started a whole new life without her. It was easier to pretend she was still in the artists' community, happily painting her weird pictures.

Love and lies, all tangled up.

'Could you let me know if you hear from her again?' I said. 'If she writes with an address or anything? Have you got a piece of paper I could write my number on?'

The woman smiled, and pulled an iPhone out of her pocket. 'We're not quite living in the dark ages here, you know. I message my sister most days to show her how the rose garden's getting on.'

~

ON THE TRAIN, I switched on my phone and saw that Tom had been trying to get me.

I messaged him quickly.

> How are the girls?

My phone rang immediately. I hesitated before answering – what if he could tell I was on a train? But I was in the quiet carriage and there was nobody else around. And he might get even more suspicious if I didn't answer.

'Hello!'

'How are things?' he said shortly. 'What have you been doing today?'

A fractional pause. 'Oh, nothing much. Resting up all day, like you said.'

'Hmm,' he said, distractedly. I could hear Edie crying in the background, Granny Vivienne hushing her. She must have given up her usual Saturday afternoon at the country club to help with the girls.

The train made a soft rattling noise as it moved over the points. Would Tom be able to hear that? Then the door into the carriage slid open – a member of staff was coming in with the refreshments trolley.

'Can I call you later?' I said. 'Need the loo.'

I ended the call, thinking I'd got away with it.

And then, like a slap in the face, I remembered. The door-bell camera. When my taxi had arrived that morning – flustering me, because it was ten minutes early – I had forgotten to leave by the back door.

He would have seen me leave the house.

33

JOANNE

Yorkshire, Present Day

Joanne pulled up the van in the car park of the vet's surgery, a square, squat concrete building tucked away in a little back street of Northallerton.

She sat there for several minutes, rain chucking itself against the windows, trying to build up the will to get out. Sometimes, these days, the useless lumps of her legs just refused to move.

Used to be, she'd get excited about collecting a new cat, taking it back to the shelter and settling it in. She'd come over all 'Joanne to the rescue', and spend an hour or two writing up their profile for the website, choosing the most flattering photos.

But now it was hard to get excited about anything. The world was a colder, greyer place now that she knew her sister was no longer in it.

Pointless.

That was the word in her head now. On good days it was a whisper, noticeable only in the quiet moments. Like when she woke up in the morning, the grey light seeping around the edges of the curtains. Or when she arrived home from work and plonked herself on her saggy sofa, wondering how on earth she would fill yet another evening. Or when she was lying in bed at night, trying yet another meditation app or 'sleep story' to try and clear her mind.

But on bad days, like today, it was a shout.

POINTLESS.

Because it was, really. Even her work. The appealing cats – the cute kittens or the bright-eyed, perky ones with engaging personalities – would find homes anyway, with or without her help. The other ones... well, she couldn't make people want them. She wasn't a magician. She couldn't make people fall in love. It was all she could do to shift her own lardy arse out of this van.

JOANNE LOOKED INTO THE CAGE. She chirruped a greeting and two little striped faces peered out, oversized ears turning towards her like satellite dishes.

'Aye,' she said, nodding to Tina, the veterinary nurse. 'These'll be snapped up like hot cakes.'

'Talking of cakes, Jenny brought in some brownies this morning. Do you want to stay for a cuppa? It's wild out there.' Tina pulled her cardigan closer around her nurse's scrubs.

'Thanks but no thanks. I'd best be getting back before it starts chucking it down again.'

The wind howled outside, while Tina entered some details onto the computer.

'Come on then, you scoundrels. Let's be having you.' Joanne turned her cat carrier on its end so the opening was at the top. She scooped up one kitten and then the other, dropping their elastic little bodies inside before they had time to protest. She righted the carrier gently and draped a paw-patterned blanket over the top.

A mournful miaow emanated from somewhere in the building.

'Ooh. Someone's not happy.'

'Oh, that's another cat that came in a couple of days ago,' said Tina.

'Want me to take a look?'

'He's in a bit of state. Not very friendly.' She held out her forearm, the skin raked with angry rows of scratches. 'Brian ran it past Mei-Ling and they didn't think rehoming was on the cards. He'll be off to the Rainbow Bridge, I'm afraid.' She gave a wry, apologetic smile.

'You mean he'll be destroyed,' said Joanne flatly.

'Builders found him. He'd been living in an old roll of carpet in the skip across the street.'

The miaow came again. Joanne stopped. Put down the carrier.

'I'll be damned if that's not Blackie,' she muttered.

Joanne clocked Tina's raised eyebrow and the slight twist of her mouth. Others were always sceptical of Joanne's ability to distinguish between cats by their 'voices'. She shrank inwardly as she recalled how the younger staff at the shelter had 'tested' her at the last Christmas party, with recordings they'd made on their phones. They'd fallen over laughing with each answer she gave, whether she'd got them right or wrong. Even Mei-Ling had suppressed a smirk, before diverting the young ones with a drinking game involving tequila slammers.

'Could I just see him?'

Tina shrugged. 'Suit yourself. I wouldn't get too close, though.'

She led Joanne along a corridor and opened a door. The yowling sounded even louder.

'What's all this, then?' Joanne approached the cage. 'That's a big story. A BIG story. Oh Lordy, you're just skin and bone, aren't you?'

The creature arched his back like a Halloween cat and hissed, the fur on his tail standing out like a brush. His black coat was threadbare and patchy, dusted with white flecks. His left eye was half-closed, weeping with discharge.

'Blackie. Oh Blackie, my love. What's happened to you?'

Brian, the vet, came into the room. 'You know this cat?'

'It's Blackie. He was at the shelter for five months. I know who he belongs to. I'll give her a call. She'll be frantic.' Joanne reached into her pocket for her phone.

Brian held up his hands. 'We scanned his chip of course, but we haven't been able to get hold of the owner listed on the database. The details don't seem to be correct. It looks like he's been living rough for several weeks, if not longer.'

That made no sense. Cheryl hadn't mentioned anything. The daft cow must have put down the wrong phone number when she registered the chip.

Joanne unfastened the cage and lifted Blackie out, his paws scrabbling against the air. She could feel the cage of his ribs under her fingers, his heart hammering.

'Shhhh-shhh,' she whispered.

'Careful,' said Brian. 'He tried to bite me yesterday when I was putting his flea treatment on.'

'You should've seen what came off him,' said Tina, screwing up her neat little nose. 'The blanket was absolutely black with them.'

Joanne thought of how it must have been for Blackie, the feeling of fleas crawling over him constantly, all day and all night. Not being able to do anything about it. Scratching himself to distraction until he was half bald.

But then another sound filled the room, low and rumbling. Blackie was purring.

'*There* now, little purrling.' Joanne knelt on the floor and put him down next to her. He stood up on his back legs, pressing his front paws onto her thighs, kneading. Then he climbed onto her lap, paws outstretched and reaching up to her neck. He pushed his face against her cheekbone. Pushed so hard that his back paws slid off her trousers and onto the floor.

She felt a flicker of... something. In the region of her heart. Like a spark trying to catch on cold, damp kindling. She cupped her hands on either side of Blackie's face and ears, gently, gently, as if trying to shelter him from the cruel world outside, and from all that he had endured. He closed his eyes in ecstasy.

She kissed the top of his poor patchy head three times.

Out of nowhere came Steffi's face, aglow with delight, her mouth fallen open to reveal neat rows of pearly baby teeth. Joanne always used to give her sister three kisses: when she woke her up in the morning, when she dropped her at play-group or picked her up. When she was trying to coax her to put her shoes on – the child would have gone everywhere in bare feet if she could. When she served up her tea of cheesy beans or buttered toast. And always, always at bedtime.

Steffi would declare it joyfully: *Fee kisses de duck!*

Three kisses for luck.

Blackie seemed to like his three kisses too, and rubbed his head harder than ever against her palm. Joanne doubted anyone had touched him with genuine affection – with love – for months. She felt her heart expand, in a painful breaching of its limits.

She looked up at Brian, her chin jutting out in defiance. 'He'll be coming with me.'

34

STEFFI

Edinburgh, Present Day

The train back from Doncaster was delayed and it was nearly midnight by the time I got home. Sleep evaded me again, lying there alone in the guest room. My brain was buzzing, trying to process what I'd learned at Chesters and what Muriel, the elderly resident, had told me about Adeline. It felt as if the conversations had taken place in some other reality, dislocated from my life in this house. And I'd have to decide what to tell Tom if he asked why I'd been out of the house for nearly eighteen hours.

I phoned Sarah in the morning. 'Would you mind being my alibi?' I asked, putting a playful, laughing note into my voice. 'If Tom asks, I was at yours yesterday. You were looking after me, waiting on me hand and foot.'

'But why?' asked Sarah.

'I went to IKEA to look at new beds for Tilly, and then to the Livingston shopping outlet to get my Christmas shopping done, and then to the cinema. But I don't want to seem ungrateful to Tom. He's taken the girls away to his mother's so I can get some rest.'

'Really? All that walking around? I thought you had hurt your ankle?'

'It's still quite sore. But it felt funny in the house without the girls. I just wanted to get out.' I hated lying to her. But I couldn't get into the whole business about Adeline. She'd think I was crazy, haring around the country like that, indulging my fanciful side.

'Steffi, are you okay?'

'Yes, of course. I'm fine.'

'Has something happened?' She paused for a few moments, and then lowered her voice. 'Did you hear back from the adoption contact register?'

'No.' Another lie. 'I don't think there were any matches.' I couldn't bear the thought of Sarah's sympathy when I told her the ugly truth. The way she'd carefully avoid saying, 'I told you so.'

What was it she'd said, when I'd told her I wanted to find out why I'd been adopted?

It will probably be sad and depressing and awful.

Tom arrived back with the girls at around seven that evening. He burst into the house with an impatient clatter of keys, shooing Tilly through the door and swinging Edie in her car seat, trying to get them in and out of the rain. I wanted to ask if he'd broken the journey from Pitlochry to ensure she hadn't slept for more than half an hour in her car seat, which would have risked her life according to the health visitor. But she looked wide-eyed and alert, gearing up for another wakeful night.

I stood in the hall, smiling and bracing myself. Would he be nice Tom, or... the other Tom? The one that made my stomach flip with anxiety.

'Did you have a nice time at Granny Vivienne's?' I asked Tilly.

'Yes, thank you,' she said woodenly, submitting to the quick hug I gave her and then (drawing in a deep but silent breath) running upstairs.

I undid Edie from her straps and gathered her to my chest, breathing her in, love chemicals flooding my body.

'God, I've missed you.' I breathed the words into her warm blonde curls. Then, with a little lurch of apprehension, I turned to Tom. 'How was your trip?'

'Fine. Good. I hope you got a good rest?'

'Yes. I saw Sarah, actually, so that was lovely.' Unable to meet his eye, I turned away and walked towards the kitchen. 'I made moussaka for tea.'

'Sorry, honey, but I've got to go into the office.'

'Tonight? On a Sunday night?'

'Yup. I've got a lot to catch up on. I'm just going to grab my laptop and go in now.'

My head told me I was disappointed, hurt that he was only just back and was rushing off again. But my body felt only relief, tension ebbing away in warm waves. A cosy evening in with the girls suddenly seemed like heaven, even if I spent most of it pacing around with Edie.

'How about we watch *The Great British Bake-Off*?' I suggested to Tilly once Tom had left. 'I've recorded it. That'll be a nice thing to do on a rainy Sunday evening, won't it?'

Her face lit up for an instant and then closed down again. 'I've got homework.'

'Okay, well, bring it down.' I forced an encouraging smile. Why the hell hadn't Tom or Granny Bloody Vivienne made sure she'd done her homework? 'You can do it in front of the television – just for once. I can help you with it if you like.'

She frowned anxiously. 'Daddy said there are too many food programmes and it's no wonder there's so much obesity.'

The word tripped off her tongue, clearly familiar. Poor Tilly. I was sure that I hadn't even heard of 'obesity' at that age.

'Oh? Well, I think it's vegan week, this week,' I lied. 'Extremely healthy.'

She went upstairs and came back down in her pyjamas, carrying her schoolbag. I fetched a warm blanket and spread it over her knees, patting it down around her as my mother had used to do for me, on cold nights. She'd never been the demonstrative type, but that had been one of her small displays of affection. Somehow, the thick wool of the blanket had reduced the awkwardness of the physical contact, providing a layer of emotional insulation.

Edie began to cry. I hoisted her high on my shoulder and stood jiggling her. Tilly watched, her expression blank.

'Would *you* like to hold her?'

She nodded and held out her arms to accept her baby sister.

'Let's walk with her,' I suggested. I let Tilly lead the way. We walked out of the living room, crossed the hall, then walked around the perimeter of the dining room.

'You seem unhappy, Tils,' I ventured.

She just kept walking, turning back into the wide hallway, giving no indication that she'd heard. As we walked past the bottom of the stairs and turned in the direction of the kitchen, she took a deep breath in and held it.

'Why do you do that, Tils? Why do you hold your breath like that?'

She made no indication of having heard me. She was concentrating hard, holding Edie so carefully, pressing her against her own chest, one hand under her bottom and the other spanning her shoulders. Her fingers were tense, outstretched to make her hands as wide as possible. Her eyes were fixed on her feet, making sure she didn't stumble or trip. Edie's cries settled, and the only sound was the rain, skittering against the windows and onto the glass of the cupola, high above us.

'And I'm worried about you. Are you okay?'

She didn't answer.

'Is there anything that I could do to help?'

When she spoke, her voice was flat, resigned. 'When will you be leaving?'

'What do you mean?'

'All the others have left.'

'Who? What others?'

'Daddy's other girlfriends and other nannies.'

What? I wondered what Tilly might have gone through, before I came. Whether she'd become emotionally attached to some of these 'girlfriends and nannies', looking for the mother figure she probably couldn't even remember having in her life. Maybe this was her trying to explain to me why she couldn't get close to me. Why she had to push me away to protect herself. It felt like an important moment, a tiny inching forward.

I chose my words very carefully. 'I see. And what was that like for you?'

She shrugged.

'It's different this time,' I said. 'We're a family. I'm not going anywhere.' But even as I said it, a cold feeling washed through me.

Tilly didn't look convinced. 'I'm tired,' she said, after we'd completed another circuit of the kitchen. 'Can I go to bed now, please?'

'Of course. But we can talk more if you like? Or just watch *Bake-Off* together?'

'No, thank you.' She held Edie out and I took her.

She held her breath again as we walked towards the bottom of the stairs, a weary little figure in her pyjamas.

For a moment I wanted to follow her up, to tuck her into bed and tell her everything would be alright. As if in warning, the staircase seemed to flex and bend, and a wave of dizziness passed through me. I lowered myself down onto the floor, holding Edie carefully.

'I'm here if you need anything,' I called up after Tilly.

Useless, useless.

As if she was adding her own complaint as to the standard of my parenting, Edie arched back in my arms and wailed.

I fed her, bathed her, changed her for bed and carried her around the house, one-handedly tidying up a bit before bed. Before Tom got back.

In living room, I saw that Tilly had left her homework books out.

God, the bloody homework. I wondered about calling up to her to remind her to finish it, but decided against it. I could write a note for her teacher in the morning, if need be.

Edie screeched, pulling her knees up towards her tummy so she was a little ball against my chest. 'Shhh... shhhh...,' I whispered, rubbing her back and kissing the top of her head.

I put Tilly's homework book in her schoolbag. There seemed to be a lot of junk in there. Crumpled pieces of paper. My heart sank. There were probably notes in there about school trips or concerts or parents' evenings that I should have replied to.

I sat down on the sofa and laid Edie down beside me. Her little arms and legs went rigid, trembling in outrage. 'Two seconds, little one.'

I took everything out of Tilly's schoolbag. I found twenty-three little pencilled notes, crumpled into balls.

> Fat = Freak
> We can see your boobs through your PE top
> Oink oink
> Hey Piggy, your thighs look like ham

The little soul was being bullied. If I was a proper mum, I'd have noticed. I'd have done something.

Useless.

TOM CAME HOME at just after eleven, bringing a squall of wind and rain and dead leaves into the house as he opened the front door. I was still walking around with Edie. She was half asleep, but every time I sat down she'd start crying again.

'I need to talk to you about Tilly,' I said.

'At least let me get my coat off,' he said, making small flapping movements with his hands. 'Don't *ambush* me.'

'She's being bullied.' I pulled the crumpled notes out of my pocket and thrust them at him.

He read a couple of them, then handed them back to me, not stooping to collect the ones that had fallen onto the floor.

'Well?' I demanded.

He raised his eyebrows and shrugged. 'This is why it's important to keep control of her weight issues.'

'Hang on, *what*? She deserves to be bullied because she's got a wee bit of puppy fat?'

'That's not what I said, as you well know.'

'Well, what do you mean, then? About her weight?'

'It affects her confidence. If she's always shying away from people, from situations, that'll make her a target.'

'She would probably have more friends at school if she was allowed playdates.'

He shot me the dirtiest of looks.

'We need to speak to Tilly about it,' I said. 'And I'll try and speak to her teacher tomorrow as well. I'll try and catch her at pick-up.'

'Let me speak to Tilly,' said Tom. 'And I'll phone the school, thanks. Besides, you won't be picking Tilly up any more.'

'What do you mean?'

'I've made other arrangements.'

I felt cold, suddenly. I remembered what Tilly had said about Tom replacing other girlfriends, other nannies.

'What other arrangements have you made?' I asked quietly.

'Deborah's daughter's going to do it.'

'Deborah's daughter? What, some teenager?'

'She's seventeen. She's studying childcare.'

'You're replacing me with a seventeen-year-old.'

'Don't be ridiculous, Steffi. It's just until your vertigo is better. And your *ankle*, of course. How are you going to cope with school pick-up? If you can't even walk up the stairs?' He looked at me pointedly.

I understood, then. This was to be my punishment for leaving the house over the weekend. It wasn't going to be mentioned. But I was to be trapped in the house from now on.

'You and Edie can just stay nice and safe at home for the moment,' he said in a soothing, cosy voice. 'Anyway, I need you to be in tomorrow. Somebody's coming to fit the rest of the cameras.'

'What cameras?'

'In the other rooms of the house.'

'You mean... even the bathrooms?'

He rolled his eyes. 'Not the *bathrooms*. Duh! But the other rooms, yes.'

'But why?'

'For security. We've got some nutter lurking about. Thanks to you,' he added under his breath.

For a moment I wondered what would become of me, if Tom did replace me. If he made me leave this house – *his* house. I had no money. No job. No real skills. Even my parenting wasn't up to scratch. I hadn't noticed what was happening with Tilly. Deborah's daughter would do a better job than me. Tom was probably right.

The wind shrieked against the windows, rattling the front door. Edie pressed her hard little head into my chest, her sleep-suited limbs tightening around me like a koala. Much as she might cry and fuss, she trusted me to look after her. She didn't know that I was completely helpless. That I might as well have been a child myself.

35

JOANNE

Yorkshire, Present Day

Cheryl must have done alright for herself to have afforded a nice bungalow in this fancy new development. Although, with its manicured front lawn and gleaming UPVC windows, it seemed more like a Lego house than a real one.

Joanne could hear the television blaring as she walked up the front path. Some kind of sports commentary, by the sound of it. It must be deafening inside the house.

It was probably just as well that Cheryl hadn't been at home on Friday, the first time she'd tried to call round. She'd been in a right mood after bringing Blackie back to Willoughby Bridge, and had even fallen out with Mei-Ling.

'I can't believe you told the vet we didn't have space for poor Blackie,' she'd shouted. 'That we wouldn't even *try* to rehome him.'

'*I* didn't know it was Blackie,' Mei-Ling had said, throwing up her hands. 'Brian said he was a black cat. A flea-bitten stray. Too jumpy to handle. How did he even end up there? The Northallerton practice is miles away.'

Joanne was calmer now. She had her head together. At least she knew Blackie was safe and warm, back in his old enclosure.

The television noises stopped when she rang the doorbell. After a few moments, the door opened to reveal Cheryl, her face blank and expressionless. It took a moment for Joanne to realise what was different about her – her coppery-brown hair was straight, in a shoulder-length bob, her Bonnie Langford curls gone. She wore jeans and a zip-up hoodie. No silk blouses or polyester trousers.

'Joanne! This is a surprise. How are you?'

'I thought I'd drop by. We had some free samples of a vitamin supplement with fish oils in it. It's supposed to be amazing. I thought you might like to try some for Blackie?'

Cheryl's mouth stretched into a smile. 'Thank you! That's very kind. His dandruff is a lot better these days, but I'll certainly give this a try.'

Joanne felt the skin prickle all the way down her back.

'While I'm here,' she said, 'do you mind if I come in and take a look at him, check how he's getting on? I never did come and do that home visit when you adopted him, and I need to catch up on the paperwork.' She was absolutely livid with herself about that. They'd been so understaffed at the time, absolutely run off their feet. And she'd trusted the bitch, more fool her.

She advanced firmly towards the doorway, and Cheryl stepped back to let her in.

'I'm afraid Blackie's out at the minute.'

'No problem. Have you got a tin of tuna?'

Cheryl stared at her, nonplussed.

'Not for me,' Joanne chuckled, patting her tummy. 'I've had my lunch. If you warm up some tuna in the microwave and put it on the back step, that might lure him back.'

Doubtfully, Cheryl led the way through to a large, open-plan living room and kitchen. It was a modern room with pale wood flooring. A large, perfectly white sheepskin rug lay unfurled in front of a fancy electric fire that was set flush into the wall. Purple flames danced slowly behind a glass screen. A purple-and-yellow-striped velvet sofa was positioned opposite a rather ugly, tall wingback chair in a dark green tweedy material, with a pair of men's slippers set down on the carpet in front of it. On a coffee table next to it lay a pair of glasses, a newspaper folded to show the sports section, and a half-drunk mug of tea. Joanne remembered the house-bound father. For a moment, she was strangely moved that Cheryl allowed him to have that horrible tweedy chair in this bright, modern room. But then she remembered the reason she was here.

'You've got it all shipshape, then?' she said.

Cheryl looked blank.

'You'd just moved in, I think you said? When you adopted Blackie?'

'Oh yes.' The woman blinked rapidly and nodded. 'Yes. That's right.'

Joanne noticed an open laptop, screen glowing on the breakfast bar. Had Cheryl been working before Joanne's intrusion? She certainly seemed impatient as she hurried to the cupboard and pulled out a tin of tuna. She forked it into a bowl, spilling droplets of brine onto the spotless worktop, and stuck it in the microwave.

'That's it,' said Joanne approvingly. 'Thirty seconds should do it. And I'd murder a cuppa, if there's one going. I'm parched.' She plonked her behind onto one of the breakfast bar stools and slid off her shoes. Because what did it matter now if she came across as rude?

Cheryl set down the warmed-up tuna on the back step outside the kitchen door and made tea for Joanne, dunking a teabag into a mug for barely a few seconds before splashing in the milk. She didn't make a cup for herself. Joanne sipped the tea in silence.

'And how are you?' asked Cheryl, adopting the whispery, quavering voice she'd used when she'd first met Joanne. 'Once again, I'm so sorry I had to give you such bad news about your sister.'

'Thank you,' Joanne forced herself to say. 'It is what it is. I've thrown myself into my work. That helps.' She glanced over to the back door. 'Any sign of Blackie yet?'

'I don't know if he's coming,' said Cheryl eventually, her eyes wide. 'In fact, I'm a bit worried about him. I haven't seen him for a few days.'

A few days? Joanne thought of Blackie's emaciated body, his threadbare fur, and tried to suppress a tremor of rage.

This woman, who had appeared out of nowhere, playing the part of someone who loved cats, could not be trusted.

This woman, who had told her that her sister was dead, could not be trusted. She wasn't what she seemed.

A tiny window of something – hope, or something like it – had appeared. Too bright, too fierce, to look at directly.

She couldn't bear it. Not again.

She felt her insides crumpling, shrinking. 'Can I use your loo?' she muttered.

Cheryl allowed herself a quiet sigh, and directed Joanne

to a door down the hall. Once inside, Joanne sat down on the loo and held her face in her hands as she counted backwards from one hundred.

Eighty-nine, eighty-eight...

Her throat tightened. She wanted to shout. No, she wanted to *roar*. To roar forty years' worth of rage into the face of that lying bitch.

Seventy-five, seventy-four...

She told herself not to be stupid. Just because Cheryl had abandoned Blackie, it didn't mean Steffi wasn't dead. That she hadn't climbed up on the banister and slid her head inside...

Joanne had a sudden flash of her sister's hair, the toddler mop that stood out like a halo around her head when she'd been sleeping.

The silky curls as they slipped through the loop of the dressing gown cord.

Those extravagant eyes. Dark sapphire blue.

STOP IT.

Sixty-five, sixty-four...

She gripped her face harder, fingers clawing the skin at her hairline.

Nineteen, eighteen...

It wasn't fair. It wasn't fair.

She let the roar in her head soften until it was waves crashing on the shore. A waterfall pounding on rocks. It would keep for later. This next bit was going to require knife-like mental precision. Total focus. She flushed the toilet, splashed cold water on her face, and went back through to Cheryl's kitchen.

The open laptop had been moved off the breakfast bar.

Interesting. *Very* interesting. Where had the cow put it? And what was on there that she didn't want Joanne to see?

The window of hope glared brighter, illuminating the way.

'Don't worry, Cheryl,' said Joanne, settling back into her chair. 'I've got a protocol for when a cat's gone walkabout.'

Protocol, my arse.

Cheryl gave a weak smile.

'Have you tried knocking on all your neighbours' doors?'

'I don't know the neighbours that well,' said Cheryl. 'But yes,' she added quickly. 'I did that last night. Nobody had seen him.'

Joanne shook her head dismissively. 'No, no. You need to make them check their sheds and garages, and wait there on the doorstep until they've done it. If you don't wait, they won't bother. Why don't you go round them again now, and I'll do a search of the databases, see if any cats have been handed in at any of the shelters.' She pulled her iPad out of her bag. 'I can do that right now.'

Joanne watched through the window as Cheryl walked over the road to the first house on the cul-de-sac. She made sure she rang the bell, then turned back to survey the room.

Now where was the bloody laptop? She hadn't heard Cheryl leave the living room while she was in the toilet, so it was probably in here. Anyway, she couldn't go looking around the rest of the house, could she? What if the ancient dad came out of his room and found her nosing around?

She checked down the sides of the sofa, and under the seat of the tweedy wingback chair. An odd thought struck her – if the old man was somewhere else in the house, why had he left his slippers behind? Why were they positioned here so neatly, side by side, in front of the chair? She imagined the old boy tripping over them as he tried to manoeuvre himself from his zimmer onto the chair. She nudged them to the side with her foot.

Next, she checked through a bunch of wanky, celebrity chef recipe books that were stacked on a shelf built into the breakfast bar. She looked in the kitchen drawers, and in the cupboards where Cheryl kept her pots and pans, and her tinned goods. She checked on the flat top of the stainless steel extractor hood. Still no laptop.

She found it in the oven.

Joanne crouched down there on the floor. At least she'd be hidden by the breakfast bar if the old dad were to come in. She would probably hear him coming in plenty of time, though, shuffling in on his zimmer frame. The laptop sprang back into life as she opened the lid, a background of a wild-flower meadow filling the screen.

Joanne clicked the envelope icon first, to see if she could read Cheryl's emails. Maybe there'd be something from the adoption contact register. But the email folder was password protected. She typed in 'password' and then 'admin', to no avail.

She nipped across to the window to check on Cheryl's progress. She was already on the third house in the cul-de-sac. She was probably just pretending to ring the doorbells, the bitch. But then the door of the house opened, and Joanne saw Cheryl talking to an elderly lady who nodded and then disappeared.

Joanne returned to the floor next to the oven. Internet search history next.

Nothing, nothing, nothing. Cheryl had looked up the weather, and the BBC news. She had looked up the *Radio Times* online.

Back to the window again... Cheryl was making her way to the sixth house now. It was the last one that was visible from the window. If there was nobody in, then Cheryl could be back in moments...

But Joanne knew she wouldn't get another chance like this, she had to take it right down to the wire. Back on the kitchen floor, she clicked on Cheryl's Word icon.

There were several folders in there, with titles that looked like people's surnames. They were all password protected.

Then, with a thump of her heart, she noticed a folder labelled with her own name. She tried a few passwords – her date of birth, her name followed by her date of birth. Her initials followed by her date of birth – and again with the date of birth in another format. And bingo. It was open.

She opened up the first document in the folder – one from September entitled 'SL-v1'.

Her heart gave an uncomfortable thump as she scanned the first few lines. Then she read them again, because they didn't make sense.

It was the letter from Sarah Livingstone, Steffi's adoptive sister, to Joanne. The one Cheryl had shown her. Why was it on Cheryl's laptop? Had Sarah emailed it to her, rather than posted it, or something?

A few minutes later she sat back on her bottom, stunned.

In 'SL-v1', Steffi had completed suicide by taking an overdose of sleeping pills. Joanne had read it three times, trying to understand. Had she completely misremembered the letter that Cheryl had shown her?

Then she'd opened document 'SL-v2', which was almost identical, but... dear God. According to 'SL-v2', Steffi had swallowed drain cleaner. It gave details about how the substance had eaten through Steffi's stomach and the soft tissues of her chest wall. And the sights and smells that had supposedly met Sarah when she'd broken the door down.

'SL-v3' had been cut back, the tone dull and restrained. It simply detailed that Steffi had hanged herself from the banister.

'SL-v4' added the detail that Sarah Livingstone never wanted to hear from Joanne again.

Joanne got up and went to the window, her head swimming. She thought she might vomit. Cheryl was nowhere to be seen. Was she at the seventh house in the cul-de-sac? Did Joanne have more time?

The folder had one more document that was simply entitled 'J-SW'.

It was a letter from Cheryl Black, Private Investigator, addressed to a Steffi Woodgrove, telling her how she'd pushed her own mother down the stairs.

She forced herself to read it line by line. *Horrible, horrible...*

She imagined Steffi reading it – yes, reading it, because she was alive, wasn't she? Wasn't that what all this meant?

Hope soared in her chest now. She tried to push it down, to keep her head clear.

And then she reached the final paragraph, outlining Joanne's tragic death from an overdose.

'Dead, eh?' she muttered. 'We'll effing see about that.'

Faint voices were filtering in from outside now – was that the neighbour from number seven calling out goodbye? Footsteps sounded on the paving outside. She was coming down the path. With shaking hands, Joanne pulled her phone out of her pocket and photographed the screen of the laptop.

She heard shoes now, the scuffing sound of them on the back steps. Joanne closed down Word and slammed the laptop shut.

The back door was opening.

FUCK...

But it was raining outside, the ground muddy. Cheryl spent a moment or two wiping her feet on the doormat.

Joanne managed to shove the laptop back in the oven. She scooched towards the breakfast bar, and rolled onto her back just as Cheryl came into view.

'Joanne? Oh, good heavens! What on earth are you doing down there? Are you alright?'

'Dizzy,' mumbled Joanne, her hands covering her face. Her instincts were clear – Cheryl couldn't find out. Couldn't find out that she *knew*.

'What can I do?' asked Cheryl, kneeling down beside her.

'Nothing,' said Joanne weakly. 'Menopause,' she added. She'd learned that it tended to shut people up.

'I'll get you a glass of water.'

'Any luck?' Joanne managed, propping herself up on an elbow to drink from the glass Cheryl handed to her.

'What?'

'Had any of them seen Blackie?'

'Nooooo,' said Cheryl, arranging her face into a sad expression.

Joanne lay back and closed her eyes again. Why had Cheryl lied? It didn't make any sense. Why didn't she want Joanne and Steffi to find one another? Why would she want to keep two sisters apart?

'Did you find anything on your database?' asked Cheryl. 'Any cats handed in?'

Joanne breathed in slowly and out again. 'No.'

Only one thing made sense. Cheryl was working for *them*... For Keith's other family.

'I'll check the database again tomorrow,' she whispered, covering her face with her hands.

'Okay, thanks *so* much. You're a total star.' Cheryl exhaled loudly. 'I've been so worried. I feel silly now that I was nervous about telling you he'd gone missing. I should have phoned straight away.' Now that Cheryl thought she'd got away with it, that Joanne believed her lies, she was all sweetness and light.

The memories were trying to squeeze back. Like the ones from that morning, just before Joanne's thirteenth birthday, soon after she'd moved foster homes, when she'd heard the doorbell ring and had gone downstairs to find a fat padded envelope poking through the letterbox. She'd picked it up and warm shit had squelched out into her hand. In the shock, she'd dropped it and it had splattered onto the carpet, up the hall wallpaper. All over her school shoes and tights. She'd even found a splodge in her hair later, during history, and had spent her lunch break in the girls' bathroom trying to wash out the smell with green paper towels, freezing water and a cake of cracked soap. The other girls in her year started a new thing that day – pulling their blazers over their noses and mouths whenever she came near.

Then there had been the time, just a week or so before Keith's trial, when a car had followed her home from school one wet winter afternoon, crawling the kerb behind her. She'd broken into a run and it had blared its horn. One endless blast followed by a staccato of short bursts. She'd darted down a bin alley between the houses, only for the car to catch up with her again when she was a street away from home. She'd let herself into the house, slamming the door behind her. It had taken four attempts to fasten the door chain with her trembling hands. And she'd hidden in the cupboard under the stairs, crouching down between the mop bucket and the Hoover. Listening to the sound of her own breath snatching and falling in her chest, and the blood thrumming through her ears.

And here she was, hiding again. Listening again. To the sounds of her body. This wet, gurgling meat cage that she lived in.

Joanne got herself up, rising slowly to her feet. She clung to the worktop as if she was still dizzy.

'Will you be okay to drive?' asked Cheryl.

Joanne held up a hand and began walking slowly towards the hall. 'I'll be fine in a minute.'

'I can call a –' The woman stopped dead, her face frozen. She was looking in the direction of the old man's chair.

'Did you... did you move the slippers?'

'Oh, yes,' said Joanne. 'I moved them. You don't want a trip hazard right there in front of his chair.'

Cheryl hurried over and rearranged the slippers, placing them neatly together, dead centre in front of the chair. She brushed their fabric tops with her hand as if Joanne might have contaminated them with her touch.

Her voice shook as she addressed Joanne: 'Please don't touch Daddy's things.'

36

ANGEL

Yorkshire, Present Day

'Useless,' muttered Daddy again.

He said it every time she walked past his chair. Last night he'd come and shouted it in her ear, waking her up at three am. Trying to calm herself down again, she'd almost wished the black cat was still around, just for a bit of warmth and company. It had hated her, though, staring at her through narrowed eyes. It could see what kind of person she really was. She'd been relieved when it had gone walkabout and hadn't come back.

'Now she knows, doesn't she?' Daddy shook his head in disgust. 'You've blown the whole thing.'

'No, she doesn't. She thinks I lost the cat and didn't fess up, that's all.'

'I watched her – turning over this room like a crime scene.

Believe me, she *knows*. It means there's less time now. You need to get on with it.'

'I did what you wanted,' Angel pleaded. 'We said we'd make her know how it feels. To lose someone by... like that.'

'I told you before. Some wimpy letter isn't enough. You need to make it happen.'

A wimpy letter? She thought of the lengths she'd gone to, to make *that* happen. The planning and the care. She'd waited literally years for Joanne to pop up on social media, to give herself and her whereabouts away. And she had done that spectacularly, wearing the Willoughby Bridge Cat Rescue fleece in her profile photo. Angel had sprung into action like a spiked steel trap.

She thought of how she'd practised the high, wavering voice. How she'd chosen exactly the right clothes from various charity shops and tonged her hair into curls like a spaniel's ears, so that she could play the part of Cheryl Black, the frumpy receptionist at the PI firm. She'd 'borrowed' Cheryl's driving license – and her drippy personality – when she'd made her approach to Joanne at the cat rescue centre. Because she knew that she, Angel, couldn't speak to Joanne direct. It just wouldn't have been possible. Joanne would have seen the hatred in her eyes. Would have heard the sheer fury in her voice.

Her heart had been hammering when she'd handed over the ID to Joanne that day. She'd been painfully aware that the address she'd written on the form didn't match the one on the driving license. That's why she'd spun the story about having recently moved.

But Joanne, the dozy cow, hadn't even looked at the ID, she'd just slid it under the photocopier and gone on with her monologue about the damned cat's dietary requirements.

Angel's job, of course, meant that she was good at being invisible. At blending in. Just today she'd spent all day at a wretched soft play centre that smelled of soiled nappies and stale chip grease. She'd been gathering evidence for a child custody case in which the instructing solicitors were representing the dad. The mother had accused him of threatening behaviour, and had convinced the family court with her wide-eyed testimony, such that he was only allowed supervised contact with his two-year-old kid once a fortnight. Angel had been waiting to see if the mother would bring her new boyfriend – who had a conviction for child pornography – to the child's birthday outing.

So she'd sat there for hours, the sounds of screaming filling her ears. Talk about the definition of hell...

It was about justice at the end of the day. She was an Angel of Justice, Daddy liked to say. But this... what Daddy wanted her to do... it went beyond that.

'I can't do that, Daddy. It's just fantasy. It's not real.' She dug her toes into the fluffy living room rug. It was dark outside now. She should really pull the curtains. The black square of the window made her nervous.

'Useless bitch.' He said it under his breath, only just loud enough to hear. 'And she wonders why the little one was always my favourite.'

Oh, he'd always made that clear, for as long as Angel could remember. He used to go over there, over to *their* house, with treats for the smug little princess – chocolate buttons, sometimes, and fizzy drinks. He'd even taken one of Angel's own teddies once. She'd cried that night, and Mum had tried to comfort her. 'He'll be back,' she'd soothed, stirring extra sugar into her hot chocolate, and tumbling in a handful of marshmallows. 'He always comes back.'

Could she make him leave, Angel wondered? Could she make him walk out into the night? Could she simply close the door, shutting him out? What would the house be like, with him gone?

She'd taken the time to get to know Cheryl Black before she'd stolen her driving license. She'd watched her habits and her routines – the way she returned from her lunch break at 1.45pm on the dot, every single day. The small KitKats she brought from home to have with her morning coffee. The way she went to the bathroom once every hour, on the hour, to apply Lancome *Touche Eclat* to the dark circles under her eyes, and a fresh coat of coral lipstick. One morning, standing by the sinks in the ladies loo, Cheryl had confided in her. She'd told her how she'd recently had to move her father into a specialist home for Alzheimer's patients. He'd cried for a week, unable to settle. She'd cried for a month, and had ended up on antidepressants and sleeping tablets.

'It was the guilt, you see,' she'd explained. When Angel had alluded to her difficulties with Daddy, Cheryl had gone on to suggest tips for making things 'more manageable' at home – keeping to a daily routine, playing familiar music, reminiscing about the old days, and so on. She'd warned about the risk of old people 'going walkabout', and how dangerous that could be.

Angel agreed with that. If she had to have Daddy living in the house, it was best to keep him in his chair, whenever possible. It was important to know where he was at all times.

She had tried using earbuds, to block out his voice, his demands. To keep the wall between now and then in place. To stop the noises, the flashes, that tried to come through. She'd given herself hearing damage by playing 90s dance music at near-top volume. Then she'd tried having the television on loud. *Match of the Day*, or the racing it if was on. Wine helped a bit, in the evenings, and 'evenings' started earlier and earlier these days.

'Just get it done, and it'll all be over.' He spoke in a soothing voice, as if he was talking about attending a dentist appointment or submitting to some horrible medical procedure.

'I can't.'

He gave a low whistle. 'Wow. So you're just going to let her be, are you? Smug Princess Steffi? Little Miss Perfect? After what she did to this family?'

She tried to think what Joy would have said, in those therapy sessions from long ago. Tried to imagine the kindly therapist sitting there beside her, with her tea-coloured tights and a calf-length skirt.

'Try to *understand*,' she would have said. 'If you understand something, it loses its power to hurt.'

'Why did you choose her?' she demanded, turning to face Daddy's chair. 'Why did you choose Steffi and not me?'

After *the incident* – that awful day when the police had come to the door – she'd found out some things about Daddy. The police had confirmed that he had purchased ferry tickets. A crossing from Dover, one way. He'd been planning to take that princessy little bitch away to start another life. And never come back. Never come back to Angel.

There was a pause while Daddy seemed to think about her question. Then a wistful sigh came from the chair. 'You should have seen her, with her round pink apple cheeks and her big eyes. The posh little voice she'd learned in that family. She was perfect. *Unused*. Like a doll, straight out of the box.'

Not like Angel, with her frizzy red hair and mottled, freckly face.

'She tricked me, pet,' he said, his voice kind now. 'She was just like all the rest of them. Out to get me.'

It happened suddenly – white light washing across the living room wall. Headlights, from a car turning in the cul-de-sac. And she was back there again. In her peeling pink childhood bedroom that smelled of damp. The maths set clattering. The doorbell ringing.

Accident... Motorway bridge.

She closed her eyes. Put her hands over her ears.

But Daddy's voice slithered into her head. It could always reach her there.

'I was going to come back for you,' he said. 'I was always going to come back.'

37

JOANNE

Yorkshire, Present Day

Albie knew something was up. Joanne had retreated to bed with her laptop and he was climbing all over her, trying to block the screen, doing his especially loud purr.

She pressed her palms to her forehead. She could hardly breathe, let alone think straight. She'd dropped into the rescue centre on the way home to check Cheryl's paperwork again. She found the copy of her driving license, remembering how she'd photocopied it without even reading it. The woman in the photograph was not the same person who'd adopted Blackie. She bore a passing resemblance to her, but that was it. Even the address on the driving license was wrong.

Joanne had never met Keith's wife or his other children. But she'd found out bits and pieces, over the course of the trial, and afterwards. Keith's son, Barry – responsible for the maggoty tongue and dog shit package – had been in his late teens at the time, and out of control. She'd overheard mushroom-haired Sharron telling a friend that he'd been sent to a young offenders' institution after knifing someone down the pub. And the younger child, Angel, had 'almost ended up in the loony bin', Sharron had added, her voice laced with malicious glee.

Joanne googled 'Angel Jones.'

One of the results took her to the website of a private investigation company. On their testimonials page, a client had written a glowing review that began: 'I'm very pleased I contacted Angel and her team about my situation...'

She tried to find a list of the company's investigators, but there didn't seem to be one on the website. On the 'Contact Us' page, however, potential clients were invited to contact 'Cheryl, our friendly team co-ordinator and first port of call.' And there was a picture of a beaming, fifty-something woman with a mass of auburn curls pinned up on top of her head – the same woman pictured on the driving license.

So Keith's daughter, Angel, had been using Cheryl's name and her identity? Was that what had happened? She thought of the tweedy wingback chair in Angel's sitting room, the empty slippers. Was Keith still alive, then, after all? Had Joanne been in the same house as him, just a few hours ago? Had she breathed his air? She shuddered.

She needed to get things straight in her head. She grabbed a notepad and jotted down what she had figured out so far.

Cheryl (or Angel, if that's who she really was) had put Joanne's details on the adoption contact register. That would have been easy, since she'd trusted that bitch with every single scrap of her personal information. She'd even handed over her passport, driving license and gas bill so that Cheryl could take copies, in case proof of ID was needed.

And Cheryl must have put herself down as the third party intermediary, so any letters would go to her. Yes that's right – Joanne remembered signing the form. Some declaration or other, giving Cheryl permission to act on her behalf. She'd barely read it, to be honest.

And then, once Steffi had made contact, Cheryl had written that shocker of a letter back to her. Passing on the lurid details about how Mum had fallen down the stairs. Pretending that Joanne was dead.

But why?

She pushed the question away.

And then Cheryl had written *another* letter, this time *to* Joanne, supposedly from Steffi's adoptive sister, Sarah Livingstone. That was the one she'd shown to Joanne that day in the kitchen. The one with the little photograph. But the photograph – that had been real, right? So there must have been a letter. A real letter. From Sarah Livingstone? No. That wasn't right.

Joanne's head hurt. She rubbed the back of her hand over her aching eyes.

Steffi must have written a letter of her own, a real one, which Joanne hadn't seen. She must have sent the photograph herself.

Joanne found she was shaking. Her sister was so close. Separated from her by only a thin tissue of lies. Steffi had put her details on the register. She had been *thinking* about Joanne.

It came without warning. Joy, surging through her chest,

taking her breath away. For a moment she felt it might shatter her, like hot water hurled onto a sheet of ice.

She folded her arms around her head, blocking it all out. The next thing she knew, Albie was on his feet, pushing his little face under her arm, his wet nose rubbing her chin.

'Oh Albie! You're a good boy, aren't you? A good, good boy.' She picked up her phone and did a search for the phone number of the adoption contact register.

The lady who answered the phone sounded confused. 'You're saying you want to amend your details to add a different third party intermediary?'

'No,' said Joanne, trying to keep her voice patient. 'I need my sister's contact details. Her name is Steffi Woodgrove. Contact has already been made. Through the third party. But the third party didn't tell me.'

'So... forgive me.' She sounded very perplexed now. '*How* do you know that contact was made?'

Joanne sighed loudly. 'I just do.'

'Can I suggest that you ask your third party intermediary to provide you with the details, then?'

'The third party is a fraudster. A con artist. She was trying to trick me. Please can you amend my form, or whatever details you have on file, and send me my sister's contact details?'

There was a long pause, and then the woman said she would have to speak to her supervisor. 'It's my first week,' she explained, apologetically.

Joanne sat, stroking Albie, waiting for the phone to ring in her hand.

One hour and forty-three minutes later, the woman phoned back. 'I'm sorry. This is most irregular. We have looked at the file and we can see that contact was made. However, since that time, the position has changed.'

'In what way?'

Joanne could hear a moist noise, like the woman was opening and closing her mouth. 'A no contact wish has been placed on the register.'

'What do you mean?'

'It means the adopted person does not wish to be contacted. We're not supposed to even inform birth relatives that this has happened. But in the circumstances...'

'But how can I get her details, then?'

'I suggest you take this up with the third party –'

'But it's BECAUSE of the third party that my sister has changed her wish.'

'I'm very sorry. This is –' She sounded like she was on the verge of tears now, but Joanne couldn't feel pity.

'Most irregular? Yes, you said. You're telling me there is NO WAY in which I can now contact my sister?'

'There may be other avenues. There are specialist inter-mediary agencies –'

'Thank you for your help.' Joanne hung up the phone.

She would have to do this another way. She started up Facebook on her laptop.

When she'd searched on Facebook previously for Steffis, or Stefanies, of around the right age, it had been like looking for a needle in a haystack. Now that she knew her surname, that would surely make things easier.

She found one profile. It hardly had anything on it. The profile picture was of a woman in a wide-brimmed sunhat. Her face was angled down so that you could only see a glimpse of her sunglasses, and the shadowed, lower part of her face. A half smile played around her mouth. Her chin was quite pointy, like a child's. The overall impression was of someone shy, mischievous. Joanne's heart thumped.

She clicked on this Steffi's friend list. There were only seventy-one listed. And there she was – Sarah Livingstone.

Sarah's own profile was private. From her photo she looked... worthy. Sensible. Slightly care-worn. Joanne nodded approvingly.

Back to Steffi. She had posted almost nothing, in the eight years she'd been on Facebook. She'd shared a petition about the rights of refugees. She'd also shared posts by an artisan cake shop, a charity for animals – Joanne nodded again, briefly – and a business called 'Little Monkeys', which seemed to offer yoga classes for mums and children.

Now *that* was interesting. She clicked onto the Little Monkeys page, and scrolled through their posts.

It seemed that Little Monkeys held yoga classes on weekday mornings, in a church hall in Stockbridge, Edinburgh. 'Mummy and Me' classes were at 9.30 am and pre-schoolers were at 11 am. There were also pregnancy yoga classes in the afternoons – leisurely, two-hour sessions, followed by tea and cake in the café across the road.

Joanne's eyes stung. She sucked in a breath. How she would have loved to have had children. To have taken them to yoga. To have gone for coffee with other mums and spent cosy afternoons fretting about weaning and tantrums and sleeping through the night. She'd have been good at it, goddammit.

In another world, another lifetime, she might have been a mother. Somebody's partner or wife. The lynchpin of a family.

But nobody had chosen her. Or at least, she'd assumed

nobody would, so she'd kept herself to herself. Her heavy body and frizzy hair. All the sadness she carried inside her.

She scooped Albie towards her and pressed her cheek against his sleek little head. Surprised, he gave a little answering chirp.

'Look at all this, Albie,' she said, trying to make him look at the screen. 'Pretty much everyone in the world is in here, somewhere.' He closed his eyes and folded a black velvet paw over his face.

There were posts with little cartoons of yoga poses that children could try at home – a soaring eagle, a cat stretch. Something called the 'sleeping dragon'. There were other posts with tips for getting children to sleep. One with little cartoon images in a circle, showing the steps for a 'wind-down hour' before bed – a warm bath followed by gentle stretches. The final image showed a bunny rabbit tucked into a comfy bed, with a yellow crescent moon glowing outside the window.

One post, a few months ago, had warned attendees that there were parking restrictions in the surrounding streets due to roadworks, and to allow a little extra time to get to class.

And Steffi Woodgrove – yes, Steffi! – had commented beneath the post:

> So sorry to have missed this week. Poor Edie's under the weather with a cold. She's been sleeping even less than usual so we were both zombies this morning and didn't make it out the house on time! See everyone next week! Xx

Edie! Joanne sat back in utter astonishment. She lifted her hand to her heart, wondering if this jumping in her chest, this bursting sensation, was normal. Was she having some kind of episode? She wriggled down the bed so that she could lie back on the pillows, take some deep breaths. Albie, purring, came and stood on her chest, kneading his paws. He circled around a few times and lay down, his flank wedged between her chest and her chin. She felt it rise and fall, warm fur pressed against her skin.

Joanne reached for Albie's front paws, holding them gently in her hands. He continued to knead, his sharp claws needling her fingers.

She clicked on a button to request permission to send Steffi a message. Her mind was racing with the possible messages she could send...

> It's Joanne here, your sister. Please can we talk? There's a lot I need to explain.

> Steffi, it's Joanne here. It wasn't me who sent that letter. I'm very much alive! Please message me so I can explain!

But an automatic response came up: *This person isn't receiving messages right now.*

Joanne closed her eyes and thought for a moment. It was clear what she had to do. First she had to call in two big favours from Mei-Ling, in the form of a week off work and some cat-sitting. Then she had to go to Edinburgh, to that church hall in Stockbridge, and simply wait. Monday morning, Tuesday, Wednesday, Thursday and Friday. Rain or shine or a bloody tornado, she'd be there. Waiting until Steffi came.

38

STEFFI

Edinburgh, Present Day

Edie had gone down for a nap, and I was just starting to drift off too, when my phone rang.

'It's Joy,' she said, through a burst of static. 'I just wanted to check in. After last time, and everything. How have things been?'

I checked Edie was still asleep in her travel cot, and made my way through to the kitchen so as not to wake her. 'It's been one thing after another, I'm afraid. Poor Tilly's being bullied.'

'Bullied? Really?' She made a huffing noise. 'Are you going to speak to the school?'

'Tom's going to do it. He thinks the answer is for her to lose weight.' I barked out a laugh.

'Ugh. So clueless.'

'And he's arranged for some teenager to collect Tilly from school. He doesn't want me to leave the house. Because of my ankle.'

'Ah yes. Your ankle.' There was a slight edge to her voice, as if she was humouring me.

I was too exhausted to lie. 'I did it to myself.'

At the end of the phone, Joy released a long sigh. 'What's this all about?'

'I needed an excuse so that I could sleep downstairs with Edie.'

'But why, dear?' Her voice was full of concern.

'I can't cope with the stairs any more.'

'What do you mean?'

'It's a sort of vertigo feeling. I shake. My heart races. My head spins. But most of all... I feel like I might throw myself down them.'

'And why would you do that?'

'I found out some stuff. About the circumstances leading to my adoption. Apparently I pushed my mother down the stairs. It was an accident, but...' I sighed and rubbed my eyes with the heel of my hand. 'She died. My father was blamed. He went to prison. That's the potted version, anyway.'

'Oh,' said Joy, very quietly. For once, she didn't seem to know what to say.

My chest felt hollow. An emotional black hole had formed inside me – too big, too heavy, sucking everything into it. 'It's just... well, it's been a shock.'

'Indeed,' she said. 'I can imagine. How desperately sad.'

'So now I sleep down here with Edie. I close the stair gates every night, in case I sleepwalk. And I have to check them multiple times before I go to bed,' I explained. 'Or after I've got up to feed Edie.'

'I see.'

'Yes. I have to keep checking things, in case I've forgotten something. I left the hob on all night last Friday – I found one of the burners on when I went into the kitchen to make breakfast. And I left the front door wide open one night, after I'd taken a nappy bag out to the bin. Tom was furious. He came down in the night and thought we'd been burgled.'

It was as if there were two of me. The one who'd pushed her mother down the stairs – shadowy, unknowable – and the present day me, terrified of what the other one might do.

I decided not to tell Joy that I'd got rid of all the sharp knives in the house. Tom hadn't noticed yet, as he never did the cooking. If he did say something, I was going to tell him I'd sent them all away for sharpening.

I'd got rid of the kitchen scissors, too, with their wicked blades. I'd replaced them with an old pair of Tilly's school scissors – safety scissors with pink plastic handles. It just seemed safer that way.

'I keep imagining Tom and Tilly coming back to the house to find us. To find me and Edie, both dead.'

Joy left a long pause. 'You need to ask yourself – what purpose is all this serving?'

'I think it must be my brain trying to keep Edie safe. An evolutionary thing.'

There was a clicking noise on the line. What on earth was Joy doing? I wondered if she was typing up notes. She was going to have to double the word length for her dissertation, after all this.

'When you have these panics, when you check the stair gates several times before getting into bed. When you lie there imagining Tom coming home to find that you and Edie have died. What would you be thinking about if you weren't thinking those things? What space is that thinking taking up?'

'What do you mean?'

'If I could take away all your fears. If I promised you that Edie would never get hurt. That nothing bad can ever happen to her. Or Tilly. Or you. That you will all live to be a hundred and die of old age, safe and warm in your beds.'

I could hear the flittering noise of an insect up near the top of the sash window. A tiny moth, perhaps. I'd have to get rid of that before Tom got home.

'What would be left?' Joy persisted. 'What would your life *be*?'

Useless.

I closed my eyes. I swallowed hard. And I saw it all. All at once, where before I'd only allowed myself to see it one crushing moment, one cutting remark, at a time.

I never believed what they said about you.

You're not going to be that size forever.

Some people are just not made for the cut and thrust of life.

'He's a horror,' I whispered. I felt a flash of panic which made my eyes water.

And then sadness, welling up from the deepest part of me. My relationship with Tom was ending. It had been ending for a long time now, ebbing away through a thousand tiny moments of disconnection.

I thought of the picture I had painted of what this family was going to be. The very softest bed linen, smoothed down each morning in sunlit rooms. Stories in the nursery, with animal noises and laughter ringing through the house. I'd pictured myself sewing dresses for the girls – one small one, one bigger one – in a lamplit corner of the living room, my mother's button box standing on the table.

Or walking along to get Tilly from school on a sweet spring day as the blossoms were coming out. Edie in her pram, staring up into the blue and pink. The fragrance of cupcakes baking whilst I cleaned Tilly's sticky fingers and the baby slept.

The idea of home. The pull of home.

I was losing it all.

My head swooped and I gripped the top of the kitchen table. 'We're working on it.'

'*We?*' said Joy. 'You and Tom? Or just you? On your own?'

I looked around the room, that perfect kitchen with the solid oak units and the Farrow and Ball walls. Tom had been making noises about getting it re-painted. One pot of that paint probably cost more than I'd earn in a day at Slater & Beeny. The thought exhausted me.

I was trapped. Trapped in this house, the dove grey walls closing in.

'I would lose Tilly if...' I couldn't even say it. 'I don't have any money of my own. I don't even have my own bank account.'

'Why not?'

'Tom opened a joint account for us when I ran out of money, after I'd used up the redundancy money. He said it was better than my old account because it had a higher interest rate, and things like breakdown cover included. But it doesn't have any funds in it. He deals with all the household stuff from his own private account. He gave me a credit card to use, which he pays off each month. But he can see... everything. Everything I spend. Fully itemised.'

Joy sighed. 'There are a million reasons *not* to leave. Many wouldn't, in your position. And nobody is saying you have to. Give yourself the time and space to make the right decision.'

I heard Edie starting to wake up and made my way back to the bedroom. 'How?' I whispered. 'How would I do it?'

'Opening a new bank account would be a good start,' said Joy. 'Walk along to the shops tomorrow and go into the branch. Build up a little fund. A few pounds a week.'

I looked down into Edie's face, staring up at me in complete trust. She had her daddy's mouth and chin. 'I can't,' I said firmly. 'Tom's getting cameras fitted tomorrow. I've got to be in.'

'You could also consider consulting a divorce lawyer.'

I flinched. Hearing those words – even just coming down the phone line – felt dangerous. 'We're not even married.'

'Just to find out where you stand. Some of them might offer a free initial consultation.'

'The notes you make about me,' I said. 'Can you confirm that they will be kept confidential?'

'Of course, Steffi.' She sounded shocked, for the first time in our conversation. 'Anything I write down is purely for the purposes of my dissertation. I'm not going to tell Tom you're planning to leave him, if that's what you mean.'

I swayed, the ground seeming to tilt under me. 'I need to stop talking about this.'

'Heart pounding? Dizzy? Hands shaking?'

'Yes.'

'So exactly how you feel when you think about the stairs, then,' said Joy, her voice full of quiet triumph.

As if she'd heard about the impending breakdown of her family, Edie began to scream in earnest. I lay down on the bed and closed my eyes, head spinning. I was unable to even pick her up. I might as well have been drunk. Drunk like my own mother, the night she died.

'The stairs are a sort of proxy for how you feel in your marriage.' Joy spoke slowly now, emphasising every word. 'Anxious. Unsafe. Not in control.'

39

STEFFI

Edinburgh, Present Day

'That was spectacular,' said Tom, pushing his plate away and stretching back on his chair. He rubbed the back of his neck and closed his eyes. 'Good job, Steff. Good job.'

'Did you have a busy day again?'

'Ugh... Robin at work was regaling me with the whole sorry saga about his wife.'

'Oh? Why, what's happened?'

'Fourteen years they've been together. Been through all sorts of shit, too. Their son's Tourette's diagnosis. His cancer scare a few years ago.'

'Oh!' I winced.

'He had a funny mole on his back. Turned out to be fine.' He waved the words away. 'Anyway, last week she came home from work and announced she was leaving him. Completely out of the blue. She had a flat all set up to move into.'

Tom's eyes were still closed, his brow deeply furrowed. He raised a hand to his eyes and for a terrible moment I thought he was about to cry.

'It's the two-faced nature of it that he can't fathom. That she was clearly planning all this, and for months. And yet they were doing all the normal things.' He opened his eyes and held his palms upwards in a gesture of helplessness. 'They played doubles every Tuesday night at the tennis club. She did kitchen suppers every Friday, for God's sake, rotating all their friends.'

For a moment I imagined their friends like rotisserie chickens; turning, heating, legs bent.

'And they're still there in the kitchen calendar, with the friends listed, right through to the end of the year. I mean, God, he's got to sit and *look* at that.' He shook his head in disgust.

'Hmm.' I wondered why he couldn't just get a new calendar. Maybe shops didn't stock them, half way through the year.

'They even went to Gleneagles for his birthday just last month. And SHE organised that. I mean, it's treacherous, isn't it. Is there any of that wine left?'

I thought of the bank account I had just opened. I'd dashed out on Monday when the camera fitters had been here, thinking it might be my last chance. My hand shook, just slightly, as I lifted the wine bottle. It sloshed unevenly into his glass.

'He's got himself lawyered up. She won't know what's hit her.' He gave a satisfied nod, as if that was a good thing. 'I'm so glad I've got you to talk to about all this. Bloody awful situation. Feel terrible for the guy.'

I looked at him, so familiar. The dimple in his chin, the small scar on the bridge of his nose. The silvered hair at his temples. He was my family. I couldn't leave him – it was ridiculous to even think it.

'Oh, I meant to ask... Did you manage to speak to Tilly's teacher about those notes in her bag?' I tried to make my voice sound light but it was the third time I'd asked him.

He took a long sip of his wine. Put it down. Took another one. My breath felt shallow. I rolled my shoulders around to try and make more space in my chest. Then he said, in a reasonable voice, 'I've got a note in my calendar to call the school tomorrow.'

'I was just going to say that I could do it, if you don't have time. And we also need to speak to Tilly.'

He held up his hands in a stop gesture. 'Just let me deal with it, okay? I've got it covered. You've got enough to deal with, with Edie.'

Later, while we were watching television, I asked Tom if he could do the bank transfer for the next block of baby yoga classes.

'I thought your ankle was sprained?'

'It is. It –' I stopped myself. I'd been about to say it would be better soon, but that wouldn't do. I wanted to put off the move upstairs for as long as possible. 'I thought I would just take Edie anyway. So she doesn't miss out on that time with her friends.'

'We don't have money to burn, you know. I suppose that fact goes right over your empty little head though, doesn't it.' He gave a sorrowful smile and reached over to stroke my hair. I felt my scalp tighten as his long fingers slid over the curve of my skull. On the second stroke, he separated a few strands of hair out from the rest, as if examining them, and I wondered for a moment if he was going to take the opportunity to tear out more 'greys'.

I knew in that instant, beyond a doubt, that I needed to go to baby yoga. I needed to go with Edie to the church hall and lay out our yoga mat on the wooden floor that smelled of warm dust and school gyms, and unroll the fleecy blanket that we used for relaxation time. I needed to take off my shoes and feel the soft grip of the yoga mat underneath my bare feet. I needed to accept one of the little lavender-scented bean bags that the teacher handed out as she walked around the class, and warm it between my hands for Edie. I needed it all with a force that welled up suddenly, bringing hot, stinging tears to my eyes.

I had about ninety pounds in my new bank account. That would cover, what, a day or so in a rented flat? Or a fraction of the deposit I'd need to pay to even get the keys? Or it could pay for a block of baby yoga classes. I could either save up to leave Tom – in about ten years' time, at this rate – or I could try and keep myself sane while I waited. Waited for what, though? For the children to grow up, leaving us alone in an echoing, empty house? For Tom to die? For *me* to die?

When he got up to go to the kitchen for a drink, I opened up the app for my new bank account. I'd managed to hide it so that it didn't appear on the home page of my phone.

The balance was zero.

That couldn't be right. I checked the transactions page. The account had been emptied, all funds transferred to an account ending 0630. I recognised that number – it was our 'joint account'.

A hot tide of dread moved through my body.

He came into the room with his glass of wine. 'Oh yes. If you're looking for that money – the money you were hiding in your *private* account – I've transferred it back to our joint account where it belongs.'

I said nothing, pretending I hadn't heard him. How had he even got into my banking app?

'Oh,' I said now, lightly. 'That's just an old bank account. I got a letter saying they were going paperless so I'd have to set up the app.'

'An old bank account that you've been making recent deposits into,' he said.

I swallowed a couple of times. My mouth had gone completely dry. 'I just thought –'

'I don't know what you've been playing at. And I don't want to know,' he said. 'But from now on, any money that comes into this household goes into the joint account. We'll say no more about it.'

But *his* income didn't go into the so-called joint account.

Seeming to read my mind, he went on: 'Who do you think pays for this house? For the food we eat? The heating? The bills for that phone you seem to spend your whole life fiddling around on, instead of paying attention to our children?'

'But the yoga class... they've got a waiting list. We might lose the space.' Maybe if I banged on about it enough, he would think the money had been intended for things like that. Not for leaving him.

'You've got a SPRAINED ANKLE,' he said, as if he was talking to an idiot. 'And vertigo – that's what you keep telling me. I'll sign you up for the next block if your mobility has improved by then. Just relax at home for now.' His voice softened. 'Stop running around all over the place and just enjoy your time with Edie.' He picked up the remote and started flicking through the channels on the television. 'Ah – the *Masterchef* final.'

A few minutes into the programme, a text message notification came up on my phone. It was from Muriel, the gardening lady I'd met at Chesters.

> Hi Steffi, I couldn't find Adeline's letter but I found a couple of the photos she sent – someone had pinned them to the noticeboard. Such a lovely gentle soul. We miss her! Muriel x

An image came through a few seconds later. Slightly blurry, it showed a baby in a pushchair.

The baby was Edie.

'What's up?' asked Tom. He'd heard me gasping in a breath.

'Oh... nothing.'

Heart thudding, I enlarged the photo on my phone screen. The pushchair was standing on grass – had it been taken in the Botanic Gardens, maybe? Or Inverleith Park? Edie looked a couple of months younger. She was wearing a light cotton hat and her pink summer coat, not her winter woollies.

I tried to think back. Had we met anyone, on any of our walks? Had anyone stopped to coo over the baby? That was assuming I'd even been there, when the photo was taken...

Another image arrived on the phone. Edie, again in the pushchair, with Tilly behind her.

Adeline must have been hanging around, watching our family. Maybe she'd even tried to talk to the children. Would Tilly have recognised her mother, if she'd seen her?

Then I thought of Tilly's 'lady' from the other day, who'd persuaded her to take Edie out of the house for a walk. Had that been part of some plan? What would have happened if the staff in Costa hadn't called the police?

And what about the 'lady' who had carved the word 'Bitch' onto my car...?

Suddenly I felt as if I couldn't breathe. As if hands were around my neck, squeezing the air out of me.

Resistant to treatment... relapsing episodes...

A rip-roaring case of psychosis.

But I was stuck, wasn't I? I couldn't tell Tom about this. Not without telling him about my visit to Chesters the other day, about going through his filing cabinet.

It was probably just as well we weren't able to go out of the house at the moment. We were safer inside, Edie and I, locked away from the world. And the next time Deborah's daughter dropped Tilly home, I'd remind her to come straight home from school, no wandering or stopping to talk to strangers.

And the doorbell camera, the cameras in the house – they seemed like a good idea, now.

I tried to calm myself down, to breathe slowly. Adeline had left Chesters, hadn't she? She'd recovered, she was better. They'd wished her well. They'd wished her all the luck in the world. I tried to remember what Muriel had said.

She was leaving for love.

40

ANGEL

On a Train, Present Day

The train was just coming up to Berwick-upon-Tweed. Angel had spent the last hour trying not to look at Daddy, in the seat opposite. She hoped he wouldn't start up with his usual mutterings. She certainly didn't want any of the other passengers to see her talking to him. Why had he insisted on coming? She stared, instead, at the glass of the window, which mirrored the inside of the carriage now that it was dark outside.

She thought for a split second that it was Joy's reflection looking back at her, and the thought comforted her. She closed her eyes and tried to conjure her up, wearing one of her patterned cardigans and a white blouse, the little golden cross and chain glinting at her throat. The helmet of white-blonde hair, and that delicate, papery-white skin that ageing ladies sometimes had.

As the train rumbled on, she remembered that day when she'd gone into the therapy room to find Joy on her feet, moving chairs around. 'We're going to try some Gestalt techniques today,' she'd explained.

Angel had waited, shifting her schoolbag from one shoulder to the other. There was a faint smell in the room, like faded farts. It was probably the grey carpet, warming in the sun, slowly releasing the smells it held inside it. Spilt coffee. Mud. Dog dirt from somebody's shoes.

'There we go.' Joy gestured to the two empty chairs she had positioned opposite each other, about six feet apart.

'So at the end of last week's session we talked a bit about your father. We discovered that you felt a sort of – BLOCK – talking about him.' Her eyes widened suddenly on the word 'block'. She looked almost excited. Angel noticed that there was a tracing of facial hair above her upper lip. For a moment Angel felt sorry for her, in her daft patterned jumper – featuring butterflies that day – moving chairs around, thinking she could make a difference.

'And I wondered if, instead of talking *about* him, you would like to talk *to* him.'

Angel stared, her mouth fallen slightly open. The woman was clearly as mad as a box of frogs, as Daddy would say.

'I'd like you to imagine that he is sitting right here.' Joy stood behind the chair and tapped its wooden back. 'And I'd like you to sit on that chair, yes, that one next to you. And I'd like you to ask him a question. Anything at all. Anything that you wish you'd had a chance to ask him.'

The smell in the air seemed to grow stronger and Angel felt her stomach contract. Had the woman actually farted?

'And then I'd like you to get up and come and sit in *this* chair.' She tapped the wood again. 'And answer the question, as if you *are* your father. Speaking from his point of view, if you will.'

Obediently, Angel put down her schoolbag and sat down in the chair nearest the window.

There was one obvious question, of course. The one Joy would be expecting her to ask, after last week's lecture about denial, anger, acceptance, blah blah blah.

'Why did you do it?' she mumbled.

'Can you put "it" into words, Angel? Try, if you can.'

She glanced at Joy briefly, her eyes sliding down again as soon as they met the therapist's. She saw that her school skirt was dirty – a splodge of mayonnaise must have dropped out of her roll at lunch.

An announcement came over the train tannoy, tearing through Angel's reverie. Joy and the therapy room disappeared, swallowed up into the dark rushing past outside.

The train slowed gradually, before pulling onto the platform at Berwick-upon-Tweed station. The carriage filled. Two teenagers, rude and oblivious, laughed raucously and slid themselves into the two seats opposite.

41

JOANNE

Edinburgh, Present Day

By Wednesday morning, Joanne was exhausted. She'd spent most of the week sitting in her car across the street from the church hall where the yoga classes took place. At the end of each class, when she saw the mums, with their prams and pushchairs and toddlers, beginning to straggle out, she would walk up and accost one of them.

'Have you seen Steffi?' she'd ask. 'Steffi Woodgrove?'

And each time, they'd shaken their heads.

It would help if she actually knew what Steffi looked like now, if she had anything else to go on other than soft blonde hair and a pointy chin.

She remembered Steffi's hair that last day – her toddler-fine curls standing out from her head in a tangled cloud. Joanne had come home from school to find her upstairs in her cot with only her 'te-vishn' for company. Joanne remembered that thing vividly. If you wound it up it played *Old MacDonald Had a Farm* and a reel of pictures juddered forward behind a scratched plastic screen. Cows and pigs and ducks. Steffi used to sing along, her face alight: 'Old MacFarmer had a pig. On that farm he had a pig...'

That day, Steffi was sitting watching it, her tartan blankie pulled around her shoulders – the room was freezing – and she was scratching her head with both hands.

Not again...

'Have you been playing with the Meyer children?' she asked. Mum was only too keen to dump Steffi on the family across the road at any opportunity. But Sandra Meyer had decided that trying to control head lice, in her family of eight, was a losing battle: 'What's the point of all that bloody combing and shampooing when the buggers just come back anyway?'

'I hungry.' Steffi stood up in the cot and held up her arms to be lifted. She was able to climb out of the cot, at nearly three years old, but she never did. Maybe because Mum had told her that a bad man would come and fetch her away if she didn't stay put.

'I'll be back in *one* minute. Promise.'

Joanne crossed the landing to Mum's room. She was asleep, her skeletal body curled up under the duvet. The curtains were drawn and the room smelled of her breath – garlic and old alcohol. Keith, who'd been in one of his good moods last night, had brought round a takeaway curry, a bottle of Jack Daniels and a litre of Coke. Just as well, because there'd been nothing else in the house for tea. Steffi had mouthed chunks of tough, yellow-stained chicken breast and put them back down again on her duck-patterned plate.

Keith had rolled his eyes and growled at her to just fucking eat it. It was good food, that.

Joanne finally found her mother's purse on the floor under a dressing gown that had a big wet patch on it, with some creamy curdled yuck around the edge. Holding her breath, she counted out a handful of change.

'I hungry,' repeated Steffi when Joanne came back to fetch her.

Joanne took her sister down to the kitchen. The fridge was empty apart from half a tub of margarine, an opened packet of ham that had gone a greeny-grey, and the end of Keith's bottle of Coke. The cupboard only had a jar of pickle in it and some boil-in-the-bag rice.

'Here,' said Joanne, pouring the Coke into a glass and handing it to Steffi. 'Drink this.' The sugar would keep her going until they got back from the shops. She hoped Steffi's teeth wouldn't start to go brown at the edges, like the Meyer children's. Because she didn't think they had a dentist. Not any more, since Mum had spat at the receptionist.

It took ten minutes to get Steffi's shoes on. She hated shoes and wanted to go to the shop in her bare feet. 'Ouchy shoes!' she cried. And to be fair, they were too tight on her. Joanne had asked Mum for money to buy new shoes, a couple of weeks ago, and she'd just laughed.

As she walked along to the corner shops, holding tight onto Steffi's hand, she knew she'd probably have to choose: would it be something to eat for tea, or head lice shampoo?

'Are you still really hungry?' she asked her sister. 'Did Mum forget to make lunch again?'

But Steffi just shook her head and swung on the end of Joanne's arm.

'Walk properly – you nearly pulled me over!' Joanne scolded. 'Pest,' she added affectionately.

They walked on past the pharmacy to the corner shop, where Joanne chose a tin of baked beans and a loaf of bread, and a pack of orange Galloway cheddar that was reduced to clear. She felt a little dancing feeling inside, like happiness – Steffi loved cheesy beans on toast. It was her absolute favourite.

Looking at the coins the cashier gave back to her – fourteen pence – Joanne knew there'd be no way she could buy head lice shampoo. With a horrible slither in her stomach, she realised she hadn't bought another bottle of Coke for Keith either.

She led Steffi along the pavement to the pharmacy. She didn't even know why she was bothering. But maybe the pharmacist would be able to give her the head lice shampoo for free or something, if it was a really desperate case. Or maybe there would be a bottle of it in the reduced basket by the till.

'Jingle bells,' said Steffi solemnly, watching the door as it closed behind them.

The pharmacist appeared at the counter, which had a plastic screen with holes in it to speak through, like in the Post Office. Joanne preferred the fancy Boots on the High Street, where there was a perfume counter and a nice shop lady who had once walked her right up to the shelf with the nappy rash cream.

'My sister has head lice,' she muttered.

The pharmacist's face didn't change. She just pointed to a shelf on the other side of the shop. Joanne went over, looked at the price label displayed beneath the bottles, and quietly led Steffi out of the shop and home.

After she'd made the tea and they'd had it in front of *Star Trek*, Joanne put Steffi into her bed.

'Night night,' she said.

'Nigh-nigh.' Steffi smiled, wrinkling her nose and showing her two rows of baby teeth – still pearly white, Joanne noticed with relief.

That's when she saw them. The pillow was crawling with them. The lice. And they were on Steffi's tartan blankie too. They must have multiplied in the few hours since she'd got home from school, dozens of them – or even hundreds, hatching silently from rows of eggs.

She sprang back. 'Fuck!'

Steffi's face crumpled. Joanne wanted to cry, too. She was so tired, and she still had homework to do. But maybe if she washed Steffi's hair she could comb at least some of the head lice out.

'Surprise! Bath time!'

Steffi sprang upright in her cot. She held out her arms, pale little stalks inside the sleeves of her bobbly yellow pyjamas. She wrapped them around Joanne's neck as she lifted her.

'Fee kisses de duck,' she demanded, her breath hot and damp against Joanne's cheek.

'Three kisses for luck,' Joanne repeated, kissing Steffi three times. She'd catch the fuckers too, now, no doubt.

On the way to the bathroom she heard voices from downstairs. 'Mum!' she bellowed. She felt a sudden whoosh of anger she hadn't even realised was there, like when you put a match to the gas cooker. 'Can you HELP?'

Her mother appeared in the downstairs hall. 'You kids stay upstairs,' she called. And then, more quietly: 'Your Dad's here.'

'Keith, you mean,' Joanne muttered. She would never call him Dad.

THE SKY HAD DARKENED and it was spitting with rain. But it was nearly half past, so Joanne got out of her car and perched on the edge of the wall outside the church. A small blonde woman emerged from the main doors, the ones out of the church itself, rather than the church hall's entrance round the side. She was holding a screaming small child in one arm and trying to push the pushchair down the church steps onto the pavement.

Joanne rushed forward. 'Let me,' she said, taking hold of the sides of the pushchair.

The woman smiled in relief. 'Thank you!'

'Steffi?' asked Joanne.

'What? No no, sorry.'

Joanne realised the woman had an accent – Polish, maybe. 'Do you know Steffi Woodgrove?'

The woman frowned, as if trying to recall. 'There *was* a Steffi. I think. She hasn't been for a while, though.'

'Steffi Woodgrove?'

'Don't know second name.' She shrugged an apology and disappeared off down the street.

A bunch of other women appeared at the top of the steps with their buggies. It was raining more heavily now. One of the women shrieked, trying to pull a rain cover over her buggy. Joanne helped them down one by one.

'Isn't there a disabled ramp round the back?' she asked after the fourth one. She was starting to feel like some kind of unpaid porter. The women had formed a little queue at the top of the steps.

'There is, but someone's been sick on the floor by the back door. Naomi's called someone to try and get it cleaned up.'

Interesting, thought Joanne.

The last woman, heavily pregnant, was pushing a double buggy. The poor cow, literally weighed down with sprogs. Joanne helped her down while the other mums stood in a gaggle at the bottom, debating in braying voices which coffee shop they should go to. The pregnant woman hesitated, as if she was wondering if she should tip her or something. Suddenly, Joanne realised that her hair was blonde, tucked up under a beret.

'Steffi?' she said, her heart leaping into her throat. But the woman shook her head. 'Morag,' she said sadly.

Joanne waited until the women had moved off down the street. Then she took a deep breath and raced up the steps – now slick with rain – and into the church entrance, then left into the church hall. 'Naomi! Naomi!' she shouted, hurrying up to the woman who appeared to be the yoga teacher. 'Morag's slipped on the steps. I think – I think she's hurt herself. She landed on her bump.'

'Shit, shit, fucking shit...' Naomi ran to the exit.

Joanne grabbed the teacher's clipboard from the chair where she'd left it. It had sheets of names and contact details but they were in bloody tiny writing – printouts from a spreadsheet or something.

She could hear voices drifting in from outside.

'No, I didn't see anything.'

'Are you sure? A pregnant woman?'

And then footsteps approaching.

Joanne shoved the clipboard under her fleece and made for the back of the hall where there was a sign for toilets. Locking herself in one of the cubicles, she took out her phone and opened the camera app so she could magnify the writing on the spreadsheet.

The second page showed the attendee list for the Thursday class, complete with phone numbers, addresses, tick boxes for attendance, and a column for special notes. And half way down the list she found a Steffi Woodgrove, who lived at 12 Hillside Park, and hadn't been to class for three weeks. In the notes section, the teacher had written a big question mark.

With shaking hands, she photographed the details.

42

JOANNE

Edinburgh, Present Day

Joanne navigated her ancient Ford Fiesta to Steffi's address, pulling up on a wide road with Victorian villas spaced along one side, shielded by drooping trees and high hedges. The house must be worth a bomb, she realised, taking in the pillars framing the front entrance, the stone balustrades at the upper windows and the two rows of chimney stacks. Did the house have... what, eight fireplaces? Jeez. Along the opposite side of the road ran a high stone wall that bordered private gardens of some sort.

Maybe they even had *staff*, with a house that size.

She took a Penguin biscuit out of her bag and shoved it in her mouth almost before she'd finished unwrapping it. The soft crunch and the burst of creamy chocolate inside her mouth gave an instant hit of comfort, but it was finished too quickly. She took out another one.

The rain stopped eventually and the sun came out, making the droplets on the windscreen into tiny diamonds. Joanne could see rainbows inside them if she moved her head in just the right way. An old man walked by with a dog, a little terrier with a straggly white coat. Joanne thought of Albie and Mitski. Mei-Ling would be feeding them, of course, but she was off to Tenerife in a couple of days. So Joanne had to get back to them soon. And Blackie, back in his enclosure at the rescue centre, would be wondering why she hadn't been in to give him his head rubs. She only had one more night booked in the Travelodge anyway, so she'd be heading back down tomorrow.

She shifted in her seat. She was starting to need the toilet.

And then... she could hardly believe it. Steffi – it must be Steffi? – came out of the house. She had a baby wedged on her hip, its little body held in place with one arm, and she was carrying a small pink plastic bag by its tie handles. She walked over to the wheelie bin, which was positioned on the edge of the driveway waiting to be collected, under the canopy of a copper beech tree. She opened the lid – awkwardly, using just one hand – and tossed the little bag in.

She was beautiful, this woman. This stranger. Joanne held her breath, trying to catch her little sister in the shape of those eyes, that nose, in the set of the chin and mouth. But this was a grown woman. She looked like the ultimate yummy mummy, with her curtain of blonde highlighted hair and her clear skin. She wore a long, fine-knit cardigan over a t-shirt and yoga leggings. Some heavy, bejewelled bangle type thing encircled her slim wrist. She was the sort of woman Joanne would normally dismiss. The sort she would refuse to feel intimidated by if she came into the rescue centre, looking for a kitten to match her curtains or some such guff. She would always find something to hate about somebody who looked like this. Who looked like they had it too easy. No bloody idea about anything.

Joanne's insides felt hollow, shrinking. This had all been a mistake. She'd lost Steffi, that night all those years ago, because of what she'd done. She'd lost the right to love her, to know her. To even know the basic details of what had happened to her.

She drank in one long, last look at Steffi as she hurried back into the house, trying to commit her to memory. That was when she noticed her feet. They were bare. She hadn't bothered to put her shoes on. Or maybe she liked the feel of the wet paving stones after the rain.

Something about the feet gave her a wild flash of... something. Something that was different from that shrinking despair. Something fresher. Shocking. Real. Like cold water flung on her face.

As the two of them disappeared into the house, Joanne heard a little shriek from Steffi and an answering giggle from the baby. *Edie*. She thought again how astonishing it was that Steffi should have called her that. The door slammed shut.

Joanne put on her seatbelt and drove away. She drove to the nearest supermarket and bought a pad of Basildon Bond, some envelopes, and a pen. And another packet of Penguins. Then she drove back to that street, and parked right outside Steffi's house, even closer this time, the copper beech dropping metallic pings of rainwater onto the car roof. And she began to write.

Dear Steffi,
I understand you have tried to get in touch

*with me. Unfortunately an estranged family
member was responsible for the letter you
received, with the incorrect information that I was
dead. Please would you meet with me and I will
explain everything. It is VERY important that you
let me me explain.*

She thought of that stranger woman, walking down the
driveway in her bare feet, that stranger who she'd loved since
the moment she'd seen the squashed-up little bundle in her
mother's arms.

*Everything is going to be fine, I promise.
Your sister
Joanne xxx*

She remembered whispering the same words to Steffi that
day, when she was about to be lifted into the social worker's
car. Stroking her hair away from her face, wiping away a
streak of tears and snot. She'd been wrong, she'd been
wrong...

But she had to be right now. She had to take a step into
the dark. A leap of faith.

With wobbly legs – did she want to be seen or didn't she?
– she walked up the driveway, up the stone steps to the front
door, and posted the letter though the letterbox. She only
posted it half way through so that one white edge of the envelope remained visible. She wanted to be able to see when

Steffi had picked it up, to know that she'd definitely got it. To know that she'd done all she could.

Back in the car, she waited. Her head began to ache with watching the white envelope. Sometimes she thought it had disappeared but then she'd blink and it was still there. Her eyes, dry and menopausal at the best of times, were playing tricks on her. She began to wonder if she should knock on the door, or ring the bell, to alert Steffi to the presence of the envelope, and then run back to the car.

After an hour or so, a black Audi pulled up in the drive, gravel crunching under its gleaming alloy wheels. A tall, dark-haired man emerged, wearing a raincoat over a charcoal-grey suit. He pulled a distressed leather satchel – some awful hipster-type thing – and a golf umbrella out from the boot. He put up the golf umbrella – enormous, covered in wanky corporate branding – just to walk the ten or so steps to the front door. Normally Joanne would despise this sort of thing, this casual display of wealth. But today she was comforted by it. At least he would be able to look after her. He would be able to afford head lice shampoo if she ever needed it. Or new shoes.

She brushed the silly thought away.

He let himself into the house, opening the door with his key. The edge of the letter disappeared. Joanne released a shuddery exhalation. She drove back to her Travelodge. It was done.

43

STEFFI

Yorkshire, Age 8

It was a dull Thursday morning at the end of the school holidays. Mum and Daddy had gone down to somewhere near Oxford for a wedding – the daughter of one of Mum's school friends or something – and Aunt Veronica and Uncle Geoffrey had come to babysit.

Steffi's throat was sore. It was very, very sore, like there was broken glass in it. She started to do some Lego, but her arms and legs were achy, so she climbed into bed with a *Famous Five* book instead. She closed her eyes and pulled the covers up under her chin. She didn't need to read, she would just think about the story – it was the one where the evil Mr and Mrs Stick and their dog, Stinker, kidnapped the children.

Downstairs, Sarah was thumping on the piano. She was learning Beethoven's death march. She'd insisted that Steffi go upstairs and stay in her room because she didn't want to catch her sore throat. She had a big competition at the week-end. Steffi pulled a pillow over her aching head. Her breath felt too hot as it moved over her face.

The bedroom door creaked and swung open.

'How are you feeling, pet?' It was Uncle Geoffrey.

'Okay.' She wondered if she could ask him for some Calpol. He might be allowed to go into the medicine cabinet.

'I've got a treat for you. We're going to go on a little trip out.'

'Why?' She popped her head out from under the pillow.

'Your mum phoned. She forgot to take her shoes for the wedding. She wants us to take them down.'

'Oh no!' Mum had been to five different shops to get those shoes – they'd trailed all around York city centre in the Christmas rush. It had been dark by the time they'd got home, rain streaking the car windows.

Uncle Geoffrey seemed to be in a hurry. Down in the hall, he held her anorak out for her to put on. Sarah was still thumping in the dining room, with the door closed against germs. The living room seemed to be in a mess – somebody had emptied the bureau drawers, and bills and papers and things were all over the floor. And Aunt Veronica was lying on the sofa, stretched back with her mouth open, her arms flung to the sides. Her skirt had ridden up so that Steffi could see the hem of her petticoat underneath. She looked like Granny, when she'd fallen asleep after the Queen's Speech on Christmas Day.

'Looks like someone's had too many lemonades,' she said, repeating what Daddy had said about Granny that day.

Uncle Geoffrey gave a dry chuckle. 'Something like that. Come on – shoes on.'

'Have you told her we're going out?'

'Yeah, I've left a note.'

They got into his car. She was allowed to sit in the front seat – something that Mum and Daddy never allowed.

They drove for ages, out of town and onto the motorway. Just boring grey road flashing past outside. She started playing 'I Spy' with herself, but it didn't really work. All she could see was lorries and cars. Muddy winter fields. The rainy sky.

There were no signs for Oxford. But they passed a sign with a picture of a knife and fork on it, and a bed.

'I need the toilet,' she said. 'And can I get a drink? My throat's really sore.'

Uncle Geoffrey didn't answer. After a while, they passed another sign, a red one with a picture of a cartoon character in a chef's hat, carrying a dish.

'I need the toilet,' she said again. She clutched her tummy, for emphasis.

Uncle Geoffrey sighed. He turned the direction of the car, fast, so that Steffi's body was pressed against the car door.

She went to the toilet – he made her used the disabled one so he could stand right outside – and they sat down at a table, in a booth all to themselves. The red seat covers felt sticky under Steffi's thighs.

Two hamburgers arrived. Steffi peered at hers suspiciously, lifting the lid of the bun to reveal a square of bright yellow cheese.

'I'm not allowed McDonalds,' she said. It was something Mum had always been very clear about.

'This isn't McDonalds. You'll need to eat something. There won't be anything else until the ferry. Look, you could have some French fries, how about that?'

The ferry? Was Oxford in France?

'I'm not hungry,' she whispered. It was sore even to speak now, let alone eat.

'A milkshake, then. Have a fucking milkshake.'

His voice had changed. Old, bumbling Uncle Geoffrey had gone. She thought of the wolf in Little Red Riding Hood. The one who'd pretended to be a granny, hiding his monstrous teeth and claws.

She felt tears pooling on her lower lids. They dropped onto the table with two tiny splashes.

'I'm sorry, I'm sorry. Come on. Come here.' He pulled her onto his knee. 'Aw, yeah. That's nice, isn't it?'

Steffi wriggled. Her skin felt scratchy, being so close to him. Like when she had to wear the jumper Granny had knitted for her, the one with the high polo neck. Mum said she'd misread the pattern and made the neck nearly twice as long as it should be. But Granny had shouted: 'It's made from *Harris wool*, Jill! She'll jolly well wear it.' Steffi, fascinated, had pictured the people of Harris, long-necked like giraffes.

'Don't touch, please,' she tried, but it came out as a whisper.

He pulled her more firmly onto his knee and locked his arms around her. It was a bit like that time she'd been on a rollercoaster. She remembered that CLUNK which meant no escape, not till the ride was over. Not unless you made an Appalling Fuss.

'I've got something to tell you,' he said.

Steffi pursed her lips. She shook her head, but so slowly that he wouldn't see and would just think she was looking from side to side.

'I know you're a big girl, now. Do you think you could keep a big girl's secret?'

His breath floated over her. How could she get away?

She clutched her stomach. 'I think I might be sick.'

'Aw wait, wait.' His voice was wheedling, but there was something else in it. Something that sent prickly waves all over her skin.

From the corner of her eye, she thought she saw something move, a figure, at the edge of the booth nearest the window. She jerked her head round but couldn't see anything.

He gave a short, disappointed groan. 'Don't tell me you're all stuck up now. Like *them*. Eh?'

'No,' she said quickly. She knew from school that there was no worse insult than to be called 'stuck up'. She'd heard people shout it at Sarah when she marched through the school yard with her music case, plaits swinging, chin jutting, and eyes fixed straight ahead.

'Well, listen up...' He pulled her in closer and she felt his breath against her ear, like he was about to whisper something.

As if from inside her head, she heard a voice.

No, Steffi! Don't let him.

Oh! It was Dodo. Steffi thought of the tartan blanket, stuffed deep into the dustbin. And how nice it had been to have Dodo, before she made her go away.

She tilted her head to the side – away from the Uncle Geoffrey's mouth – and listened carefully.

Make a fuss! Run!

Steffi took a deep breath. 'DANCE, then, whoever-you-may-BE!' She sang it as loud as she could. Uncle Geoffrey started in surprise. She pushed down hard and suddenly on his legs so that her bottom slid off his lap.

She ran up to a waitress who was standing by a hatch into the kitchen, lifting plates piled with food. 'Call the police!' she cried. 'That man took me in his car. I need to get home.'

The woman put the plates down and crouched in front of her, taking her shoulders.

Behind Steffi, there was a clatter of chairs and then a waft of cold air. She turned and saw the double doors to the restaurant swinging closed. Uncle Geoffrey had gone.

IT WAS VERY, very late by the time she got back home.

She'd spent hours – literally hours – at some sort of police place. There'd been a room with a dolls' house in the corner with one disappointing wooden doll that was basically just a clothes peg with a dress on. And a car garage with plastic cars and a ramp and a barrier that tinged. They'd asked questions and then more questions. And then the same questions all over again. They'd been really pleased when she'd managed to remember that Uncle Geoffrey's car was grey, and that the first two letters of the number plate had matched that because they'd been 'GR'.

She'd never felt so hot in her life. And her throat had been so sore that she'd started to cry – a croaky, squeaky cry like the tin lion in the Wizard of Oz. They'd let her lie down on two hard plastic chairs pushed together. She vaguely remembered Mum and Daddy arriving, and Mum snatching her up into a hug, holding on tight, tight. The thick, cloying scent of her roll-on deodorant, the faint smell of onions on her hands from making last night's mince.

She'd slept in Mum's arms while she and Daddy talked to the police. Then Mum had used her cross voice: 'This child is burning up! She needs to be in bed!'

Steffi didn't want to burn up, like Miss Havisham in her wedding dress. She'd seen that on television, one dreadful Sunday night.

She'd started to cry again. But then another policeman had come into the room and muttered something to the other ones about an 'incident'. Something to do with a motorway bridge.

So now she was home in bed. She'd been given Calpol and a cold flannel for her head.

She wasn't stupid. She'd gathered, by now, that Uncle Geoffrey was some sort of kidnapper, like Mr and Mrs Stick in *Five Run Away Together*. Didn't he realise Mum and Daddy didn't have any money? They couldn't even afford to replace their rusty old car, let alone pay some huge ransom.

And poor Aunt Veronica had been duped, Daddy had said in the car. Steffi wondered if that was the word for when you'd drunk too many lemonades, but didn't ask. She could barely speak at all now, with her throat. Tonsillitis, Mum was saying. She'd phone the health centre first thing in the morning.

The door to her room creaked open and she felt the bed shift as Sarah climbed in behind her. She looped her arm around Steffi's waist and pulled her body close against hers. She didn't seem to be worried about germs any more. Perhaps the piano competition had been cancelled.

The bed shook, ever so slightly. Sarah was crying, her face buried against Steffi's hair.

Steffi reached up and took hold of her sister's fingers.

'I'm okay, Big Sarah. I won't die. You don't die of tonsillitis. Mum said.'

She felt hot, like her head might explode. So very hot and tired.

Then she became aware of Dodo. She imagined that she was standing by the bed, that she stooped to kiss Steffi's forehead. Her eyes were squeezed shut and she held her lips there on Steffi's hot skin for a long time before she stood up.

'Where are you going?' Steffi whispered.

'I've got to go now,' said Dodo.

'But why? You only just came back.'

Dodo sniffed, and Steffi realised she was crying too. 'I'd only get in the way. You're safe now, with your family. Look – Sarah's got you.'

Steffi laid her head against the cool cotton of her pillowcase and let sleep take over.

THE NEXT DAY, on the way back from the health centre, Steffi asked what had happened to Uncle Geoffrey. Had the police found him?

Mum was quiet for so long that Steffi thought she hadn't heard. She continued to drive the car through a set of traffic lights and then a roundabout. Then she said, 'Don't worry about him. We won't be seeing him again.'

'But why –' began Steffi.

Next to her in the back seat, Sarah gave her a wide-eyed, urgent look and shook her head. She drew her finger across her lips, as if she was closing a zip.

Steffi understood. Uncle Geoffrey was one of those things they weren't supposed to talk about. Like Granny's operation last year, or the tube of cream Mum had once left on the side of the sink.

Or Dodo.

Steffi thought of the burger restaurant on the motorway,

the shape in the corner of the booth. The urgent, whispered instruction to run.

'Anyway, I have something exciting to tell you,' said Mum. 'That job Daddy was offered a few weeks ago – the Head of Music one up in Edinburgh? Well, he's decided to take it after all.'

'So we're moving?' said Sarah flatly.

'Yes,' said Mum. 'And don't worry. Dad knows of a brilliant piano teacher up there. She used to teach at the conservatoire in Glasgow.'

'What about George*ina*? My *friends*?'

'You'll make new friends,' squeaked Mum. For a second, Steffi thought she sounded like she might cry. But that was stupid. Mothers didn't cry.

Not this one, anyway.

A new school...?

Steffi tried to summon Dodo, to see what she thought of all this. She tried to picture her strapped into the middle seat, between her and Sarah. She imagined an eye-roll. A huffy sigh.

But something had changed. She could imagine Dodo if she tried hard enough, but she knew she wasn't really there.

It was funny, wasn't it, the things that you saw out of the corner of your eye? Sometimes they were real and sometimes they weren't. And then there were the things that had once been real, which were somewhere in between.

44

STEFFI

Edinburgh, Present Day

Tom had woken up as Mean Tom that morning. Some days it took a while to see which version of himself he'd be. But today I'd seen it in his face as soon as he walked into the kitchen.

'Have you taken my earbuds again?'

My muscles tightened. Had I? Had I taken them and forgotten?

'No,' I said. 'No, I don't think so. When's the last time you saw them?'

He scrunched his face in irritation. '*I* can't remember, Steffi.'

'I haven't seen you wearing them over the weekend. Did you have them on Friday, when you went to the gym?'

'I *definitely* had them at the gym,' he said, as if that

somehow proved I had taken them. He crouched down by the cupboard that housed the crockery. He sighed heavily and pulled all of the cereal bowls out, clunking them onto the tiled floor one by one, so that he could re-stack them on top of the pasta bowls. I winced, wondering if something would break, imagining shards of china thrown across the room. A broken edge slicing a pale neck. Instinctively, I moved in front of Edie's high chair.

It was ridiculous. Tom would never hurt us. Even Mean Tom.

Finally, he stood up, chosen bowl in hand, and poured himself some cereal. I appeared behind him, holding the milk, and he jumped back.

'For Christ's sake!'

'Sorry.'

'Steffi?' came a small voice from the doorway.

I spun round. 'Tilly!'

'Can I get some toast?' Her body was stiff as a board, her hands clenched in front of the waistband of her school skirt.

'Of course, sweetheart. What would you like on it? Nutella?'

Tom's back radiated silent disapproval.

'How about Nutella and *banana*?'

'Yeh,' nodded Tilly.

Later, at the front door, Tilly stood obediently while I kissed the top of her head.

As she proceeded down the front steps, Tom turned to me. 'Listen,' he hissed. 'I want those earbuds back on my desk by the time I get home.'

'But –'

'I don't care. Just get it sorted.'

An hour later, I'd turned over the downstairs of the house and still hadn't found them.

I strapped a sleepy Edie into her bouncy chair. 'I'm sorry, little one, but you're safest there.'

There was no choice but to get on with it and climb the stairs, which I achieved by holding the banister with both hands, counting three steps and then stopping, then doing three more, until I reached the top.

I checked Tom's study – the top of his desk and the bookshelf. The drawers of his desk were locked, as usual. And the filing cabinet. A thought passed like a shadow across my mind – had Tom taken the earbuds to work with him? Had he *wanted* me to spend all day looking for something I would never find?

Edie began to scream from the sitting room. She'd woken up properly, furious at her confinement in the bouncy chair. I'd have to go and get her, resume the search later.

The stair carpet seemed to ripple and bend, like an optical illusion. I wondered, wearily, when this was going to end. Was it going to go on for the rest of my life? Easing myself down on my bottom, I caught sight of Tom's Burberry raincoat hanging from the coat stand in the hallway. He had gone to work in his wool overcoat today, but Friday – when he'd last remembered seeing the earbuds – had been rainy. I went and checked the pockets, calling to Edie that I was coming.

The earbuds weren't there, but there was a piece of paper. An envelope, with my name printed carefully on the front. For a moment I thought of 'the lady', of Adeline. Was she finally trying to make contact? Had Tom intercepted her letter?

I opened the envelope and read the note three times while Edie's cries rose higher and higher.

'I'm coming, my love. I'm coming.'

I HAD the strangest sensation that I was observing myself – or being observed – as I manoeuvred Edie's pushchair through the doors of the coffee shop. I could have been in an episode of that TV show – *Long Lost Family*. Once out of the rain, I leaned forward to unzip Edie's cosy-toe cover, letting my hair fall over my face.

When I stood up I saw Joanne – the woman who was supposed to be dead – sitting at the table in the corner, as she'd said she would be. She was facing the doorway, eyes wide, like she was scared she would miss something if she even blinked. Hands clasped on the table in front of her, waiting. I registered straggly greyish-brown hair, features thickened by middle age, a bulging chin, before I glanced downwards, needing to avoid eye contact.

The queasy, sinking feeling in my stomach told me that it had been a mistake. This woman, she had nothing to do with me. She was a stranger.

She stood up as I approached, her umbrella clattering off her lap.

There was nothing for it but to look up. To look at her. I'd stay a few minutes and then make my excuses.

'I'm Joanne.' Her voice was tight, her forehead creased into a frown. She held out a hand and I shook it. Her palm was moist with sweat.

'Steffi,' I replied. 'It's nice to finally meet you!'

So it wasn't going to be like the telly then. There weren't going to be hugs, or tearful outpourings.

For some reason I pictured Tom, his expression a mixture of pity and suppressed glee: 'Oh Steffi, I did warn you. It was a tiny bit naïve, wasn't it?'

Then I heard Dodo's voice in my head for the first time in weeks.

Fuck off, asshole. This doesn't concern you.

I drew out a chair and sat down.

45

JOANNE

Edinburgh, Present Day

Joanne nodded towards the pram. 'Is this –' She stopped herself before saying 'Edie', not wanting Steffi to know she'd been stalking her on Facebook. 'Is this your baby?'

'Yes, her name's Edie. She's asleep at the moment.'

'Ah, bless,' said Joanne, adopting the soft, cooing voice she normally used to talk to cats. She leaned forward to peer into the pram. Edie was facing away from her, the hood of her coat pulled up. Joanne glimpsed a rounded pink cheek, a whisper of blonde hair.

'I can't wait to meet her.' Was that too twee? Too presumptuous? Maybe Steffi would wheel her straight out again once she'd heard the miserable tale Joanne was about to tell.

'She can't wait to meet *you*,' said Steffi, with a shy, tight smile.

A few beats of silence passed while Steffi unzipped her

jacket and smoothed down her hair, tucking it behind her ears.

'Is it just the one you've got?' asked Joanne.

'I've got a step-daughter too. Tilly. She's my fiancé Tom's daughter from his first marriage.'

'Ah, lovely.' The cooing voice again. 'And you're well?' She swallowed hard. 'Happy?'

Steffi nodded and smiled. Joanne exhaled a long breath.

'What about you?' asked Steffi. 'Have you got family?'

She tried to make her voice cheery. 'It's just me and my two fur-babies,' she said. 'Albie and Mitski. I'm a bit of a mad cat lady!' She raised her eyebrows and pulled the corners of her mouth down to make a sort of comical face. 'I work in a cat rescue centre in Willoughby Bridge, in North Yorkshire.'

Her legs were shaking so hard that her knees were jumping off the chair. She pressed them down with sweaty palms. She knew that in a moment Steffi was going to ask her what had happened, about the circumstances leading to her adoption. This was it. There was no more skirting around it. It had to be met head-on.

'So...' said Steffi. 'You said you wanted to explain some things?'

'Yes,' said Joanne. 'So. It came to my attention that another family member had contacted you, informing you of my demise.' She could hear that she sounded oddly formal, like a social worker or a police officer. 'But as you can see, I'm not dead quite yet.'

For a moment, Joanne thought Steffi was about to giggle. But then she nodded and matched Joanne's serious expression, pressing her lips tight together. Little dimples appeared around her mouth.

'And you might as well know that the same family

member also told me that *you* were dead. That you'd died by suicide.'

Steffi's mouth fell open. 'Jesus...'

'So I wanted to explain what really happened.'

'I'd like to know,' said Steffi. 'But it's okay. Take your time.'

A waitress appeared beside them with a notepad, wanting to take their orders. Joanne ordered builders' tea and Steffi asked for a vanilla latte with two extra shots.

'Edie keeps me up at night,' she explained with a little shrug and a laugh. 'I live from one cup of coffee to the next.'

There was a playfulness in her facial expressions, her mannerisms, overlaying a restless, nervous energy. Joanne scoured her face, trying to make sense of it. Trying to match up the woman in front of her with the child she remembered. Trying to find some connection that would make this easier.

'Keith,' she managed to say eventually. 'He was your father. Mine, technically, too. Or so our mother said. He didn't live with us – he had another family – but he used to come round one or two nights a week. They liked to drink together.'

Benders. That's how Joanne had thought of it, even as a twelve-year-old. They'd gone on benders together. She'd heard Keith saying that his wife – Mum's rival – was a fat, moaning cow who didn't know how to have a good time.

'The night it happened, I'd used up the last of his Coke and I hadn't had enough money to buy a new bottle because I needed to buy some food. You had head lice, too, but there was no money to buy head lice shampoo.'

Steffi nodded, watching her intently.

'You were ready for bed, but I decided I'd wash your hair with normal shampoo and try and get the worst of them out.

So I put you in the bath and did your hair with the shower hose.'

Joanne remembered the little black insects, swirling in the water and disappearing down the plughole. Steffi with her palms over her eyes as the water dripped down. 'No more effant,' she'd cried. She'd always thought the rubbery shower hose was like an elephant's trunk. 'A WHITE effant,' she'd warned Joanne once, her eyes like saucers, as if its paleness made it especially terrifying.

'Then I got you out of the bath. I was trying to dry you off so I could put you in your pyjamas, but you weren't having any of it. You were running around on the landing. Then I heard a noise from downstairs.'

It had been Keith, his voice practically shaking the house, or so it felt: 'Where the FUCK is my Coke? Did you drink it?'

Joanne remembered the familiar clenching in her gut. She remembered hoping, simultaneously, that he wouldn't blame her, and that he *would*. Because then he wouldn't blame Mum. She heard his footsteps in the hallway below, his boots pounding the stairs. Coming closer.

Usually, Joanne blocked off the memory there. She'd learned to do that, like pressing STOP on a video tape. But today she had to let it play.

So she took a deep breath and told this strange, adult Steffi how she'd grabbed the small, two-year-old Steffi, still slippery wet from the bath, up into her arms. How she'd stood there on the landing and answered Keith: 'I gave it to Steffi. She hadn't had any lunch and she was really hungry.'

Keith hesitated.

'Weren't you, eh?' Joanne added, talking to her sister in a daft baby voice. Even when Keith was in the worst of moods, Steffi could usually win him over with one of her cheeky smiles or her breathless giggles. Out of the three females in the house, she had the most power over him and she didn't even know it. But Steffi just hid her face and wrapped her arms more tightly around Joanne. She could feel the heat coming off her little body.

'So hungry,' Joanne added, to reinforce the point.

'Fucking useless cow,' said Keith, presumably referring to Mum. He tried to lift Steffi out of Joanne's arms. 'Come here, Princess.'

'Don't touch, please,' said Steffi, just as Joanne had taught her.

She felt a swell of satisfaction, followed by uneasiness as she saw Keith's face darken.

'I wouldn't.' She tried to sound bold. 'She's got head lice. Could we have some money for head lice shampoo, please?' She could feel her sister's heart beating against her own chest, thrumming as fast as a little bird's.

Keith didn't answer. He turned and went back down the stairs. Joanne took Steffi back into the bathroom. She gently unfastened her arms from around her neck and tried to get the pyjamas on her. But then Keith reappeared behind them, brandishing the kitchen scissors. They had rubber black handles and steel blades that glinted wickedly in the light.

'It'll all have to come off,' he said. 'All of it.'

'No,' said Joanne. Not Steffi's curls. She placed herself between Keith and her sister, holding her arms to the sides like wings.

Then she heard her mother's voice, slurred with drink already. 'Whass going on up here?'

'*Christ!*' Keith whacked the scissors down on the side of the sink. He spun round and went onto the landing. Joanne stood in the bathroom doorway, hands either side on the doorframe, blocking the way to Steffi in case he came back.

'Steffi's got nits.' His voice was charged with accusation.

'How's she got nits?' Her mother's face was gormless. She swayed to the side and steadied herself with a hand on the wall.

Keith took a step forward, his dark bulk towering over her. 'How do you think?'

'It's not my fault,' Mum wailed. 'She's your kid just as much as mine. You expect me to do *everything*!'

Keith punched her across the face, whipping her head to the side. She cried out and doubled over. Joanne could see strings of blood and drool stretching from her mother's open mouth, a pool of it collecting in her cupped hands.

'You knocked out my fuckin' tooth!' She spat into her hands and wailed again. It was a wild, animal sound, like when Mrs Meyer had gone into labour with her last sprog. Joanne had heard her noises from across the street.

'Shut up, you useless bitch!' bellowed Keith. 'Cut their fucking hair! Do it fucking now!'

Mum took a step back, steadying herself on the banister post at the top of the stairs.

Steffi shot out from behind Joanne and onto the landing. Still naked, she was clutching the kitchen scissors, her fist wrapped around the blades.

'No, Steffi!' Joanne bolted after her.

'Mama!' shouted Steffi, her voice alight with terror. Almost as if she already knew what was about to unfold.

Steffi launched herself at her mother, making contact just as Joanne managed to grab her little sister around the waist. But Mum's hand slid off the banister post. She put a foot back to steady herself but it missed the top step and met thin air.

Now, sitting with Steffi in the café, Joanne put her hands over her ears. She didn't want to remember those noises. The slippery, thunking noises of hips and elbows and knees glancing off the stair treads and the banister on the way down. The splintering of bone and cartilage on the tiled floor below. The wet, sucking noise as Mum took her last few breaths through a ruined face.

In her mind, Joanne pressed STOP. She looked up at Steffi. 'So that was that. She died from the fall. And I told people... I said it was Keith who pushed her. I told that to the police and I lied in court.'

It was the first time she'd ever said it out loud. She watched her sister's face carefully, but Steffi just nodded.

'You see, I wanted them to take him away and lock him up. That's what I wanted. So he couldn't bother us again. And the jury believed me. There was blood on the upstairs landing – and the broken tooth – so it was clear that he'd hit her. That he was in a violent rage. The jury didn't take it kindly when he tried to pin the blame on... well, you. He was convicted of manslaughter in the end. They weren't convinced he'd actually intended to kill her.'

Steffi said nothing. Her face was white.

'The problem was, with our mother dead, and Keith in custody, there was nobody to look after you. To look after us. We got taken into care, but into separate families.'

Steffi looked to the left, following Joanne's line of sight.

'Sorry,' said Joanne, returning her gaze to Steffi.

She couldn't explain that she felt as if there was someone else there with them. A figure who couldn't be counted. Maybe it was because of Edie, sleeping in her pram. Or maybe she could sense the long-dead players of the story, come back to witness her account.

'Keith always protested his innocence. As if a man like him could ever be described as innocent. His family was... well, angry doesn't begin to cover it.'

'Was it one of them who wrote that letter?'

Joanne nodded. 'His daughter, Angel. She came to Willoughby Bridge, saying she was a private investigator. She reeled me right in. I gave her the details she needed to track you down. I'm so sorry, Steffi. The closed adoption, the privacy – it was to keep you safe. I realise that now. And I just handed everything over like a complete mug.'

'And Keith... is he still alive?'

Joanne shook her head. 'I'm not sure, now. I did some searching online a while back. Ancestry sites and whatnot. I thought he'd died – in 1991, a few years after the accident.' She remembered the relief she'd felt, when she'd found that nugget of information. 'But Angel – she said she lives with her dad.' Joanne thought of the wing-back chair, the weirdly positioned slippers. 'Although she's clearly a pathological liar. Nothing she says can be trusted.'

'But the letter she sent,' said Steffi. 'The things in that were true. It was me who killed my mother, and not him. I was responsible for her death.'

'You were a tiny child, caught up in a domestic violence incident,' said Joanne sharply. 'You weren't responsible for anything that happened around that monster.'

Steffi shook her head. She looked utterly lost. Her blue eyes seemed to darken, the pupils enormous. A single tear ran down her face and quivered on the soft curve of her jaw line, next to two little freckles. And suddenly Joanne could see her, just for a second. Her toddler sister, sheltering inside the woman who sat opposite her now.

Joanne reached down and pulled something out of her

bag – a little package wrapped in tissue paper. She handed it over to Steffi, who unwrapped it.

'It's your tartan blanket,' explained Joanne. 'You used to take it everywhere. The social worker forgot to put it in your bag when you left. I've hung on to it. Just in case.'

It was just a tiny thing. Only about the size of a tea towel.

Steffi picked it up in both hands. She buried her face against the fabric. Joanne heard her take in a breath, saw her shoulders heave. Watched her sobbing like her heart was breaking in two.

Joanne stood up suddenly, her chair screeching on the wooden floorboards. She took two steps over to Steffi and crouched down in front of her.

'Look at me,' she said urgently.

Steffi shook her head.

'Listen,' said Joanne. 'Everything is going to be fine, I promise.'

46

STEFFI

Edinburgh, Present Day

The floorboards blurred and swam as I listened to Joanne's words. Unable to look at her, I lifted my arms instead. Held them out awkwardly, unsure, like a child saying sorry, the little tartan blanket still clutched in one hand. And then I felt her arms, bulky in their anorak sleeves, closing around me. One wrapped tight around my ribcage and one reaching up, her hand cradling the back of my head. I felt her shake, heard the catch in her breath as she suppressed a sob. I inhaled her – the damp, hot, powdery scent from the crook of her neck.

I thought of my tartan blanket, the one I'd got my mother to make after I'd spotted the fabric in the haberdashery shop. I thought of how I'd thrown it away, had shoved it deep into the bin, burying the love I didn't know what to do with.

'Jo-Jo's here,' she whispered. 'I'm here now, darling. I've got you.'

I saw flashes of my old life, caught in a glancing light. A shadowy room with tall doors and pale yellow walls. A white wooden panel – the side of a cot? – printed with faded giraffes. A sun-dappled garden with pansies and the gnarled roots of a tree. A mossy plank strung up with knotted rope to make a swing. Bare feet on cool evening grass. The faceless shape of a sister. And her voice, warm in my ear, so close that it seemed like part of me.

Jo-Jo.

Dodo.

Like a heartbeat, I'd carried her with me my entire life.

I pulled her against me in a sudden, urgent movement.

'I'm so sorry I let you go,' she said, all in a rush, as if the words had been waiting years to come out. 'I'm so sorry. Forgive me. Please forgive me.'

47

JOANNE

Edinburgh, Present Day

'There's nothing to forgive.' Steffi shook her head. 'Nothing at all.' It was the fourth time she'd said it. They'd ordered fresh drinks and Steffi had wiped away the trails of mascara from her face.

It was growing dark outside now. Joanne hoped Steffi wouldn't realise how late it was getting and start talking about school runs or something. She wanted to stay there in that bright bubble of the coffee shop forever, hearing Steffi forgive her over and over again.

'I should have made them listen,' said Joanne again. 'I should have made them realise we needed to be together.'

'You didn't have a choice. You were too young to have any say in it.'

'Did you have a good life, though?' Joanne tried not to

sound too desperate. 'Was it a success, the adoption? Were you a close family?'

'Yes,' said Steffi carefully, looking down at her hands. 'It was a very stable upbringing. I was very sheltered and safe. My adoptive parents didn't want me to know about the circumstances, so I didn't even know I was adopted until a few weeks ago. They've both died now, but my sister, Sarah, lives nearby. How about you? Where did you go... afterwards?'

Joanne shrugged. 'Oh, various foster placements and then a cousin of Mum's took me in. It was fine.' She wasn't going to tell Steffi about how Sharron and Dave had moved out and changed the locks when Joanne had turned sixteen. How she'd lived in the store room at Mr Singh's B&B.

'Were you happy?' asked Steffi.

'It's always haunted me,' said Joanne. 'I mean, how things would have turned out if I hadn't lied. Would we have been kept together? Would it have made a difference if they'd known it was an accident? If there hadn't been a trial?'

Steffi shrugged. 'Maybe he would have taken us in. *Keith.*' She wrinkled her nose.

'He might have taken you, but not me – he hated me. And then I wouldn't have been able to protect you. And it wasn't just him I had to worry about. His other family – his wife and his other kids – they were hardly going to welcome you with open arms.'

'Was he violent often?' she asked.

'It was mostly mind games. Head-fuckery. He'd be nice one minute and then he'd just turn on you the next. Eviscerate you with just one or two words. He had a special talent for that.'

She nodded uneasily.

'But he'd hit Mum before. Once when he was tanked up after his brother's funeral. Once on her birthday when the dress he'd bought her didn't fit. One time he threw the kettle across the kitchen when it was full of boiling water. Mum was scalded all down her arm.'

'Did he take drugs, as well as drink?' Steffi looked about five years old with her round eyes and shocked expression. Safe in her nice, middle class life, she'd probably never even met a drug addict. Good. Joanne felt a flicker of satisfaction.

'No. He prided himself on the fact that he didn't take "any of that muck" as he called it. He saw himself as a business-man, you see. He co-owned a nightclub with some other dodgy bloke.'

'Did you ever tell anyone about him? Weren't there people who could help?'

Joanne shrugged. 'There was a social worker who came round when Mum was taken to hospital once after a bender. I told her about Keith, that we were afraid of him.' She'd been so scared, afterwards, of what Keith might do if he found out, that she'd barricaded herself and Steffi into the bedroom, pushing the chest of drawers against the door. 'Someone came round a few days later and asked a bunch of questions. But nothing happened.'

'Maybe it wasn't seen as high risk, or something.'

'I don't know. The service was overwhelmed, I guess. I also told the school nurse about him once.' She'd fainted during gym class because she hadn't eaten for two days – Keith had emptied Mum's purse so he could take some 'busi-ness associates' out for a curry. 'Again, nothing came of it.'

'That's awful.'

'Mum adored him, that was the thing. She thought he

was going to leave his other family and come and rescue us. She thought he'd get us a nice house to live where there wasn't mould on the walls. He could be charming, you see, when he was in a good mood. Although that was almost worse.'

It slithered into her mind – the time he'd pulled her onto his knee when she was trying to watch *Grange Hill*. His eggy whisper about her being a special girl and a princess. She'd elbowed him in the stomach and shouted 'Fuck off!' before grabbing Steffi from her playpen and hurrying away upstairs.

'Because his mood could change in a second. We never knew what he was going to do next. Honestly, he was like a shadow hanging over the house. I grew up in a state of constant high alert.'

Steffi sat very still, eyes cast down, fiddling with her hands. One of the dimples in her chin deepened and she pressed her lips tighter together.

'Are you okay?'

Her chin began to quiver. She snatched in a breath through her nose.

'What's wrong, Steffi? Please tell me what's wrong.'

'It's what you said about high alert. And the mind games. I don't want my children to grow up like that.'

'Oh, love. No, no, don't cry. It's okay.' Joanne fussed around her, pouring a glass of water and offering a bunch of napkins to use as tissues.

'What's this all about?' she asked, once Steffi had blown her nose and the tears had stopped.

'It's Tom. I'm not allowed to leave the house any more. I shouldn't even be here now. I'm going to have to say I was at the dentist – an emergency appointment or something.'

'Not *allowed*? What do you mean?'

'He's arranged for a colleague's daughter to pick Tilly up from school and he's stopped me from going to my baby yoga classes. He says it's because of my ankle and my vertigo, that it's not safe.'

'Slow down! Your ankle? Vertigo?'

'I had a... a *thing*... about the stairs. For reasons which are now obvious.' She pulled a face and blinked several times. 'So I said it was vertigo. And that I'd slipped and sprained my ankle on the stairs. It was an excuse so that I could sleep downstairs. But he's jumped on it as a reason why I shouldn't go out by myself. And he's put cameras all over the house. He says it's for security but it means he can see what I'm doing.'

No. No. It wasn't possible. She hadn't got Steffi away from Keith only to let her walk into *this*.

'He won't let anyone visit the house, except Sarah, sometimes, and even then he moans about it. Tilly can't have friends over. He says it's because they'll make a mess of the house.' She was talking faster and faster, the words spilling out. 'But if I'm not allowed to go out, and I'm not allowed to have anyone over, then it means I can't see *anyone*, doesn't it? And nobody can see me. I'm an invisible woman. Sometimes I feel like I don't even exist.'

Joanne thought of the dark-suited man she'd seen getting out of the Audi in Steffi's driveway. She wanted to wrap the strap of his wanky distressed leather satchel around his neck and bloody garrotte him with it. Then she'd shove his golf umbrella so far up his arse his eyeballs would pop out.

She took a deep, shuddering breath. 'Go on.'

'I opened my own bank account to make a few small savings – to make me feel a bit more independent, you know? – but he found out about it somehow. He transferred all the money out to our "joint account" which I can't even access. I wanted to pay for more baby yoga classes and he wouldn't give me the money.'

'How do you think he found out?' Joanne asked. 'I mean, I presume you've checked your phone?'

'Checked it for what?'

'Spyware? Tracking apps? Have you noticed anything odd?'

Steffi frowned. 'Hmm. One of the baby yoga mums mentioned something to me the other day. She said she'd been trying to message me through Facebook and couldn't. I had a look at my phone and realised that some of my settings had been changed.'

Joanne carried out a search on her own phone – *How can you tell if your phone has been hacked?* 'Okay,' she said to Steffi. 'Has your battery been draining too fast? Have apps been running slower than usual? Have you had any strange text messages or verification requests?'

Steffi nodded. 'Yes.'

'Have you noticed any strange noises on the line – clicking noises, or echoes?'

'Yes! It was doing that the other day when my sleep coach lady phoned.' She unlocked the phone and pushed it across the table to Joanne. 'You have a look at it.'

Joanne went into settings and scrolled and clicked through the menu until she found where to check the battery usage. 'According to this, there's something running in the background, using up your battery. Something called Admin Manager 15Z.'

'What's that?'

'I don't know.' Joanne shook her head. Next, following the advice she'd found online, she checked the phone's location.

'So your phone is showing as being located in two places

at once. One is here in this coffee shop and the other is...
there.' She showed Steffi the map screen, pointed to a pulsing
blue dot.

'Tom's office,' Steffi whispered.

Joanne powered Steffi's phone off and pushed it back
across the table. 'It looks like he's installed some kind of
spyware onto your phone. It's tracking your location and
probably your activity on various apps.'

'Then he'll know where I am. He'll know I'm not at the
dentist.'

'You're scared of him,' Joanne observed. It was unbelievable. Here she was, sitting in this ordinary café, with the
noise of the coffee machine and clinking crockery, and the
hum of people chatting. And yet at the same time she was
back *there* again. Back in the bathroom in that house,
stretching her arms across the doorway. Trying to protect her.
Failing.

There was a cry from the pushchair. The baby had woken
up. Steffi reached into the pram and lifted her out – a sleepy,
curious little creature wearing a miniature blue corduroy
dress and soft stripy tights. Wispy blonde curls standing out
like a halo. Dark blue eyes.

'Would you like a hold while I sort her bottle?' Steffi came
around to Joanne's side of the table and placed Edie onto
her lap.

It reawakened something in her, the weight of the padded
little bottom on her knee. The warm, golden scent of her hair,
like hayfields at the end of summer. She found she knew the
exact cadence for bouncing her knee, to make the baby settle.
Noises emerged from her lips, soft little nonsense words from
long ago.

When Joanne looked up at Steffi, she could see that her

face had changed. It was as if Edie had jolted her back into her role – the good mother, the good wife. Joanne could see she was going to try and make light of her situation.

'But we're okay, honestly. Tom's never been violent, or threatened me, or anything like that. God, no. It's not like *that*.'

Edie began to fuss a little. Joanne lifted her under the arms and laid her flat against her chest, stroking her back gently, smoothing the soft corduroy of the dress under her fingers. The baby settled again, resting her cheek against Joanne's shoulder.

Joanne thought for a moment, focusing on the tiny movements of Edie's body as she inhaled and exhaled. Then she said, very gently, 'Have you thought about leaving him?'

Steffi shook her head. 'I gave up my job before having Edie because... because things had gone wrong at work. My stress levels were just through the roof and I had to get signed off. I don't think I could get another job, let alone hold it down while looking after a baby. I could never cope on my own. He'd take Edie. He'd take me to court and say I was an unfit mother. And as for Tilly – forget it. Tom and I aren't married so I'm not even her stepmother. I'm nothing to her. Nothing. I would never see her again. I can't just *abandon* her, can I? With a man like that?' Her voice tightened, disappeared into a squeak.

Joanne tried to speak as slowly and calmly as possible. 'There's a name for this behaviour, Steffi. It's called coercive control.' She paused, allowing the words to sink in. 'It's a criminal offence.'

'But it doesn't make any difference what it's called, does it?' said Steffi. 'Because I can't leave Tilly.'

'I can't pretend to know how this all works. But I think a

family court would take all of the circumstances into account, including the abuse.'

Steffi frowned, and opened her mouth to speak.

'Yes, the abuse, Steffi. Because that's what it is. Coercive control is a form of domestic abuse. A court might decide that you should still have contact with Tilly. Or even that she might live with you, if they thought it was in her best interests. You need to speak to a solicitor. As soon as possible.'

'Maybe if I talk to him, though? Tell him that he has to change? Maybe we could have counselling.'

Joanne felt prickles of sweat break out on her forehead and down the back of her neck. Edie began to whimper and she set her down on her knee again, bouncing her gently.

She thought of her mother's face meeting the tiled floor at the bottom of the stairs.

Run, she wanted to scream. *Run as fast as you can.*

'You need advice,' she said. 'Advice from experts. About finding a safe way to leave him.'

Steffi was shaking now. She wrapped her arms around herself. 'I didn't come here for this. It was supposed to be like *Long Lost Family*.'

'Can you go somewhere with the children? Can you go to your sister's, or another relative, and just tell Tom you're visiting for a few days? Then you could take some time to decide what you're going to do.'

Come to me, she wanted to say. *Come home with me.*

Steffi stood up, scraping her chair back. 'I need to go home now. I need to be there for when Tilly gets back from school.'

'Let me come with you,' said Joanne, although in truth she didn't know how she would manage that. She had to head home. Mei-Ling would be in Tenerife by now, and Albie and Mitski would need feeding tonight.

Steffi shook her head. 'He wouldn't like that. We'll speak again. Soon. I'll call you once I've got my phone sorted out.' She held out her arms to take Edie. Joanne ignored the gesture. She wasn't ready to let Edie go.

'Shall we go to a phone shop? I could buy you a pay-as-you-go phone. Then we could stay in contact without having to worry.'

'That's very kind. But I really don't have time. I need to get back.'

'What will you tell him about today? If he realises you haven't been to the dentist?'

'I'll tell him I've been meeting a friend. One of the baby yoga mums. He might not like it, but it's not as if he can do anything about it now.'

'You need to get out of that house.'

'I'll phone Sarah. I'll tell her what's going on and see if she can help. She might be able to help me find a lawyer to talk to.'

'Go and stay with her. Take the children. Please.' Joanne let Steffi take Edie. She watched as she tucked her back into the pushchair and zipped up the cosy-toe cover.

Suddenly she was back on her knees, on the pavement outside her mother's house. Needles of rain slashing through the glare of headlights. She was letting Steffi go, letting someone pull her away and into a car. She was calling out above Steffi's screams. Promising that everything was going to be fine. That she would see her very soon.

'Promise me you will.'

'I need to go,' said Steffi now, her face pale. 'I'll be in touch.'

Joanne watched them leave, clutching the edge of the table in both hands, dread washing over her in cold, sick waves.

48

ANGEL

Edinburgh, Present Day

Whater a performance. Tears. Histrionics. And lies, yet more lies.

In the corner booth, just a few feet from where Steffi was bundling the baby into the pushchair, Angel nursed her cold cup of coffee, turning the cup around in her hands.

Who was going to stand up for Daddy, in all this? Joanne had made him sound like some sick psycho. She'd made it sound like what she'd done was justified.

And Steffi, with her round eyes and shocked face, looking like butter wouldn't melt. She didn't even seem to know what she'd *done*.

There had to be accountability. There had to be a reckoning.

Angel squirmed in her seat, her body writhing with restless energy. She watched as Steffi pushed the pram out of the door. She watched Joanne stack their dirty cups and plates onto a tray and carry it to the counter. Even from across the room, she could see that the woman was shaking.

Good.

It was getting dark outside and the rain was heavier now, rivulets running down the windows. The booth was filling with shadows, despite the fairy lights strung across the coffee shop's walls and ceiling.

Joanne, the hard-faced bitch.

Steffi, the perfect princess.

It's time now, pet. It's time.

His voice wormed around inside her head. How was it possible to long for someone, the way she longed for Daddy, and yet also to wish he'd go away?

But if he went away – if he really went away – what would be left?

It came to her again, the scene she had been starting to remember on the train yesterday. That September afternoon in Joy's therapy room when they'd done the Gestalt technique – the so-called empty chair exercise – where she'd had to face an imaginary Daddy.

She let the memory run now. She couldn't stop it any more. It was humming in her brain, the way the tracks hummed when a train was approaching down the line.

49

ANGEL

Yorkshire, Age 13

'Why did you do it?' she mumbled, in the direction of the empty chair.

She said it to pacify Joy, but really, she just wanted to fly out of the fart-smelling therapy room and far away. Away to somewhere she'd never have to think about this stuff again.

'Can you put "it" into words, Angel? Try, if you can.'

She glanced down at her dirty school skirt, twisting her 'A' necklace around her neck. 'Why did you kill yourself?'

'Good. Now say it to him.' Joy tilted her head towards the chair.

The words came out in a dull, muddy voice: 'Why did you kill yourself.'

It was barely even a question. Angel knew perfectly well why her father had done it. He hadn't been able to face going back to prison. It was as simple as that. He'd served his four years for manslaughter, for a crime he hadn't committed. That was enough for anybody.

And then, after just a year back at home, he had risked everything to try and make a new life. A new life, with a new name. With the pretty, perfect princess – and Angel too, of course. She was sure he'd been planning to come back for her when the time was right.

Daddy always came back, after all. He always came back.

The police said he'd driven off in his car, after Steffi had alerted the staff at the Little Chef near Huntingdon. He'd made it most of the way down to Dover. He would have made it onto the ferry to France. But the police had pulled him over for speeding. He'd got out of the car and made a run for it. He'd run up a slip road and onto a motorway bridge.

And then he'd jumped.

It was all because the pretty, smug princess had tricked him. She'd shopped her own father to the police – just as the other, older bitch had set him up for the manslaughter, years before. But it was the princess who had finished him off.

'Now go and sit in your dad's chair,' said Joy.

Suppressing a sigh, Angel went and sat down in the chair, crossed her legs.

'I'm sorry,' she said, in Daddy's voice. 'I wasn't thinking straight when I did it. I was mentally unwell.'

It was what the social worker had told her. And what her mother had told her. Her mother hadn't said that at first, though. She hadn't said that when the police had rung the doorbell that day. She hadn't said that when she'd collapsed on the living room floor, making that sound that left no room for other thoughts.

Angel put her hands over her ears. She stood up and walked back to her own chair.

'Good,' said Joy, nodding. 'Have you got another question for him?'

Angel sat in silence, listening to the clock on the wall ticking. The shouts of children from the playground over the way.

Red rover, red rover, let LINDSAY come over...

The question seemed to erupt from deep inside her, like vomit: 'Why did you do it?'

'Do what, Angel?' said Joy quietly.

But Angel couldn't say this one out loud. She flashed back to that day, not long after Daddy had come home from prison. She'd been reading the latest issue of *Just Seventeen* in her room. Lying on her stomach with her feet waving in the air in time to *Total Eclipse of the Heart*. Her father had come in and closed the door quietly, saying he had a special job for her.

'I'm having some important people over to the club this evening,' he said. 'Businessmen. They're thinking about investing in the business. I could have nightclubs all over the country – imagine that! Your old dad!' He snickered softly. 'We'd be able to pay for proper medicine for Mum, to make her better again. Proper doctors and that. But I need *your* help.'

Angel nodded. If you cut out tokens from the back of the magazine you could send off for a full-sized nail varnish, a red glittery one called 'Cherry Pie'. She'd cut out two so far.

'What are you smiling at?'

'Nothing. What do you want me to do?' She definitely wanted to help. Yesterday, Mum's knees had been so bad that she hadn't been able to walk at all, even with her sticks. She'd lain in bed all day, crying in shame at the size she'd become. She'd never be able to re-start her job in Tesco, while she was like that. And Angel – although she knew she shouldn't complain – would never be able to get her piano lessons.

'The thing is,' said Daddy, 'I need you to be nice to them. Know what I mean? Make sure they have a good time. A *really* good, fun time.'

She sat up on the bed, paying attention now. He budged up and put his arm tight around her. He dropped his voice to a confidential whisper. 'I'm asking *you* – not the girls at the club – because, let's face it, you're special, aren't you? No offence to them. But I know you can do this better than anybody. You, as pretty as a picture, eh?'

Angel shrugged. The boys at school had started called her 'Ginger', starting the word with a hard 'G'. Someone had even shouted 'Ginger pubes' at her in the canteen last week, when she'd gone up for seconds of jam sponge. Some of the boys had actually cried with laughter.

'People at school don't think so,' she muttered.

'What people?'

'Just *people*.'

'Well, they're pathetic, aren't they? Stupid little boys. You're my gorgeous Angel and I know you'll help your dad out. We can do this together, can't we, love?' He made his hand into a fist and bumped it off her leg. 'Get this family back on track?'

'But how will I make sure the businessmen have a good time?' Angel asked.

'Just play with them, whatever games they want to,' said Daddy. 'Grown-up games, maybe. But you're a grown-up girl now, aren't you?'

Back in Joy's room, Angel squirmed on her chair, the memory of pain moving up through her body.

'Why did you do that?' she whispered. 'Why did you let them hurt me?'

Joy, merciless, pointed to the other chair.

Angel walked over to the chair, slowly, trying to think of what she would make Daddy say.

I wasn't thinking straight.

I was mentally unwell.

You're so bloody sensitive.

What are you talking about? What businessmen? You're imagining things. Yet again.

She sat down in Dad's chair, ready to hear something. Ready to feel something.

Nothing.

There was only emptiness. A black, howling void.

She put her hands over her ears and it just howled louder.

With black nothing shrieking through her ears, she got up off the chair and ran out of the room, Joy calling out at her to wait, to come back. To please come back.

50

STEFFI

Edinburgh, Present Day

I arrived home just before Deborah's daughter rang the bell to drop Tilly back. Once I'd waved the teenager off, I stepped out onto the doorstep and scanned the street.

Uneasily, I thought of Adeline. Was she somewhere nearby? What would she do, if I left Tom? Would that be her chance to lay claim to Tilly? What with her at large, and Joanne staking out the house and the baby yoga class, not to mention Tom's cameras, it was no wonder I felt like I was being watched.

'What's wrong?' asked Tilly.

'Nothing, darling. How was school?'

She shrugged and kicked her shoes off. One of them bounced against the wall.

'Oh no!' she dropped her bag and rushed to see if it had left a mark on the paintwork.

I heard a tiny whirring noise, coming from the corner of the ceiling above me and to my right. It was one of the surveillance cameras, swivelling around to track the sound.

'It's fine,' I said quietly, ushering her away and into the kitchen. 'Would you like a piece of toast?'

I made her a plate with eight small squares of crispy, golden hot-buttered toast and some slices of banana. While she waited, she attempted to play *A sailor went to sea, sea, sea* with Edie, who flapped her hands obligingly, propelling herself back and forth in her bouncy chair.

It seemed unbelievable that I could be here doing this, behaving in such an ordinary way, after this afternoon. The hours in the coffee shop with Joanne seemed like a dream. How could I have told her all those traitorous things about Tom?

I set the plate in front of Tilly with a glass of juice, and handed a square of toast to Edie, who solemnly plastered it to her cheek.

Tilly looked down at the food anxiously. 'Is this not carbs? Do we have anything that's not carbs?'

'You could have a yoghurt?'

'But that's dairy, isn't it? Have we got anything that's not dairy or carbs?'

I sat down opposite her. I couldn't let her struggle on alone any longer.

'I saw the notes in your schoolbag, Tilly. I want to help. Do you know who has been writing them?'

She looked down at her hands. 'Just people.'

'What people?'

'People like Aurelia and Annabelle. Don't tell Daddy.'

'Daddy already knows, darling. He's going to speak to the school.'

Her face spasmed in distress. 'But he'll make things worse. Can *you* speak to them?'

'Daddy doesn't want –' I stopped. I felt utterly helpless.

'What?'

I was tired of second-guessing what Tom wanted or didn't want. But there was one thing I could say that was indisputably true. 'Do you know that you are absolutely perfect? Just the way you are?'

I wanted to reach across the table and take her hands. But I held back, because she would probably pull them away. She might even get up and wander off, and then we wouldn't get to finish our conversation. But it was one of those endlessly defeating circles, wasn't it? I was stiff and unnatural with her, and so she was like that with me.

For some reason I thought of my mother, and how it must have been for her, trying to settle a three-year-old stranger into the family. Not knowing how to be with me – whether to hug and cuddle me or give me space. Because I must have been stiff too, when I arrived. Bewildered and homesick. Always looking for Dodo, and not for her.

I was beginning to understand what it was she'd tried to take on. I was filled, suddenly, with sorrow, for the relationship we'd never quite managed to have. I saw her in my mind's eye – the vertical grooves between grey-green eyes. The defensive, thin line of her mouth. A mouth that had to keep so many things unsaid. Impossible things about loss and love and belonging.

So I did it – I reached across the table and held out my hands to Tilly. For a second she froze. Then, carefully, she laid her palms flat on mine. She regarded me with fearful, trusting eyes. I wrapped my fingers around hers, tight and warm.

That was the moment I realised there was no option. I had to break the grip of Tom, one way or another. I had to step up and be the person Tilly needed me to be. I had to do it for her, and for that old, lost version of me that I could see when I looked at her.

It would have to start with a conversation. I would have to lay it all out for Tom, and give him the opportunity to change. I would have to make it clear that I considered Tilly to be my child, as well as his, in all the ways that mattered. And that I would fight for her. And for me. I would finally fight for me.

'How about we go and speak to your teacher tomorrow? Together?'

She nodded. Her eyes went shiny with tears.

'I'm going to go upstairs and phone Auntie Sarah. I think we might stay there tonight. Then we can have a good, proper chat about things and I'll take you into school tomorrow. We'll sort everything out. Would you watch Edie for me, just for a few minutes?'

I WENT into the downstairs bathroom – where there were no cameras, as far as I knew – taking the landline handset with me. I dialled Sarah, knowing she'd be at work.

'H-hi Sarah.' My teeth were chattering as if the room was freezing.

'Steffi. Everything okay?'

'Could I bring the children over in a bit? Could we possibly... stay? For a night or two?'

There was a long silence.

'You're welcome any time, Steffi, of course. It's just

tonight's not brilliant since Ben's maths tutor is coming and they'll need the kitchen to work in.'

'Oh...'

'Is everything okay?' she repeated.

'I'm having a few... problems. With Tom. I need to have a conversation with him. A very serious one. I was hoping to get the girls out of the house for a bit so that we could talk properly.'

'Conversation... as in a splitting up type conversation?' Sarah's voice rose in disbelief.

'Potentially.'

'Does Tom know about this?'

'Not yet,' I said quietly. 'We've been having problems for a while now.'

'But you have a baby. However would you cope on your own?' I could hear my mother's voice in hers now. 'What's he done, anyway?'

What an Appalling Fuss.

'It's hard to explain over the phone. But he's being controlling. He won't let me leave the house. He's monitoring my phone. Not letting me have any money.' I hated the sound of my voice – bleating, complaining, a victim.

'*What?* Are you sure this isn't some sort of misunderstanding? Something that can be cleared up?'

'I *want* to clear it up,' I said. 'That's why I need to talk to him. And I need the children not to be there. I need them to be somewhere...'

Somewhere safe.

'You can't pull a stunt like this. You can't just... *abduct* his children. There's no going back from that. It would be like... like exploding a bomb in the middle of your relationship.'

'I'm not abducting them. They're my children too. And they would only be going to your house.'

Abduct.

A half-memory stirred at the back of my mind. Rainy grey motorway stretching on forever. Red plastic chairs. Bright yellow cheese on a burger.

I'm not allowed McDonald's.

'Steffi?' said Sarah. 'Are you listening to me? It'll put him on the defensive. It'll set the whole discussion off to a terrible start.'

I swallowed down a lump in my throat. 'I have to do something,' I whispered. 'I'm so unhappy. Please, Sarah. Help me.'

'I want to help,' she said. 'I just don't think you should rush something like this. Why don't you wait until next weekend? You can tell him in advance that the girls are going to stay here for a sleepover. And then you can talk to him when you're both relaxed. Would that work?'

'Okay,' I said, trying to sound bright. Although I knew there was no way Tom would agree to both the girls going to Sarah's.

'Why didn't you *tell* me?'

'I met Joanne today,' I said. 'My birth sister. Talking to a stranger made me see things from a new perspective.'

'Your *birth sister*?' She inhaled sharply. 'God, Steffi – I didn't even know you were in touch.'

'I'm sorry. I'll explain everything.'

'I can't keep up.' She sounded lost, bewildered. 'I feel like I have literally no idea what is happening in your life.'

I thought of it all – the stairs... the scissors... psychosis. Gaslighting and coercive control.

'Joanne thought I should bring the children over to yours. To make sure they were safe. She made me promise I would.'

There was a long pause. There was a shuffling noise followed by the trumpeting sound of a nose blow. 'Okay,' she said finally. 'Bring the children round tonight. About dinner time.'

I opened the door to the hall and nearly fell over Tilly. She'd been sitting just outside the bathroom, her back against the wall, holding Edie in her arms.

'Tilly! You gave me a fright!' I hastily wiped the tears from my face using the back of my hand. 'I thought you were in the kitchen.'

'If you and Edie leave here... if you leave Daddy, I mean... can I come with you?'

I caught my breath, looked up. The hall camera was swivelled towards the area by the front door. Hopefully it was far enough away that it wouldn't have picked up what she'd said. I wanted to comfort her and say nobody was leaving anybody. But all I could do was buy time. I dropped my voice to a murmur. 'What do you mean, darling?'

'I don't want to stay here alone with him and Mummy.'

Seconds passed. I swallowed. '*Mummy*? What do you mean?'

'Yes – Mummy. She's here. She's under the stairs.'

51

STEFFI

Edinburgh, Present Day

My legs felt weak, suddenly. I put a hand on the wall and lowered myself down beside her. 'What are you talking about, Tilly?'

'Mummy came back one time.'

I was right. I'd been right about Adeline.

'Was this a couple of months ago? Did she take photographs of you and Edie? Is Mummy the "lady" you talked about?'

Tilly shook her head. 'No. It was before you came to live here. I heard her downstairs, late at night, shouting and screaming at Daddy.'

'But... how did you know it was Mummy? It could have been another lady.'

'Because I came out of my room. I hid at the top of the stairs and looked through the banister. I do know what she looks like.' She eyed me reproachfully. 'I've got a photograph of her in my drawer.'

So Tom hadn't destroyed all the photographs, after all. He'd missed one.

'Maybe she had come to talk to Daddy?'

Tilly nodded. 'I think so. But she didn't look very well.'

I moistened my lips. 'What do you mean? How didn't she seem well?'

'She was sleeping.' The last word emerged as a tight squeak. I heard the shudder of her breath leaving her body. 'She had been shouting. And then she was sleeping.'

'It's okay, darling.' I tried to sound calm. 'And what did Daddy do?'

'He took her into the cupboard under the stairs. Like, half carried her, sort of thing.'

I shook my head soothingly. 'No, no. There's nothing in that cupboard. I've been in there. It's just boxes and things. I think it must have been a bad dream, sweetheart.'

She turned her head and looked nervously down the hall. It struck me suddenly – the breath-holding, the way she would always run from the kitchen all the way to the top of the stairs. It hadn't been the stairs she'd been frightened of. It had been the door – the plain, wooden, very ordinary-looking door to the cupboard under the stairs.

She wrapped her arms tighter around Edie, who wriggled and began to cry. 'He came out, after a while.'

'Okay...'

'But *she* didn't.'

I swallowed again. 'Well... did you ask Daddy about it?'

'No. He looked very stressed. It's best not to bother him when he's stressed.' She bit her lip, started worrying it between her teeth.

Edie writhed uncomfortably in her sister's arms, drawing her knees up to her tummy. I hoped we weren't in for a bout of colic. Not tonight of all nights. 'Did you tell anyone?' I tried to keep my voice light and matter-of-fact.

She shook her head doubtfully. 'I didn't want Daddy to get into trouble.' She raised her eyes to mine. 'Is he in trouble now?'

I looked at my watch. It was half past five. Tom wasn't due back until around seven. I would have time to check the cupboard under the stairs. To put Tilly's mind at rest.

The door to the cupboard opened easily. There were some cardboard boxes in there, and a shelf with a box of screwdrivers and work tools, a variety of torches and electric lanterns and a gas camping stove. Fixed onto the wall above the shelf was the fuse box for the house and the garage. There was nothing unusual in there at all. The inside of the cupboard was carpeted – in the same thick oatmeal twist as had been used elsewhere in the house. But I would need to pull the boxes out if I wanted to check what, if anything, might be under it.

I started to lift the first box, the cardboard base bulging with the weight of whatever was in it. I put it back down and picked up one of the torches and shone it behind the boxes, into the back corners of the cupboard.

The piece of carpet had been neatly cut and fitted to the shape of the floor. The torch caught the glint of something that looked like a carpet tack, just visible along the furthest edge. When I shone the torch along, I could see that there were a few of them. But there were no tacks or staples on the area of the carpet I was standing on, the part nearer the door. It was as if half of it had been professionally fitted, and half had not. Or maybe it had once been lifted and re-laid.

I bent down to try and move the box again. I'd have to move them all out into the hall to have a proper look. But then I remembered the cameras.

Pocketing one of the torches, I emerged from the cupboard and went to talk to Tilly. I crouched in front of her and spoke in a low voice.

'I'm going to turn off the power to the house, okay? I just need to check something and there are wires in the way,' I lied. 'But first, I'm going to take you and Edie upstairs.'

Easier said than done, of course. I took Edie from Tilly's arms and fastened her into a baby sling on my chest. I ascended one step at a time, both hands on the banister. Tilly walked up behind me, matching my pace. I tried not to think about my birth mother. The collision and fall.

It was just a couple of carpet tacks, I told myself. Hardly anything at all, really. But I could feel my heart jumping behind my ribs.

There was a walk-in cupboard at the back of Tilly's room, lined with clothes rails. The floor was piled with cuddly toys and Build-a-Bears and the flimsy little garments that made up their extensive wardrobes.

'Now, I want you and Edie to wait in here. Like hide and seek, okay? The lights will go out, but I'll come back up soon. Actually, wait...' Tilly had a rechargeable night light by her bed – a squidgy white polar bear that gave off a soft blue glow. 'Look, you take this.'

Tilly nodded and sat down cross-legged in the furthest corner of the cupboard. I took Edie out of the sling and settled her in her sister's arms.

'Okay?'

She nodded again. Her eyes were black holes in the dim light.

52

STEFFI

Edinburgh, Present Day

I n the cupboard under the stairs, I flicked the main switch on the circuit board and cut off the power to the house. Then I heaved the cardboard boxes out of the cupboard and into the hall. I had to get a move on – I couldn't leave the poor children in Tilly's toy cupboard for more than a few minutes.

After I'd pushed the fourth box out into the hall, I had enough space to pull up the carpet, using one of the tools in the tool box to pull out the staples.

There was a wooden trapdoor underneath – a modern-looking one with a steel ring-pull handle recessed into the wood. I took hold of it with both hands, pulling it up to reveal a set of narrow, steep stone steps, leading down into the darkness.

Then I heard a noise, a rattle.

I froze. I strained to listen, but all I could hear was my own heartbeat, the blood thumping through my ears. Was there someone down there?

The sound came again. This time I recognised it as the handle of the back door, the door to the garden room. It was being turned back and forth, the mechanism being stopped by the lock again and again.

Holding the torch in front of me, I forced my legs to carry me through to the garden room.

There was a shape outside the glass door. Something was out there, on the patio. I saw a pale-coloured head, the hair falling over its face as it stooped to examine the door handle. For a moment I thought of a scarecrow with a mop head, moving in the wind.

The figure stood upright and I saw that it was Joy.

For fuck's sake.

I opened the door. 'What are you doing here?'

She looked taken aback, a little hurt. 'It's Thursday. I came over earlier for our session but you weren't here. I thought I'd come back and just check everything was okay. I knocked but there was no answer and I thought you might be busy with the little one. I thought I'd just let myself in.'

I exhaled. In the drama of meeting Joanne, I had completely forgotten Joy was due to come round.

'You still want me to use the back door, don't you?' she asked. There was a note of tiredness in her voice, of patience stretched just a little bit too thin. As if she could no longer keep up with me and my neurotic requirements.

'I'm so sorry,' I said. 'I forgot about our session. It's been quite a day. And the power's out. Sorry.' I stepped aside to let her in.

'What on earth is going on?' asked Joy.

'I'm in a bit of a panic.'

'Yes,' said Joy. 'Indeed you are.'

I glanced at my watch. It was ten to six. Tom could be home in half an hour, if he was early. I didn't have time for this.

'What can I do to help?' Joy reached out and gently held my upper arms.

'I think there's a fucking corpse in the cellar.' Tears of terror spilled down my face.

I couldn't see her expression in the dark, through the blur of tears. But I heard a clicking noise as she swallowed.

'Shall we call the police?' Her voice was oddly calm. Flat, even.

'I need to check the cellar first. The children are upstairs. I told them to hide in Tilly's toy cupboard.'

'I see,' she said. 'Do you want me to go up and make sure they're okay?'

'No. Tilly's never met you. She might get a fright.' Not just a fright – she'd be terrified if some stranger appeared in the dark.

'Shall I come down to the cellar with you?' For a moment I wondered about her voice – it could have been the trained voice of someone dealing with a person who was having a psychotic break. Keeping things calm until help arrived.

'No.' I lifted one of the chairs from the dining alcove in the garden room, and gestured for her to follow me into the unlit hall. I placed the chair at the very back of the hall. From that position, the door to the cupboard under the stairs was half way down the hall on the right, and the front door was straight ahead, so she'd be able to keep an eye on both.

'Please can you wait here and listen out for the children?

If Tom comes back, please keep him busy. Tell him you're babysitting.'

She nodded.

'Keep him out of the cupboard under the stairs. That door there. *At all costs?* Okay?'

Joy sat herself down on the chair and smoothed down her skirt. 'Understood,' she said. 'Go and do what you have to do.'

She sat there quietly, looking straight ahead in the direction of the front door, as I pushed the cardboard boxes, one by one, into the guest bedroom. I couldn't risk Tom seeing them there in the hall, if he came back early.

Then there was nothing to do except walk down the narrow stone steps. The air grew colder as I descended, and smelled damp. It made me think of a school trip to an old castle where we'd all gone quiet inside the stone dungeons, with their dank, drainy stench.

At the bottom, I shone my torch around. There was nothing much to see. I took in a long wooden work bench along the side wall, with tins of paint stacked on top. A twin tub washing machine and a roll of old carpet. Some sacks of something that looked like sand or grit.

The tightness in my chest began to ease a little. In a few moments I could go back upstairs, replace the carpet and the cardboard boxes and turn the power back on. I could fetch the girls from Tilly's toy cupboard and make out that it had all been a game. I could have a cup of tea with Joy and talk about weaning and sleep routines.

My imagination had clearly run away with me. I'd done Tom an injustice by even thinking he might be capable of something like this. I owed him the chance to try and make this relationship work. It would all be fine, a happy ending.

We could all stay here in this expensive stone tomb of a house forever.

But I couldn't ignore the fact there was another door, a smaller one, in the far wall of the cellar. I forced myself to check it. The handle was stiff but it opened and I emerged into a second room.

For a moment I thought of a school locker room or a swimming pool changing room. There were modern blue storage lockers set against the left hand wall, wide tall ones that reached almost up to the ceiling. A couple of wooden stools against the other wall.

The storage lockers were locked tight. But I remembered the paperclip trick I'd used to open Tom's filing cabinet. Ignoring my thudding heart, and the nausea that tugged at my stomach, I went back up the steps into the cupboard under the stairs and searched in the tool box for a piece of wire. I cut it with pliers and twisted it into the shape I'd learned the last time.

Then I stopped to listen, trying to detect any sound coming from outside the cupboard. All was silent. I thought of Joy in her chair, her face vigilant, keeping watch for me. I descended the narrow staircase again.

Down in the second basement room, it took several attempts to open the first locker. The mechanism seemed more robust than the one in the filing cabinet in Tom's study. My hands were shaking and the piece of wire kept springing out of my fingers. I had to scrabble for it on the floor several times, wildly swinging the beam of my torch. The door finally swung open to reveal a figure-like shape towering over me – something tall and white. I gasped and sprang back. But it was just a wedding dress, suspended from a padded hanger, its thin cellophane cover rustling with the movement of the air.

I unlocked the second storage locker and in there was... a thing.

A thing wrapped in grey plastic sheeting.

A thing in a sort of foetal position, with loops of duct tape around it like a web around a fly. The shape suggested bent legs and a torso. And at the top, a more tightly wrapped shape, rounded and totally black with tape, like the spent head of a match.

I took my piece of wire. I wriggled and poked it through the layers of plastic until I tore a hole in it. A hole through to the thing inside. When the smell hit me, it was indescribable. I turned and vomited onto the stone floor.

53

ANGEL

Edinburgh, Present Day

The woman sitting on the chair in the hall tugged down on the ends of her wig, teasing a few of the ashy blonde strands in front of her ears and stroking them into place.

She adjusted her glasses and smoothed down her skirt, making sure the hem sat properly below her knees. She'd be a strange sight to anyone who opened the front door and came into the dark hall. An apparition. She wondered if her glasses would reflect the light from the street and glare back. Like a thing she'd once seen in a horror movie – a dark thing with white light streaming out of its eye sockets.

A strange sight indeed, as Joy would say.

Or, as Joy would have said if she had still existed, rather than dying of a heart attack several decades ago.

It had been necessary, of course, to be someone else, in

order to infiltrate Steffi's life. Just as she had used Cheryl, her colleague, to be Joanne's private investigator, she had used her old therapist Joy – frumpy do-gooder Joy – for Steffi. Sliding into other identities seemed to be a special talent of hers. She hardly knew who Angel really was, these days. It was hard to remember what Angel should think or feel.

I need this to end.

It was the one thought, the one feeling, that was indisputably true. She held onto it like a rock. If she did this thing, then she would no longer have to think about whether she was going to do it. Daddy could sleep quietly in his chair.

She tried to summon some enjoyable thoughts. Like how she'd found Steffi months ago, not long after Mum's funeral. All it had taken was that one comment Steffi had made on the baby yoga class Facebook page, moaning about her lack of sleep. Angel had made the journey to Edinburgh and followed her home from the next class. And then she'd followed Steffi's car one evening, when she'd been driving around with the children in the dark. She'd had to get a proper look at her. And she hadn't been able to resist scoring that word – BITCH – onto the side of her car.

She had proceeded to join multiple Facebook groups for Edinburgh parents and new mums, hoping that Steffi might post some request for help or advice. When she had, Angel had been ready to spring into action. It had taken her mere minutes to clone some baby sleep guru's website and insert Joy's name and photo into the 'About Me' page, and then message Steffi with an offer to help.

Then she'd read a baby-whispering book on the train on the way up to Edinburgh, and tried to imagine how Joy would have handled a fragile new mum.

She replayed the look on Steffi's face when she'd

answered the door to Joy that first time. How she had practically fallen to her knees in relief. Angel had nailed it, standing there in her sensible coat, radiating the calm experience of an older woman. She had absolutely nailed it.

Poor little Steffi. Poor little perfect princess, with her perfect princess of a baby who (shock, horror –she was a baby!) wouldn't sleep. Boo hoo.

But tonight, Angel felt she could collapse with exhaustion herself. Just fall off that expensive antique dining chair onto the floor and simply lie there. And maybe it wouldn't matter. With darkness all around, you couldn't see the things that might be moving in the corners of your eyes.

I need this to end.

At the start of it all, she'd thought the letters might be enough to satisfy Daddy – the letters she'd faked between Steffi and Joanne.

When that hadn't proved to be the case, she'd embarked on a plan to simply ruin Steffi's life. Her dossier of notes – which she'd been planning to offer up to Tom, once she'd talked Steffi into leaving him – should be enough to convince a judge that the children shouldn't be placed in her care. Through her PI work, she'd gathered enough evidence for parties in child custody cases to know what boxes would need to be ticked.

It had hardly even been necessary to embellish the notes very much. Steffi had been quite unstable enough, all by herself. And Joy had arranged some useful 'third party corroboration', starting with the calls to the police: the concerned neighbours reporting a distressed child and a mad woman on the roof.

It had been easy to buy a duplicate bottle of Steffi's vitamin tonic – already bitter-tasting with its fermented fruit extracts – and stuff it full of crushed valium tablets. Joy had practised swapping it for the real one, and swapping it back, while Steffi tended to the baby and its tiresome whims. It had worked perfectly, the day Steffi had fallen asleep and Tilly had gone walkabout with the baby, encouraged by Joy through the letterbox.

She had the duplicate vitamin tonic with her today, in her bag. She didn't suppose she'd get a chance to use it now, with all these comings and goings.

Daddy had rewarded her with a thin smile when she'd painted the picture of Steffi, her life ruined, her children torn away from her by the courts. But he wouldn't budge from his original plan. He wanted her to drug Steffi and then drown her in the bath, for Tilly to find. Or use a funnel to pour drain cleaner down her unconscious throat. The perfect princess with her insides corroded to slime and mush.

You couldn't shop your own father to the police, like Steffi had done that day in the Little Chef. You couldn't *ruin a whole family* – and expect there to be no consequences.

Was that somebody outside? A rattle of keys in the lock. The creak of the front door. A shaft of sodium light fell across the decorative Victorian floor tiles as the door swung open.

Ah, it was Tom.

Angel sat quietly in her chair as he moved towards her in the darkness. Again she wondered if the light would reflect off her glasses and give her away. Or if he could hear the hiss of her breath.

But he turned to his left and pushed the door to the cupboard under the stairs. And then he was gone, just another shadow, slipping away.

It was ideal, really. She could just let him finish things off now. She sat back in the chair and closed her eyes.

54

STEFFI

Edinburgh, Present Day

A creak came from somewhere up above. From the cupboard under the stairs, I realised.

'Joy?' I called. 'Is that you?'

'Steffi?' called Tom in a hide-and-seek voice. 'Ste-ffeee?'

The blood in my veins seemed to crystallise – an instant freeze, like some catastrophic chemical reaction. I switched off the torch and stood there in the darkness, trying not to breathe.

'Oh, Steffi,' he said when the opened the door into the room, shining his own torch up and down my body, and then over to the tall locker, and the thing inside. His voice had affection in it, and exasperation. As if I were a child who'd disappointed him. 'What are you up to down here? Where are the kids?'

'They're...' I nearly told him that they were upstairs, and

that Tilly knew I was down here and might come looking any moment. But my instincts told me to stop. I didn't want Tom to know she'd told me about Adeline being under the stairs. 'They're at Sarah's. She came to get them when the power... when it went out. And Ash is on his way round. He's coming to... to sort out the power.'

He raised one eyebrow in mild amusement. 'Really?'

'Yes. And my friend Joy is upstairs.'

Where *was* Joy? Had she seen Tom come in? Why hadn't she distracted him, like I'd asked? Or was she on his side in all this? For a mad moment I wondered if Tom had 'turned' her, like some Cold War spy, and she was working for him. I thought of her dossiers and notebooks, logging my 'instability' and questionable parenting.

He just laughed. 'Nice try, Steffi. I'm afraid your imaginary friend isn't going to save you now.'

'*What?* She's real. Joy is real. She's just upstairs.' My voice squeaked like a child's.

'God, Steffi. Why did you do all this?' He gestured to the vomit on the floor, the locker, the plastic-wrapped shape. '*Why?*'

I thought quickly of an explanation that didn't involve Tilly. That played into his view of me as a wayward child. 'I've been checking around the house. Gradually, for weeks. For clues. One of the neighbours mentioned they had a cellar and I thought we must have one too.'

He frowned. '*You?* Talking to the neighbours? Since when?'

'I've figured it out,' I said. 'You sent those photos, didn't you? The photos of Tilly and Edie. You sent them to that therapeutic community place. Chesters. To avert any suspicion. To make it seem like she was still alive.' I could hardly get the words out. I didn't have the breath.

He pursed his lips and tipped his head to the side, contemplating the question as if I hadn't framed it quite right.

'And her letters,' I said. 'Her birthday and Christmas cards to Tilly. *You* wrote them.'

Horror washed over me, again and again, as it started to become clear. He must have deliberately chosen inappropriate presents he knew Tilly would hate – the garish eyeshadow sets and tacky dolls. And had he drawn the sketch of the screaming face himself? Only to lift it between his thumb and fingertip and drop it in the bin?

Poor Adeline had to be mad, even after he'd killed her.

We were all pieces that he had to control. Pawns on a board.

I realised that I would die here in this cellar. And that Tom would tell Edie and Tilly that I had been mentally ill, beyond saving. That it was best not to mention me. All photos of me would be destroyed. After a while, Tilly would barely remember I'd existed. Edie wouldn't remember at all.

'Come on, then,' I said, my voice challenging now. 'Tell me why you did it.'

'What do you know?' he asked, sitting down on one of wooden stools. I got the sudden, freakish sense that that he was in a chatty mood. That we could almost have been gossiping about friends or colleagues and he was filling me in. 'How much did you find out at Chesters?'

'I know that it's some sort of mental health facility and she lived there for a few years, trying to recover. And that she left, because...'

She was leaving for love.

'She came back for Tilly. She came back to fight for her.'

He raised his eyebrows and pulled the corners of his mouth down, as if it was an interpretation of the story he hadn't heard before.

'I know she came here, to the house,' I continued. 'You had an argument. You killed her and then brought her down here. She's been down here for *years*.' I gasped in a sob. The same thing was going to happen to me. I just hoped to God that he would look after the children. That they would be okay. That they would have decent lives.

A few hours ago, I'd imagined us thrashing things out in front of divorce lawyers. Making sure of the best outcome for the children. I longed for that now. Longed for it so much it hurt my chest.

Then I had another realisation. 'That's why you couldn't marry me, isn't it? Why you kept fobbing me off about setting a date? You couldn't get a divorce from Adeline because she was dead. She was decomposing in your cellar.'

'I was *trying* to get a divorce,' he said tetchily. 'That's exactly what I was trying to do. I'd written to her at her commune.'

'It's a mental health facility, Tom. The woman was trying to get herself well again. But it suited you to call it a commune, didn't it? Then she could just stay there forever, cut off from the world, and nobody would question it. Nobody would wonder why she'd never come back.'

'I'll call it what I like,' he snapped back. 'It was a monstrous indulgence. Navel-gazing and finger-painting and whatnot – all at my expense. I wasn't going to keep paying for all that after the divorce. And she didn't like that. But instead of getting a lawyer involved like any sane person would have, she came round here unannounced, all guns blazing, the usual. Wanting to take Tilly away then and there, saying she'd go for full custody. And she would take me for every penny I had. I was only trying to get her to calm down.'

'Calm her down how?'

'I put my hand over her mouth to stop her screaming and shouting. I didn't want her to wake Tilly. Can you imagine how that would have destroyed the poor child? To come downstairs and see this woman, this mental case, who was supposed to be her mother? She'd idealised Adeline, you see, in her mind. Thought she was some great artist.' He rolled his eyes in gentle amusement, smiling at me as if we were both in on the joke. For a crazy moment, we felt like a partnership again. As if he was bringing me into his confidence so that we could find a way through this.

'So what happened? You grabbed her and...?'

'I was too rough. I frightened her. I'd forgotten her heart condition. She just stopped, Steffi. She just stopped.'

He shook his head regretfully. But there was something else in his face, a gleeful spark he was trying to suppress.

'I don't believe you.'

'I felt dreadful.' He spread his hands in a *mea culpa* gesture. 'But what could I do? It was damage limitation from then on.'

Damage limitation. To suppurate inside plastic sheeting. The gruesome mess held in with neatly wrapped tape.

Suddenly, I understood. 'You tidied her away.'

'I *did*,' he nodded, seeming surprised that I understood. 'I did.'

All I could think of was how big he was. Those meaty hands. The thick jaw. The heavily lidded eyes. Behind his well-spoken voice and his trappings of wealth, he was nothing but a thug.

'The question now,' he went on, with a faux-apologetic grimace, 'is what do I do with *you*?'

I glanced behind him, wondering if I could slip past him and get to the trapdoor. I could slam it shut behind me. I could call the police.

He took a step closer, his bulk towering over me, blocking my exit. I could smell something coming off him, some hot, animal scent. The chemistry of his body was changing, pumping him up for what he was about to do. I felt the crotch of my jeans become warm, and wetness down the inside of my leg.

I wasn't going to get away from him. It was impossible.

Suddenly it flashed into my head – a blurred impression of myself as a very young child, flying at a shape at the top of the stairs. I'd been so scared of that shadowy, half-understood version of myself. Scared of what she had done and what she might still be capable of. Now I realised that she'd only ever needed me to protect her.

I stood up tall.

He tugged his sleeves up from his wrists and took another step forward.

55

JOANNE

Edinburgh, Present Day

J oanne felt like some mad stalker or something, following Steffi home from the café.

She'd spent twenty minutes in the car first, calling the rescue centre and asking Paul, one of the spotty teenage volunteers, to help out with Mitski and Albie. There was no way of getting house keys to him, not now that Mei-Ling was in Tenerife, but he was going to lower two bowls through the cat flap and attempt to pour some dried food into one, and some water into the other.

Mitski, in particular, would be affronted if she saw a strange man's hands reaching through the cat flap. Joanne wasn't quite sure how he'd manage it. She imagined Mr Tickle from the *Mr Men* books, with his rubbery orange hands and arms. But Paul – a geeky lad who was doing science A-levels – had been delightful on the phone and had risen to the challenge. She tried to remember if he'd been one of the ones who'd laughed, when the young ones had been taking the piss out of her at the Christmas party for being able to distinguish between the cats' voices. Even if he had, she was ready to forgive him now. Needs must.

The truth was, she had a bad feeling about all this. About Steffi and what was going on in that house.

First, all the lights in the house had gone out at once. Could there have been a power cut? But none of the other houses on the street – or the streetlights – had been affected. Or maybe a fuse had blown? Twenty minutes later, she'd seen a woman arrive and go around the back of the house.

Good, she'd thought at first, thinking it must have been Sarah, and that Steffi must have told her to go round the back to avoid the cameras. But then she'd remembered Sarah's profile picture on Facebook – her dark wavy hair caught up into a twist. This woman had white-blonde, old-lady hair. So who was she?

Then, just before six, she'd seen Tom pull up in his Audi and enter the house, all in a hurry. Hadn't Steffi said he wasn't due back until seven?

The thing was, he hadn't even parked it straight in the drive, or lined up the wheels. That bothered her. It really bothered her.

And now, a few minutes later, the lights hadn't gone back on.

Steffi, the children, the old-lady-hair person, and Tom. All in the house in the dark.

She sighed heavily and swung open the door of the car. Steffi was going to think she was a raving nutter, if there was a reasonable explanation for all this. But she couldn't ignore the crawling sensation in her gut.

The doorbell jangled, somewhere deep within the house. But nobody answered. She saw there were stained glass panels on either side of the front door – flimsy, antique-looking things that they probably hadn't been able to get rid of because of listed building regulations.

She'd broken into houses before, to rescue cats. Once, when an old lady had been taken into hospital suddenly and had phoned the centre in tears. Once, when a postman had dropped into the centre to report distressed miaowing in an empty house. There wasn't always time to go through the official channels. She wrapped her hand in her coat and punched it through the stained glass. She shook off the fragments, then reached through and turned the lock from the inside. She was in.

At the end of the hallway, a figure sat in a chair. Joanne could just make out its shape in the dark, and as her eyes adjusted she could see it was the woman with the old-lady hair.

The woman stayed perfectly still, frozen, the way animals sometimes did when cornered in a small space. Joanne took out her phone and turned on the torch. She shone it into her face.

'Piss off!'

Joanne's heart nearly jumped out of her chest. It was *Cheryl*. Or Angel, or whatever she was called. Wearing a wig, for God's sake.

'You?' Joanne cried. 'What the fuck are you doing here, you silly fool?!'

Her fight-or-flight instincts were firing all over the place. But somehow, she wasn't scared of this woman, sitting here in dress-up. There was a monster in this house, but it wasn't her.

'You shouldn't be mucking around here!' Joanne scolded. 'Why are you here?'

Angel's face moved as she ran her tongue around the insides of her cheeks. It made Joanne think of a face Steffi had used to pull, as a toddler, when she was in trouble. 'She's my sister,' said Angel. 'I wanted to get to know her. I'm minding the children for her.' She blinked slowly.

'Where is she?'

Angel's eyes widened and her hand moved up to her neck. There was something glinting there, reflecting the light from the torch – some sort of necklace. At first, Joanne thought it was a gold cross and chain but it was a flimsy pendant in the shape of an 'A'. Angel took it between her thumb and forefinger and twisted it. 'She's in the cellar.'

'What cellar?'

'Under the stairs.' She said it almost sadly, inclining her head towards a door – the under-stairs cupboard, Joanne supposed.

'What's she doing down there?'

Slowly, Angel shrugged.

Joanne went to the door and pulled it open.

Oh Christ. There was an open trapdoor in the floor, with a narrow staircase leading down. For a moment she thought she could see a flicker of weak light down there, but then it went black.

She shone her phone torch down, but she couldn't see what was at the bottom. She could feel Angel standing behind her, the woman's breath on her neck.

She took a moment to think. If she was going to go down there, she should really find something she could use to protect herself – and Steffi, if needed. She scanned the shelf that ran along the far wall of the cupboard. There were screwdrivers there. She grabbed one of them – a small one with a sharp point.

'Call the police,' she hissed at Angel.

She began to make her way down the steps. With the forefinger and thumb of her left hand – which was also clutching the screwdriver – she kept hold of the narrow banister rail which was fixed to the stone wall. On the other side of the steps, the wall only extended a few feet. Beyond that there was a drop to the right. A black void.

She paused and swept the phone torch beam down there, making out the pattern of the flagstones below. Then she pointed the light back down at the narrow, uneven steps. She had to make sure she didn't lose her footing.

By the time she'd heard the sound – shoe leather whispering against stone – it was too late. She swung round to her right just as two hands shot up out of the darkness and grabbed her ankles.

The back of her head hit a sharp stone edge as she was pulled down into the black.

HOT, sharp pain exploded through her head. She thought she could smell burning. Or something molten, metallic.

It took her a moment to realise that she was lying on her back on the cellar floor, near the bottom of the steps. There was a weak, white light coming from somewhere – she'd dropped her phone with its torch still on.

'Who the fuck are you? And what are you doing in my house?' Tom was standing above, looming over her. There were several long, deep scratches, running all the way down his face. Steffi must have put up some fight. She'd managed to catch one of his eyes, too – the eyelid was torn, the cornea blood red.

'I'm her sister,' she managed. There was hardly any breath in her lungs. 'And the police have been called, by the way.' She had no idea if this was true. That psycho woman, Angel, could be on her way down here to help Tom finish her off, for all she knew.

'Well, you've made a big mistake,' said Tom. 'This has nothing to do with you.'

'You've made a big mistake too, pal.' Because he hadn't noticed the small, sharp screwdriver, still clutched in Joanne's left hand. Somehow, fuelled by pure adrenaline, she managed to lurch up and drive it into the side of his abdomen. He howled and pitched forward, trying to grab her around the throat. She managed to knee him in the groin and push him off, the effort sending a bolt of pain through the back of her head.

He curled onto the floor, moaning and holding himself. Joanne managed to get herself onto all fours, and scanned the shadowy corners of the dark cellar. There she was – Steffi – lying on her side in the doorway to a second cellar room, one arm extended out as if she was trying to reach for Joanne.

She began to crawl over to Steffi, inching her way over the flagstones. Red-hot pain fired down the nerves in her back and across her shoulder – she must have wrenched something as she'd fallen. And her head... her head felt like it would burst.

She was almost there... almost. Then she heard a shuffling behind her. A muttering.

'You've asked for it now, you bitch.'

56

ANGEL

Edinburgh, Present Day

A ngel felt as if she was hovering above herself. Watching.

She waited for a thrill of satisfaction. She tried to summon the glee she used to feel when she imagined the hard-faced bitch and the perfect princess getting what was coming to them.

It wouldn't come.

She waited for a few moments at the edge of the trapdoor. She heard thuds. A muffled shriek. A full-throated roar.

Finally, she exited the cupboard and went back to sit in her chair in the hall. Steffi had instructed her to sit there, after all.

She supposed Steffi would die now, and Joanne. Maybe it would be better for the baby if it were to die too. To disappear, like dirty water down a plughole. Her father's blood was mixed into this family too, running through its veins. Hiding in its DNA. If you thought about it, he'd been here in this house for some time.

She could feel him now, a black shape amongst the writhing shadows. And she could hear him, in the sounds coming from the cellar.

It kept coming into her mind again and again – her thirteen-year-old self trapped in that torturous therapy session with Joy. The empty chair exercise where she'd allowed herself to think, just for a moment, about the businessmen. About why Daddy had done that.

Apparently, Joy's heart attack had happened later that week. She'd never seen her again. Nobody had even bothered to tell Angel. She'd turned up for her therapy session as normal and sat on a grey plastic chair in the waiting room for an hour before anyone realised.

Now, sitting there in the dark in Steffi's hallway, Angel sighed. Here she was in yet another chair that didn't belong to her. In a body that hadn't felt like hers for a million years.

I need this to end.

It seemed to have gone quiet in the cellar now. But there was another faint noise coming from somewhere. From above, now. A thin little wail coming from upstairs.

It was the baby crying. Angel climbed the stairs and followed the sound into Tilly's bedroom.

'Hello-ooo?' she called out softly in Joy's voice. 'Don't worry. Steffi's asked me to check on you.' She opened the door of the toy cupboard and peeked in.

A little white face in the corner, peering out from behind a pile of stuffed animals. Tear streaks like slug trails down her face.

Dear oh dear.

And the baby in the child's arms, fussing and wriggling.

'I'm Edie's sleep lady,' she told Tilly. 'Would you like me to help settle her? Steffi said it's important we're quiet.'

Tilly nodded. Angel reached for Edie, feeling the stretch of her little body as she lifted her under the arms. It would be easy, she thought, as she looked down at the baby. She could just cover its nose and mouth with her hand. She could press gently, sealing off the air, until she went still. Edie wouldn't even know anything about it. She would slip out of this life easily, without ever knowing anything about the things that could happen. About prison sentences and social workers and suicide. About businessmen and Cherry Pie nail varnish and the empty chair technique. She would never have voices shouting in her head.

She would never have to know that her mother had been killed by her father.

I need this to end.

But there was something about Tilly, crouching there in the corner. So scared, the poor mite.

For a moment she wasn't sure if she was Angel or Joy. Or if she was both. Or some other person altogether.

The baby stopped crying and settled against her body. She realised she'd been gently jiggling her, shushing her. She'd learned to do that when she'd helped Steffi. She was surprised to feel something flicker inside her chest, briefly. Something that was not nothing.

'Please help,' said Tilly simply. 'Me and Edie, we're so scared.'

The child trusted her. The child thought she was Joy, here to help Steffi. So she decided she might as well be. For today. Until all this was over.

'Has Edie got a baby monitor?' she asked.

Tilly nodded.

She pondered. 'Here's what we're going to do.'

57

JOANNE

Edinburgh, Present Day

J oanne knew she was in bad shape. She guessed that the back of her head had split open. She could feel something soft, something pulsing. It hurt like a bastard. If she moved even slightly, it made her want to vomit.

She'd managed to get across the floor to Steffi and was lying on top of her now, trying to keeping most of her weight on her knees and elbows so she wasn't squashing her. In the space between the two of them and the cellar stairs, she could make out a shadowy hump on the flagstones that she thought was Tom. He'd managed to shuffle a few more feet towards them, but now he was lying still. She hoped he'd lost consciousness, was bleeding out. But it was possible he was just gathering his strength. Biding his time.

She didn't know what the fuck he'd done to Steffi, but

even in the dim light, she could see the marks on her neck. And he'd messed up her face. She wasn't conscious any more. Joanne cupped careful hands around the curve of her sister's head. If Tom wanted to finish Steffi off, he'd have to get past her first.

The pain in her head was expanding like a balloon. Her mind started to slip and slide, as if she was falling asleep.

But Tom's face – ruined, diabolical – was burned into the insides of her eyes. It reminded her that she had to stay awake. And she had to try and wake Steffi up, too.

'Well done,' she whispered into Steffi's ear. 'You did really well. You helped me get him.'

If the screwdriver had gone deep enough. But where was the effing screwdriver now? She must have let go of it in the struggle. If Tom did try and attack again, she had nothing to use against him but her bare hands. She managed to raise her head a bit. Might it be over there by the steps? But the floor was too dark to see. She could make out some sort of wooden work bench along the side wall. She wondered if she could crawl over there to see if there was anything else she could use as a weapon. Perhaps, if she could summon up some strength, if she could push through the pain, she could finish Tom off. But she couldn't leave Steffi. She couldn't leave her alone.

She needed help. Backup.

'Angel!' she called, her voice little more than a croak. 'ANGEL!'

There was no reply.

She thought, suddenly, of her cats. If she didn't get out of this cellar, she hoped Mei-Ling would make sure they were looked after. She hoped their next owner would stroke Albie behind the ears in that way he liked, and would learn the language of Mitski's various chirps and chirrups. She'd hoped that they would keep them together.

'Stay awake, love. Stay awake now.'

Joanne realised she couldn't feel Steffi's breathing any more. She tried to silence the rasp of her own breath so she could listen harder. She held her cheek close to Steffi's nose, straining to feel warm air against her skin.

Nothing.

She closed her eyes. Their life – their short, sweet life together – reeled through her mind. The tartan blankie, trailing everywhere behind them. Bare feet and summer pansies. Pushes on the swing. Three kisses for luck.

Was that a child's cry? Maybe it was just a trick of the mind as her brain began to shut down.

'Shhh,' she whispered to Steffi, stroking her hair. 'It's okay. I'm here.'

Then there was a shifting noise. Unmistakeable. Joanne forced her eyes open. The shadowy hump moved. Tom was getting up off the floor.

Then she heard the little voice more clearly. It was coming from somewhere above.

'Daddy?'

Oh please, God. No...

58

ANGEL

Edinburgh, Present Day

Angel stood in the cupboard under the stairs, two steps back from the trapdoor.

In one hand, she held a heavy marble rolling pin. She'd gone to the kitchen looking for a knife, but they'd all been put away somewhere. This was all she'd been able to find. In her other hand, she held Edie's baby monitor. The little green lights on it cast an eerie glow onto the walls of the cupboard. Just enough to see by.

'Daddy?' said Tilly's voice through the monitor. 'Daddy? Are you there?'

Angel turned up the volume to full and placed the monitor at the edge of the trapdoor.

'Again!' she hissed. 'Shout it this time.'

'DA-DDY?'

There was a rustle and a shuffle from the darkness below Angel's feet.

'Is that you, darling? Daddy's coming.' And then a bark of instruction: 'Stay where you are.'

A loud cry burst through the monitor. Tilly must have given Edie a little pinch, just as she had instructed.

Torchlight came from the hatch below, slicing the darkness. The voice came again, closer this time: 'Hold on, my princess.'

And there it was – anger. It roared through her like a fiery furnace. Insatiable. Destroying everything in its path.

It was him she hated. It had never really been the others.

His head emerged from the trapdoor. 'Who the fuck –'

He shone the light into her eyes. Half-blinded, she lunged forward and swung the rolling pin, aiming for his face. But he ducked, and it only glanced the top of his head. He swore and dropped the torch – she heard it slide down the cellar steps and clatter onto the floor below. She lifted the rolling pin again, trying to locate his face as her eyes struggled to adjust. He launched himself out of the trapdoor and grabbed her around the legs.

She heard the sound of her own shriek, as if it was coming from someone else, from some place outside of herself. She landed smack on her back at the bottom of the steps. It took a few moments before she could draw a breath. She hauled herself onto her elbow, then instantly sank back down as dizziness overwhelmed her.

She could see Joanne lying on the floor. The back of her head was a nasty mess – gashed open and bleeding. She was covering Steffi with her body, her hands making a trembling cage around her head.

My sisters.

How different it all could have been.

She closed her eyes for a moment, her head spinning. Then she sensed something moving above her. For a moment she wasn't sure which man it was, standing over her, raising the rolling pin up, about to bring it down on her head.

She only knew that it was the darkness, claiming her now. The shadows made flesh, finally. She closed her eyes, and her body flooded with relief.

I need this to end.

59

JOANNE

Edinburgh, Present Day

Joanne heard a terrible cracking noise. A crunching of bone.

And then another distant shriek: 'DA-DDY!'

Dear God in heaven. Surely he hadn't gone for the child?

She managed to raise her head again. She tried to understand what she was seeing.

The brute had managed to get up. It was the Angel woman he'd hit. He was standing over her, holding a great big bastard of a rolling pin.

Summoning every last ounce of her strength, Joanne moved herself off Steffi's body. She got onto all fours and then she forced one foot flat onto the stone floor and pushed herself up into a standing position. The pain was like an axe in the back of her head. But she couldn't give in to it. Not yet.

Tom began to lift the rolling pin again. Adrenaline flooded Joanne's body like a bright white light. She flew at him, launching herself onto his back.

'Jesus!' he roared. 'Fuck off, you bitch!'

He tried to shake her off but she clung on tighter, arms and legs wrapped around him. He swung the rolling pin behind his head, trying to make contact with her. She sank her teeth into the side of his neck.

He howled in fury. Joanne held on tight. Still clinging to him, she jostled her body weight back and forth, her mouth filling with his hot, metallic blood. His legs folded under him and he sank sideways to the floor. Scrambling free, she wrenched his right shoulder back against the floor and climbed on top of him. She pressed down on his upper arms using the full weight of her body, and pushed her knees into his abdomen. For the first time in her life, she thanked her stars that she was a well-built lass, that there was a bit of meat on her bones. She could feel the sticky wetness where she'd stabbed his side with the screwdriver, and she ground her knee deeper into that spot.

He bucked and tried to throw her off him. A thin stream of vomit erupted from his mouth.

Just when she thought she couldn't hold him any longer, a dark shape appeared at the left of her field of vision. It was Angel, crouching like an animal, holding out the rolling pin. Joanne grabbed it and pressed it horizontally across his neck. She felt the springy resistance of cartilage and pushed harder, hoping she was crushing his windpipe.

Tom made a choking noise, inched his head to the side. The rolling pin was flat against the side of his thick neck.

Joanne became aware that Angel was behind her, sitting on his legs. She could hear the woman grunting.

He managed to grab the ends of the rolling pin, trying to force it off his neck. She pushed down more firmly.

'You rotten shit,' she spat into his face. 'Why did you have to do that to her, eh? All she did was try to love you, to make a nice family for you.'

She thought of all the things she'd wanted for Steffi, when she'd given her up. The life she could have had.

Tom's eyes bulged. He sucked in a gurgling breath. 'She was a sneak and a liar.'

Was. The word was like a blow to the heart.

'She tried to make it work with you, you controlling prick.' A long string of sticky red drool stretched from her open mouth down onto his face.

'Bad blood,' he managed. 'There's nothing you can do... about bad blood.'

'You cowardly thug. Pick on someone your own fucking size.'

She pressed down with all her might on the rolling pin. His eyes rolled back in his head and his body began to jerk in a frenzied dance.

60

JOANNE

Edinburgh, Present Day

Nobody could call Joanne a people person. She wasn't fussed about people at all and she had her reasons.

But somehow, these days, she was able to like the people Blackie liked. And Blackie seemed to like Mrs Kumari.

Joanne found a free plug socket amongst all the gubbins behind the hospital bed. She plugged in the grey, fleecy heat pad, turned it on to its most gentle heat setting, and placed it in the hollow of the bedcovers next to Mrs Kumari's poor wasted legs. Next, she patted the heat pad and Blackie came out of his carrier and jumped up onto the bed. He began walking around in a circle, kneading his paws, finding the best position for curling up.

And this was the bit Joanne liked. Mrs Kumari had suffered a catastrophic stroke and was hardly able to move.

She was doubly incontinent. She couldn't talk. The poor soul couldn't even ask the nurses to turn off that confounded nonsense that was blaring from the television. But when Blackie flumped down and began to purr, one side of her face contracted into a half-smile.

'There we go,' said Joanne, stroking Blackie. 'Good *boy*.'

This was his third month of being a therapy cat. The charge nurse said she'd never seen anything like it. The mood on the whole ward lifted on Thursday afternoons, when Blackie came.

And Blackie seemed to like Mr Hartley, too. Mr Hartley wasn't really supposed to be here – his stroke had been mild and he'd regained most of his physical functions. But he had advancing dementia and his wife, his main carer, had died a few weeks ago. So he hadn't been able to go home, and the powers that be were trying to work out what to do with him. Blackie nestled on the bed with his front paws on Mr Hartley's chest and allowed the old man to cry into his fur. Joanne let this continue for three minutes until she decided some distraction was in order. She patted Mr Hartley's hand and asked if he'd seen that new BBC documentary about cats.

Tilly rushed in at quarter past four, clutching her schoolbag, a battered charcoal sketch of a lion and a bar of Dairy Milk. Sarah waved to Joanne from the doorway, calling out something about being late for fencing, and disappeared. That woman was always rushing everywhere.

Joanne pulled up an extra chair and flapped at Tilly to sit down. 'I was just telling Mr Hartley about the benefits of dry cat food versus wet. And I thought he might be interested to hear how we introduced Blackie to the others in stages.'

Tilly nodded earnestly.

'What a right to-do that was, eh?' said Joanne, shaking

her head. 'Blackie nearly lost a piece of his ear when he tried to sleep on Mitski's blanket that time. But they're all good now. Oh, and Tilly's brought your chocolate, Mr Hartley. And she's done a very fine picture of a lion, I see.'

As they made their way to the car park later, Tilly grabbed Joanne's sleeve and pointed to another low hospital building that stood on the far side of the complex, on the other side of a scrubby triangular area of grass.

'Can we go and visit Daddy?'

'Not today, Tilly.' Joanne's voice was firm. 'You know the rules. You're allowed to go with your Granny Vivienne, once a week.'

'But I don't like Granny Vivienne.'

Join the club, thought Joanne. Join the sodding club.

But she spoke sweetly to the child: 'Why don't you draw a lovely picture for Daddy when we get home? A nice picture of Mitski. I'm sure he'd love to see her, with her beautiful stripes and everything.'

Like hell he would.

'Maybe,' said Tilly, considering.

Sometimes she looked down at the child and saw Steffi as she would have been. If she hadn't been taken away, if Joanne had known her at age eight, age nine. If she'd been able to keep her beside her, through all those lost years. She knew Tilly wasn't Steffi's blood but she'd picked up some of her mannerisms, her little turns of phrase. Her gentleness.

She could see that Steffi had been building something of herself inside that motherless child. Some lasting edifice of love. Something to comfort her, and to fall back on.

'Will Daddy mind? About Albie and Mitski and Blackie being in our house?'

'I'm sure he won't,' murmured Joanne. Truth be told, Tom

wasn't in a position to mind about anything. He'd sustained a traumatic brain injury, that night in the cellar. It had been caused, most likely, by the pressure of the rolling pin against his carotid artery, blocking the flow of blood to his brain. According to the two doctors who'd given evidence in court, his short-term memory was almost non-existent and he had the mental capacity of a seven-year-old.

It had been determined by the court that he didn't have capacity to stand trial – he was 'unfit to plead', to use the legal jargon. But the lawyer had explained that there was going to be a sort of trial called an 'examination of the facts', because it was important for all parties involved to understand what had happened. The judge would decide whether he was satisfied, beyond reasonable doubt, that Tom had committed the offences of murder and serious assault that he'd been charged with. If he concluded that Tom *had* committed the offences, he would go on to consider whether there were, on the balance of probabilities, any grounds for acquittal, such as diminished responsibility. It was an unusual case, the lawyer had said, because Tom had lost capacity *after* committing the offences, and not before.

Joanne had struggled to absorb the legal ins and outs of it all. But one thing was clear – Tom couldn't be convicted for the things he'd done, for the suffering and devastation he'd wreaked on his own family. Following the examination of the facts, the judge might give an order specifying that he should undergo supervision or treatment. At worst, he might be detained in a secure psychiatric facility. But he was in hospital anyway, undergoing rehab for his brain injury. As well as trying to help him to recover some mobility, they were trying to retrain his brain, to get his childish outbursts and inappropriate behaviours under control. It was likely he would need full-time care for the rest of his life.

She hadn't faced charges for the injuries she'd inflicted upon him. The Procurator Fiscal's office had been satisfied that she'd used reasonable force only, and had been acting in defence of herself and others. It helped that she'd instructed Angel to make that emergency call before she'd gone to the cellar to confront Tom. And Angel had actually done so, thank goodness. She'd told the call handler that there were three women in imminent danger, and two small children upstairs. Joanne remembered how relief had washed over her when she'd heard the sound of the sirens, distant at first and then closer.

Angel had been unconscious by the time the paramedics had arrived. Tom had crushed part of her skull with the rolling pin, and she'd needed sixteen screws and a metal plate fitted. She'd been left with neurological issues, including problems with her balance. As if that strange woman hadn't had enough problems already.

'Granny Vivienne', the bitch, had been appointed Tom's guardian, and she'd offered to pay a substantial settlement, including paying for treatment at some fancy rehab centre. She'd been terrified, seemingly, that Angel would raise a civil case against Tom.

Joanne had got away comparatively lightly, with just a few staples for her head wound, and a concussion that made her vomit for a week. No settlement had been offered to her, but she didn't care. She often thought of those moments in the cellar, her hands around her sister's head, trying to listen for her breathing.

She'd have given up her own life in a heartbeat. She

would have given it up to save her. Or just to be there. To make sure Steffi hadn't been alone, facing that monster.

Joanne shook her head to dispel the memories. She unlocked the car and transferred the cat carrier into the back seat, poking a few cat treats through the bars. Then she bent over and kissed the top of Tilly's head, squeezing her eyes tight shut for a moment. 'Let's get home now, shall we?'

61

ANGEL

Yorkshire, Present Day

If you needed to do therapy, Angel had to admit this was a nice room to do it in. According to Bea, it had originally been the library of the old house, back when a Lord and a Lady had lived here with servants and everything.

A huge bay window looked out onto the rose garden, with wooden shutters that creaked sometimes when the sun shone full into the room. The other walls were lined with bookcases. On the upper shelves, where nobody could reach, were ancient-looking volumes – hunting and fishing almanacs, sets of law reports, a twenty-four-volume series about the history of the Napoleonic wars in mould-green bindings. And on the lower shelves, a higgledy-piggledy collection of modern non-fiction and novels. Angel could see a row of Danielle Steel novels and the latest Harlan Coben. There was even a block of short, white books at the end which she recognised as *Mr Men* books.

These walls had heard some of Angel's deepest secrets. She'd cried in here about the loss of her mother, just a few months before, and the 'break with reality' that had occurred afterwards. She'd cried about what she'd tried to do to her sisters. She'd cried for the loss of her father, all those years ago. And now there was no avoiding it.

'So, after our last session,' said Bea, 'you decided you wanted to revisit the empty chair exercise that you began with your previous therapist many years ago, when you were a teenager.'

'Joy,' nodded Angel. 'Her name was Joy.'

'And you didn't want to sit in your dad's chair, but you wanted to try it with me playing the part of your dad?'

'Yes,' said Angel. 'And with me facing him.'

'So, I'll use the information that we now have?' Bea raised her eyebrows and gave a slow, meaningful nod. 'That we got from your social work file, and the police reports after your father died.'

'Yes,' said Angel again.

'And I'll try to answer your questions from the point of view of your dad. You can tell me if what I'm saying sounds right. You can nod or shake your head. Or you can correct me. The important thing is that you're in control, yes? You're in control now, Angel.'

Bea moved two chairs into the centre of the room so that they were facing each other, and helped Angel to walk over to one of them. The room swam around her and she had to sit with her eyes closed for a few moments.

'Whenever you're ready,' said Bea.

Angel reached back through the years for her unanswered question. 'Why did you do it? Why did you let them hurt me?'

'I'm going to answer based on what we have found out, okay?' said Bea gently. 'Just the facts.'

'Yes.'

'So, I'm speaking as your dad now, okay?' Bea cleared her throat. 'I made certain contacts when I was in prison serving my sentence. That is, my sentence for the manslaughter of Steffi and Joanne's mother. I learned that there were possible ways – illegal ways – that I might find out where Steffi had been placed for adoption.'

Angel gave a tiny nod.

'I co-owned a nightclub. I found out that one of the case workers involved in Steffi's adoption had an adult son who was a town councillor.'

'Yes,' whispered Angel.

'The son frequented certain types of clubs. Adult-only clubs. So when I got out of prison I decided I would try and use blackmail against the case worker and her son.'

'Yes,' said Angel again.

'Are you okay?' said Bea. 'Do you want me to stop?'

Angel shook her head.

'So, I'm being your father again now.' Bea paused, and Angel could hear her swallow. 'I groomed you.'

Angel took in a breath and held it.

'Which means I manipulated your emotions and thoughts over a period of time, so that you would do what I wanted. Then I deliberately placed you in a situation where I knew that the members at the club would take advantage of you.' Bea swallowed again. 'Do you want me to go on?' Her voice sounded hoarse now.

Angel nodded. The breath she was holding was hurting her chest.

'I arranged for photographs to be taken of the abuse that took place. By which I mean, the case worker's son – and others – sexually assaulting you, a thirteen-year-old girl. I used the photographs for blackmail. To get Steffi's new surname, and certain other details, from the case worker. And then I tracked her down and infiltrated her family circle. Once I'd gained their trust, I attempted to abduct her and take her out of the country.'

'But –'

But you were going to come back for me.

Safe in Bea's office, she allowed herself to recognise that she no longer believed that. She'd held it to her chest, like a shield, all of these years. But he'd left her. Daddy had used her and he had left her.

A single tear shot down the side of her face. 'But why? Why did he do it?'

Bea shook her head. Her eyes were shiny. She seemed to be on the verge of tears herself. 'Do you want to try sitting in the other chair?'

Angel didn't move. Mucus ran down her chin and she wiped it off with the back of her hand. 'It's like sacrificing one child for another.'

'I can see why it might feel like that to you.'

'It must be because he loved her more than he loved me.'

Bea sighed. 'I would challenge that, Angel. I would say that love is very, very far away from all of this. Very far away from what your father did. I would say that love doesn't come into it at all.'

'So what, then? Why did he do it?' Angel remembered the time she'd sat in Daddy's chair, doing the exercise with Joy all those years ago, and tried to answer the question. The great howling nothing that was his response.

She saw it this time, she noticed it – the trick her mind tried to play. The way it tried to jump onto another track. How it tried to focus on the perfect princess and how she'd tricked Daddy. To superimpose her smug face onto the howling void.

It was easier to feel anger than sadness.

But Steffi had only been a child.

And she, Angel, had only been a child.

'Why?' she whispered to Bea. 'Why would someone do something like that?'

'Perhaps, Angel, what this shows is that you *can't* figure out why.'

'But Joy, my old therapist, said this empty chair exercise would help me to get over it. She said that putting Daddy in the chair would help me to feel in control.'

Bea frowned. 'The empty chair exercise can be a powerful therapeutic tool, but it must be conducted with enormous care. It's about allowing yourself to feel raw emotions, perhaps to confront uncomfortable truths, but in a safe, controlled space. Perhaps that's what your therapist meant. I suspect the issue was that the exercise got interrupted. You said you ran out of the session? And there was never an opportunity to complete it, or have a proper debrief?'

Angel shook her head. She'd been trapped inside that exercise, alone with that empty chair, all these years. 'I still... I just need to understand *why*.'

'You may never understand why he did it. You may never understand who he really was. But you can try to figure out who Angel is.'

Angel looked at Bea helplessly. 'How?'

'You do this in tiny, tiny steps,' said Bea. 'Talking of which, I think Sarah will be waiting. We'll pick this up again next time.'

Bea took Angel's arm and led her carefully to the recreation room where Sarah was sitting, reading a battered copy of *The Railway Children*. Her face was rapt, creased into a frown of concentration.

Angel hadn't been able to face the others since it had happened. She'd barely been able to think about them. But Sarah had travelled down from Edinburgh once a fortnight, to offer the one thing that she could. Company. Without having to make conversation. Without having to explain, or justify.

Outside the window, clouds were scudding across a pearly-blue sky. The breeze moved through the trees, shifting the bare branches of the magnolia tree that stood outside the window.

'Hello,' said Angel softly.

Sarah's head shot up. When she saw Angel, she smiled.

And that was nice, wasn't it? For somebody to be happy, simply to see you.

Angel smiled back.

'Are you ready?' asked Sarah. 'Shall we start your lesson?'

She helped Angel to sit down at the piano – on a high-backed chair so she couldn't fall backwards – and then pulled up a chair beside her.

'We were learning *Angels*, weren't we?' said Sarah. 'The Robbie Williams song?'

Angel nodded happily, feeling the seven-year-old Angel inside her. The ten-year-old Angel. The ones who had never had the chance to grow. She said simply, 'I wanted to learn a song with my name in it.'

'Okie dokie,' said Sarah, spreading out the music on the stand.

Suddenly Angel asked, 'Do you ever see... *her*? You know. Joanne?'

'Yes,' said Sarah.

'Can I tell you something to tell her?'

Sarah nodded. Angel leaned in close and whispered something into her ear.

She sat back on the chair and stared at the music in front of her. She felt Sarah's hand, warm and hesitant, on her shoulder. *Real.*

Angel began to play the first, halting notes of her song. The shape behind her, the one in the corner, the howling nothing-shape, began to fade. Until it was just a shadow, a flicker on the wall. Just the pale winter sunlight moving through the branches of the old magnolia tree.

62

STEFFI

Edinburgh, Present Day

There was cat hair everywhere, all over the house. It seemed to float invisibly in the air, only to land on any surface as soon as it had been mopped or vacuumed.

Which wasn't very often, these days, I had to admit. The side of the expensive designer sofa in the living room was all tufty where Mitski had used it as a scratching post. As was the carpet on the bottom step of the stairs. And there was a discoloured patch on the upstairs landing where Albie had vomited up a slug he'd tried to eat. He'd never been much of a hunter, Joanne had explained, in a whisper, as if he'd have been upset if he'd heard.

Tom would be apoplectic if he ever returned to the house. But we would cross that bridge if and when we came to it. Which seemed unlikely.

Whenever I asked Vivienne how he was, she muttered, 'No change.'

The court had made an interim order which meant that the girls and I would stay in the house for the time being, at least until the position regarding Tom's future was clearer. The judge had decided it was in the best interests of both children to continue to reside with me for now, and he saw no reason to disrupt the status quo regarding their living arrangements. My lawyer had said this boded well for the future. I repeated her words, like a mantra, in the dark hours of the night when my mind raced with anxious thoughts.

Vivienne, who'd been appointed Tom's legal guardian, and was now in charge of his practical and financial affairs, had raised no objections – it was probably a good thing that she had her hands full with Tom. And she paid across the decreed sum each month for the children's care and maintenance.

I longed for the day we could leave this house and find somewhere to live that didn't have stairs, and a trapdoor, and the lingering memory of that smell which had emanated from the locker in the cellar. One step at a time, Joanne always said.

I heard the front door go. That would be Joanne and Tilly, back from their pet therapy session.

Holding Edie by the hand – she was toddling now – I went to let them in, even though Joanne had her own key.

Poor Tilly looked exhausted, weighed down by her heavy schoolbag. She'd struggled to sleep since it had happened – 'The Accident' as we called it. It was she who woke in the night, now, and not Edie, who had finally started sleeping through.

School was going better, though. The bullying had

stopped, once the brisk but kindly Head of Year had become involved. You have to speak up about bullies, she'd told Tilly.

I dropped a kiss onto the top of Tilly's head while Joanne fussed around, taking her coat and schoolbag and hanging them up. She picked up the fleece jacket that she'd hung over the radiator earlier and held it out for Tilly to put on, one arm and then the other.

'There,' she said, crouching in front of her, pulling up the zip and then tugging down on the cuffs so that the sleeves sat properly. 'There.'

'Come and see, come and see.' I led them through to the kitchen where I'd set out the cake I'd managed to make earlier that day, complete with my attempt at piped white icing: 'Happy First Birthday Edie!'

Joanne gasped. 'Look at that, Tilly! A masterpiece!'

'Yummy. When can we have it? Do we have to wait for Auntie Sarah and the boys?'

'They'll be here any minute,' I said. Sarah had promised to come, saying they had a forty-minute window between Airfix modelling club and gymnastics.

'I still find it astonishing that you called her Edie,' said Joanne, shaking her head, as we set out the cups and plates on the coffee table in the living room.

It was something she'd said again and again, over the last few months. It turned out that Edie had been our mother's first name.

'I think some deep-down part of you must have loved her,' persisted Joanne. 'Despite all her... her struggles. It's a pity she's not here to see all this. She'd have been tickled pink at the idea of grandchildren.'

'It's such a shame I can't remember her. What was she like?' It was something I'd asked several times, noticing that

Joanne seemed to like it. Perhaps she wanted to make our mother live on in some way, by remembering and talking about her.

'Darling, can you fetch the cake slice and the cake forks?' Joanne beamed at Tilly, who rushed through to look for them. The child hung on her auntie's every word. 'Our mother had a lot of problems, as you know. But she had hopes and dreams, just like anyone. She'd worked in a beauty salon before she had us – did I tell you that?'

I nodded and smiled. She'd told me at least ten times.

'She was great at doing make-up and nails, and all that. She used to do our nails sometimes, too. I remember her dotting the polish so carefully onto your tiny fingernails. And she always said she wanted to get back into it again, maybe even have her own salon one day.' She stopped and frowned, shook her head. 'But every time she tried to summon up some willpower, some grit, to get herself out of her situation, he would somehow empty that out of her. He emptied her out, again and again. I think he preferred her that way.'

She sighed. 'Look at me. Whenever I talk about Mum, it always comes back round to *him*. Bloody Keith.'

'I can't remember him either, not really. I can't even picture him.'

'Good,' said Joanne warmly, taking the cake slice and cake forks from Tilly. 'Thank you, darling.'

Keith, long dead, had lived on only in tricks and reflections. The imaginary 'Daddy' conjured by Angel's trauma. The violent bully who stalked Joanne's worst memories. The fairy-tale wolf I'd glimpsed behind Uncle Geoffrey's façade. Or something standing in the shadows, some familiar shape summoned by the darkest of Tom's moods.

'I can't remember my mum either,' piped up Tilly.

The child was still processing things. Like me, she wasn't sure how to grieve a mother she couldn't remember. But it turned out she loved these discussions, the kind that took place between sisters.

I pulled her onto my lap – all elbows and knees, she was getting so big. And I squeezed her tight. Now that I had started hugging her, I wasn't able to stop.

She gave a little squeal of a laugh.

'Sit still, you monkey,' I said. 'Do you know what I think? I think there's a part of you that remembers your mum. Just like I remembered Joanne, but didn't realise.'

'But I was only two when I knew her.'

'Two-year-old Tilly is still there, though, somewhere deep down.'

She looked at me sceptically. 'Where?'

'Inside you,' said Joanne, knowingly. 'It's like your bones. You can't see them, and you don't really know what they look like.'

'Unless you get an X-ray,' said Tilly.

'That's right,' said Joanne. 'Well done. *Unless you get an X-ray.* But you know they're there, right? They're still part of you.'

'How did you remember Joanne but not realise?' Tilly asked me.

'I kept a little version of her inside of me, all those years. She kept me safe, all the time.'

'Even when you were asleep?'

'Yes. And when I couldn't sleep, as well. When Edie was tiny and I didn't know what to do.' My throat tightened, remembering those lonely nights.

'Is someone keeping me safe while I'm asleep?' asked Tilly.

'Yes,' cut in Joanne. 'I am. And Steffi is. And Edie.'

'Edie's only a baby.'

'Edie loves you,' Joanne said gruffly. 'And that keeps you safe.'

'What about Daddy? Is someone keeping him safe while he's not well?'

I swallowed. 'Um...'

'Granny Vivienne and the nurses,' spat out Joanne. 'They're looking after him. Don't worry, darling.'

The doorbell rang, saving us from further conjecture about Tom's psychological safety.

At the door, Sarah held me in a hug that was a few seconds too long to be a simple hello, while Ben and Adam ran around us and into the house like a little SWAT team. Adam was clutching a dripping carton of Ribena, as usual.

'How are you?' Sarah whispered into my hair. She seemed different these days. Lighter, yet more fearful, after what had almost happened in the cellar. Quicker to laugh, but sometimes her eyes would fill and she'd go silent.

Uncle Geoffrey had been the final piece in the puzzle of our relationship. The hidden factor in the unsolvable equation of our family. Sarah had confessed, after The Accident, that she'd known he was my father. She'd known it since the day he'd tried to take me away to France and had ended up running from the police and hurling himself off a motorway bridge near Dover, his blood and brain matter splattered over the tarmac. Our parents hadn't even needed to warn her never to tell me. Even after I'd learned the bare facts of my adoption, that had been a tale too awful to tell.

Sometimes I tried to piece together that strange fever dream of a day. I could only remember fragments: the red sign of a motorway food stop, the queasy smell of the burgers with their plasticky cheese slices. Dodo's instruction to run. The whump of air from a swinging door. Somehow, in the most wretched of circumstances, my twelve-year-old sister had instilled in me an instinct for self-protection. And it had come to the fore in that crucial moment, overriding the unspoken rules of our family. To be a good girl. To do what I was told. Not to make a fuss.

I thought of my eight-year-old self, who'd been brave enough to make a fuss that day. Who had, perhaps, been trying to keep me safe through this whole business with Tom. Offering up her imaginary friend, because it was the only way she knew how to help.

Ben zoomed around the living room in circles, holding a toy helicopter aloft and making 'doof-doof-doof' gunfire noises. Tilly eyed him warily and shrank back against Joanne. Then she noticed Edie, cruising her way around the end of the sofa, and seemed to decide that intervention was required. She took her sister's hands and walked her along until they reached the safe zone around Auntie Joanne.

Joanne hauled Edie up onto her lap and locked her arms around her middle. Edie tried to grab for her sister, saying 'Diwwie, Diwwie.' Tilly went and fetched one of the fabric-covered books Edie liked to chew.

'How's work?' I asked Sarah.

'Oh, you know. Manic as usual. I've had to take two days off this week because Adam's had a tummy bug.'

'Oh dear,' I said uneasily. Adam was lying on the floor by the TV, finger buried deep inside his nose.

'And Ash is busy with some big project at work. What about you? How's the new business going?'

'It's going well, thank you.' Joanne and I had started a pet-sitting service, caring for people's cats and rabbits and guinea pigs while they were on holiday. We shared the visits between us since Joanne was also working part-time at the local cat rescue centre, as well as doing her pet therapy volunteering. Edie sometimes came along on the visits. This week we'd been looking after Antonia, a big, fluffy, lop-eared rabbit who she absolutely adored.

And Tilly, if she didn't have too much homework on, made up a 'care plan' for each pet, adding a pencil sketch of the animal in question so there would be no confusion as to who was who.

'I don't think we'll be making our first million any time soon,' I said, with a wry laugh. But then I saw Tilly's face fall slightly, so I changed tack. 'But actually, we've made a really good start. Lots of our clients have recommended us to their friends. I think we're going to be very busy, come summer. And they all love Tilly's sketches. Tilly, why don't you go and get that one you did of Antonia?'

She flew out of the room to get it. Ben zoomed after her, followed by Adam, the half-crushed juice carton still in his hand. Edie, not wanting to be left out, climbed off Joanne's lap and toddled towards the door. I scooped her up and gave her a kiss. She kicked her legs in protest.

'I saw Angel at the weekend,' said Sarah, speaking to Joanne now. 'I went down to Chesters again. She asked me to pass on a message.'

Joanne frowned. 'What message?'

Sarah leaned in close and whispered something in Joanne's ear. Something that sounded like: 'She said you did the right thing.'

Joanne kept looking straight ahead, and for a moment I wondered if she'd even heard the words. She held her eyes wide open. The muscle in her jaw tightened and a quivering dimple appeared on one side of her chin.

Albie, who'd been watchful in the corner while the boys had been running riot, now approached with a sharp miaow. He stood up tall on his hind legs, placing his front paws on Joanne's knee. She detached his claws from her trousers and lifted him, clutching his furry body against her chest. She smiled around the room, just one single tear escaping down her cheek. 'Where have those children got to? And have you got the matches, Steffi? I think it's Happy Birthday time.'

LATER THAT NIGHT, about three in the morning, Tilly crept into bed beside me. This was a frequent occurrence, since 'The Accident'.

'I had a terrible dream,' she whispered, her breath hot against my ear. 'I can't get back to sleep.'

'It's okay, sweetie. Come on, cuddle up.'

I caught myself wondering what Joy would say, if she'd known we were all sleeping in the same bed – me, Edie, Tilly and whichever cat had stretched itself out by our feet. Blackie probably, since he was completely soft on Tilly. I reminded myself – as I'd had to do many times – that Joy wasn't a real person. As Sarah had tried to explain, Joy was a product of Angel's troubled mind, the trauma she'd buried. And maybe – probably – of her obsessive desire to hurt me.

And she'd tried to explain how thirteen-year-old Angel hadn't coped, after her father's death. How I'd been the easiest person to blame. How people could tie themselves in knots, could believe almost anything, to try and get the impossible to make sense.

Tilly pressed her face against the sleeve of my pyjamas. I heard a muffled voice: 'Tell me about Daddy. What did he do?'

I placed my hand on the back of her head, stroked her hair, still damp with the sweat from her nightmare. 'What do you mean, sweetheart?'

Tilly had never asked any questions about what had happened in the cellar and why. And we hadn't forced information upon her that she might not be ready to hear. We'd simply said there'd been an accident.

But that was untrue. It hadn't been an accident at all.

I thought of all the things Mum and Dad had held back over the years, trying to protect me from my past. They'd layered silence over the pain, and it had thickened like scar tissue.

Tilly lifted her face and gave me a strict, no-nonsense look. 'I want you to tell me what Daddy did.'

I took a few breaths. 'He told me that when your mother, Adeline, came to visit – that night a couple of years ago when you heard them fighting – he tried to stop her shouting. He did that by putting his hands over her mouth. And she died in the struggle, because she had a heart condition. Then he hid her...' I swallowed. I owed it to her not to gloss over the truth. 'He hid her dead body in the cellar, so nobody would find out. But the police aren't sure if he's telling the truth, or if he killed her on purpose. So there's going to be a court case about it.'

Tilly gasped in a breath, her hand over her mouth.

'Oh darling. Oh, it's okay.'

'But why would he kill her on purpose?'

I sighed. 'Maybe he thought she was going to make things difficult for him.'

'Was it because of me?' she asked in a tiny voice.

I chose my words incredibly carefully. 'They might have been arguing about you, and the arrangements for you. I'm not sure. Sometimes that happens, when parents break up. But if they did, it was *definitely not* because of anything you did.'

'And he hurt you, didn't he? And Auntie Joanne? And that other lady?'

'Yes. He did. There was a big struggle and we all got hurt, including Daddy.'

'And who was that other lady? The one who had come to help you with Edie's sleeping?'

'She was my half-sister, which means we shared the same biological father. And I didn't know.'

Tilly nodded, absorbing this information. 'Why didn't she tell you? That seems weird.'

'It was complicated, darling.'

'But that lady helped you with Edie's sleeping.'

'She did. And I was feeling sad about things, after having Edie, and she helped with that too.'

It was the way I'd decided to think of it. I knew that Joy – or Angel – had wanted to hurt me, and that was why she'd come into my life. But I liked to think that some of the kindness she'd shown me, some of her compassion and understanding, had shone through from a better place. From kindness that she'd once been shown herself, at some point in her life.

Maybe one day I'd be able to tell her – my other sister – that I saw it all clearly now, the things she'd been trying to make me understand. I saw that of course I hadn't been able to cherish every moment of motherhood because I'd been exhausted. Unsupported. I'd been trying to do something that was never meant to be done alone.

And I'd felt empty because I'd been with someone who preferred me to be empty. Any time I'd tried to express something of myself – something that didn't have to do with him – he'd crushed it like some dirty household pest. He'd tried to clear and tidy me away, just as he'd done with Adeline.

And as he might have tried to do, eventually, with Tilly. And with Edie. A cold feeling went down my spine and I pulled them closer, my two, tousle-haired little loves.

'Thank you for telling me,' said Tilly. She exhaled long and loud, as if the tension of weeks or months was being released.

'That's okay. You can ask me anything and I promise I will always tell you the truth.'

'Is it still okay for me to love Daddy?' Her voice quivered.

'Yes.' I felt exhausted, suddenly, thinking of the long road ahead of us, trying to work through all this. This was only the very start.

'We won't all live together again, will we.' Her voice was hollow – a statement, not a question.

'No, darling. And once things are sorted out, and we know where Dad's going to live, we might go and live in another nice little house or flat somewhere. You, me, Edie and Joanne.' It was probably better to plant the seeds of that idea now. This house would have to be sold, in all likelihood, to pay for Tom's care.

'And the cats.'

'Yes. And the cats.'

'Are you going to be my mum now?' she asked.

I hesitated. I could hear worry in her voice. 'It's tricky, isn't it? I mean, Adeline will always be your mum, I guess. But what do you think? What would you like me to be?'

'You could be more like a sister,' she said. 'A big sister who looks after me. Like Joanne looks after you.'

'That sounds like a very good idea,' I said, trying to keep my voice steady.

'And like I look after Edie,' she added. She stretched her arm over my chest and pressed Edie's button nose with one finger.

'That's settled, then.'

'I might go back to sleep now.'

'Okay, darling. I'll be here.'

There in the dark, with my girls tucked on either side of me, and Joanne asleep upstairs – probably with the other two cats piled on top of her – I realised that I was doing it, without even trying. I was cherishing this moment, with all its difficulty, its impossible knots of love and pain.

I'd finally found the thing I'd been looking for. I'd tried to find it in Tom, and in the bricks and mortar of this expensive house. I'd searched for it from the windows of trains and way, way back in the pages of family photo albums.

Home.

Here it was, woven into these moments. In the warm press of Edie's skin against mine. In the rhythm of Tilly's breathing, slowing as she relaxed back into sleep. And in the sound of my own heart, beating with the love I'd carried inside me, all the years of my life.

A NOTE FROM LUCY

Thank you for reading *The Child Upstairs*! If you would like to find out what happens next, I have written a mini-sequel called *Adeline's Promise,* which I would like to offer you as a free gift and a thank you!

Download it by copying this link into your browser and following the instructions: **https://BookHip.com/NPAKDFC**

Reviews are so important to us authors, especially those of us who publish independently. I would be really grateful if you could spend a moment to write an honest review on Amazon (it doesn't need to be long or detailed – even a line or two would be great).

Also, if you enjoyed *The Child Upstairs*, then you'll love my other psychological thriller, *The Child In My House*, which is available now on Amazon!

If you would like to get in touch, I would be delighted to hear from you – please email me at lucy@lucylawrie.com

ACKNOWLEDGMENTS

To Matt, thank you for your unwavering belief in me and my writing, and for lighting the entrepreneurial spark I needed to get it out into the world. I could never do this without you.

Thank you, Charlotte, for bringing Steffi, Sarah and the Sleep Fairy to life with your drawings. And to Emily, who needed a real life Sleep Fairy – I realise now that you were only trying to help with future research!

To Arlene Eves and Sheila Wallace – thank you for being the most amazing supporters and cheerleaders. And thank you, Vicky Newham, for your help and solidarity in all things relating to book marketing.

I simply couldn't have written this book without my friends Jane Farquharson and Lesley McLaren. You are so talented and so generous with your time, your ideas and your creativity. You have gone above and beyond to help me with this especially 'needy' book (including the shameless encouragement of violence!)

Finally I want to thank every single one of you, the readers who've come on this journey with me. And particularly those of you who have left an encouraging review, signed up for my newsletter or dropped me a lovely message. You're the reason I do this and I am more grateful than I can express.

ALSO BY LUCY LAWRIE

THE CHILD IN MY HOUSE

A family riddled with lies. A little girl who won't speak. What if keeping her safe means losing her forever?

Juliet only wanted to see her childhood home one more time – to look at it from the street. She never intended to meet the new owners, let alone talk her way into a position as their new live-in nanny. But it's too late now to tell the truth about who she really is.

Six-year-old Kitty has progressive mutism and cannot speak. Nobody knows why she keeps making silent phone calls to the police. Juliet makes it her mission to find out.

As Juliet settles into the house, nostalgia for her childhood gives way to uneasiness, as troubling memories surface. She begins to realise that her new employers have a connection to her own past, and family secrets she has tried hard to forget. And she is horrified to learn that they have a secret too – one that could blow their world apart.

Juliet faces an impossible choice. Keeping Kitty safe could cost her everything.

The Child In My House is available now on Amazon.

Made in United States
Orlando, FL
28 December 2023

41838934R00264